W9-BZB-780

Scowling at the prisoner, the *doshin* barked an order. The giant's legs had been left free, the net roped around his waist, while two tethers around his neck were held by men on either side of him. One of the patrolmen saw the giant's eyes and gestured urgently to the *doshin*. "Excuse me, Hasegawa-san, but the prisoner is blind!"

"What!?" The *doshin* stopped the procession and stepped around to look at the prisoner from the front. The Yngling "stared" at him, eye-lids open wide. There could be no doubt. The man's eyes were not even remotely human. The *doshin* waved a hand in front of Nils's face, then poked a finger almost into one eye. And got no flinch, not even a blink.

"He is blind!" he said.

"Excuse me, Hasegawa-san," said the senior patrolman, "but he is reported to have run around inside the yard, dodged and threatened people, and then run to the gate, raised the bar . . ."

Hasegawa stilled the man with a gesture, and turned back to Nils. "What is your name, and where are you from?"

"My name is Tetsu-te. I am from across the sea."

The *doshin* frowned. The name Tetsu-te—Iron Hand—sounded like something some rough *ronin* might take on himself, but this foreigner could not be a *ronin* or any other kind of samurai.

"What kind of eyes do you have?" he demanded.

"They are eyes given to me by Okuni-nushi."

Okuni-nushi! So important a god! Most of the patrolmen backed away, but the *doshin* stood his ground. If this was a *kami* of some sort, how had they succeeded in capturing it?

Unless it had allowed them to capture it.

BAEN BOOKS BY JOHN DALMAS

The Regiment
The White Regiment
The Regiment's War
The Yngling and the Circle of Power
The Yngling in Yamato
The Lizard War

JOHN DALMAS

THE YNGLING IN YAMATO

This is a work of fiction. All the characters and events portrayed in this book are fictional, and any resemblance to real people or incidents is purely coincidental.

A Baen Books Original

Baen Publishing Enterprises
P.O. Box 1403
Riverdale, NY 10471

ISBN: 0-671-87634-1

Cover art by David Miller

First printing, December 1994

Distributed by Simon & Schuster
1230 Avenue of the Americas
New York, NY 10020

Typeset by Windhaven Press, Auburn, NH
Printed in the United States of America

For

Jon Inouye, Jan & Jerry Numata, Yaska Huff,
John Nishimura, Paul Koshi

and most particularly for

Jess Roe: cowboy; swordsmith; scholar
and practitioner of the martial arts,
both armed and unarmed;
and friend

PROLOG

The Black Castle of Osaka, though considerably smaller, was scarcely less handsome than the Emperor's palace, and much more ancient. Its massive outer walls were thirteen centuries old, far older than any written record in Yamato. Within them, of course, the original buildings were long gone, burnt during the Great Plague. But some of their older replacements, whose jet-black roof tiles gave the castle its name, dated back as far as three centuries.

High in the residence of its lord, two men sat in a comfortable chamber, with wall panels open to the evening breeze. The day had been hot, was still hot, and they'd exchanged the formal *kami-shimo* of the wedding ceremony for light kimonos. Both were *takai daimyo*—lords over lords. One was Arakawa Hideo, master of the castle and father of the bride. The other was Kyushu Tadaki, a maternal uncle of the groom, Ten-no-Suji Terasu.

Even given the groom's ambivalent status with the imperial court, one might have expected a wedding between such elevated families, traditionally less than friendly, to be attended by *daimyo* and their retainers from numerous districts. This ceremony, however, had been small, attended mainly by members of Arakawa's immediate family and senior retainers, and those of Lord Kyushu.

Absently, Kyushu sipped *sake* from the delicate porcelain bowl he held, then muttered, "It's as if we were hiding the wedding."

He said it sourly. Arakawa grunted. "What we're doing is dangerous enough already. It is best we made small of this ceremony."

"Hikari will hear of it soon, nonetheless. And it calls attention to itself by its very smallness."

1

"True. But it also shows deliberate avoidance of anything resembling imperial ambitions, and thus disarms his suspicions to a degree. Hikari may be reluctant to act, but he is not a fool. And what he lacks in steel is made up for by the men around him—and by the restrictions his father imposed on us."

Arakawa said this last with distaste. The older man scowled but did not argue. He simply said, "I do not care for subterfuge or delay. They are foreign to my nature."

"I understand. But if the blood-bath comes to pass before we are ready, it will be our blood, and the blood of our armies. And our families will be wiped out, root and stock; we will have no second chance."

ONE

Fanns allri nannan som Ynglingen han—
milt som mjök (önar leene),
stark som storm (men allri rastne),
vis som jodens sälva annen.

Å varelse var han, ej dykt.

There was never other like the Youngling,
mild as milk (his eyes smiling),
strong as storm (but never raging),
wise as the spirit of the earth.

And living man he was, not myth.

Prefatory verse of *The Järnhann Saga*,
Kumalo translation

3

Matthew Kumalo didn't wonder why he was playing chauffeur to a Neoviking chieftain. It paid off: the big barbarian had been their entry into remarkable areas of study. And of course, there was the Northman's charisma: you tended automatically to do what he wanted.

Besides Matthew and Nils Järnhann, a woman and two men rode the pinnace, skimming some fifty meters above a rolling sea of grass. Grass turned tawny by drought and late-summer frost. Waves swept it, the heads of fescue and deschampsia bending to a fresh breeze.

He flew on manual, guiding on an ancient, overgrown highway, its cuts and fills still evident. Its pavement, though, had long since disintegrated and been buried by dust storms. In these times it knew only the hooves of saddle mounts, the tough splayed feet of pack camels, and the infrequent herds of sheep and cattle being driven to China.

Nils Järnhann watched as if the blank glass eyes in his sockets were functional, then spoke to the pilot in front of him. "Fly higher," he said. "We'll be there soon."

Matthew Kumalo pulled gently on the control and soared to five kilometers, gaining speed. Ahead, the undulations became rounded hills. Beyond them, from his new altitude, he could see a broad basin, and on the far side, mountains high enough that the upper slopes were dark with forest. Moments later, the pinnace left the final rounded hill behind, and Matthew slowed.

The basin was a broad valley, a river flowing through it in wide looping curves, with groves and strips of woods along its banks. In the distance westward, a vast dust cloud rose. As seen from the pinnace, it could have been a great herd of cattle being driven to new pastures, but in fact, the khan's personal *tümen* was in training there, 10,000 strong. Much nearer, on the south side of the river, was a large encampment, laid out in orderly lines and rectangles like a city of the ancients.

"Is that it?" Matthew asked pointing.

"That's it," Nils answered. "That's Urga. Stop above it, and I'll find which is the *ger* of the khan."

After her husband had parked five kilometers above it, the

senior ethnologist, Nikko Kumało, set the viewer on "scan." Then she moved aside to let the eyeless barbarian operate it. She was still not entirely used to the ease with which Nils used equipment. Nor did she stop to wonder why, with his psionic vision, he even bothered with the scanner.

The Buriat encampment was an orderly set of sub-camps distributed over an area several kilometers on a side. The Northman adjusted the magnification until it occupied almost all the screen. A brief scan showed which *ger* was the khan's: the largest—a felt tent a dozen meters across, shaped like an inverted serving bowl. It was whitewashed like most of the others, but a banner hung from a pole in front of it.

Nils didn't at once lock onto it. A little apart from the others, outside their pattern, was another splendid *ger* scarcely smaller than the khan's, with other, lesser *gert* close around it, their arrangement different from that of the Buriat camp. Nils recognized it as the camp of the Chinese ambassador, though it was larger than when he'd seen it last. Near it was a paddock a hectare in size, the horses in it notably bigger and finer than the tough Buriat ponies. Only after several seconds did Nils return his attention to the khan's *ger*, and lock the viewer on the ground in front of it.

"There is something wrong here," he said to Matthew. "Take us down to ten doubles,[1] and I'll hail them."

Pinnace *Alpha* began a silent descent, accelerating down a gravitic vector that intersected the ground within meters of the khan's door. There was activity in the camp—women and some older children pursuing duties, other children playing, and male slaves tending lactating mares in the vicinity—but no one noticed the descending pinnace till it was within three hundred meters of the ground and slowing. These were not a people who looked upward much, except when falconing. Then a child saw it, and called out. Others looked up, first children, then their elders, and the *Alpha's* sound pickup caught the spreading shouts. People scattered, some ducking into *gert*, others running away. Some emerged with bows in hand. At

---

[1] A double is a length measurement equal to about 1.7 meters. It is called a double because it is two strides long.

fifty meters the pinnace stopped, and Nils used the loud-hailer, speaking Buriat.

"I am the Northman," he boomed, "come from the sky to find my *anda*,[2] Achikh."

A woman had emerged from the khan's *ger* with a bow and quiver, a broad heavy woman of perhaps fifty years. Nils recognized Dokuz, the khan's mother.

"Achikh is not here," she shouted. "Go away!"

He answered her in the formal style: "Then I will speak with his brother Kaidu, the khan. Achikh's brother, the Great Khan Kaidu, who was my friend. Noble Kaidu, the Great Khan who hosted me and gave me rich gifts, and asked me to be his shaman."

She didn't answer at once, squinting upward, afraid but brave, her wide mouth slightly open. It wasn't necessary to be a telepath like Nils to see her mental wheels spinning. "Kaidu is hunting," she called at last, "with a large party of warriors. Achikh is with him."

"Hunting where?"

"In the Changajn Nuruu, far to the southwest. He will be impossible to find."

"I will be back," Nils answered, then switched off the hailer and turned to Matthew. "Rise and go north."

Ted Baver, the junior ethnologist, spoke then. He knew Buriat, and had understood Dokuz. "North?" he asked. "She said southwest."

"She lied. He is hunting, all right, but in the mountains southeast of Baikal."

Matthew didn't question. Presumably the Northman had read her mind. Releasing the vector lock, he began to climb, swinging northward. At 5,000 meters, the planetologist leveled off, called a map onto the screen, then on it set and locked cross-hairs over the general area Nils had asked for. That done, he set the pinnace on auto-pilot.

Ted Baver looked curiously at the Northman. "Lied? Why?"

"She was afraid for Kaidu. Since we left, Achikh killed Fong,

---

[2]*Anda*, in the Mongol dialects, means blood brother or soul brother, someone to whom special loyalty is given.

the Chinese ambassador—drew his sword and cut him down inside the khan's *ger*, which is a serious violation of the *yassa*. The usual punishment for that would be suffocation, or exile in special cases, but Kaidu has made him a slave, instead, adding the humiliation of wearing a yoke."

The fifth person on board, young Hans Gunnarsson, stared at Nils, his angular juvenile face shocked. "Kaidu did that to his brother? When he could have exiled him instead? Achikh would much rather be exiled than wear a yoke."

"Fong had long since put a spell on Kaidu," Nils replied. "Also, Kaidu fears the Chinese emperor."

"Just a minute," Nikko said. "The woman you spoke to is Kaidu's mother, right? And Achikh is his brother. Doesn't that make her . . ."

"Dokuz is not Achikh's mother; Kaidu and he are half-brothers. The Buriat do not differentiate."

Matthew held the pinnace to subsonic speed to avoid sonic boom, but even so, in half an hour they were over the Jablonovyj Chrebet, land claimed by the Yakut-Russ but often encroached upon by Buriat hunting parties. These were low but intermittently rugged mountains, their forest interspersed with lobes and islands of grassland. The AG generators raised the pinnace to twelve kilometers then. From there Nils panned the land with the viewer, while the others watched a monitor. If this failed to find the Buriat hunting party, they could fly a search pattern.

They spotted the camp in an open draw, not far above a broad grassy valley. Seventy or eighty leather shelter tents had been set up in the orderly rows typical of Mongol hunting camps. A creek ran past it at a little distance. Nils examined the camp at increasing magnifications; numerous horses grazed in the vicinity, remounts and pack horses. There were also men, not a lot of them. Slaves they'd be. Some tended fires, and large racks where meat dried and smoked. Others, perhaps camp keepers, seemed to have little to do. Some fished with spears, and those who worked, worked leisurely.

One of them wore a yoke. *Achikh*, Ted decided, though from twelve kilometers, image waver precluded recognizing the face. "Shall we go down and get him?" he asked.

Nils shook his head. "We'll wait for Kaidu to return. I don't want to steal Achikh from him. Let him be released formally. That way, at some future time, Achikh can come home if he'd like."

Nils began to scan the country round about. Soon enough he found a large party of horsemen, slowly sweeping the length of a steep-sided valley whose grassy bottom contained a brook. Other horsemen, barely glimpsed, rode through coniferous forest on the slopes. Conifer groves bordered the brook, and he glimpsed animals trotting through them: elk[3] and wild horses.

Not long afterward he found a force of men, five or six hundred of them, mostly on foot. They were perhaps twenty-five miles from the Buriat camp, hiking along a sparsely forested ridge crest. These were not Mongols of any tribe; their hair hung in heavy braids. "Yakut-Russ," Ted guessed aloud, and Nils nodded. They carried bows and quivers, and swords rode at their belts. They seemed to know where the Buriat camp was, at least approximately; the ridge they were on would lead them near it.

Aboard the *Alpha*, everyone napped intermittently, but with someone always on the viewer. Hans found another, seemingly smaller hunting party riding toward camp, pack horses loaded with game, mostly elk. Nikko and Matt casually discussed projects they might undertake after delivering Nils and Hans back to their clan. Ted suggested they explore the situation on the Japanese islands. Japanese was one of the languages he'd deep-learned before leaving New Home, and the history and culture of pre-plague Japan had intrigued him.

The sun was low, coloring the clouds, when the larger party of hunters returned to camp. Matthew turned to Nils. "Shall we go down?"

"Not now. Take me to Urga, first. There is something there I want to have with me when I meet Kaidu."

---

[3] The term "elk," as used here, refers to Siberian animals (the Altai maral) of the genus *Cervus,* closely related to the European red deer. They are much larger, however, equivalent in size to the North American *Cervus* commonly termed elk or wapiti.

Matt frowned but swung southward, setting the controls for Urga. When they got there, Nils waited till after nightfall, then had Matthew put him down some four kilometers from the encampment. There was no moon. The opaqued pinnace, hidden by darkness, sat on the steppe in the shelter of a force shield for more than six hours. After the first two, Matthew and Nikko had grown increasingly uneasy at Nils's continued absence, but surprisingly, to them, Ted Baver seemed quite relaxed. Hans had begun the wait a bit sourly; he'd wanted to go with Nils, but the eyeless giant had refused, saying that in this, stealth was vital, and numbers a disadvantage. But having had a strenuous and sleepless night, the night before, Hans had soon fallen asleep, curled on the deck like some long angular animal.

When Nils returned, only Matthew was awake. The Northman stood just outside the force shield, and spoke in Swedish, as if to establish his identity without question. As soon as he was inside, Matt re-formed the domed shield. Nikko had wakened, as had Ted; Hans still slept. Nils appeared to have been sprayed with blood, obviously not his own or he wouldn't be there. He'd taken with him a clear plastic bag. Now he tossed it on the deck. Matthew looked, and almost threw up.

"I'll need it later tonight," Nils said. "Now I want to go back to Kaidu's hunting camp." He turned to Nikko then; she looked pale enough to faint. Gesturing at his leather breeches and bare torso, he said, "When I had the chance, I wiped myself off with grass as well as I could, but it had mostly dried by then."

They were all awake when the autopilot brought them to the coordinates of the khan's hunting camp. Matthew stopped above it at 1,000 meters. "Now what?" he asked.

"Lower to a hundred doubles, then light all the inside lights, and make the hull one-way transparent."

That would make the hull opalescent, seen from outside. The Northman warrior, it seemed to Matthew, never forgot anything he'd seen or heard, assimilating it all as part of his mental universe, ready for use in analysis or action. And he'd shown more than once a mastery of dramatics. Matt nodded. "Right," he said, and began to take the *Alpha* down.

Aibek, son of Elbek, stood guard outside Kaidu's tent. Not that the khan was in danger here, for aside from the double handful of slaves, the men were sworn *nökür* to Kaidu. But guards were always set. It was the latter part of the night, in the time of the new moon, and very dark, so when the light flashed on in the sky, Aibek looked up immediately in alarm. Overhead, at some uncertain distance, an object shone like a brilliant oval moon.

His shout came unbidden from his throat, at the same moment as the other guard's, and as he stared, it seemed that the glowing object was slowly lowering. Then two bright fingers of light speared down from it, focusing on the tent of the khan, and at once Aibek's skin rucked with chills. It was all he could do not to duck inside to hide. Other shouts followed, as men emerged sleepily from tents and looked upward. They stood transfixed, no one drawing a sword or stringing a bow, for surely this was a very powerful god, perhaps even great Tengri himself.

Finally, a short stone cast overhead, it stopped. And spoke! Then Aibek knew fear beyond imagining, his knees quaking so that he almost fell. He was aware of the khan standing beside him now in his sleeping robe.

"KAIDU!" called the glowing god, much louder than necessary. "I AM THE NORTHMAN, COME TO SEE MY *ANDA*, ACHIKH! BRING HIM OUT TO ME!"

Aibek remembered the Northman, a giant wizard, hugely muscled. He'd been impressed then. But now, to see his true form! . . .

Kaidu called out that Achikh be brought forth. Half a minute later, the Mongol veteran stumbled into the light, impelled by a guard. Achikh's neck was bent from the yoke he wore, and his hands were tied to it, as they always were at night.

"IS THIS WHAT YOU HAVE DONE TO MY *ANDA*? YOUR BROTHER?"

Kaidu's voice cracked, but he answered. "He drew his sword in my *ger*, which is against the *yassa*, and killed a man there, the Chinese ambassador, which is also against the *yassa*. The law called for his death. I have spared him."

"YOU LIE TO ME! YOU COULD HAVE EXILED HIM! I WARNED YOU ABOUT THE CHINESE AMBASSADOR. HE WAS AN EVIL WIZARD, WHO'D COME TO YOU ONLY TO BEGIN THE ENSLAVE-MENT OF THE BURIAT. ACHIKH DID THE BURIAT AND ITS KHAN A GREAT FAVOR BY KILLING HIM, BUT AFTERWARD YOU WELCOMED ANOTHER CHINESE VIPER TO YOUR BREAST, A NEW AMBASSADOR. DO YOU STILL HOPE TO ALLY YOURSELF WITH THE EMPEROR?"

Kaidu gathered himself in defiance. Squinting upward against the light, he called, "I have already allied myself with him."

"AH, KAIDU! MISGUIDED KAIDU! YOUR ALL-POWERFUL ALLY DIED IN HIS PALACE LAST MORNING AT DAYBREAK, ALONG WITH HIS TROLLS AND MOST OF HIS CIRCLE OF POWER. THEIR BLOOD SPRAYED THE WALLS, AND RAN ACROSS THE FLOOR LIKE A RIVER!

"NOW! FREE ACHIKH!"

The khan stared a long moment, then turned to the keeper. "Free him," he husked. The man slashed the thongs that held Achikh's hands, then drew the pins that held his head enyoked. His torso bare, Achikh stood like some mythical mountain troll, his thick body knotted and sinewy, his neck and back crooked. He had to twist and look sideways to see the glowing god above them.

"EVERYONE BUT ACHIKH AND KAIDU! FLAT ON YOUR BELLY NOW, THAT YOU DO NOT SEE THAT WHICH MIGHT BLAST YOUR SOUL FOREVER!"

Aibek dropped on his belly without hesitating, wrapping his arms around his head that no light should get in. Only Kaidu, with Achikh, remained standing. He'd known the Northman was a powerful wizard, but he'd never imagined such power as this. The glowing light settled to the ground, and now he could see what form it had. In shape it was somewhat like an oblong *ger*, but smooth as steel. It had stubby legs to stand on, and a stalk stuck out the top. Two great eyes stood out on shorter stalks; it was from them that the fingers of light came. It settled on its feet with a hiss.

"Achikh, come here." The voice was softer now, but still not truly human. Kaidu saw Achikh walk toward it, unfaltering, and wondered if he could have done as well himself. He saw a mouth open in the side—no, a kind of door!—and the giant Northman stepped out. Perhaps not a god then, but a magical vessel. The Northman helped Achikh into it, then turned and looked out at the Buriat khan.

"Kaidu," the Northman said loudly, in his own voice now, "I commend you to your people. In most matters you have been a great khan. Only in the matters of the emperor and Achikh have you seriously erred, and that because the ambassadors were wizards who laid a spell on you. I now declare you free of it.

"Meanwhile a strong force of Yakut-Russ is on its way. They can arrive tomorrow; be warned!

"And here! I have brought you a gift from Urga tonight!"

The Northman threw something toward Kaidu that landed almost at the khan's feet, then he disappeared inside the vessel of light. The door closed behind him. After a moment, the fingers of light went out, and the glowing vessel began to ascend back into heaven, while around Kaidu, his warriors still lay prostrate. When it had risen a short way, it paused. One of the fingers of light reappeared, moved, found the object the Northman had thrown. And the vessel spoke again. "OPEN YOUR GIFT, KAIDU! THE GIFT OF FREEDOM I BROUGHT TO YOU FROM URGA!"

Kaidu bent and picked it up. It was a bag with something in it, something hard. He found the opening, reached in, and pulled the object out.

By its blood-encrusted hair. It was the new ambassador's head.

TWO

As the pinnace lifted, Nils seated Achikh cross-legged on the floor. Then he knelt behind him on both knees, kneading and pummeling his neck and shoulders while Ted Baver watched. "We need to straighten your neck and back," Nils told him. "As they are, it would be difficult to fight." After a bit, his large powerful fingers and even his knuckles, began to explore the muscles. Occasionally they dug hard, so that the Buriat winced. It took more than a little pain to make Achikh wince; Ted knew that from a year of close association. After a while though, Achikh's spine was straight, and the probing stopped. Nils began to rub again, and Ted could see the residual tension drain from the Buriat, who got down on the deck and lay slack while the Northman finished the treatment.

By that time they were 450 kilometers above the Earth, parked on the gravitic vector through the hunting camp. Matthew had turned away from the pilot's panel to watch. "Nils," he said at last, "you're familiar with the sanny. Your friend might enjoy a session in it; it ought to feel good to him. And he may have brought some, uh, bugs with him. Lice, maybe, or fleas. Have him strip, and you can show him how to use it while I run his breeches through the cleaning drum. I should probably run your things through, too. You might have picked up some while you gave him that massage."

Achikh understood Anglic, but not this; key words were unfamiliar. Nils explained, and in a minute, Achikh stood nude. Then Nils demonstrated the sanny to him, motioned Achikh inside, and closed the door behind him. Ted Baver waited, curious. It seemed to him the small booth might waken a latent claustrophobia in the Buriat, who was, after all, a man of the open. A moment later they heard a muffled shout, and some thumps against the wall. *The spray took him by surprise*, Ted thought. But Achikh did not come bursting out. After a few Buriat oaths and a few more bumps, they heard only the soft hum of the water recycler till the door opened and a dripping Achikh stepped into the cabin, a grin on his face. Nils shooed him back into the sanny, showed him how to turn the drier on, and closed the door again.

Then the Northman too stripped, to wait his turn. Matthew handled their clothes at arm's length, tossing them into the drum and setting it on wash and microwave. It troubled him to have Nils walking unabashedly naked in the pinnace, certainly more than with Achikh. The Northman was always imposing, almost intimidating in his size and muscularity, but one got used to that. Completely naked though . . . It occurred to him then that it wouldn't bother him if Nikko weren't there, even though she sat pointedly facing the windscreen. *You're jealous, Matthew Kumalo!* he told himself, and the thought disturbed him. So far as he knew, Nikko never thought of Nils sexually, and surely he'd know; there'd have been some sign. Or was it a different sort of jealousy? Perhaps he simply didn't want her to see Nils's—equipment, so much larger than his own, as Nils himself was so much larger. And why should that trouble him? The course in psychology he'd taken, at the university, had insisted that penis size was not an important factor with most women. Most women; that meant not all of them. And important? How important did something have to be, to be *important*? For that matter, how did the textbook's authors know?

He shook himself out of it when Achikh walked into the cabin and Nils disappeared into the sanny. Matthew handed Achikh a robe, then took the cap from the bottle of delousing compound, and had him sit on a chair while he worked the compound into his scalp. To kill any little biters, he explained in Anglic.

By the time Matthew was done, Achikh's breeches were ready. The Buriat showed no sign of the cangue now, the yoke he'd worn, except for heavy callus on his shoulders. Nils had come out of the sanny while Matthew was finishing the delousing treatment. Nils and Hans had been deloused the day before, when they'd left Miyun, so Nils waited patiently, naked but with his back to the pilot's seat. Matthew reddened slightly; it seemed to him the Northman must have read his mind earlier. Except that he was sitting with his back to Nikko, however, Nils acted as if he'd read no thoughts at all. Perhaps he hadn't, Matthew told himself. Perhaps he tuned people out most of the time. Otherwise things could get pretty confusing, even for him, at least where there were a lot of people.

Nikko had glanced over her shoulder just as Nils stepped from the sanny, and her head jerked back to the windscreen at the sight of him naked. An after-image stayed with her for a moment, and irritated, she banished it by rapping keys on her console. Calling up data: the inventory of their edibles and potables. She looked it over critically. They were adequate for two or three persons for a while, but wouldn't last long for six. They shouldn't postpone a return to Varjby or some other supply base, any longer than they needed to.

I wonder what Nils has in mind for Achikh? she thought, then wondered if Nils had read the question in her mind. She still didn't know how much of the time he was aware of the thoughts around him, nor did she know him well enough to read his body language. She wasn't even sure he had body language, he was so different from other people. Including his own. Similar but different.

She remembered, too, his thoughtfulness that evening in the Neoviking encampment, when new to him and to Earth, she'd made such a fool of herself. He'd had real eyes then, with pupils, not the opaque eyes of pale blue glass they'd machined for him on board the *Phaeacia*, after he'd been blinded in Kazi's dungeon.

With Achikh on board, Matthew had felt uncomfortable as they'd lifted. Would the Mongol panic, lose control? But it had been dark, moonless; he couldn't see the ground receding beneath them. And Nils had been massaging him; though the Mongol was obviously very strong, Nils could have controlled him.

Still— The planetologist spoke to Nikko, who got up and

sedated Achikh with a mild morpheate. The Buriat blinked at the spot on his arm where she'd pressed the applicator, then lay down on a pallet by the boat's side and was asleep in a minute or two. Nils laid out pallets for himself and Hans, and followed Achikh's example.

"Why don't you sleep, too," Matthew suggested to Nikko, and glanced at the chronometer in one corner of his screen. "I'll set the wakeup for a little before noon."

"Aren't you going to sleep?"

"In a few minutes."

She opened her sleeping compartment, little more than a cabinet containing a shelf-like bunk with a storage net above it. Ted opened one of the spares. Matthew rotated the pinnace a hundred and twelve degrees, till east was in front of him out the wrap-around windscreen. He could see the moon now, a hair-like crescent sitting on the eastern horizon. From the ground it would be invisible in the morning light. Even from 450 kilometers up, the horizon outshone it, another silver thread, but broadly curved and scintillant, lit by a sun not yet visible to him, and bordered above by a band of powder-blue atmosphere.

He became aware of Hans crouched beside him, also looking. "It's beautiful," the boy murmured, then pointed. "What is that which shines like the sun on a sword edge?"

"It's the curve of the Earth, with the sun shining on it from the other side. If you watch for a minute or two, you can see the sun rise."

"But—the sky is still dark. It's not dawn yet."

"This high, the sky is always black. The sun will shine like a bright bright moon or a very large star, but the sky stays black."

Hans said nothing for a moment, staring at the vivid stars. "How high are we?" he asked then.

Matthew touched some keys, converting kilometers to measurements more familiar to the young Northman. "Two hundred and seventy *tusen*,[4] he said, adding, "I brought us so high because it's safe up here. No orcs, no trolls, no storms.

---

[4] A Neoviking *tusen* is 1,000 doubles, or about 1,700 meters— roughly 5,580 feet in the old British and American systems.

And because it gives me—perspective." He doubted the boy knew the Anglic word; he himself didn't know the Scandinavian word, assuming it had survived the primitive centuries since the plague.

Then the limb of the sun topped the horizon, spilling light across a stretch of sea. He reached, adjusting the windscreen to filter the sunlight. In a minute or so, the sun's entire disk had risen free of the horizon. In another minute Hans spoke again, his voice hushed with awe.

"I think I should sleep now."

A few minutes later, Matthew locked the controls and got ready for bed himself. Already Hans was asleep, and the planetologist wondered what his dreams would be like. Achikh, he felt sure, was out for a few more hours at least, and there was no reason to suspect he'd explore the controls if he woke. But locking them cost nothing.

THREE

The high-pitched beeping of the wake-up drew Matthew from his bunk and Nikko from hers. Ted, he supposed, was awake but not yet emergent. A blurry-eyed Hans sat up on the deck, where he'd either crawled or rolled off his pad in his sleep. Achikh seemed not to have stirred. Nils had awakened earlier; he sat in a lotus, head upright, eye-lids exposing uncanny-looking, featureless blue glass. *God knows where his mind is*, Matthew thought. Matt himself had been dreaming. Already the threads of it were gone, but it had been about the Northmen. Beyond that, a single word remained from it in his mind: *perspective*. If the Northmen had a word for it, Nikko would probably know.

It was his turn to make breakfast: Danish barley and oats ground together in the pinnace's own mill, and pre-baked. He moistened it with Danish milk, dried and reconstituted in the pinnace's liquids processor, then served it with Danish cheese on the side, and Danish apples processed into sauce. He'd gotten used to that kind of fare—palatable in an uninspiring way, and most of all nourishing.

When they'd eaten, they talked: Matt, Nikko, Nils, and Ted. Achikh still slept, while Hans gazed raptly out at the Earth below. Matthew might have switched the hull to one-way transparent for him, but feared the sight might panic Achikh when he awoke.

"I presume you want to take Achikh with us back to the Balkans," he said to Nils.

"Ted Baver would like to visit Jih-pen first."

Matthew blinked, then realized. Japan. "We can go there after we take you home."

"I would like to visit Jih-pen too. There is someone there I'd like to find, someone Jampa Lodro told me about."

18

It was Ted Baver that answered. "It might be hard to find one specific individual in Japan. What's his name? Where does he live?"

"Jampa called him Chicho-san, and said he usually lives in the mountains."

Ted frowned. *Chicho-san*. The name meant nothing to him—unless—*I'll bet that's Shisho-san, respected teacher*, he thought, *as mispronounced by a Chinese or Tibetan. Not really a name*. He became aware of Nils's eyes on him.

"He is also called Ojiisan Tattobu," the Northman added.

Ojiisan Tattobu—Revered Grandfather, more or less. In Japan, a lot of people might be called Respected Teacher, or Revered Grandfather. And as for living in the mountains—

"Ninety percent—nine parts in ten—of Japan is mountains," Ted replied. "Or probably more. And Japan has a lot of islands; four main islands. Which one of them? Did he say?"

Nils shook his head, answering in Swedish. *"Nej, sa ikke."*

Ted turned to Matthew. "If we go, I could ask about him. Assuming the language hasn't changed too much. He could be someone everyone knows about."

Matt felt resistance within himself; he didn't want to go. And recognized the source: He was uncomfortable with landing at unfamiliar places. Back on New Home he'd fought, so to speak, for his place on the expedition. Then, when the *Phaeacia* was due to go home, he'd argued to stay, and won out. Earth was where the excitement was, the potential for learning.

Yet he was afraid, or perhaps anxious was the word, after the traumas they'd gone through with the orcs, those first weeks on Earth. But fear wasn't something to give in to. As best you could, you considered its sources in the mind, and the external factors, consulting with others if need be. Then you acted accordingly.

"What do you think?" he asked his wife.

"Let's do it. Exploring fits our job purpose; it's why we're here."

"Um." Nothing about risks or— But then, there were risks everywhere on Earth. Though they were worse in some places than others, sometimes much worse. He dismissed the question for the time being and dredged his memory. He'd not only been the expedition's senior planetologist; he'd been in charge of all ground operations. And for years had crammed ancient information about the mother planet, preparing. Commonly he didn't have to check the computer for geographic information. "Honshu's the main island," he said, "and along with Kyushu it's closest to the mainland. To Korea, specifically. That makes it a better prospect for finding—" He paused, groping for the name. "Shisho-san.

"And the Kanto Plain is most likely the major population center," he went on. "It has the biggest concentration of agricultural land, and the initial flyover found towns and villages there."

No one else had anything to add. "Okay, we'll go. Secure all gear." The map was still on the screen. He set the controls for a gravitic vector through southeastern Honshu, and when Nikko and Ted had finished securing, they headed southeastward, gradually losing altitude as they went. Nikko sat in the co-pilot's seat beside him.

"How do you say *perspective* in Scandinavian?" Matt asked her.

She looked at him as if wondering what brought that question up. "*Pehr*-spehk-TEEV," she answered, putting the main stress on the third syllable and secondary stress on the first.

"Is that old Scandinavian, or modern?"

"Both, but it was Latin originally."

He grunted. So the Scandinavians still had the concept. Surprising, considering the post-plague collapse into primitivism, nearly eight centuries past.

When they arrived at forty kilometers above southern Honshu, the sky below was almost innocent of clouds. He stopped above Omori Bay, and took the *Alpha* down to 10,000 meters. There was no sign at all of the ancient Tokyo-Kawasaki-Yokohama megalopolis. Matthew traversed the area more closely, with the scanner at intermediate settings, changing to higher magnification at times, while the ship recorded what he saw. One would have expected most of the city to have fallen, a victim of weather and molecular decay. The great majority of it would have been the disposable, recyclable construction of the period 2015 to 2105. But where older sections had been retained, he'd expected visible ruins, and there were none. Pre-plague European cities had preserved neighborhoods of ancient masonry buildings, and after eight centuries, parts of old walls still stood, occasionally even a shell. But not here. Perhaps Japanese cities had retained little of the old. That and scavenging, and Japan's earthquake frequency, might account for the lack.

There was a living town on part of the site; he guessed its population at fifty thousand or more. It was well laid out along wide streets that were dirt but nearly unrutted, perhaps serving as much for firebreaks as for traffic. He saw no vehicles beyond handcarts, but pedestrians were numerous, and there were people on horseback. Most of the buildings seemed classically Japanese, wooden, with shake or tile roofs. Many windows— indeed many whole fronts—were open to the early autumn air. At one end stood a palace, with gardens and high protective stone walls.

Interesting. He lowered to 5,000 meters and circled more widely over the Kanto Plain, remaining high enough not to draw attention. If anyone down there happened to examine the sky closely—which was unlikely—the most they'd see, if they noticed the pinnace at all, they could explain away as a hovering bird too high for its wings to be seen.

There was extensive farmland on the Kanto Plain, though commonly there were strips of woods and brushland along its streams and flood channels. Small villages were frequent, and small towns were scattered here and there, occasionally with a castle by them. And here, at least, agriculture was no longer dominated by rice. In September, rice paddies would still be green, unharvested, and he did see some. But mostly he saw vegetable crops, stubble fields, and pastures.[5]

---

[5] Even in medieval Japan, arable land was in short supply, and rice, though requiring much more labor, could produce much heavier yields per hectare than barley or wheat. With Yamato's much smaller population, labor, not land, is in short supply. Thus barley has become the staple grain, and rice something of a luxury.

He swung west-southwest then, paralleling the coast. Here the country was mountainous and forested, with clusters of farms in the larger valleys. And—it struck him then, and he turned to Nikko.

"Who did the overflight here when we first got to Earth?"

"If it wasn't you, it was probably Chan."

Matthew shook his head, wondering how anyone could overfly southern Honshu and not notice, or noticing, have failed to report it: Fuji, beautiful Mount Fuji, was dead ahead—*and utterly changed*! Its stately, symmetrical cone was gone! While Nikko manned the camera, he called up the data on Fuji as it had been before the plague, then angled downward to examine the mountain more closely, busy with his instruments, muttering his observations to the computer. The old crater had been 600 meters across; now it was 4,100 meters across, and still nearly circular. Its high point, on the southwest side, stood only 2,350 meters above mean sea level; the old height had been 3,776. It had blown! Sometime after the plague had ended travel between Earth and her colony on New Home, Fujiyama had erupted, and the explosion had been stupendous. Given the various measurements, he had the computer estimate the volume of mountain that had blown off: approximately 5.9 cubic kilometers! Then he called up what the computer library had on the eruptions of Tamboro and Krakatoa: This one seemingly had been even greater—the largest, then, in human history. And clearly, from the asymmetry of the present crater, she'd blown northeastward, in the direction of the Kanto Plain. The damage from the blast, followed by the meters-thick ashfall, must have been terrific.

Now her flanks were forested again. Even on the northeast slope, the trees were large and old, so it had happened centuries ago, perhaps not long after the plague. In her cone, a large lake spread marvelously blue, with two small cones emergent, also forested. Mount Fuji still was beautiful, but now it spoke not of cool symmetry. Now it said, "*See what I have done, and remember. For I can do it again.*"

What effects the event must have had on Japanese culture! A post-plague, sub-technical culture! Certainly the story would have lived on in folk tales. The sound itself would have been cataclysmic. The nineteenth century Krakatoa eruption in Indonesia had been heard in Japan, 5,800 kilometers away; this would at least have matched it.

And what must worldwide weather have been like, the next year or two? Surely there'd have been no proper summer; perhaps snow flurries in Paris in June, night frosts in Chicago in July. And crop failures throughout the north temperate zone— the sort of thing that had followed the great Tamboro eruption of—when had it been? 1815, the computer told him. Of course, when Fuji had blown, there'd been no Paris or Chicago, not in the pre-plague sense of great populations. Encampments perhaps, of miners digging through the rubble for metals, and villages with people numbering in the dozens or possibly hundreds.

From Fuji they flew on to the sites of old Osaka, and farther west, Hiroshima. There were towns on those old city sites, too, the new Osaka perhaps half as large as the town near old Tokyo. It occurred to him that a smaller town might be preferable for their first landing, or the countryside near such a town. He swung back east and north, and after a time, circled one that he guessed might hold three or four thousand, standing near the mouth of a valley entering the Kanto Plain. After briefly discussing sites with Nikko, Nils, and Ted, he lowered the *Alpha* toward a pasture or hay meadow about five kilometers east and north from the town, and a few hundred meters south of a small village. On the road between village and town, perhaps a hundred meters from the landing site, was a farm cottage with a steep thatched roof.

In an adjacent field, people were at work hoeing weeds from what appeared to be a late crop of some vegetable. The pinnace reached fifty meters without being noticed, so Matthew, wanting their attention, touched a key on his console. A horn ululated, an uncanny sound to anyone not familiar with it. The field workers glanced up toward it, and almost instantly were either prostrate or fleeing wildly.

He settled the last few dozen meters, and put the pinnace down gently on its hydraulic landing feet. Then, with two key strokes, he generated a force shield.

It occurred to Matthew that somehow he didn't feel good about this. *I'm afraid*, he told himself. *I've got a tinge of anxiety. Well, fear can be appropriate sometimes.*

FOUR

From—"*Yamato*," by Ndambe Predtechensky. Pages 137-151, In *Ethnological Summaries of Earth Cultures at the Time of First Contact,* Heine Katsaros, ed. University Press, A.C. 816.

. . . The huge cultural differences between pre-plague technological Japan, and Imperial Yamato 770 years later, resulted very largely, of course, from the enormous loss of population and the virtually total loss of pre-plague technology. More interesting, however, are the striking cultural parallels between Yamato and *pre-technological* Japan, most notably with Japan of the Kamakura period, AD 1185-1333.

In fact, these similarities can easily over-impress the student when first she encounters them. But on further familiarity, the differences become equally striking. Yamato is no mirror of a distant past, but a unique culture of its own, whose similarities and also its *differences* with the past provide numerous entry points for study, analysis, and insights.

Once they were on the ground, Matthew switched the hull to one-way transparent, which would enable them to see out in every direction without being seen inside. Ted sat down in the study seat, put on the "student cap," called up the "cramming program" —the deep-learning program— and did a refresher on the 21st-century Japanese language. There'd be a wait, probably substantial, before anyone of authority arrived. The review would make good use of the time.

Presumably some of the farm workers had run to the village and informed the headman, or whatever authority they had there. The headman, finding the report hard to believe, would come out, presumably soon, perhaps only near enough to see with his own eyes. He in turn would send someone hurrying to the magistrate in town. Then, depending on the rules of procedure here, the magistrate would either send out an assistant with some constables to investigate, or he'd send a messenger to the *daimyo* at the castle. Probably the latter.

Whichever. Someone would be out to investigate. Ted hoped the language wouldn't be too changed for at least limited understanding—at least enough to enable a computer analysis of the changes, and an update of its Japanese language memory. The next step, he decided, would be to establish some sort of ambassadorial status for himself. From that base, he could try for the information Nils wanted, and begin compiling general ethnological data as a basis for planning research.

While Ted crammed the language refresher, the others ate. Not a lot though: Given the state of the larder, Nikko didn't put out a lot. The cram took less than an hour, and outside, no one had shown up except a boy of about twelve years, who'd crept along a shallow ditch that passed within twenty meters, to crouch staring at the pinnace from the cover of long ditch grass. So Nils got in the chair to begin his first cram in Japanese, or in anything else. An hour later he'd finished the pronunciation drills at the end of Section One, and still no one in authority had arrived. Several adults had approached to within fifty or so meters, and dozens more stood where the road passed, a hundred meters off. The boy in the ditch stepped out of it and seemed about to walk up to the invisible force shield. Then some woman, no doubt his mother, rushed shouting from the yard of the nearby farmhouse and hauled him away by an ear. Nils began Section Two.

Matthew began to fidget. Surely the authorities had been notified by now. Were they gathering an armed troop? They couldn't possibly force their way through the shield, though. He settled himself to wait as long as it took. Achikh awoke from his drugged sleep, and Hans, speaking Buriat, gave him what Matt assumed was a one-minute summary of the day so far. It would be interesting, he thought, to understand what was said.

Nils had finished Section Two before anything developed outside. Then, as he began on Section Three, a party of mounted men turned off the road by the farmhouse and rode slowly across the hay meadow toward the pinnace. The farmers, seeing them come, scurried to line up facing where the riders would pass, dropping to hands and knees and bowing their heads, their straw hats like a row of small shields.

Nikko focused the scanner on the horsemen; their expressions ranged from worried to stony. Some carried lances, and others longbows; sword hilts projected from their sashes. Their helmets were individualized; Nikko, harking back to her course on Japanese history, guessed they were made of lacquer.

Without being aware of it, Captain Iwatoku Kunio tightened his grip on his lance. The object on the ground ahead had obviously been crafted by the gods. It shown in the sun like polished steel, but with a subtle shimmer that suggested it was more. The report was that it had lowered gently from the sky. Which was hard to believe, but how else could it have come here? Magical.

He spoke tersely to his men, his voice low: "Take no action without my order! Say nothing without my order!" Then he nudged his horse's barrel with a heel, speeding its pace a bit. It wouldn't do to seem hesitant.

At thirty meters he stopped. The strange object sat without moving. A *boat*, he told himself, and examined the thought. A boat with legs? Not legs that walked, surely; they were short and seemed to have no joints. He frowned. It looked not at all like any boat he'd ever seen, but it felt to him like a boat. From the sky. It had what might be eyes on short stalks, and from the top what could be a stubby flagpole, though there was no flag on it. Something transparent—glass perhaps?— curved around the front of it. A window. He glimpsed movement through it, but what had made the movement was difficult to imagine.

Iwatoku looked down at the kneeling farmers, and reining in his horse, called out sharply. "You! Peasants! Has anything come out of this object? A person perhaps?"

No one answered for a moment, each waiting for someone else to reply. Then a young man rose on his knees and spoke apologetically. "Please excuse our ignorance, my lord, but I have not seen or heard of anyone or anything coming out of it. But just before it came to the ground, it made a terrible sound, like ghosts, but very loud! Some of us were in the field there" —he pointed— "hoeing potatoes when it happened. We all heard it, and were greatly frightened."

Iwatoku scowled, then touched heels to horse again and rode on to within ten meters of the sky boat. From there he called out to it: "If anyone is inside, we will be honored, should you be willing to speak to us."

For a long moment there was no answer. Then: "We have come from heaven," said the sky boat, "to see how the Buddha Amida's people are doing."

The words were human, but the voice—was not. Not quite. And the speech was strange, archaic, like something written by the scribes of early chiefs. Iwatoku understood it though, and was awed. *This was a boat from Amida's Heaven*! Dismounting promptly, he knelt on all fours, his men following his example as quickly as they could. Behind them, the peasants too pressed their foreheads to the dirt.

The Heaven Boat bade them rise, and Iwatoku talked with it at length, feeling more and more at ease. It asked many questions, most of them ordinary. Some of what it asked— most of it—he would have expected Amida to know. Frequently it was necessary to repeat slowly, and to rephrase things before the Heaven Boat understood. It seemed to him it was some sort of being he spoke with, not the Heaven Boat itself. At times he discerned what seemed to be other voices, too faint to understand.

Finally the Heaven Boat said it would now return to Heaven. "We shall come back soon," it added. "Be prepared to meet us here. There will be things we want of you, mostly knowledge."

With that, its legs withdrew into its body, the boat itself hanging there as if the legs still held it. Then slowly it rose, its speed increasing smoothly, and within a long minute, it had disappeared into the sky.

Iwatoku stared after it. Why would Amida send a Heaven Boat to Yamato? What did it mean? He shook his head. The gods had intentions and plans of their own. Well. Lord Matsumura would want to inform the Emperor at once. As a descendant of the Sun Goddess, the Emperor would know best how to deal with a visit from Heaven.

He looked around at the others. "Shigeru!" he ordered. "You, Eiji, and Takumi stay here in case the Heaven Boat returns before I do.[6] I am going to report to Lord Matsumura."

He turned his horse then, leading the rest of his party to the road and back toward town. The peasants dispersed, some of them returning with their hoes to the potato field. The three samurai left in the hayfield watched Iwatoku and the others out of sight behind the roadside row of trees.

Izuhama Eiji ground his teeth. This was no time to be left behind. Lord Matsumura and the Emperor would surely try to profit from this Heavenly visit. It was up to him to inform Lord Arakawa as quickly as possible. Perhaps if he feigned illness, Shigeru would excuse him and he could return to his quarters. Then he would send Yasuo to visit his "ailing mother" —they'd established her fictional condition for contingencies like this—and in six days, Yasuo could be in Osaka, if he rode hard.

Nikko had set the controls for 15,000 meters. That would take them well out of sight of the ground. Meanwhile the computer ran a linguistic analysis of the conversation, developing a vocabulary and grammar for 29th century Yamatoan. Yamatoan because the people here used the ancient name Yamato for their country. Japan had never been more than a name used by foreigners, borrowed by Europeans from the Chinese. And for whatever reason, the official pre-plague name "Nippon" seemed to have lost its standing. As they lifted, Ted turned his attention to a terminal, watching diagrams flash on and off the screen. Linguistic analyses based on sound prints were not simple, and if the computer gave him a prompt, which was possible, he was there to handle it.

---

[6] In Yamatoan, the strictures on the use of given names such as Shigeru and Eiji are looser than in pre-plague Japan. In fact, the language as a whole is less formal and stylized, though still considerably more than Anglic.

Meanwhile, Matt turned to Nils. "Did you read anything interesting in their minds?" he asked.

Nils nodded. "Interesting yes, but nothing urgent. They are warriors, and consider themselves above other people. Also they're suspicious of foreigners."

"Suspicious of us?"

"Not of us. Concerned, but not suspicious. They believe what Ted Baver told them—that we came from heaven. And they wonder why Amida sent us."

"And none of them was telepathic, you said." That was something Matthew had asked about earlier, before Ted ever addressed the samurai. He would never forget the trouble caused by telepaths among the Orcish greeting party at the City of Kazi.

Ted interrupted. "The analysis is finished, and the computer is printing out instructions for further questions. Do I have time to cram the update?"

Matthew nodded. "Sure. Go ahead. Then we'll go down and see what we can learn about Nils's Shisho-san. And ask the questions the linguistics program wants answered."

FIVE

Då kom modern hans å grätte
för att han blev 'klarad frejlös.
"Gråter ikke mor," sa Järnhann,
"de ha jort mej tjänst, de dom're.
Ja' har alltid velat att ja'
skulle se vad ligger på den
söra sidan Jötasjö'n.
Ja' ä ikke född att stanna
hem bland dem ja' växte upp vä.
Hellers ska ja' vannra över
joden, trots d' faror fanns där.
Sitt' ja' ikke hem i trygghej.
Fara ut i vääden ja' å
träffer vad de öder ville."

Then his mother came a-grieving
that the ting had named him outlaw.
"Don't cry, mother," Ironhand told her,
"They have served me well, those judges.
I have always wished to travel
south across the Jöta Sea and
find what's to be seen and done there.
I was never born to stay
at home among those I grew up with.
Rather would I wander 'cross
the world, despite the dangers found there.
I could never sit in safety.

Rather travel o'er the world and
meet whatever may confront me.
           From— *The Järnhann Saga*
                    Kumalo translation

When Ted was done, Nils asked to cram an update on Sections One and Two of the basic course, and they stayed at 15,000 meters till he was done. Then they rode the same gravitic vector to the ground. The three left-behind samurai still waited, watching intently as the pinnace settled. The one named Eiji was more exploratory than the other two. Casually and on foot, he approached the pinnace, till he bumped into the force shield. Though first contact was made by a forearm, it was so unexpected, he struck his face against it, and recoiling, fell on his buttocks, one hand to his nose. His companions laughed uproariously. Eiji scowled first at the pinnace, then at the other two samurai. The leader, Funakoshi Shigeru, stepped to where the grass was pressed down by the invisible force, and extending one hand in front of him, felt the unseen shield.

"We apologize for any injury your friend may have suffered," Ted said in his updated Yamatoan. "We overlooked that a human being cannot see the protection Amida has given the Heaven Boat. Has Captain Iwatoku returned yet?"

"No," said Funakoshi, impressed by the Heaven Boat's courtesy and concern. "And soon it will be dark. Perhaps he will not return until morning." He gestured at Eiji, who still held his painful nose. "Please excuse our comrade for colliding unintentionally with your spell of exclusion."

They continued talking for a while. Dusk was settling, and Nikko opaqued not only the hull but the windscreen, in order to have lights on inside without sacrificing privacy against the locals. The Yamatoans, it turned out, were not acquainted with the name Shisho-san, but they knew of Ojiisan Tattobu, whom they said was a very holy man. They did not know where he was, or when he would appear. His comings and goings were unpredictable, and the best place to hear of him was at the castle. Wandering Zen monks often stopped there when passing through; Lord Matsumura invited them to meals with him, and often talked with them late into the night. If one of them had encountered Ojiisan, or perhaps only heard about him—where he might be, what he might be doing—they might well have mentioned it.

Ted got the computer's questions answered then, and speaking for Matthew, told the samurai to return to the castle. After a long several seconds of hesitation, Funakoshi bowed acceptance; clearly, orders from Amida's emissaries outweighed those of their captain. The three samurai mounted their horses and rode away.

"Now what?" Ted asked.

Briefly Matthew thought about it. "We'll stay on the ground tonight," he replied. "It's possible that a representative of some other faction, a peasant perhaps, will come out to talk this evening and give us a different viewpoint. Meanwhile, when the linguistics program has finished its new analysis, we can all cram an update on Yamatoan."

The analysis was done almost before he said it. Nils took the first turn in the chair, and each of them ate a small supper. By the time all were done, it had been dark out for a while.

"Matthew," Nils said, "I wish to go outside and explore."

"Do you think that's a good idea? You told me yourself they don't trust foreigners, and you certainly look foreign here."

"I will be cautious."

Nils stepped to the door and waited. He wore the deerskin breeches and shirt he'd sewn the winter before in the Altai, his sword at his left side. Matthew chewed a lip, hesitating. For the Northman to go out without some sort of facilitating pre-arrangement with the locals seemed foolhardy. On the other hand, Nils Järnhann was virtually a force of nature, who came and went as he pleased and had survived repeated dangers. And hopefully his size—nearly two meters and 118 sinewy kilos—would give potential attackers pause for thought. But . . .

"I will go with you!" Hans announced.

"And me!" Achikh said. "We are *andat*, you and I, and you need someone who can protect your back if there's a fight."

Nils grinned at them. "It's good to have friends you can rely on, but this time I'll go alone. I'm looking for information, not a fight. I'll use my psi, not my sword, and stealth, not strength.

And one alone can be more stealthy than three or two." He turned back to Matthew.

Matt returned his look, then shrugged. It was Nils's own life Nils risked, and he was, after all, a barbarian. All three of them were. Impulsive, independent-minded barbarians. The odds were that none of the three would live to middle age.

A smile played around Nils's mouth, and Matt realized the Northman was esping him. Nodding, the planetologist killed the lights, then touched the latch release on his console. The door slid silently open, and Nils stepped out. Another touch closed it after him, and Matt turned the lights back on.

The three project personnel and the two remaining barbarians watched on the viewscreen as the Northman, the *yngling* of his people, strode away into the night. He made no effort at stealth. Of course, Matthew told himself, he'd know if anyone was around to see him. It occurred to him then that Nils could have opened the door himself, using the release beside it, and hadn't. He'd known the lights should best be out first.

A remarkable man, Matthew thought; he adjusted easily to technical and project considerations, and easily accepted whatever people might think of him. The planetologist turned to Baver.

"Ted, what was it like, a year traveling with Nils?"

Ted grunted, then smiled. "It was an education. On at least a couple of levels."

That wasn't the kind of answer Matt had been looking for. He wasn't sure what kind he *had* been looking for, but that wasn't it. Perhaps it should have been though, because Ted was clearly a much different man than he'd been before. *Ideally I should have debriefed him yesterday morning, then viewed his cubes,* Matt told himself. *But on Earth,* ideally *doesn't often apply. I'll debrief him tomorrow, and start setting time aside to view what he recorded.*

Nils moved without uncertainty. Given the way they grew up, the way they lived, Northmen were hard to disorient. Mostly, any maps they carried, they carried in their heads, and having seen the district from the air, he had a mental map.

There was no moon at all, nor would there be tonight;

he knew that from the progression of the phases. But overhead was the Milky Way—what the Yamatoans called the River of Heaven and his own people the Winter Road. The very different, earthly road that ran from the village toward town was lined by trees. His psychic vision didn't need the starlight to see them. He approached them at an angle, bypassing the farmhouse by some fifty meters. His psionic sensitivity told him that no one was awake close by, except the farm wife who sat barefoot on the floor, weaving a straw mat by the light of a lamp—a shallow bowl containing oil and a wick.[7] For just a moment, through her mind, he smelled the fragrance of its smoke, and watched admiringly the quick deft movements of her hands.

Then he entered the road without hesitation and turned left toward town, moving now at an easy, swinging lope. The exchange between Ted and the samurai had told him there was a temple in town,[8] and at least a pair of inns. Either was likely to provide information.

Just how he'd get that information without drawing a crowd, he'd decide when he got there.

The road he was on ended at a wider road a kilometer eastward—the royal road between the district's castle town, Momiji-joka, and Miyako, the capital of the Emperor. There was a *sake* house at the junction, with three somewhat inebriated farmers and the proprietor. They were talking about the Heaven Boat that had landed in Ushi's hayfield. The proprietor hadn't seen it, but the farmers had, and they were busy arguing over what the *kami* inside had said, and what it all meant.

It seemed to Nils there was little prospect there of information about Ojiisan Tattobu, so he took the right turn and loped on toward Momiji-joka. This royal road, running east and west, had trees only on the south side, the sun side, again mostly tall poplars, and again with occasional chestnuts and thick-boled, coniferous *sugi*. As he neared the town, he twice met people

---

[7] Vegetable oils, particularly camellia-seed oil, are used in lamps.
[8] The Yamatoans have several names for "temple," varying with the type. This was a *do*, a temple for public worship and instruction.

on the road. Once it was three well-to-do farmers, walking home from the pleasure district. They gave him a wide berth, stopping and standing aside well off the track. The other time it was two samurai, *ronin*, also going to Momiji-joka, but moving less swiftly than Nils. He'd slowed to a walk eighty meters before he caught up to them, and overtook them with long swinging strides. They weren't aware of him till he was about to pass them, and the nearest one started aside with a jerk, bumping into his companion, then both stood staring at Nils's back. He felt their momentary alarm, their confusion and chagrin at having been startled. After a moment, one of them called after him, but he neither stopped nor turned to look back. He didn't need to turn to see behind him, and it might have been taken as confrontational. Nor were they displeased that he didn't, for they had never seen so large a man, nor one who felt so dangerous.

When Nils was fifty meters past them, he was almost out of sight, for the road was shadowed by overhanging trees. He began to trot again, the same swinging lope as before.

Fifty meters short of town, the trees left off. Ahead was a river, and a bridge built of timbers resting on stone piers. He stopped at the end of the trees, examining the situation. The town was not walled, as a European town would have been, but he discerned two guards at the far end of the bridge, unseeable to normal vision in the darkness. Not far beyond the bridge, the road became a street lined with businesses. A few shops were still open, lamplight spilling through opened panels to illuminate the thoroughfare. Not far from the bridge, one of the buildings was larger than the others, and it seemed to him it was an inn.

Nils slipped off across a field of sweet potatoes, tripping once on vines, and approached the river upstream of the bridge. The bank was riprapped with stone, against erosion, but just now the eighty-meter-wide streambed was mostly dry, water flowing in a pair of shallow channels ten to fifteen meters wide. Holding his scabbarded sword in front of him, he waded them without difficulty, then climbed the riprap on the far side.

Here in every direction were minds, thoughts—a mental bumble. In such a confusion, he'd have needed to get fairly close to one to read it, but there was nothing to mark any of them as especially worth his while. He turned left in the direction of Bridge Street, no longer loping, slinking now. Here the street was dark, most of the houses set back behind gardens and screened by bamboo fences, some of them overgrown with vines. It seemed well to avoid the lights of Bridge Street, so a block before he came to it, he turned right. He'd approach the inn from behind.

Another block brought him to it, or rather to the yard behind it. It too was fenced, the fence taller than he was, of stout bamboo woven together with hemp rope. The bamboos had been cut with a slashing stroke that left the tops sharp as punji stakes. There were outbuildings inside the enclosure; by the smell, one of them was a stable. He found a gate closed and barred, with a guard asleep inside it, but a dozen meters along the fence grew a young chestnut tree large enough to take his weight. Carefully he climbed it, till he was higher than the fence. The chestnut began to bend, and he hung to the side toward the fence as he climbed, until he overhung it. Then, quiet as a cat, he dropped inside.

Taking advantage of the dark and the drowsing gate guard, he crossed the yard and crouched beside the inn. Again his mind scouted, selecting, and he crept farther, to a window shuttered against the night air. Inside was a room with five men, drinking *sake* and talking.

He crouched there and eavesdropped, paying heed primarily to explicit thoughts, largely ignoring the images, concepts and beliefs stirred by the conversation. On Earth, perhaps no other telepath could have done what he did, and even Nils focused mainly on one man at a time. One of them was a samurai, two were local merchants, and one a sword polisher. The other was a traveling priest devoted to the worship of Amida. The priest was offended by some of the things the samurai said— things he considered disrespectful to the Buddhas—but he held his tongue. The samurai seemed at the point, in his drinking, where he might easily be roused to violence. He was, the samurai boasted, in the service of Lord Fukumori. His father having recently died, he was traveling to his home district near Nagoya, to see to his inheritance. Actually he lied. He was a *ronin*, and had recently left a robber band which preyed on travelers and backcountry hamlets in the mountains.

The traveling cloth merchant wanted to talk about a boat that was said to have come down from Heaven and landed near the village of Omugi, not far away. The priest considered it the talk of some drunken peasant, but the traveling grain merchant entered into the argument, insisting that numerous farmers had seen it, and that a squad of samurai had gone there from the castle to investigate. They reportedly had found it just as the farmers had said. The priest declined to argue further then, for it was the merchants who were paying for his drinks.

Nils crouched outside, listening for half an hour without learning much of value, then insinuated a notion into the priest's mind: that perhaps it would be wise to leave this party, to go to the local temple and request lodging from its rector. The priest, who was less than sober, took the thought from there: True the two merchants had invited him to stay with them, but who knew how long they'd sit drinking before they went to bed. Or what unpleasantness might develop with that surly samurai who considered himself better than any of them.

With that, Nils had gotten a notion of where the temple was—on the lower slope of the ridge, just above town. He decided to go there, make himself known, and ask about Ojiisan Tattobu. He turned and slipped through the darkness toward the gate.

The guard was still dozing, squatting on his haunches with his back against it. Nils considered slipping up and disabling him, but he might harm the man, who'd done nothing to earn injury from him.

The stable was near the fence; on one side its eaves overhung it. Quietly he went to it, and found a ladder leaning against the opposite side. Boards and bundles of fresh thatch were stacked by it; apparently workmen had been repairing its roof. He climbed the ladder carefully, testing each rung with his weight. It held. The roof was too steep to climb without help, but the help was there—another ladder lay on it, extending all the way to the crest. He climbed it too, and at its upper end, found it secured by large ell-shaped brackets hooked over the ridge pole.

He examined the slope on the other side. He could pull the ladder up, transfer it to the far side, then climb down it to the eaves and jump into the alley. But the transferred ladder would be a problem to the roofers in the morning, and he could just as well lie on his back and slide down. Though the slope was steep, it seemed to him he could control his speed by spreading his arms and digging in his heels. In a few seconds he could be in the alley again, and on his way to the temple.

He swung his legs across the ridgepole and began his slide—and broke through the roof! For several seconds he hung half through, feet walking on air, struggling for a firm grip to pull himself back up. Old thatch and pieces of rotten board rained down on the mare beneath him, the animal snorting and stamping in alarm. Somewhere in the darkness below, the stable boy wakened, and ran outside shouting: "Help! Help! Someone is stealing the horses!"

This jerked the gateman awake. He blew three piercing blasts on the alarm horn that hung beside his post, then ran toward the stable, sword in hand. Nils broke the rest of the way through and fell, landing on the mare's right rump before hitting the dirt floor. The mare, recoiling, whinnied loudly, and a pile-driver hoof caught the back of Nils's shoulder as he rolled to his knees, propelling him to the middle of the floor. There he got to his feet, and limping, ran toward the end of the stable opposite the inn.

This end, open like the other, led onto a manure pile that was more bedding straw than animal waste. Beyond it was the bamboo fence, but the manure pile was too soft a base for jumping from; Nils ran over the pile, turning right and running through the narrow space between stable and fence, in the direction of the gate.

By now, men were running from the back of the inn, some freshly wakened, some half drunk, several with swords long or short. Drawing his own sword, he ran to the gate. The running men gave way to him, then two samurai closed in behind him. The gate opened outward, and he burst through it—to find a street patrol almost upon him, drawn by the alarm horn.

With their spiked, barbed staffs they surrounded him, and before he could act, a net was thrown over him. He did not struggle. He read nothing like blood lust among them, or even brutality. Unlike the street patrol that had captured him in Pest, that night several years earlier, their intent was to take him unhurt if possible. The samurai who'd followed Nils through the gate, were kept away from him by the patrolmen, the *doshin* in charge warning them off sharply. Nils found himself being wrapped around by cords, his sword taken from his hand and returned to its scabbard.

While they worked, the gate guard came panting out with the stable boy in tow. The guard had the boy describe what had happened, or what he thought had happened, then the *doshin* asked questions of them both. The proprietor of the inn was there too, by then, and described thefts that purportedly had taken place recently. The *doshin* listened to them intently, then banished them with a wave. People were always ready to dump all recent misdeeds on the first available miscreant arrested. Matsumura-sama's magistrates would want proofs or a confession. The giant's only established misdeed seemed to be trespassing. Probably he'd come to steal a horse, as the stable boy said, but suspicion was not evidence.

Scowling at the prisoner, the *doshin* barked an order. The giant's legs had been left free, the net roped around his waist, while two tethers around his neck were held by men on either side of him. The senior patrolman prodded the giant with a staff, and the patrol walked him down the alley to Bridge Street, marching him off toward prison. But on Bridge Street, in the light from a *sake* shop, one of the patrolmen saw the giant's eyes and gestured urgently to the *doshin*. "Excuse me, Hasegawa-san, but the prisoner is blind!"

"What!?" The *doshin* stopped the procession and stepped around to look at the prisoner from the front. Nils "stared" at him, eye-lids open wide. The *doshin*, disbelieving, pushed close to the Northman, being careful not to breathe on his face—a normal courtesy performed without thought—then stepped back. "Take him into the *sake* shop," he muttered, "where the light is better."

Inside, there could be no doubt. The man's eyes were not

even remotely human. The *doshin* waved a hand in front of Nils's face, then poked a finger almost into one eye. And got no flinch, not even a blink. Cautiously he touched one, and still got no response.

"He is blind!" he said.

"Excuse me, Hasegawa-san," said the senior patrolman, "but he is reported to have run around inside the yard, dodged and threatened people, and then run to the gate, raised the bar . . ."

Hasegawa stilled the man with a gesture, and turned back to Nils. "What is your name, and where are you from?"

"My name is Tetsu-te. I am from across the sea."

The *doshin* frowned. The name Tetsu-te—Iron Hand—sounded like something some rough *ronin* might take on himself, but this foreigner could not be a *ronin* or any other kind of samurai. It was the words "from across the sea" that directed the *doshin*'s thoughts now. In his youth he'd traveled to the west coast, and stayed awhile in Shimonoseki. Several times he'd seen Korean seamen in the harbor, and once a ship from China, driven there by storm. This man looked nothing at all like any of the sailors, and he spoke Yamatoan, albeit strangely, which the other foreigners had not.

"What kind of eyes do you have?" he demanded.

"They are eyes given to me by Okuni-nushi."

Okuni-nushi! So important a god! Most of the patrolmen backed away, but the *doshin* stood his ground. If this was a *kami* of some sort, how had they succeeded in capturing it? And why would it have fled from the people who chased it? At most it could only be a very minor *kami*.

Unless it had *allowed* them to capture it. In which case, what could its motive be, and how seriously might it be offended with them? He decided to take it to his superior's office. The *yoriki* might criticize him for imposing, for not handling this himself, but if he mishandled it . . .

The *yoriki* questioned first the *doshin*, then briefly the prisoner. When he was finished, he glowered at the junior official. "This is obviously not a *kami*," he said, "but a demon, and in either case is the business of the priests. Take him to the temple and turn him over to the rector. Making sure he does no violence."

The *doshin* was humiliated at the implied criticism, but at the same time relieved that it hadn't been worse. He bowed deeply, and marched out with the prisoner. He did not believe this was a demon; it did not behave as a demon. It was probably a very minor *kami*, he decided. But in either case, the *yoriki* was right: the rector was the proper authority to deal with it. He suspected that propitiation would be the correct handling.

It was nearing the hour of the boar—approaching midnight— when they arrived at the temple. The rector was not delighted to be wakened, and like the *yoriki*, snorted at the suggestion that this might be a minor *kami* sent by Okuni-nushi.

"It is a demon," he grumped, "one that has lost most of its powers by exposure to some very holy person. The Abbot of Mamori-no-Tera passed through the district a few weeks ago on his way to Miyako, to report to the Emperor on Osoroshii-yama. The demon probably saw him passing and was weakened by it."

The *doshin* kept his eyes on the well-rubbed plank floor. To him, the rector's explanation seemed dubious in the extreme, though not impossible.

"Tie it to the big *sugi* in the back garden," the rector went on, "being very sure it cannot get loose. I will dispose of it in the morning. But be careful not to kill it; it must be killed with proper ritual, in such a way that its spirit cannot get out of the body and do further damage." He arched an eyebrow. "Very probably it would seek you out and possess you."

Then he went back to bed.

Borrowing a lantern, the *doshin* led his men, with the prisoner, to the *sugi* the rector had spoken of. He continued skeptical, but took no chances. The net was left on the prisoner, but nooses were slipped through it, drawn tight over each wrist, and the arms pulled across the body. Then the rope ends were tied behind the thick tree trunk. Another rope, provided by a temple servant, was wrapped around the prisoner's legs and waist, with spare loops around his shoulders and neck, tight enough to keep him from moving.

When they were finished, the *doshin* looked his prisoner over unhappily. The deerskin breeches were torn on one leg, and stained somewhat with blood—something that had happened before he'd passed into their hands. "Please excuse me if you are a *kami*," said the *doshin*. "I have only been obeying orders."

"I excuse you," Nils said slowly, still unpracticed with the language. "But will Okuni-nushi excuse you? If my body is made dead—executed—bad things will happen to this place—this entire district. The worst will happen to those responsible."

The *doshin* kept his eyes lowered and turned away. Snapping orders, he left, his men following, carefully not looking back.

Okuni-nushi! The rector lay on his thick futon with his eyes closed. He didn't believe in Okuni-nushi, or in most of the other gods, hadn't believed in them since his youth. Not even Amaterasu-omikami, something he wouldn't admit to anyone. They were, he told himself, superstitions passed on from ancient times. Not that he'd stand for anyone saying such a thing to his parishioners; it would shock and upset them needlessly, and if believed, would certainly reduce income. But in fact there were only two real gods: the Buddha Amida and the Buddha Sakyamuni; the rest were myths. It was that which made him so certain about the captive demon. It was clearly neither human being nor Buddha, which left demons as the remaining alternative. For example, "Osoroshii-kami" was a demon instead of a god, he was reasonably sure.

For a time he lay considering possible deaths for the captive demon. Beheading wouldn't do, nor burning nor quartering; it would escape from the body. Perhaps the rumen or bladder of a cow could be slipped over its head and tied tightly around the thick neck. He could even have it suffocated that way. A butcher could supply the rumen, and it was customary to have a butcher do executions anyway. Only unclean persons were assigned to execute prisoners, and of unclean persons, butchers were the best qualified.

Then a complication occurred to the rector. The demon would simply escape into the rumen, and if the rumen ruptured . . . He could have the creature hung, of course, but he'd heard of thick-necked persons surviving after being cut down seemingly dead.

No, he'd have it garroted. The butcher was a powerful man, with stout arms and thick, short-fingered hands. Using a leather thong, perhaps twisting it tight with a stick to defeat the demon's powerful neck muscles . . .

These were the rector's thoughts as he drifted toward sleep. Then an eerie howl reached his ears, startling him wide awake. Throwing aside his quilt, he sat bolt upright, eyes wide. It repeated, as much roar as howl now, and it came from behind the temple. *The demon!* he thought. Heaving to his feet, he waddled angry and resolute along the hall to the rear door. There he took down the lantern that hung beside it, and stepped outside. As his feet found his slippers there, his eyes found the demon. The creature howled again, a great coarse-voiced sound that must have wakened everyone in the temple. Tight-lipped, the rector hurried down the steps to confront it. The gate guard came running up at the same time, but the rector sent him back to his post; it wouldn't do to leave the gate unguarded against thieves. Besides, three *ronin* who'd been given shelter for the night came out the back door just then, swords in hand.

The rector glared at the demon. "What are you howling for? Have you no manners? People are trying to sleep!"

"I wanted you to come out and set me free," it said. Its voice was remarkably calm.

"Set you free? You're a demon! Anyone can see that!"

"I am not a demon," the demon answered reasonably. "I am a human, sent by Okuni-nushi to talk with people here, to see how they live and what they think about."

"There is no—" The rector had almost said there was no Okuni-nushi, right in front of the *ronin*. "Why would Okuni-nushi send you?"

"Okuni-nushi rules the invisible, and I am his retainer. He chose me because I had no eyes, having lost mine defending the good name of the Buddhas. And having no human eyes, I can more easily see the invisible, with the help of the god's eyes he gave to me.

"It was recommended that I speak with someone known as Ojiisan Tattobu. Perhaps you can tell me where he is."

The rector scowled, avoiding the demon's eyes. He disapproved of Ojiisan Tattobu and his troublesome opinions, and was glad he seemed relatively inactive these days. "Ojiisan does not choose to keep me informed of his comings and goings. You have not answered my question: Why would Okuni-nushi send you?"

One of the *ronin* had also brought a lantern, and stepping up beside the rector, raised it to get his own look at the captive's face. He inhaled sharply at the sight—it was strong-boned, with powerful jaws (from chewing tough meat since childhood), straw-colored hair and sparse cottony beard. *And blank, pupil-less eyes, their blue as pale as a red-start's eggs.*

"I do not see as you see," the prisoner went on, still speaking to the rector, "but I see things others cannot. I see your soul, and the spirits in the swords of these samurai. I see your thoughts, and the things you have done. I see you with the young acolyte, Heimatsu, and with the serving girl . . ."

"*Enough!*" the rector shouted, angry at this demon who would expose his private activities before some grinning *ronin*. "If you'll be quiet, I won't have you killed in the morning. I'll have you taken to the castle instead, and let Lord Matsumura decide what to do with you. He is notoriously affable. He will probably have you released."

No sooner had he said it than it struck him that this—thing— might well have seen in his mind the treachery he planned. For he had no intention of keeping his promise.

The prisoner said nothing for a long moment, but it seemed to the rector he could *feel* the blank eyes regarding his soul. "I will be quiet," the prisoner said at last, "and—commune with Okuni-nushi. But the patrolmen tied my wrists too tightly. You must first have them loosened. Otherwise my hands will begin to rot, and it will do me little good when Lord Matsumura frees me."

So. The demon couldn't see into his mind after all, had only been guessing. Lips pursed, he peered at the demon's hands; they were indeed swollen, and if he didn't loosen them, who knew what he might say to these *ronin*. "Excuse me," the rector said to the *ronin*, for they were samurai, even if currently unattached, and courtesy was owed them. "If you will loosen his wrists, not too much of course, and watch him during the night . . . One of you can watch at a time, while the others sleep. When you leave in the morning, I will pay each of you five silver *chogin*."

A *lot of money!* thought the senior *ronin*, then said aloud, "And a jug of *sake* tonight."

"Of course."

"We will do it then." Without looking at his comrades, the senior *ronin* examined the prisoner's bonds. Wrapped in the net as he was, and wound around by rope, there was little danger from him. The *ronin* loosened and retied the thick wrists one at a time, then watched the prisoner's face intently. The return of proper circulation in the hands must sting intensely, he thought, but the prisoner showed no sign of it. The rector looked the work over carefully, then nodded and turned to leave.

"Hoshin," said the senior *ronin* to one of his comrades, "please accompany the rector and receive the money for us. Also the *sake*."

The rector turned angrily toward him. "You must watch him through the night first!"

The *ronin* bobbed a shallow bow. "So sorry for the misunderstanding. The *sake* tonight, the money in the morning."

Still angry, the rector nodded stiffly, then walked toward the temple with Hoshin a step behind. The other two samurai grinned at each other. "Do you wish me to take the first watch?" asked one.

"Thank you for asking, but I will stay awake for a time and speak with this person. Or demon or *kami* as the case may be."

"I also, for I have never seen one like him before. But first I will go inside and bring our cloaks. These nights are getting chilly."

He turned and trotted toward the temple. The senior *ronin* examined the prisoner thoughtfully, saying nothing, however, until his companions had come back, one with their traveling cloaks, the other with a jug of *sake*. They put the cloaks on and sat down on their feet, close enough together to pass the jug back and forth. Each had a drink. The *sake* was not warmed as it should have been, but it was good regardless.

The senior *ronin* smacked his lips, then looked at the figure tied to the *sugi*, and spoke to it. "Do you know what I think? I think that fat rector was lying. I think he plans to bring up the butcher before breakfast, to kill you."

"Thank you for the courtesy of telling me. I am quite certain of it. For I did look into his soul, as I said earlier."

The *ronin* cocked his head curiously. "What are you, really?" he asked. "*Kami* or demon?"

"I am a foreign samurai, one who has wizard sight. But the rector would never believe the truth, so I lied to him."

The three of them eyed him for several seconds without speaking. That he was foreign was obvious from his appearance. And certainly he had the assurance of a samurai. As for wizard sight—his eyes were uncanny enough. "The rector is sure you are a demon."

"The rector sees demons where there are none."

Hoshin spoke then, the *ronin* who'd gone after the *sake*. "Please excuse me, but I do not believe a human being can see into souls, not even a wizard. You must be a demon after all."

"Excuse me for disagreeing, but it is by the grace of Okuni-nushi that I see into souls. He brought me to Yamato to look into the souls of men and see how they live."

"If you are a demon, that's exactly the sort of thing you would say."

"True. But Okuni-nushi would not send a demon. He sent me also to find a wandering holy man called Ojiisan Tattobu."

The three inhaled sharply, the sound hissing. "That one is very holy! He can be dangerous to you. If you are a demon, it would no doubt kill you to look at him."

The prisoner interrupted them. "Is there a wizard in this district? If there is, and if he's powerful enough, he can look at me and see the truth."

The senior *ronin* looked at his friends, then back at the prisoner. "We do not know. We are strangers in this district. Some *daimyo* keep a wizard in their household, but wizards of any real power are very rare."

They passed the jug again.

"Excuse me if I am imposing on your generosity," the prisoner said, "but may I also have a drink of that?"

The one holding the jug looked at the others, then got to his feet and, lifting it to the prisoner's mouth, tilted it carefully. The prisoner took a swallow.

"Thank you for your generosity. That is good _sake_."

"Please excuse me for disagreeing, but it is quite ordinary _sake_."

"Ah. By the standards of your enlightened country, perhaps. In mine it would be considered exceptional."

If this is a demon, the senior _ronin_ told himself, _he is strangely well-spoken. As far as that's concerned, if he's a demon, why doesn't he put a spell on us and shrivel us all down to vermin?_ "You said Okuni-nushi brought you to Yamato. Not sent, but brought. Did you misspeak yourself?"

"Not at all. He brought me."

"From a foreign land? How? In what way did he bring you here?"

"In a Heaven Boat. It still sits in a pasture near the village of Omugi, not an hour's walk from where you sit now. Lord Matsumura knows of it. He sent a party of samurai to speak with Okuni-nushi's retainers who fly it above the sky."

The three were no longer surprised at anything the prisoner claimed. As for his truthfulness, he no doubt told the truth when it suited him, but some of the things he said . . .

"If one of you climbed the hill to the castle," the prisoner went on, "you would find that what I said about the Heaven Boat is true. Of course, I could simply know about it, and be lying when I said I came on it. But Lord Matsumura will want to question me."

The senior _ronin_ looked him over carefully. With someone who looked so foreign, it was difficult to guess what he was up to. "Excuse me for saying it, but you have told us things that sound very strange."

"True. And as far as you know, all that I said could be lies. But if you were to describe me to Lord Matsumura, I believe he would want to examine me for himself. And if I were in fact a demon, would I not have put a spell on you? And on the rector, who is unworthy to serve the Buddha Amida? All that is necessary is that Lord Matsumura's men arrive before the rector brings the butcher up to kill me in the morning."

The senior *ronin* didn't answer for a moment, then laughed, his decision made. "You are correct about the rector, at least. We have heard that he sodomizes his maid servant so that, if anyone accuses him of laying with her, he can deny it, saying she still has her maidenhead."

He turned to the others. "I am going to the castle, and tell them what we've seen and heard here. Do not tell the rector. If the *tehon daimyo* sends men here to collect this"—he paused— "this person, let the rector think he learned of him from the *yoriki*'s office. And when you pass the jug, give the prisoner my share. He will get cold, tied to that tree all night."

The first light of dawn was thinning the darkness when armed men arrived. They were not Lord Matsumura's men, however, but a street patrol led by a *doshin*. The *ronin* had not been let into the castle at so late an hour, nor would the gate guards disturb their master or his captain with a message from some unknown *ronin*. So he'd gone to the *yoriki*'s office. That seemed far better than leaving the prisoner to be strangled by the butcher.

The *yoriki* knew of the Heaven Boat, and while he didn't believe the prisoner's claim to have arrived on it—the giant had said nothing about it earlier—he would have him brought to prison and questioned. No doubt they could inspire him to confess that he was lying. If not, *then* perhaps he'd send word to Lord Matsumura, asking if he wished to examine him himself.

The guard let the patrol through the gate, and they went straight to the *sugi*. The jug was empty on the ground, and the two *ronin* on watch lay huddled beneath their cloaks, snoring. The prisoner had been cut free, and lay beside them, sleeping as if covered with furs.

Once more the *doshin*'s men threw a net over the giant and tied him. Then they led him back down the slope into town, to the prison compound, where, with lances and swords at the ready, they untied him and fastened a cangue around his neck, leaving one hand free so he could feed himself. Then he was put into a dirty cell with another prisoner, to await interrogation.

SIX

The first week of August had been dry, and the train of men and horses raised puffs of dust on the mountain road. Like the other poorer travelers in the caravan, Hidaka Satoru was afoot. But unlike some, for Satoru, hiking was no hardship. He was tall, even for someone from the Hidaka District—184 centimeters—with long muscular legs and arms, tough feet, and a strong and craggy face with bristly brows.

Whereas the other foot-travelers wore broad, nearly flat straw hats, Satoru's head was bare, protected only by a mane of coarse black hair. All in all, his appearance matched his rough Hokkaido dialect; in another time and place, he might have been referred to as a jack-pine savage. The others would have treated him as a primitive, except for the aggressive intelligence behind his features, his eyes. Intelligence and ambition, and something more. Something indefinable.

By standards on this road, the caravan was sizeable. Thirty-six men rode or trudged in the heat and humidity: six merchants, eight armed servants who tended their masters and their master's horses; thirteen other travelers, all armed, ten of them afoot; and nine mounted *ronin* with lances and swords—samurai not currently pledged to any *daimyo*. In addition, there were twenty-four pack horses. Eight carried the merchants' travel equipment—tents, bedding, clothing, and food. The others carried merchandise.

The ten men afoot slowed the party, but the merchants, all of them frugal, had been unwilling to hire more *ronin*. Instead they'd gathered other travelers, expecting that bandits would avoid so large a party, as most would have. The merchants would provide the other travelers with barley, *miso*, and bean curds. As well as weapons—lance-like *naginata*; who was to know that most of them were totally undrilled with them?

The road wound largely through coniferous forest: usually pine or *sugi*, but occasionally *tsuga* or fir. Along exposed crests and in saddles, there sometimes were meadows, while at lower elevations, beeches, oaks, and other broad-leafed trees shared space with the conifers. In draws and ravines, mountain streams rushed and tumbled. Seeps and rivulets were numerous on the slopes along the road, and thirst could usually be quenched without unstoppering a flask or water skin. Every few miles there were rude log shelters—three walls and a roof—but the small caravan normally camped where dusk found them, the servants setting up their masters' tents, with help from the unmounted travelers who were rewarded with a bowl of heated *sake* after supper.

Especially on the passes, the dog days of August were less oppressive in the mountains than on the coast, but hiking the sometimes steep road made the sweat ooze from both horses and the men afoot. The "road" was little more than a broad trail. It had never known a wheel, and a party such as theirs would occasionally travel all day without meeting other travelers. On most days, though, they met two or three parties, generally smaller than theirs. Invariably the most important merchant— the one who'd paid for three of the *ronin*—would ask any travelers they met whether they'd seen or heard of bandits on the road. For back in Toyama there'd been stories. The reply, though, had been "no" in every case, and his party felt increasingly relaxed. And when, on the fifth morning, they met a cavalry patrol, it seemed to them that the danger was indeed slight. The troopers' faces were hard and haughty, while their fine armor and red laquer helmets signified status and reputation. Besides two swords, each of them carried a long bow in a boot by his saddle. Surely any bandits would have been intimidated and left the district.

It was only three hours later, not long after eating the midday meal, that Hidaka Satoru sensed danger, an ambush close ahead. He thought to shout a warning, then didn't, for this was a difficult place from which to escape. The road sloped down to cross a rowdy creek, after which it climbed sharply; it was

uphill both ahead and to the rear, and steep on both sides.
And he felt something else, something in the future, beckoning.

So what he did instead was separate himself from the nearest
of the mounted escort, watching alertly, and when the first
arrows sliced from the forest's edge, he threw himself flat on
the ground.

He didn't hide his head though; he watched. Within two or
three seconds, seven of the nine *ronin* guards had been shot
from their saddles, most with multiple arrows. The other two
had dismounted, swords drawn. Satoru could see numerous
bowmen who'd stepped from the concealment of trees.

The travelers made no attempt to counter-attack. Some of
the bandits came down onto the road then, to disarm them,
and the party's two remaining *ronin* fought. Clearly the bandits
too were samurai, however, or most were, and the fight was
quickly over, the two guards lying dead in the blood and dust.

After that, the *honcho* of the robbers came down and
demanded to know who was the caravan's leader. The principal
merchant stepped forward, straight-backed but swag-bellied.
If the value of loot was sufficient, he was told, they would all
be let free, to hike out of the mountains as best they could.
Otherwise they'd be held for ransom, and killed if the ransom
demands weren't met. Satoru read in the *honcho's* mind, though,
that prisoners and ransom dealings were a nuisance. Any who
made no trouble were to be let go; it was a policy of his chief.
To the *honcho* it made more sense to kill them.

Meanwhile, bandits were examining cargo packs and
saddlebags, while others roughly searched clothing. All six
merchants carried considerable cash on their persons, in
silver *chogin* and gold *koban*. On the pack animals were
found, among other things, five loads of richly embroidered
silk, a small pack of carved ivory, and three loads of woolen
cloth from Korea.

And sewn into his traveling kimono, the senior merchant
had a number of pearls of the first water, a small fortune in
themselves.

The bandits tied the saddle horses into the string of pack
animals, preparing to lead them away. Then Hidaka Satoru
walked up boldly to the *honcho*.

"Excuse me," he said, "but I would like to join you."

The *honcho* stared for a moment, taking in the long, rugged body, the strong face and intent gaze.

"Are you skilled with weapons?"

"I am not a samurai, as you can see," Hidaka answered, "but I am from Hokkaido, and was trained as a militia man. I am skilled with both *naginata* and bow. And more important, I was born a wizard into a family of wizards. I was brought up in its skills from childhood, and excel in them."

The *honcho*'s brows drew down like dark furry caterpillars, as if in disapproval, but he shrugged. "If you come with us," he answered, "you will be required to demonstrate your skills and willingness as a fighting man. And if they are not satisfactory, our chief will no doubt kill you himself."

Satoru laughed, an act of astonishing audacity for a peasant conversing with a *ronin*. "There is as little chance of my failing," he said, "as there is of that body rising to its feet." He gestured toward a fallen escort, who had an arrow through one eye and two others through his corselet.

The bandit scowled, but instead of drawing his sword, he pointed. "Wait there until I tell you what to do."

Satoru smiled as the *honcho* walked away. He was a man of destiny, had known it all his life. This encounter with bandits would prove a major step on his way to wealth and power, he had no doubt at all.

Minutes later the travelers watched their horses and all their goods disappearing up the road with the bandits. They wondered glumly what they'd eat, and the merchants in particular wondered how their feet and legs would stand the road, for they were not used to walking.

SEVEN

Not only Matt and Nikko were concerned when Nils had not returned by sunup. Hans fidgeted restlessly, while Achikh brooded. Matthew told himself that a telepath with a sword, and remarkable skill in its use, was less subject to harm than the average foreigner. On the other hand, Matt had crammed what the computer had on pre-plague Japan, including its history. At least during the Tokugawan Period, foreigners had been feared and hated, particularly Caucasians, and Nils was clearly both. Further, a peculiar and often unreasonable sense of honor had prevailed then, even more extreme than among the Neovikings, while armed men had been everywhere, skilled and quick to fight. And it seemed to Matt that some of them might take offence simply at Nils's size and coloring.

He tried to shake off his concern. Anyone who'd survived the things that Nils had . . . On the other hand, how long could someone tempt death without paying with his life?

The morning was warm and humid, for mid-September. High clouds had moved in, and the breeze had freshened. It seemed likely to Matthew that they'd have rain before the day was through.

At 0853, Captain Iwatoku arrived with a smaller party than the day before. Without Nils to monitor the Yamatoans' minds, Matthew felt ill at ease with them. The expedition's early experiences, including his own, with orc telepaths and dungeons, had traumatized him. And then the *Phaeacia* had been parked above the atmosphere to back up the ground parties. Now there was no backup; he and Nikko and Ted were on their own.

Matthew stayed on the ground only long enough for Ted to ask the questions that they and the computer had listed. Then, at 0937 and with minimal formality, Ted bade goodbye to the small party of samurai. Matthew raised ship to twelve kilometers, far beyond ordinary telepathic range, and above the landscape of clouds below them. By that time the computer had completed its analysis of the new Yamatoan words, and incorporated them into the language bank. They now had a strong basic Yamatoan vocabulary and grammar which, augmented with 21st century Japanese, should permit effective communication across a broad spectrum of subjects.

Nikko reinventoried their food and water; they'd need to replenish somewhere, soon, and Matthew didn't want to do it in Yamato. "We've implied that we're gods," he said. "We can't tell these people we're running out of food and water."

Nikko shook her head. "Lots of primitive people, maybe most of them, assumed that their gods ate and drank like everyone else."

"Including the pre-technological Japanese," Ted put in. "They used to leave offerings of food and *sake* for the gods. We could tell them to do that for us, and one of us could sneak out after dark and get it, so they wouldn't see that we're ordinary humans."

"Or one of us could go out in an EVA suit," Nikko suggested. "Helmet and all. That would certainly impress them."

Normally an image like that would have amused Matthew; now he simply gnawed fretfully on his lip. The suggestions made sense, but he felt ill at ease with them. What he really wanted to do was return to the Northmen, to a part of this world where he felt reasonably secure.

Matthew Kumalo, he told himself grimly, *you're losing your grip*.

But the fact remained that they were running low on food, and were restricting water to drinking and cooking. There was a limit to what the pinnace's recycler could do with waste water. By making the trip above the atmosphere, they could be back in Varjby in an hour, dealing with people they knew. Allow an additional hour—two or three at most— for actually getting what they wanted, and another hour to get back. Meanwhile they could be cramming the language update while they traveled.

Perhaps Hans and Achikh would even agree to stay behind

in Varjby, so the *Alpha* wouldn't be so damned crowded. That would . . .

Ted interrupted Matthew's thoughts. "Matt," he said, "don't you think we ought to be on the ground? In case Nils comes back?"

Matthew felt a bit like a football with the air leaking out of it. He nodded reluctantly. "I guess we should." *I'll send the Yamatoan greeting party home when we get down though*, he added to himself. It was the possibility of psi-snoops that worried him most.

But when they landed, the Yamatoans had already left, all but the peasants working in the field, most of whom only looked up for a minute or so, this time, before turning their attention back to their work. The Heaven Boat was becoming old hat.

Ted was the first to cram the Yamatoan language update. Then he turned the student cap over to Nikko. Matthew sat down with him in the pilots' seats, and began debriefing him on his year-long trek, on foot and horseback, from the Danube to Mongolia, and thence to China. Lacking the privacy desirable in debriefs, they murmured in undertones.

When Nikko was done on the deep-learning program, she coached Achikh through a turn on it, and then Hans. Matthew announced he was ready to return to the Balkans, to the Northman settlers there, to take on supplies, and found no one else happy with that. Nils might come back while they were gone, they complained, then wander off again.

"No," Matt said, "if he comes back while we're gone, he'll know enough to stay around. He'll know we wouldn't abandon him."

"Suppose he arrives with someone chasing him?" Ted asked.

Matt had no answer to that, and reluctantly agreed to stay where they were till the next morning. Nikko and Ted, in turn, agreed to go willingly back to Varjby then, even if Nils hadn't returned.

The rest of the day went slowly. They ate once, sparingly. Matt, Nikko, and Ted took turns on watch, in case some Yamatoans showed up again. All that actually happened though, was that the peasants left the field, as if driven out by the brief spattering rain shower that swept through just before they left. Which seemed reasonable; the air did feel as if a storm was coming. The two not on watch watched Ted's cubes of the trek. Hans and Achikh watched with them, but neither seemed happy with the waiting. Then Hans took out his pocket stone and added, if possible, to the razor sharpness of his sword.

As evening began to settle in, Achikh said he was going out and hunt for Nils.

"You have no sword," Hans pointed out.

"You will lend me yours."

Hans shook his head. "I'll need it if I go out."

"Then I will get one out there." The Buriat gestured with his own head.

"The people here aren't used to foreigners," Nikko pointed out. "They probably don't trust them. And they're more ruled by custom than many people, and quick to take offense."

"Not more than my own people," Achikh said stubbornly.

Matthew tried to get him to wait till near daylight, hoping that Nils might return by then, but the best he could get from him was agreement to wait till after dark, when he wouldn't be seen coming out of the pinnace. Achikh squatted beside the door. Hans spoke to him in Mongol, and Achikh replied tersely.

"What did he say?" Matthew asked.

"He told me he plans to go to the village."

Slowly dusk thickened to twilight, and twilight to full dark, which was dark indeed, given the now thick cloud cover. By then it was raining again, and the wind had worsened. Matthew let himself hope that, given such weather, Achikh would change his mind. But shortly the rain paused, and the Buriat got to his feet.

"I will go now," he said.

Matthew nodded, switched off the lights and force shield, and opened the door. Achikh stepped out, and Hans moved as if to follow him.

"Hans—" Nikko began, and the tall adolescent turned to her.

"I will go with him," Hans said. "He may be Nils's *anda*, but it's my duty to write the Järnhann Saga, so I must find him and stay with him. Besides, Achikh and I shared hardship and danger for a long time. It would not be right to let him go alone."

With that the boy followed the Buriat warrior, while Matt and Nikko watched. When both Achikh and Hans were clear, Matt switched the force shield on again and belatedly closed the door. The air that had blown in smelled of rain.

"At least we've got more room," Matt said. Nikko nodded, glancing at Ted, who looked definitely unhappy, as if he felt he should have gone with the two barbarians. As much as his cubes and debrief, as much as his performance in the showdown at Miyun, this told her how greatly the junior ethnologist had changed from the young man ridden by self-doubts. The timid young man who couldn't relate to the Northmen, or to the other realities of primitive, present-day Earth.

The storm made it too dark to see the row of trees by the road, and no light shone in the windows of the farmhouse. But with a barbarian's sense of orientation, Achikh and Hans angled northwestward, to strike the road on the side toward the village. Hans would have preferred not to cross the potato field; the Star People wouldn't want human tracks crossing the freshly hoed ground from the sky boat. But Achikh was in no mood to be reasonable, and there might as well be two sets of tracks as one. Besides, the air felt as if there'd be enough rain tonight to wash their tracks out.

The road was puddled, and the trees that flanked it, thrashing in the wind now, made it even darker than the field had been. In the village, they saw only occasional thin cracks of lamplight; the storm shutters had been mounted. They didn't attempt stealth; it seemed needless. The wind continued to increase, driving intermittent rain. Surely no one was likely to be out without good reason.

"Where are we going?" Hans asked.

"To some house where there will surely be weapons. A big house; a headman's house."

Hans shrugged. He supposed that was as good a plan as any. An image came to his mind then, the village seen from the air: Its forty or fifty houses were mostly strung out along the road, mostly within twenty meters of it, and typically nearer. One had been considerably larger than the others, with more and larger outbuildings. The trick would be to find it in the dark.

Shortly they came to a yard fenced with stout bamboo, more than head high beside the 188-centimeter Hans, and woven together with rope. *This must be it*, Hans thought. Ahead, from the other side of the fence, they saw torch glow, and slowed till they came even with it. There was a gate there, with the torch inside.

Achikh raised the gate latch. Hans felt his scalp prickle. Without a word, the Buriat pushed the gate wide and pounced in, half crouched. From inside came a shout, and drawing his sword, Hans followed.

He was no sooner clear of the gate than someone kicked it shut, and Hans's eyes darted 'round. Achikh was struggling in a net, and three men were trying to subdue him. He was substantially larger than they. One had him around the knees, while the other two were trying to wrap him with a rope. Two others, swords in hand, faced Hans, while another ran toward them across the compound. Hans turned and fled, danger lending speed and strength to his long legs. As he ran, he tossed his sword over the fence beside him, and at the corner leaped, grasping the tops of two bamboos and vaulting. Pain seered his hands, and he landed in an off-balance crouch, falling. He was on his feet in an instant, turning back along the outside of the fence. His sword should be about half-way back to the gate.

It was too dark though; he went most of the way to the gate without finding it. And stopped, chagrined. How had this happened? These people couldn't have been waiting for them. And now he had no sword! He shouldn't have thrown it. But he couldn't have vaulted with it in his hand, and hadn't dared slow enough to sheath it.

Another rain shower burst upon him, this one harder, its large cold drops pelting like gravel stones. He huddled against the fence for what protection it gave. What should he do? What could he do? *Try to find my sword*, he decided. *Without it I'm helpless*.

The possibility of going back to the pinnace never occurred to him; he had to help Achikh.

Three samurai dragged the enwrapped Achikh toward the house. Others came out on the low veranda to question him. "Who are you?" one of them demanded. "Why did you trespass?"

"I am Achikh, son of Korchi. I came here to ask help."

A fist struck him on the nose, making his eyes water, and he felt the blood start. "Tell the truth! You were sent by Matsumura to spy on me!"

"I am looking for my friend. My—soul brother. This seemed to be a headman's house, so I came in to ask if you knew of him."

The fist struck him again, this time in the mouth. "Do not contradict me!"

Another man spoke who'd come out of the house. "Excuse me, Akawashi, but I do not think this man was sent by Matsumura. He is a foreigner. His clothing is foreign, and he speaks like a foreigner." He turned to Achikh. "Who is this friend you claim to seek?"

"His name is Tetsu-te Nils. He can be recognized by his very great size; I stand only to his shoulder. And he looks strange in other respects."

"What did the wretched foreigner say, Takada-san?" asked Akawashi impatiently. "I did not understand all of it."

"That his friend's name is Tetsu-te something, and that he is very tall and foreign-looking."

"He is lying, trying to get us to release him. Then he will go straight to Matsumura. We must kill him. Tetsu-te! That is no name! It is the sort of thing peasants call each other because their real names carry no honor."

Takada Chiu shook his head. "Iron Hand. It is the sort of name a barbarian might choose. A barbarian like this one." He turned back to Achikh, whose nose and mouth were bleeding. "This Tetsu-te. Is he a warrior?"

"Among his people, he is a chief, famous both as warrior and wizard. And his hair is the color of sunshine. If you had seen him, you'd know who I speak of. Also he has wizard's eyes."

Wizard's eyes? Takada regarded this indigestible lump for a moment, then put it aside. "Who are his people?" he asked.

"They are the Hokkitami."

Northmen? Takada Chiu had never heard of anyone called Northmen. He turned and said to the others, "That could be any of various foreign people."

Akawashi Kata grunted disgustedly. "He is making it all up. Matsumura sent him."

Takada looked intently at the captive. Kata could be right, but it seemed to him that this was something more than lies. This man had secrets, perhaps to do with Matsumura, but also quite possibly of greater matters. "You are a foreigner. How did you come to Yamato?"

Achikh could have said in the Heaven Boat, but he said simply, "In a boat."

Takada glowered; this was getting him nowhere. Of course he'd come in a boat; he was a foreigner, after all. "*Why* did you come here?" he demanded.

"Nils came here to find a holy wizard who is called Shisho-san. Also called Ojiisan Tattobu. We came here together, but got lost from each other."

Akawashi broke in then, scornfully. "You say this Tetsu-te is your friend, and a great chief. Yet you do not even wear a sword."

"I have been a warrior in different lands. I had a sword, but it was taken from me when I was made captive. Nils only rescued me two nights ago. I've had no chance to get another."

"Made captive by whom?" Takada asked.

"By my brother, who is the chief of the Buriat. Because I slew the emperor's ambassador to him, an evil man."

It struck Achikh then that they might think he spoke of their emperor, yet it seemed to him he could feel the hostility lessen.

Takada turned to Akawashi, who stood perplexed, as if he'd been cheated. "I believe my business here with you is complete for now," Takada said, his tone suddenly haughty. "We will leave at once, although the weather is really too foul for travel." As if to emphasize his comment, thunder rumbled across the sky, and a gust of wind slashed rain at them beneath the veranda roof. "If this storm is the *taifu*—perhaps even if it isn't—the river will become impassable, and I do not wish to be caught on this side of it. This one's companion has escaped, and Matsumura's man or not, he may go to him. And if Matsumura sends a platoon of cavalry here . . ."

Akawashi blanched in the torchlight.

"I will take this captive with me," Takada went on. "It is possible that Lord . . ." He paused. It would not do to name his lord before these men. Let them think he meant his *daimyo* brother. "That my lord may wish to question him. Have road rations packed quickly; we will saddle our own animals." He turned to two of his men. "Bunji, watch the prisoner. Yukio, prepare a horse for him; he'll ride it on his belly."

Crawling in the mud, Hans found his sword by feel. Fortunately it was the hilt his hand touched. Both palms were already sliced by the tops of the bamboo he'd grasped in vaulting over the fence.

There was no torchlight inside the gate now, but he decided against opening it. Instead he explored the perimeter of the fence, slowly, looking for a way to cross it without further injuring his hands. Lightning pulsed continually in the east now, distant enough that most of the thunder was drowned out by the growing wind. He circled it completely, back to the gate, finding nothing. Perhaps, he thought, he could find something in some other yard nearby, a pole perhaps, long enough to vault the fence in back.

Before he could leave, though, he heard the sound of men inside, and saw the glow of torches. Quickly he ran to a front corner of the fence, hid behind it and peered around. A short column of men rode out. At the moment, the rain was not intense, but the worsening wind threatened to blow the torches out. Still, they gave enough light that Hans could see a bundle across one of the horses, a horse not part of the short pack string. *Achikh!* he thought. He dared think nothing else, for if it was Achikh, there might be a chance to follow, and rescue him in the dark somewhere, when his captors rested. The last of the horses came through the gate and turned after the others up the road. Hans followed them, jogging, stumbling in the dark, guiding on the torchlight ahead of him.

The road left the village, and shortly after entered woods along the Gara-gara River. It was in the woods he lost sight of the torchlight. He also lost the road, floundering among poplar trees, stumbling over a fallen branch, headlong into mud. He stopped then. He knew in which direction the river lay. He could hear it. But where were the horsemen?

The storm had continued to worsen, and the lightning was no longer distant. It strobed the sky in a rapid sequence of white and black, blinding him alternately with glare and darkness, while its thunder boomed and rolled. The wind shook the poplars like a mastiff shakes a chicken, and he heard a tree fall. Turning his back on the river sound, he pushed forward till his feet found the road again. The way the storm raged now, surely the torches had blown out. Reluctantly he turned left, back toward the village.

Soon he was out of the woods again, and lowering his head, clawed against the wind. The rain no longer simply poured; it lashed and battered, stinging like hail. Lightning pulsed incessantly now, and the thunder threatened to burst the world. He first realized he was coming to the village when part of a house blew past him, a flurry of thatch and matting fleeing the storm. He squinted, and by the storm's strobing thought he glimpsed a shed. Staggering, he fought his way to it. It was made of rough boards, with a board door leaking light. He opened it and ducked in. A family was huddled there, with its cats and chickens, its cow and pigs. No one spoke, to welcome or reject him. He went to a corner by himself, squatted down and began to shiver.

EIGHT

Sväädkunni glödde krytt på pojkan,
nybörjan bland de äldra pojkarn,
de som flinte på den yngste
lärling i d' hela skaran.
Knappt fyllt treton år d' ungan,
men stod liksom lång som de
som fyllit sjutton år i liven.
Lång å jängli, men i kroppen,
stark å vig, mer än de visste.

Sjefen såg en ledlös pojke,
träsvärd i d' långa handen,
pojkuppsynen lugn å munter,
utan iver, ingen märke.
Då rinkte tränaren sin panna.
Ryktbar kjämpen, härdad räd'ren,
kjennte väl vad livsslås 'hövde.
Nikkte sjefen då, å mente,
d' var dragen som kunn' bli
gutts styrke, om man skölte rätt ham.

Matts the Swordwise eyed the novice
standing 'mongst the older boys who
leered at one they all expected
to make sport of in their training.
Newly turned thirteen, although as
tall as almost any of them.
Long and gangling, looks deceiving,
strong and agile more than seeming.

64

The drill chief saw a loose-limbed
boy, whose long hand held a
wooden sword with neither nerves nor
avid hunger. Calm and cheerful.
The scarred brow wrinkled.
Famous warrior, hardened raider,
was to blood and death no stranger,
knew the attributes of heroes.
Calm could be the special strength
of this young boy if he was taught well.
From— *The Järnhann Saga*
Kumalo translation

Captain Iwatoku Kunio looked up sharply from the petition he was reading. "Yes, Shigeru?" he said.

The guard corporal's manner was laconic. "There is a *ronin* who wishes to speak with Lord Matsumura."

"There is always a *ronin* who wishes to speak with Matsumura-sama. Why do you bother me with this one?"

"He came the night before last, to tell his lordship of a giant, yellow-haired foreigner supposedly held in prison." The guard thumbed in the direction of Momiji-joka, below the rocky hill on which the castle stood. "He claims that the giant is a wizard, with wizard eyes, and arrived on the Heaven Boat. Fumio didn't believe him, and sent him away. He came back yesterday, and Fumio informed me; I sent him away. Now he is here again."

Iwatoku straightened with a grunt. *On the Heaven Boat. That makes it my business, I suppose. But yellow haired? Unlikely.* "What does he mean by 'wizard eyes'?" Iwatoku asked.

"Excuse me, Iwatoku-san, but he didn't explain. He insists that the foreigner is also a wizard of considerable skill. And that he'll leave only after he's spoken to his lordship. If you want me to, I'll have him sent down the road with as many bruises as necessary."

Iwatoku shook his head. Truly this was an arrogant *ronin*, but— If he actually knew something about the Heaven Boat— And Matsumura-sama had given orders that *ronin*, if they showed proper respect, were to be treated courteously—after all, they were samurai—although all too often they were a nuisance, working angles to get employment. With an expression of distaste, he got to his feet. "And he is now at the gate?"

"Yes, Iwatoku-san."

"I will go down and speak with him."

Iwatoku paused at the door to slip his feet into straw sandals, then walked with the guard down a short hall and onto an outside walkway. The equinox had nearly arrived, and although the days still were hot, they'd held a welcome hint of autumn recently. The humidity had been lower than in proper summer weather, and the mornings notably cooler. Although today the humidity was high again; in this season that could mean a storm coming.

The *ronin* was waiting, seated in the grass just outside the main gate. Seeing a captain coming with Shigeru, the man bowed deeply. He had not let himself go, as many *ronin* did; he was clean-shaven, and his hair was properly tonsured, with the samurai lock neatly tied. His clothes were dirty, of course, but that was to be expected of someone who slept where opportunity presented. No doubt beside the road, as often as not.

"Your name?" Iwatoku asked.

"Kamoshika Akira," the *ronin* answered. "I was in the service of Lord Shimano for five years, until last spring's required reduction in forces."

Shimano. That was a long way from Momiji-joka. "You told Corporal Funakoshi of a giant foreigner, a wizard you said, who'd come to Yamato on the Heaven Boat. How do you know those things are true?"

"Excuse me, your lordship, but I do not *know* it. But surely he is very strange." He shrugged. "It seemed to me you should be told."

"Mmm. How large is this giant? Does he appear to be dangerous?"

"He stands about this tall." Kamoshika Akira motioned at arm's length above his head, reaching to perhaps two meters. "Also he looks very formidable, but he seems remarkably mild-mannered, lacking ferocity. And his eyes are unlike other men's. They are blank, without any iris, the featureless pale blue of a red-start's eggs. He appears blind, yet he sees—through the spirit he claims."

Iwatoku examined the information. Yellow hair. Eyes blue and without irises. Outlandish; he got no mental image from it at all. Suspicion formed. "Having told me all this," he said, "I suppose you want breakfast now."

The *ronin* bowed again. "It would be welcome. But before I eat, there is other information I must deliver to Lord Matsumura."

"What information?"

"Excuse me. I am only an unworthy *ronin*, and you are an elevated personage. Nonetheless, I do not feel free to tell anyone but his lordship."

Iwatoku scowled. "I am his lordship's marshal. You will see him only if I decide you should. And if you do not tell me, I will assume you lack confidence in what you've come to say."

Once more the *ronin* bowed. "That may be. But I am unwilling to tell anyone except a *tehon daimyo* like Lord Matsumura. I can only tell you that it is something I personally saw and heard. And that it has to do with the imperial family."

Iwatoku looked long and hard at him, then turned to the guard corporal. "Shigeru, send a squad to the prison and have it bring the foreign giant here, if there is one. Manacled. I will question him." He looked back at the *ronin* then. "Wait here. I will see what I think of your giant. Then perhaps I will speak to his lordship about you."

The captain turned back inside, half expecting the *ronin* to leave, once he was left alone. Certainly his story sounded unlikely. But the Heaven Boat had been real; perhaps the giant was too. And perhaps he actually had arrived in it.

Standing in Matsumura's audience chamber, the giant was more impressive than Iwatoku had expected. Partly it was his musculature, and partly the bloody welts left on his back during his day of questioning in prison. It was the sort of questioning his lordship had never condoned. Withholding food for a few days was one thing, but flogging was only to be applied after the hearing, as punishment, and never to force confessions.

Lord Matsumura Shinji regarded the foreigner thoughtfully,

and had him turn so he could better examine his back. The man did an admirable job of ignoring the pain, and the flies attracted to the raw and seeping surface. The *daimyo* told himself that someone else would taste that heavy strap—the jailer, or the *yoriki*, or possibly both. Whoever was responsible. The emperor himself had forbidden questioning under torture. Not that an imperial edict could stop such barbarities, where a *daimyo* allowed it, but it set an example, and made it easier to discontinue.

When the foreigner had turned to face him again, Matsumura asked: "Your name!"

"I am called Tetsu-te Nils, your lordship."

Nissa. A name he'd never encountered before. "And you are a wizard?"

The man stood straight, his expression mild but alert, showing no sign of the abuse he'd suffered. "I have certain small skills not shared by most men, your lordship. Some persons might consider me a wizard."

"And you came here on the Heaven Boat at Omugi?"

"That is correct, your lordship."

Matsumura looked at the strong young face, its new growth of downy beard white as cotton, its eyes seemingly blind. The *daimyo* raised a hand. "What am I doing?" he asked.

"You are holding up three fingers on your left hand."

"Hmh!" Clearly there was something, at least, to the man's claims; he'd give some thought to this, and question him at length. The *daimyo* looked at the senior of the guard escort. "Take the foreigner and wash his back. Then hold him in custody till I call for him again. He is not to be abused. And see that he is well fed."

When the giant was gone, Matsumura turned to the *ronin*, who'd been brought to him with the foreigner. "What indication of wizardry did you observe in him?"

Kamoshika Akira bowed. "Your lordship, at the temple he looked into the soul of the rector, and saw things which seemed accurate to us. Certainly they embarrassed the rector deeply, causing him to speak quickly to forestall further comments. Also it seemed clear that the giant could see, despite the strangeness of his eyes."

"Nothing more than that?"

The *ronin* bowed again. "No, your lordship."

The *daimyo's* brows drew down in a scowl. A shrewd man with no wizard skills at all might make observations regarding the rector's character. He himself had. But the eyes ... "Captain Iwatoku says you had more to tell me. Some secret which you refused to speak of to him. What is this secret?"

"This has nothing to do with the foreigner, Matsumura-sama. In the spring, Lord Shimano reduced the number of his samurai, according to the schedule the emperor had ordered, and I was let go, along with several others. Later I was employed at the castle of Lord Sumikawa Tomi for a time, breaking horses. While I was there, a young samurai came to the castle, wearing a large mustache and dressed like a hundred-*koban* samurai of ordinary family. With him were eight others, similarly dressed, but they acted toward him as if he was someone of very high rank. As if his quite ordinary clothing was intended to fool people."

He paused, glancing up at the *daimyo's* wide face, then averted his eyes again, as courtesy required. "On an occasion four years ago, I traveled with Lord Shimano to Miyako, to the imperial court. While there, I chanced to see Prince Terasu, a handsome young man of particularly proud carriage. And while I am hardly worthy to say so, I am sure the youth at Lord Sumikawa's castle was Prince Terasu."

Matsumura opened his mouth as if to speak, perhaps angrily, but Kamoshika Akira continued talking. "The next day I was with two other *ronin* at a tea house, when a man came in, a man with flaring eyebrows like a crow's wings. I recognized him at once as a companion of the handsome young lord. All three of us carried our paired swords, and wore our hair in the samurai style, and seeing us, the man came over. He ordered *sake* for us, and asked if we would take employment with him. When he was asked what we'd be expected to do, he would only say it was difficult and sometimes dangerous work, but in the long run would bring us honor.

"My two companions agreed, but I did not. For it seemed to me there was something about this job that I would not like. I told him I was already employed. The man was somewhat insulting to me then, implying that I feared danger, but I said nothing about it. His manners were elegant, as if he was some elevated personage."

Matsumura had sat back listening, eyes intent, no longer on the verge of interrupting. "The next day," Kamoshika went on, "the handsome young lord whom I believe is Prince Terasu left with only seven of his companions, plus my two friends. I did not see them again, but the next day I heard that the stranger with large eyebrows was still in town, looking for *ronin* to hire.

"Because you are a *tehon daimyo* and *tenshi-no-kobun*,[9] it seemed I should tell you this. I do not know what it means, but . . ."

With that he stopped, and Matsumura questioned him no further; the *daimyo* could add two and two as well as anyone. Matsumura ordered Iwatoku to have Kamoshika Akira lodged and fed with the guards for the time being. Iwatoku was also to send for the *yoriki* who'd been on duty when the foreigner was taken to prison. Afterward he'd question the so-called wizard further.

It was afternoon before the *daimyo* spoke with the *yoriki*. Afterward the foreign giant was brought to him again. Deeply worried and chagrined, the *yoriki* sat in a rear corner of the chamber beside the *ronin*, Kamoshika Akira, in case Matsumura-sama had further questions for them.

Matsumura spoke to the foreigner. "You claim to have come here in the Heaven Boat, is that correct?"

"That is correct, your lordship." Then, as if replying to the

---

[9] *Tehon daimyo* is not to be confused with *takai daimyo*. No period in pre-plague Japan had equivalent ranks. *Tehon daimyo* ("paragons of nobility") had demonstrated their dedication to the emperor, and were assigned rich, non-hereditary fiefs buffering the vast imperial territory. There they kept four times the number of samurai allowed ordinary *daimyo*. They were expected to shield the imperial territory against possible rebellion.

The title *tenshi-no-kobun* carries even greater honor. It means "like a son to the emperor."

daimyo's unspoken doubt, he repeated part of the exchange between the Heaven Boat and Captain Iwatoku.

Matsumura looked at Iwatoku. "Did he recite that accurately?"

"As closely as I can recall, your lordship."

Matsumura turned back to the foreigner. "What is your relation to the Heaven People?"

"They are a kind people, a peaceful people, and a people of great knowledge. I had become a guide to them, in my part of the world. They intended to come here, and I asked if they would bring me with them. In China, a very holy man, Jampa Lodro, had told me of a great holy man here, whom he called Shisho-san, or Ojiisan Tattobu. I wanted to meet Ojiisan, and the Star People agreed to bring me with them."

Matsumura frowned. "You are charged with trying to steal a horse. What were you doing in the stable at the inn?"

The giant chuckled. "First I was falling through the roof. Then I was being kicked by a horse. Then I ran out the back door into a manure pile." He chuckled again, and shrugged. "I had been listening to conversations in the inn, and found myself in the back yard. Wanting to leave, I climbed onto the roof—there was a ladder there—with the intention of sliding down the other side into the alley. It was the only way I could see to get out of the yard without harming the guard, who was sleeping with his back against the gate."

Matsumura looked at him bemused, and tried to sort his way through the odd set of claims. "Kamoshika said something about Okuni-nushi, and wizard sight. What is the truth of that?"

"Honorable Kamoshika told the truth about what he heard, but what he heard was not all true." The foreigner paused to let the *daimyo* examine and grasp what he'd said. "I spoke the truth about my wizard sight, but lied to the rector when I said Okuni-nushi had sent me. The rector had already decided I was a demon. He'd had me tied to a tree, intending to have me strangled in the morning. I hoped to make him change his mind."

Matsumura's gaze had sharpened. "You admit, then, that you lied to the rector!"

"And to the *doshin*. I hoped to confuse him, make him unsure.

I preferred to avoid the kind of treatment that came to me anyway."

The *daimyo* pursed his lips. "You told Kamoshika that you are a wizard. For every real wizard, there is a score or a hundred who claim to be one. Why should I believe you? A confessed liar."

"A point well taken. But most men lie, now and then. Not all of them admit it." He paused. "What do you see when you look at my eyes, your lordship?"

"Eyes like no others I've heard of."

Nils raised his unbandaged left hand to his face, and when he lowered it, his eyes were in his palm. "Now what do you see?" he asked.

Matsumura's breath hissed out. The foreigner's lids lay sunken. He got from his seat and stepped forward to peer more closely. Empty! Beneath those sunken lids could be no eyes, and as if to prove it, the lids opened for a moment. Nils held out to him the irregular, pale blue orbs of glass he'd worn there. "The people of the Heaven Boat gave them to me," he said. "In the sight of most people, I was ugly with the sockets empty."

Matsumura looked at the glass eyes, then back at the empty sockets. "If you are blind, then how . . ." He stopped.

Nils nodded. "I have wizard sight. I do not need eyes to see."

The *daimyo* shook his head as if to dislodge a fly. Nils spoke on. "Let me tell you what I see in this room. You, first of all. You stand this tall" —he gestured— "and are thick chested. Your robe is golden, and the short garment over it is sleeveless, with wide stiff shoulders. Its color is blue, the shoulders being the darker. Your breeches are golden, with diamonds outlined in blue, and figures of birds and flowers in various colors. Your mustache is more gray than black, your hair more black than gray. And from your left hand, you've lost the last joint of your least finger."

Without looking aside at Iwatoku, he went on. "Captain Iwatoku is taller than you but less heavily built. His face is narrower and shaven, his nose thin and curved, and— And just now you wonder if I can also fight without eyes. It seems your empire has many excellent swordsmen. I'll be happy to fight one of them, if you wish. For I am more than simply a wizard."

He paused. "And yes, it would be well to fight with wooden swords, for my sake as well as the captain's. For wizardry plays no part in my swordsmanship, except as it allows me to see."

Matsumura stared thoughtfully for another moment, then barked an order to someone waiting outside the open door, and there was the sound of the person hurrying off. For a long minute none of them spoke, then a servant entered, carrying two wooden fencing swords—oaken rods made to simulate the weight and balance of steel—and handed them to Iwatoku.

"Captain," Matsumura said, "it will please me to have you test him. You are as skilled as any swordsman in my service."

Iwatoku bowed. He had mixed feelings about fighting the foreign giant—there was something about the man—but he would not decline. At any rate it would be an interesting experience. He offered the foreigner his choice of the two training swords. The man simply took one, not examining the other, and handled it, testing its weight and balance, then stepped back, ready. Iwatoku took the other, slashing the air with it, for its cross-section and aerodynamics were different from those of the *katana* he customarily carried in his sash. It was just a hair less quick.

"I do not wish you to injure each other," Matsumura said. "If I tell you to stop fighting, you must do so at once." He paused, looking at them. The foreigner was more than a full head taller than Iwatoku, who was somewhat tall for a Yamatoan. "Are you ready?" Matsumura asked.

Both swordsmen nodded.

"In that case, please begin!"

Iwatoku used the *gyakufu* opening, balanced and relaxed, sword poised, leaving his opponent to commit himself with the first move, which he would then counter. But Nils's opening was like nothing he'd seen before, and in a moment they were trading slashes and thrusts in what seemed a standoff. The captain then changed his rhythm, attempting to throw the foreigner off his own, but his opponent adjusted smoothly. Shortly, Matsumura called a halt, and peered at Iwatoku. "What did you think of him?"

"Excuse me, your lordship, but I believe he has *fudochi*—the mind that does not tarry. He did not try as hard as he might have. Otherwise he would have beaten me, I have no doubt."

The *daimyo* turned his eyes to the foreigner. The man was facing directly at him. "And you, Tetsu-te Nissa! What do you say to that?"

"Matsumura-sama wished us to fight in order to learn whether I am able to, without eyes. I have shown that I can."

Matsumura regarded him for several seconds without saying more, then changed the subject: "In addressing me, a *daimyo*, you do not fully express all the courtesies appropriate to my rank. Do you not respect rank and authority in the land you come from?"

"We do, but we show it differently. In many ways my people are different from yours." He paused. "Among a numerous and wealthy people, you are a *tehon daimyo*, and a *tenshi-no-kobun*. My own people are neither numerous nor wealthy, and we have no ranks comparable to your own. But among them, I am a major personage.

"A long time ago, a young warrior whom they called their *yngling*, saved the tribes from destroying each other in war. After his death, they told themselves that, in another time of great danger, he'd reappear, be reborn to them to save them once again. That time of danger came, and it was I who led them through it. They therefore believe I am that *yngling*, and though I am not the leader of any tribe or clan, I am, when I'm with them, their speaker of the law."

"Umh." Matsumura grunted, then waved to the servant who'd brought the wooden swords. The man moved to reclaim them, but Nils's was stuck to his right palm, and the servant stared big-eyed at it.

"What is the matter?" Matsumura demanded.

"His hand, your lordship! It is—something is wrong with it!"

Matsumura beckoned preemptorily to Nils, who peeled the sword free and handed it to the servant before stepping over to the *daimyo*. He showed his hand. Beneath the thick sword callus, the palm had been a single large blister, which had cracked and leaked during the swordplay. The serum had stuck the hilt to his palm.

"How—did that happen?" asked Matsumura.

"The jailer placed a stone from the fire on it, as punishment. On the magistrate's order; he wanted me to confess that I was trying to steal a horse." Nils chuckled. "It was a lie I was unwilling to tell, which angered him. And because I am a foreigner, he considered it no crime to do what he did."

Matsumura's face darkened with anger as he examined the injury more closely. The burn did not seem dangerously deep, but it might easily become infected, and at any rate, scar tissue could leave the hand curled, unfit for the sword. The *daimyo* shot a glare at the *yoriki*, who tried to wish himself invisible. Raising his voice, Matsumura called another servant in, and sent him after the physician who dwelt in the castle. He peered up at the Northman's face then, curiosity replacing anger.

"Such a burn should be very painful. Do wizards not feel pain?"

"Wizards are human beings. We are born, and sooner or later we die, like anyone else. Some do mostly good, a few mostly evil. Some are more foolish than wise, others more wise than foolish; some are brave, others cowardly. Brave or cowardly, if you cut them, they bleed, though some can stem their bleeding, if it's not too severe. But stab them to the heart, and life departs them.

"As for pain—it's a feeling of the flesh. When the hot stone was laid on my hand, I cried out with pain. Then I was able to change my mind about it, call it simply a feeling, a strong feeling. Something I could examine in detail. That was wizardry. But it did not greatly lessen the injury, though it will help it heal much more quickly.

"Had the torturer poured molten lead on it, though, no wizardry of mine could have saved it. Any more than I could grow new eyes, when those I was born with were punctured by a torturer in a land far from here. Nor could my mind have stepped away from so great a pain to examine it with calm."

Matsumura stared at the foreigner with respect verging on awe. Then a door slid open in its grooves, and the physician arrived with a straw bag of soft cotton cloths, boiled and dried, and a pot of healing ointment. His apprentice carried an urn and basin, and soap. Matsumura spoke to the physician, who examined the hand. Tight-lipped and frowning, he had the apprentice pour water into the basin, then carefully but thoroughly washed the hand, shaking his head at the burn as if disapproving such a thing. Even more carefully he dabbed the hand dry, then spread it with ointment and wrapped it loosely. The Northman never winced.

"You must keep it clean!" the physician said emphatically, then turned to Matsumura. "If it doesn't become infected, and if he flexes it gently from time to time, it should be all right. Otherwise it could draw up like a claw." With that, he and his apprentice gathered their paraphernalia, bowed to Lord Matsumura, and backed out of the room.

Matsumura chewed his mustache for a moment, thinking what he'd say to the magistrate. Certainly the man would have to be discharged and flogged. The jailer too. *I should offer Tetsu-te Nissa the privilege of wielding the strap*, he told himself grimly. But wouldn't, for it seemed to him that punishment and revenge should be separated. It also seemed to him that the giant would decline the offer if he made it.

He looked at the foreigner again. "What did you say your rank is, among your people? What is it they call you?"

"I am their *yngling*."

"Ah yes. *Inrinu*.[10] Please sit down, Inrinu-san. I will have tea brought to us, and you will tell us about your land and people."

Nils Järnhann talked with the *daimyo* at length, answering his questions not only about the Northmen and their homelands old and new, but about the places he'd traveled and people he'd met in those travels. Dusk was settling when he'd finished, they'd had supper as well as tea, and the fringe of the great storm had arrived, the *taifu* which would so drastically affect the Northman's friends this night.

Then servants showed him to a guest room, which Kamoshika Akira would share with him for companionship.

---

[10]*Inrinu* is an approximation of the word *yngling*.

Matsumura Shinji had inspected the feverish storm preparations before retiring, the placing of storm shutters, and the moving of loose out-of-door objects to shelter.

Now he lay on his futon, thinking against the backdrop of hooting wind, of thunder and snarling rain. But it wasn't the storm that held his attention, for the buildings had been built of stout timbers, and each of its heavy roof tiles fastened to the one beneath with a trowel of cement. In Matsumura's youth, they'd withstood the worst typhoon of memory, without damage.

Rather it was the foreigner he thought about, the foreigner and his wizard powers. How far did they extend beyond seeing without eyes, and bearing pain? With the empire restless, and many *daimyo* unhappy with the Emperor, a *tehon daimyo* could be well served by a wizard—by one who was honorable, that is. And in its way, the foreigner's behavior had seemed both honorable and civilized.

Matsumura considered himself a man not susceptible to charm. Honorable men were numerous in Yamato, though fewer than one might wish. Honorable men who were also civilized. Then why, he wondered, had he been so impressed with the foreigner, who was after all a barbarian? Was it wizardry? Or character? He reviewed his two meetings with the man, and what the *ronin*, Kamoshika Akira, had said of him. None of it really smelled of wizardry, as one thought of it. Not even when Nissa took the eyes from his face and held them out for inspection.

What wizards had he known before, to judge by? Real wizards. Ojiisan was said to have strong wizard powers, but he'd never met the old holy man, whose powers were from Heaven, at any rate. He *had* seen, indeed talked with Juji Shiro several times, and surely the famous abbot required wizard powers to commune with the soul of the terrible mountain.

How did one distinguish wizardry from holiness? By skin color or eyes? Juji Shiro's eyes were the color of ripe strawberries, almost as uncanny as the *Inrinu's*, but at least they had pupils. The *Inrinu* had said his eyes had been crafted for him by people from Heaven, but then—what was wizardry and what craft?

He brushed the thoughts aside; they would get him nowhere. When the storm was over, he decided, he'd ask the *Inrinu* to take him to the Heaven Boat and introduce him to those who sailed the heavens upon it. If indeed he was connected to them, and certainly he'd sounded convincing.

With an action decided on, his attention went to the story Kamoshika Akira had told him, of the man who'd seemed to be Prince Terasu, and the recruitment of *ronin* by the man's retainer. Why would Terasu recruit *ronin* in Sumikawa, a district backed up against wild mountains? And many days' travel from the states ruled by either his father-in-law or uncle. Or had it in fact been a matter of mistaken identity? Or had Kamoshika lied?

I need to ask him more questions, he decided. But it sounded like something the emperor should be told about.

The storm was worsening, taking his attention. The *taifu*, almost surely. Muttering, he got to his feet and padded down a hallway lit by fragrant lamps, to the windward end of the building. There rain had penetrated between the storm shutters, wetting the polished planks of the cedar floor. He wanted to see the storm, and considered going downstairs, out into the courtyard. Everything would be barred though, and who knew what would happen if he opened a door? If the Wind God got a finger inside, he might pull out a wall. Had the servants set out the paper birds for the god to take away with him? Of course they had. It was not something they'd forget.

A particular gust shook the shutters. *Ho, Susa-no-wo!* Matsumura thought, and chuckled. *You heard me thinking of you! I can almost see the shutters bow from your pummeling!*

He turned back to his room, his mind cleared by the storm. Tomorrow would be soon enough to worry about wizards and princes.

Kamoshika Akira lay with his neck on his padded wooden pillow. Thunders rolled, rumbled, and occasionally banged. The wind roared, shaking the stoutly built building. The *taifu* beyond a doubt. He was grateful to be inside the strong walls of Matsumura's mansion.

He turned his head and glanced at the foreigner, Nissa the

Inrinu. Nissa lay on his stomach to spare his flogged back, and had shoved his pillow aside, cradling his head on an arm. Kamoshika had never been flogged. Caned a few times as a boy, but nothing that drew blood.

Matsumura-sama had accepted the foreigner with remarkable readiness, though *tehon daimyo* were supposed to be especially suspicious, for they were charged with the Emperor's security. There was something special about this Nissa that went beyond his size and strength, beyond his swordsmanship. Perhaps beyond even his wizardry. In himself and in Matsumura-sama, it gave rise to admiration and trust. In people like the rector and the jailer, on the other hand, it gave rise to suspicion and fear.

It would be very good to serve a lord like Matsumura-sama, he told himself. *Surely there must be duties here for another samurai, even if he has all the fighting men allowed him by law. Breaking and training horses, perhaps.* It was he, after all, who'd brought word of Nissa, who might otherwise still be in prison, without food or perhaps even water, his back festering, and perhaps his hand. Tomorrow he'd say something to remind Iwatoku of that, if he saw him. Ask the marshal to be his intermediary, and find a position for him here.

The *Inrinu*! That was a story he'd like to hear more of. And what a fighter! With a hand like his was! That by itself should convince anyone he was a wizard.

By dawnlight, Matsumura Shinji stood in the rain on the castle wall, looking down on Momiji-joka. Or what was left of Momiji-joka, for most of its buildings had been flattened, their roofs and walls strewn over the landscape. Including the quarter immediately downhill of the castle, where many of his own people lived: servants, samurai, and officials. There was much to see to. The Heaven Boat would have to wait for a day or two; then, perhaps, he could find time to visit it.

NINE

Nils and Kamoshika Akira were invited to remain for a time as guests in the castle of Lord Matsumura Shinji. Nils had requested that wooden practice swords be brought to their room, and he and Akira had practiced—Nils with his unburned left hand!—demonstrating and explaining to each other the strategies, tactics, and techniques of their very different styles.

The serving girl who brought their breakfast could hear their hoarse grunting and the clashing of their swords as she came down the hall, and was almost afraid to open the door. Fortunately, the rooms on either side and across from theirs were unoccupied.

Nissa, it seemed, was ambidexterous. Thus, though considerably less practiced with his left hand, he used it quite well. And it seemed to Akira that had they fought in earnest, this huge foreigner, even fighting left handed, might well have killed him.

After eating, the same serving girl had brought basins and a pitcher of hot water. They'd washed their hands and faces, rinsed their mouths, then began scrubbing their teeth with soft sticks rendered brush-like by chewing. A page boy came to their door and told them they were wanted in Matsumura-sama's audience room when they were finished.

Three minutes later they were met by Captain Iwatoku in the corridor leading to the audience room. It was Kamoshika Akira he spoke to. "I believe you are looking for service with a *daimyo*. Is that so?"

Akira bowed. "That is my profound desire. And although I am unworthy to be considered, I would particularly like to serve Lord Matsumura Shinji. Unfortunately there are so many abler *ronin* to be found, it is doubtful that anyone would sponsor me."

Iwatoku looked him over, approving his modesty. "I am willing to sponsor you. Lord Matsumura has already commented that such an able and honest samurai should not have to wander around the country, sleeping beneath the sky and wondering where his next meal will come from."

Nils managed not to grin: the conversation was a charade, part of a complex but effective system. Akira knew he was good, and Iwatoku knew that he knew. Further, Matsumura had told Iwatoku to broach the matter with Akira, who being familiar with such matters, understood this. Assuming that nothing intervened, Akira would be hired as soon as a suitable post had been decided on; Iwatoku would work this out with Matsumura.

And once employed, Akira would be committed not only to Matsumura, but to Iwatoku, because if he failed to satisfy the *daimyo*, then Captain Iwatoku, as his sponsor, would be humiliated, greatly intensifying Akira's own disgrace. Akira bowed deeply; Iwatoku, as marshal, bowed slightly in return. Then Akira and Nils followed him to Matsumura's door. A guard opened it, admitting the captain, who announced the two guests. They also entered, Matsumura receiving their bows with a nod.

"Inrinu-san," the *daimyo* said, "I have just received a message from the magistrate. Not the one who troubled you. He says a tall foreigner was brought to the prison last night, accused with assault on a samurai." He raised an eyebrow. "A tall foreigner *with red hair*! The charge is not as serious as it sounds, because the samurai is also in prison, charged with public drunkenness, disturbing the peace, and drawing his sword without reasonable cause.

"It has occurred to the new magistrate that, given this foreigner's height and unusual hair color, there might be a connection between him and yourself."

Nils laughed. "I came on the Heaven Boat with a tall red-haired boy sixteen years old; this must be him. He is a poet's apprentice who has travelled with me for more than a year, sharing my hardships and adventures. His master assigned him to complete my saga—the poem of my life—and give the tribes of Northmen something new to recite on winter nights."

Now both of Matsumura's eyebrows rose. Was Inrinu-san that important to his people? On a table there lay a sheaf of rice paper, an ink block, and brush. He had Iwatoku write a message to the magistrate: This new foreigner was believed to have come on the Heaven Boat. He was to be brought under guard to the castle and delivered to the sergeant at arms.

When Iwatoku had written it, Matsumura called a guardsman and gave him the message to deliver. When the man had left, the *daimyo* turned again to Nils. "Let me see your injured hand, please."

Nils held it out. He had already peeled and trimmed off some of the dead callus. Matsumura examined it thoughtfully, then looked up. "It shows remarkable healing."

"There is a procedure for that. Taught me by my wife, who is a powerful healer."

"Your wife? You had not mentioned a wife."

"She has left this world. She has gone with the great heaven ship to its place in the sky."

"Ah!" Matsumura's face closed in a slight frown. He wasn't sure if that had been like dying or more like taking a sea voyage—whether it called for condolences or not. "Well," he said at last, "I have urgent matters to attend to, petitions to hear. I will send for you when this red-haired person has been brought to me. And perhaps later today I will have time to visit the Heaven Boat."

Nils didn't return to his room. Instead, he and Kamoshika Akira walked to the wall above the gate, to stand in the sun and talk, and gaze across the battlement for a look at the red-haired foreigner. Nils was describing the events leading to the first Orc war, when a squad of guardsmen marched into sight from the town, up a road newly cleared of branches and fallen trees. Nils gestured. "That's Hans they have," he said, but didn't call or wave. The boy's hands were behind him as if tied or manacled; he was still under arrest. Instead, Nils turned and went down into the courtyard to wait for him, while Akira hurried off to find Iwatoku and tell him.

Nils stood grinning as the squad marched up the final length of road and through the gate. "Hans Gunnarsson!" he called. Hans turned his head at once, breaking step and stumbling. "Nils!" he shouted.

Without warning the jailer with him slugged the side of his jaw, hard, knocking the boy down. It took Nils only half a dozen strides to reach them. The man was bent over Hans, pulling him to his feet, when a large hand grabbed the collar of the jailer's tunic and jerked him backwards. Another hand gripped his arm and jerked it hard, backward and upward into a hammerlock, while a voice growled in his ear, "I may kill you for that."

Already, a sword or two had slid from their scabbards, then the *honcho* shouted an order, and they slid back in. Nils jerked upward just a little harder, and the jailer squealed. "Shall I pull it out of the socket?" Nils asked him. "Or—" Abruptly he let go the man, who spun away, already drawing his sword. A shortsword, for he was no samurai; the job of jailer was unclean. A heavy palm struck the side of the man's skull, knocking him sprawling to the cobblestones, head ringing. With one hand, Nils pulled him to his feet by the hair. The sword lay on the cobbles.

"Why," Nils asked reasonably, "did you strike the boy?"

The man's eyes were wide. He'd never imagined anyone so large as this, so fierce looking; it had to be the giant whose interrogation had resulted in yesterday's dismissals and floggings. The hand had let go of him again, but now a sword waved before his face like the head of a snake. "I—" The jailer's voice was hoarse. "He called out. He should not have!"

Nils's voice was patient. "Why should he not have?"

"I—had not given him leave to."

"Ah. And who gave you leave to hit him for calling out? I am Lord Matsumura's guest, and this is my student . . ."

"Nissa-san!" The crisp voice that interrupted him was Iwatoku's, and the tone was one of command. "*I* will speak to this creature."

Nils stepped back, and got a lesson in Yamatoan cursing. The drift of it was that Lord Matsumura had ordered, orally and in writing, more than once, that prisoners not be abused while awaiting trial. And this particular prisoner was thought to be someone from the Heaven Boat. "That was explicit in the message. I know. I wrote it myself. I presume the magistrate told you?"

The face was in shock. The head nodded.

"Very well. I now take delivery of the prisoner. Return to the prison. I will see to you later."

The jailer turned away, stumbling on the cobbles. "Do not forget your *wakizashi!*" Iwatoku said. Robotically the man bent, picked up the shortsword and sheathed it before stumbling out the gate.

Nils didn't move to release Hans. He left that to Iwatoku, who cut the rope with a knife like a razor. Then, grinning, Hans and Nils gripped hands, arms pumping.

"Where is Achikh?" Nils asked, and Hans's face fell. He didn't need to answer, for now Nils could read the basic fact in his mind: Achikh had been taken away captive by unknown men.

"Come!" Iwatoku said. "We will take him to Matsumura-sama. He will want to see him." Together they crossed the courtyard to the *daimyo*'s residence, and climbed a long flight of open stairs. As they walked, Nils briefed Hans in Swedish on Matsumura's rank and character. At the entrance to the audience room, they were admitted with the same formality as before. It was Nils who introduced the youth.

The *daimyo* looked the boy up and down. "Inrinu-san tells me you are sixteen years old. You are already very tall. Are you still growing?"

"I believe so, your lordship."

"I hope to visit the Heaven Boat today."

Again Hans's face fell. "Your lordship, I regret that it was no longer there, the last I looked. It was there shortly before the storm, but the next morning it was gone. And it did not come back all day. I know. I was hidden where I could see if it did."

Matsumura frowned. "Hidden? Where were you during the storm?"

Hans told him the main features of his story, from leaving the pinnace to being thrown in jail. Omitting that he and Achikh had intended to steal a sword. When he'd finished, Matsumura gazed at him intently.

"How many men were there who took your companion away?"

"Eight. I counted them. Exactly eight."

"Eight? Akawashi Kata has only six samurai. And they went west?"

"Yes, Matsumura-sama."

"Westward, the road crosses the Gara-gara River. During the *taifu*, they could not have crossed."

"It was just beginning to rain hard then."

Matsumura looked hard at him, then nodded thoughtfully. "That may be why they left in the middle of the night. Otherwise they could not have crossed for at least two days. But to leave in such a storm, and in such darkness . . .

"Yet there were samurai there the next day, you say. Then Akawashi must have had samurai visiting him from elsewhere. And hardly wandering *ronin*, if they had horses. What traveling party of mounted samurai would visit a minor functionary of no reputation? And without coming to me first! This is very curious! Very interesting!"

He turned to Iwatoku. "Captain, go at once and bring Akawashi Kata to me. I wish to ask him questions. But do not tell him what I am interested in. That would give him time to compose lies. Tell him I'm interested in the storm damage to his village. Which is true, as far as it goes."

Iwatoku bowed, and left the room at once. Matsumura turned again to his guests. "You will wish to bathe," he said. "After that, return to your room. I will order tea sent, and something to eat, all you might wish for. The food in prison is notoriously poor, and seldom sufficient for a young boy's appetite. I will send for you when Captain Iwatoku arrives with Akawashi Kata."

The three of them left: Nils, Hans, and Akira. "What will be done with my jailer?" Hans asked in the hall.

Akira chuckled. "Perhaps nothing."

"Nothing?" Hans asked. "It sounded as if he was in trouble with Captain Iwatoku, at least."

"He insulted Matsumura-sama by treating his orders

contemptuously. In turn, Iwatoku-sama humiliated him for it, in front of us and a whole squad of guardsmen. And although he is unclean, it is quite possible he will commit *seppuku*."

Hans paled. To a Northman, suicide was a function not of honor, but of insanity. These people were stranger than he'd realized.

A groom led Iwatoku's horse to the stable, where impressed village labor was helping Akawashi's own people replace the roof. The gate guard had hurried to Akawashi when Iwatoku had ridden in, and the bailiff was waiting on his feet when his visitor entered, conducted by Sergeant Nirasaki, Akawashi's deputy. Akawashi bowed deeply to his *daimyo*'s marshal.

"Please be seated," he said. "You honor my humble residence and my unworthy self with your elevated presence. I will have tea brought, and . . ."

Iwatoku ignored the chair, raising a hand in restraint. "Do not go to so much trouble, Akawashi Kata. I have come to conduct you to his lordship. He wishes to discuss with you the storm damage to your village, and to the crops stored here."

Akawashi's heart stuttered. "It is most generous of Matsumura-sama," he said, "to think of us in our time of trouble. But it is hardly necessary to spend his valuable time worrying about our unworthy selves here in Omugi. We will get by nicely, and the tax will be paid. I will write up a complete report."

Iwatoku's eyes nailed him. "Matsumura-sama will be interested in your report later. Today he wants to talk with you personally. I am to bring you with me. Do not keep me waiting."

Akawashi bowed deeply. "Of course, Iwatoku-sama. Let me but wash, and change my clothes." He gestured at himself. "I have been inspecting construction today, and as you see, my clothing is quite soiled."

Iwatoku nodded curtly. "Quickly, then. I will wait here." His strong jaw clamped shut. Again Akawashi bowed, then hurried from the room.

In the hall, he motioned urgently to Nirasaki to follow him, and in his room whispered rapidly: "I am leaving with Iwatoku-sama, to be questioned by his lordship. I have no doubt they have learned something of what I've been doing, and wish to confront me with it. When they learn nothing from me, they will wish to question you, you and the men. Someone is likely to break, and that must not happen. As soon as I have left with Iwatoku, take the men and cross the river into the mountains. Go to Takada, and report to Chiu. He will see that you are taken care of."

"The river is high. I am not sure we can cross it."

Akawashi drew himself to his full height. "You must do it. I order you to. Do you understand?"

Nirasaki bowed deeply. "I understand, Akawashi-san. We will cross the river and go to Takada, to Chiu."

Quickly, Akawashi opened a strong box and took from it a purse of silver *chogin*, enough to feed them and buy cheap lodging at inns, where there were any. He pushed it into Nirasaki's hands, then hurried from the room, leaving it for the *honcho* to close the chest again.

After padlocking the chest, Nirasaki went to the stable, and from there watched until Iwatoku and his three men left with Akawashi Kata. Akawashi wore his *kataginu*, appropriate to a serious audience with his lord. Nirasaki gave them time to ride down the road a short way, then hurried to round up the five other samurai in the bailiff's service. While they gathered their gear, he'd have the cook pack food for them.

He did not look forward to the next two or three weeks.

As they rode to Momiji-joka, Akawashi twice complained of feeling dizzy and sick to his stomach. Iwatoku looked at him with little sympathy, considering it the result of a guilty conscience. When they reached the castle gate and dismounted, Akawashi asked to be allowed to visit a *chozuba*. "I'm afraid I must relieve my bowel, either willingly or not."

There was a *chozuba* near the gate, for the use of guards and travelers. Iwatoku motioned toward it. "Do not take long," he said. The bailiff nodded gratefully and disappeared inside. Iwatoku waited impatiently for several minutes, then followed him into the latrine. Akawashi Kata lay on the floor in his own blood and guts, his hands still half closed on the handle of his shortsword.

Matsumura Shinji sat with brush in hand, writing a letter to the Emperor. His eyes scanned what he'd already written: the evidence that Akawashi had been connected with bandits. As evidence it was hardly compelling, but the Emperor might have other evidence that would make this more meaningful. For a moment now, Matsumura hesitated, then wrote on, brush flicking busily.

"Also, a *ronin* in whom I have some confidence, has told me of seeing a man who closely resembles Prince Terasu at the castle of Lord Shimoda. Please excuse me for writing this, but he believes that this person, who could hardly be the prince, may have been recruiting bandits among the *ronin* at Shimoda-joka."

When the ink was dry, Matsumura folded the letter, sealed it with wax, and impressed the wax with his ring. Not many would have dared write what he just had, but he was *tenshi-no-kobun*; it was his responsibility.

TEN

The first two-thirds of the day had been more than eventful, beginning with Hans in jail, continuing with Akawashi's suicide, and ending with the discovery that the bailiff's men had fled. Then, suddenly, nothing was happening, and the two Northmen decided to walk to the landing site. Perhaps the *Alpha* would be there again.

They could have ridden; Lord Matsumura had no shortage of horses. But traditionally, Northmen were hunters, men of the thick forests, dark swamps and hidden trails of Scandinavia, and they had pride in their range and speed and tirelessness afoot. Since they'd transplanted themselves to the fire-climax grassland of what once had been Rumania and Bulgaria, horses had become central in their lives, but old traditions and values still were strong, and they made a point of foot treks.

Akira could understand their walking by choice. *Ronin* commonly traveled hundreds of miles afoot, not only because they had no horses and were searching for suitable employment, but because, being unemployed, they were free to travel, to explore their homeland. Yamatoans in general might walk long distances on pilgrimages to shrines and other holy places. To walk was to show greater respect to the *kami* and the souls of the dead, while being in closer communion with the earth. Samurai might walk on pilgrimages to old battlefields, and to the birthplaces and death places of heroes and ancestors.

Nonetheless, today Akira rode behind the two Northmen. Their legs were so long, who knew how fast they might walk? A squad of Matsumura's household troops rode along too, because Nils and Hans looked very foreign indeed, and Matsumura didn't want them subjected to possible trouble on the road.

At first the two Northmen didn't talk a lot. Momiji-joka was a beehive of rebuilding, and there was a lot to watch as they walked through the town. Hans called to a carpenter at work, framing a building. The man turned, to stare with open mouth at the red-headed youth, his huge blond companion, and their escort. Waving, Hans wished him good weather and good building, and the carpenter, suddenly beaming, waved back.

But when they'd crossed the bridge into the countryside, Nils and Hans began to talk at length, mostly in Swedish for privacy, using Yamatoan words here and there where no Swedish word quite fitted.

"Tell me the rest of what happened after you lost Achikh," Nils said.

Frowning, Hans recalled the eight men on horseback, their torch flames whipping in the wind. Recalled losing sight of them in the woods, being forced to give up on rescuing Achikh, and finding shelter in the shed at the edge of Omugi.

The rest of that night had been little better. Hans hadn't been in the shed long before the roof tore off. There was a hayloft overhead, which gave some protection, but even so, water was quickly trickling on them between the planks of the loft floor, with no room between the leaks where a person could rest dry.

He'd spent the night shivering, sleeping neither much nor well, and left the shed in the half-light of dawn. It was still raining steadily but not hard, the rain colder.

After scanning the gray and sodden desolation, he trotted off down the road. The village around him had been demolished. Its dwellings had been built for comfort in the hot and muggy summers. Many had had floors raised above the ground for ventilation; interior walls, and some exterior walls, had consisted of movable panels; there'd been large windows, with storm shutters too frail for the *taifu*. There'd been "wind eyes" beneath the ridge pole at both ends, open in summer to let air through and heat out. In some poorer homes, walls had been of woven reeds or split bamboo. In winter, hempen cloth could be hung inside, to help keep in heat.

Now all of it was gone, including raised floors, and the debris strewn widely.

Some of the outbuildings had been sturdier, a few of logs, some of planks. But most of their roofs had been thatch, and no roof had withstood the storm. A few people had already emerged from wherever they'd sheltered, to pick through the debris while rain fell on the sodden straw rain capes they wore. One man had upended a timber; he shouldered it now, and began to carry it to where, presumably, his house would take shape again.

Hans trotted through the devastation without stopping, speeding up as he passed the high fence where Achikh had been captured. On its windward side it was half pushed over. He would go to the pinnace and report what had happened to Achikh, then try again to find Nils.

Beyond the village, most of the roadside poplars had been damaged: tops broken out, or major branches torn off. Some had been uprooted and flung down. He left the road before he came to where the farmhouse had been, picked his way through the debris, and stopped abruptly as if struck. The pinnace was gone! He ran to where it had been; perhaps there'd be some message, some sign at least. When there wasn't, he straightened, looking first up, then around. He'd emerged from the shed hungry, and unconsciously had suppressed the discomfort in his belly as well as in his lacerated hands—a barbarian response. Now, suddenly, he felt the emptiness in his gut.

Without conscious decision, he trotted back to the village. People would have food—some food, anyway. He'd seen large crocks in the shed where he'd sheltered, as if the family there had carried them from the house. He'd help them begin reconstruction, and ask to eat when they did.

The property of the bailiff, Akawashi Kata, had also taken heavy damage, but he'd had a special "storm building" in which he'd sheltered, along with the six samurai in his employ. By the third hour of daylight, the rain had decreased to light and fitful showers, and the clouds had thinned enough that, standing in the low doorway, Akawashi could see where the sun was hiding. He scowled at his roofless stable and sheds, and the wreckage of his house. Its frame still stood—in that it had fared better than any other dwelling in the village—but the walls were mostly gone, and the roof.

He went to a roofless shed, where his household staff had sheltered beneath two tents, and rousted them out. Then he ordered his sergeant to round up twenty villagers, to hunt down shakes from his roof and do other things he needed done.

Sergeant Nirasaki bowed his salute, called two of his men to him, and left the yard. They would start at the upper end of the village, he decided, and take one person from every household until he had twenty. That would distribute the burden and lessen the resentment.

Approaching the farthest place, he saw that the occupants had already gathered wreckage into piles, one of structural timbers, another of boards . . . *And there, with them, was the tall trespasser of the evening before, the one who'd jumped over the fence!* The sergeant hadn't himself seen the youth, but it had to be him. Yasu had gotten a good look, and described him. But had the trespasser gotten a good look at Yasu?

He stopped his men, and questioned Yasu to be sure. There could be no doubt of it, Yasu told him. That was the man. The sergeant murmured instructions then: They were not to kill the youth. Akawashi-san would want him alive, and able to answer questions. Injure him if they must, but take him alive, and if possible undamaged.

He wished they'd brought bows. The long legs which had jumped the fence last night could surely outrun any of his men, while strung bows with arrows nocked could stop a fugitive without the bowstring ever being bent. As it was, subterfuge would have to suffice; subterfuge and surprise.

They walked toward the people then, the sergeant wearing his most affable expression. "Good day!" he called incongruously.

They straightened from their work. Now they bowed, even the trespasser, though his was delayed and awkward. Deliberately the sergeant avoided more than a glance at him; anything closer might alarm the youth. But that glance had shown him more than the red-copper hair. The boy's complexion was very light, and his eyes gray-blue. Foreign indeed! What might such a one be doing here? Who had sent him? More than Matsumura-sama might be behind this.

"Akawashi-san needs one of you to help hunt shingles and rebuild his house," the sergeant said, and turned to the trespasser. "You are tall, and a tall person can be most useful, especially if you have carpentry skills. Come with me. You will be in time to eat, and drink a cup of warm *sake*, and if you work well, there will no doubt be a few *zeni* for you to buy something with."

The family peered furtively without raising their faces discourteously to the sergeant's. Hans, who still hadn't eaten, was unsure what these men had in mind. Nor did he realize what an unlikely scenario the sergeant had portrayed—breakfast and *sake*! And coppers to spend! His major questions were: had these men come from the place he'd fled the night before? If so, had he been or would he be recognized? They'd shown no sign of recognition. Perhaps the men who'd seen him the night before had left with Achikh.

By then, samurai stood on two sides of him, and closer than he liked. Best he went with them, ready to run if necessary.

It wasn't until they were passing the bamboo fence, and the lead samurai turned in through the now open gate, that alarm coursed through his limbs. At the same time he heard swords hiss from sheaths, and a strong arm shoved him roughly through the gate.

He went through without resistance, then broke abruptly into a sprint toward several of the bailiff's servants who were gathering useful debris. This time he left his sword sheathed. The servants scattered at the approach of this remarkable apparition, who was taller than anyone they'd ever seen, and had red hair! He snatched up a drying pole that one of them dropped, and veering, ran toward the fence at the east end of the yard. This time he used the pole to vault with, sparing his wounded hands further damage from the sharply cut bamboo tops. The last the samurai saw of him was his back, as he disappeared over the fence again.

The sergeant shouted angrily for his men to get horses and pursue him; never mind saddles, just bridle them and ride.

The horses had been removed from the stable, however, and released in the paddock. It took a few moments to first get bridles, then catch and bridle three of the animals. The sergeant took time to saddle one of them, take a bow, and sling a quiver of arrows over his shoulder. Then he galloped after his men.

He caught them at the lower edge of the village, looking down at the muddy surface of the road.

"Where is he? Why haven't you caught him?"

"Honcho-san! He ran so fast, he was gone before we could catch sight of him. We cannot find even his tracks."

If he'd stayed in the road, Nirasaki told himself, they could see him even now. Perhaps, screened by trees and debris, he'd run off across the field, or—he might be hiding in some wreckage in the village.

He had his men leave the road, picking their way through and over broken tops and fallen branches, to look beyond the wind-ravaged trees. They saw no one. The wheat stubble offered no cover. Could the trespasser be lying flat among the potato plants farther south? It seemed unlikely; the plants had been beaten down by the storm.

He ordered his two men to hunt behind tree trunks, and under the broken tops of poplars. Then, feeling pessimistic, he rode back into the village to look amongst the wreckage and question villagers.

Had the men he'd left behind looked carefully enough, they might have found where Hans had hidden his sword, in the once-tall, storm-flattened grass beneath a fallen poplar top. That would have given them a clue. As it was, they were as pessimistic as their sergeant, and expecting not to find anything, didn't.

ELEVEN

From—*The Folklore of Earth: Metaphysical Beliefs at the Time of First Contact*, by Jean-Erik Apodaca. University Press, A.C. 839.

. . . Not only did the eruption of Fuji-yama devastate a great area of southern Honshu. It must also have traumatized severely the primitive, superstitious survivors. Among a people with a traditional love of nature, Fuji-yama had been the mountain, indeed the natural object, most beloved by the pre-plague Japanese for more than a millenium. With its near-perfect symmetry, it had been an object of veneration, and the subject of innumerable poems, wood-block prints, and ink paintings.

Yet after the eruption, the very name Fuji-yama was lost, suppressed by the enormity of the explosion, and the earthquake and ash-fall that accompanied and followed it. The mountain, so greatly altered in appearance and image, was given a new name, Osoroshii-yama—Terrible Mountain. In fact, in modern Yamatoan, the term *osoroshi* is more intense, symbolic of a greater fear, than our word "terrible" or any of its synonyms.

The popular Buddhism of Yamato is not the popular *Jodo Shinshu* sect of pre-plague Japan. The basic features are similar, and some of the sutras have even survived, but various animistic elements have been incorporated, some of them survivals from pre-technological Shinto. Thus it is not surprising that popular belief assigns a soul, a godhood, to Osoroshii-yama. And a most terrible god it is, for in a moment of wrath it had laid waste a large region, decimating its population.

The god of the mountain is not clearly differentiated from the geological entity, the great volcano. In fact the mountain's soul, its godhood, is widely thought of as simply an aspect of the mountain. Yet that godhood is given a name of its own— Osoroshii-kami—when the speaker wishes to emphasize the mountain's godly aspect.

Various beliefs have formed about Osoroshii-kami. One is that, from its throne in and on the mountain, it rules eruptions and earthquakes throughout the empire. Not surprisingly, fear and worship of Osoroshii-yama is strongest on Honshu— especially in the elbow of the island, in the shadow of the mountain, so to speak. But even on distant Hokkaido it is influential, and when a sharp temblor shakes the ground there, or some local volcano burps, the prayers to Osoroshii-kami are many and fervent.

Again not surprisingly, certain rites and practices have grown up to propitiate Osoroshii-kami. One of these is the planting of a tree species known as *sugi*, the coniferous *Cryptomeria japonica*, especially along roadsides. Supposedly the *sugi*—a very handsome tree—is beloved by Osoroshii-kami, and by planting it, it was believed that the god was less likely to cause destruction in the vicinity. At one time, reportedly, the lowland roads on Honshu were lined with *sugi*.[11]

The propitiation of Osoroshii-kami tended to grow somewhat lax, however, when volcanic and seismic activities had been absent or mild for a time. And as individual *sugi* inevitably died along the roads, victims of root rot, decay or storm, fast growing poplars (*Populus* spp.), or sometimes fruit-bearing chestnuts (*Castanea crenata*), were planted instead, if for no other reason than their ease of propagation.

At the time of first contact, no major quakes or eruptions had occured on Honshu for nearly a century—a calm of unusual duration. And along many roads, only scattered *sugi* remained. That would change, of course . . .

Hans had heard the two samurai who hunted him, but had hardly glimpsed them, for he was high in the top of a large

---

[11] In the mountains, the roads are generally walled with native forest, and there the roadside trees are whatever nature provides. Stands of *sugi* are not infrequent, however.

sugi, the central of three veterans that stood side by side, forty meters tall. Long adjusted to windstorms, and having healthy root systems, and long crowns that distributed the wind pressure over their entire length, they'd withstood the *taifu's* fifty-meters-per-second[12] gusts.

The *sugi* had been pruned to four meters from the ground, to allow summer breezes through to the road; the Yamatoans, like the ancestral Japanese, did whatever they could to ease the steamy summers. That pruned length, and diameters of about ninety centimeters, made them highly unlikely candidates for climbing. But Hans, long-limbed and sinewy, had climbed one anyway, keeping to the side away from the village, and hidden himself in its dense foliage, three-quarters of the way to the top. Behind and in front, the other two *sugi* further screened him. A casual glance would hardly have picked him out; he might even have escaped a diligent examination.

As it was, it occurred to neither samurai to look up. And as hungry as he was from the start, and as thirsty as he became, he didn't come down till dusk had thickened to near twilight. Then he retrieved his sword and trotted off toward the castle town, Momiji-joka, staying behind the trees on the east side of the road, ready to hide at the first sign of anyone.

The sky was clear. There was starlight, and in the west, a pale thread of moon like a silver eye-lash. Thus he didn't need Nils's psychic vision to spot the guards at the other end of the bridge. The Momiji River gathered its waters from steep mountain watersheds, which drained quickly, and even now, less than twelve hours after the rain had stopped, its level and force had begun to fall. Also, though considerably larger than the Gara-gara, it was less violent here, and seemed swimmable.

He followed the shore upstream, watching for something that would float—something stranded. He'd have swum for it unaided, had it not been for his sword. After a bit he found a board lodged among shrubs. Using his sword belt, he tied his

---

[12] Approximately 110 miles per hour.

sword to it, then waded into the river. At once the current swept him off his feet, and he began to swim, holding on to the board. His progress across the swift current was slow, and he was most of a kilometer below the bridge before he reached the far shore.

The town was not as ravaged as the village; many buildings had been more strongly built, and their frames had survived, or in a few cases entire buildings. But even so, the damage was extreme, and in the darkness, people worked by the light of lamps and torches, piling debris and salvaging goods. Some sites had already been cleared, and canopies of hemp or cotton set up on guyed posts. A few businesses had opened again, and Hans could smell something cooking, a stew made with beef.[13] Following his nose, he soon came to a large tent on the site where a tea house had stood. Its raised floor was still in place, though by what artifice he didn't know. Passersby could sit on the edge of it to eat, with their feet outside, thus not having to take off their sandals. Or they could take off their sandals and go in. This evening all the customers were inside.

Hans had never before seen an eating house, but he'd heard of them from Nils and others, while gathering stories for the *The Järnhann Saga*. The procedure seemed simple enough: one asked for food and paid for it. He had no money, of course, but he could pay in services, if the proprietor was willing.

So he went in. Being barefoot, he had no sandals to take off. And while his feet were muddy, the whole town was muddy from the storm, and the usual strictures relaxed. There were several low tables, and people sat on the floor with their feet tucked under them. The two tables in the rear had no one sitting at them, and he went to one of them. He tried sitting as

---

[13] Before the plague, Japanese Buddhist traditionalists declined to eat beef, and many would not eat wild game, other than fish and birds. By first contact, however, these compunctions had either disappeared or become unusual, probably because of the contingencies of early post-plague survival. In fact, Yamatoan foods and eating customs differ in various ways from pre-plague traditions of whatever era.

the others did, but his ankles weren't used to the strain, so instead he sat crosslegged.

The proprietor came to him, leery of his extreme height and foreign appearance, and asked what he wanted. Hans's crams had included polite pre-plague usage, and Ted had warned him of what the people here considered proper behavior. Also, his vocabulary and usage updates were strongly influenced by the speech patterns of Captain Iwatoku, who'd thought he was speaking to heavenly messengers. Thus Hans's reply was suitably obsequious and self-deprecating.

Without getting up, he bowed as best he could. "I have no money," he said, speaking carefully, "and am unworthy to ask your esteemed favor. But if you would be so kind, I would like something to eat. I have only this evening arrived in your excellent town, and have not eaten since before the storm. My poor skills are nothing, but I would be happy to work for my meal."

The proprietor sized him up, then turned away without speaking. Hans didn't know what that meant, but a couple of minutes later, a pretty girl about his own age brought him barley and a bowl of *miso*. It wasn't beef stew, nor was it enough, but it was food.

Ordinarily, so strange an apparition as Hans would have snagged and held every eye; most people would have been concerned at his strangeness, and upset at his being there. But their town had been physically devastated. So much had been lost, and there was very much to do, and somehow this had weakened the barriers between people. The usual forms of behavior had been loosened, at least for the day.

Thus, once Hans had seated himself, people's attention had pretty much returned to their eating and conversations. Most glanced at him only occasionally if at all. Nor were the glances hostile, though some were unhappy to have an armed giant among them. One who watched him more continually was a solitary carpentry contractor, who had a good view of him without turning. The remarkably tall foreigner, with the remarkable hair and skin color, clearly had no concept of proper eating manners; he ignored his chopsticks, putting his food in his mouth with his fingers. Yet the carpenter enjoyed watching him, even felt friendly toward him—he'd had more than a little to drink—and fingers or not, the foreigner's eating movements were deft and tidy.

He appeared strong, too, as well as tall; although he was slender, his bare arms were sinewy. Thus it occurred to the carpenter that the strange youth might be very useful on a building crew. There would be jobs which other men did on a ladder or platform, which the foreigner could do with his feet on the ground. And there'd be very much work, rebuilding from the storm.

The carpenter beckoned to the proprietor, and when the man came over to him, gestured toward Hans. "It was very good of you to give the foreigner barley," he said. "Even foreigners must eat. Let me also be generous to him, for he is clearly very young, and the young are always hungry. Bring him a bowl of your stew, and some pickled radish. I will pay."

The proprietor bobbed a shallow bow and left. A minute later, as Hans was finishing his *miso*, the man reappeared with a steaming bowl of stew and set it in front of him. Hans looked up and began to thank him; the proprietor shook it off. "The carpenter sitting there paid for this," he said gesturing. "He ordered me to bring it to you."

Hans looked questioningly at the carpenter, then nodding, smiled his thanks. The carpenter grinned, and while Hans began to eat, went over to him, squatting to speak. "Excuse me for asking," he said, "but are you looking for a means of making your living? I am a master carpenter. Perhaps I could employ you on my crew. There is much building to be done in Momiji-joka before winter."

Hans stared, but the carpenter was not offended. He was usually good natured, and the *sake* had made him more so. Besides, the stare felt neither arrogant nor disrespectful.

Behind it, the Northman youth was evaluating his immediate prospects, and the man who'd offered to hire him. If he was employed here, he could learn about the town, ask questions, and perhaps find Nils.

"Thank you," he said, the word patterns flowing more easily now from the cram imprints. "You are more than kind. I am most happy to accept your generous offer, and only wish I were worthy of it. I have helped to build houses before, but not the kind you have here. I've helped fit the corners on buildings made of logs, and put roofs on."

The carpenter laughed. "Good enough! You will do well!" He looked toward the serving girl and got her attention. "More *sake!*" he ordered, when she came over. "For me and my helper." He grinned at Hans as she left. "We will celebrate, you and I, and then we will go to my house. It has lost its walls and roof, but part of the frame still stands, and I have spread canvas as a shelter."

That wasn't their last drink together that evening, and the carpenter, who'd had a large head start, soon was drunk. He wasn't the only one. A *ronin* came in, walking stiff-legged in an effort to look sober. Having worked that day on cleanup, he had money. He turned surly when he drank, and had already spent an hour in a *sake* shop; now he ordered roast pork with soy sauce, which would have horrified a samurai of the Tokugawa Period, twelve hundred years earlier. The soy sauce would serve to keep him thirsty, and sharpen his enjoyment of the *sake*. While he waited, he had another bowl of *sake*, and more when the pork came, and more again when that was gone.

By that time the carpenter had begun to be loud, talking, laughing, and gesticulating, and the proprietor asked him to leave. Getting to his feet, the carpenter stumbled into the *ronin*, who rolled over backward, spilling his drink and swearing.

The carpenter turned to apologize, and seeing it was a samurai he'd knocked over, went pale. The *ronin* struggled to his feet, already reaching for his sword hilt. He drew it. By that time Hans too had stood, and drew his own. The *ronin* never noticed; he was focused totally on the carpenter.

"On your knees!" he shouted, and the carpenter knelt, sobered now, hoping to be spared. The *ronin* raised his blade as if to strike. Then the Neoviking youth spoke, sharply and loudly.

"Touch him and you die!"

The *ronin* turned and stared, for just an instant astonished. Drunk, he hadn't noticed this remarkable creature before. This remarkable, non-samurai apparition! Then the enormous discourtesy registered, the unbelievable insult. His face contorted, and he stepped to face his challenger.

The proprietor, meanwhile, had shooed a servant into the street with the establishment's alarm horn, dented from the storm but still functional. He could hear it blaring. "Please, *kunshi!*" he begged.[14] "Do not kill one another." He turned his attention to the samurai, though careful to stand out of reach. "Excuse me, my lord, but it was all an accident. This person" —he gestured toward the carpenter— "has drunk a great deal, and inadvertantly stumbled. He is anxious to make it up to you. No doubt he has *chogin* in his purse, and—"

The *ronin* slashed the proprietor with his eyes. "Both of them are common dogs without value. They must die."

During the exchange, Hans had glanced around, sizing up the possibilities. He'd trained with both Nils and Achikh, during their year together, but he knew his sword skills were far from expert. Nor was fighting his muse. Though not averse to fighting, he was a poet; spinning words was his special talent. And while the madman in front of him was considerably drunker than himself, it seemed to him the *ronin* might very well outmatch him.

Nonetheless he'd committed himself. Now he'd have to make the best of it. "If you are not a coward," he said calmly, "then you will first fight the man who has a sword. If you attack my friend first, I will cut you down from behind." Hans stepped back to the edge of the raised floor. "I will fight you outside," he added, "that the proprietor need not scrub your blood from his floor."

He hopped out backward then, without taking his eyes from the *ronin*—who a moment later followed him. It was dark, and the *ronin* was drunk, and the floor was two feet above the ground. Hans had expected the man to stagger on landing, giving him a momentary advantage. Actually the *ronin* fell, sprawling on all fours. Hans could have killed him then, and might have, had intended to. But beside him was a pile of salvaged lumber, and without conscious decision, he lay aside

---

[14] "Kunshi" means gentleman, singular and plural, in the sense of the superior man, one given to self-control and proper behavior.

his sword, snatching up a length of five-by-ten-centimeter studding. The samurai was just getting up when Hans hit him with it, hard, harder than necessary, sending him sprawling sideways to lie still.

Then men came running through the tea house, and jumped out. Patrolmen. One of them stumbled on the fallen *ronin* and also fell. A net was thrown over Hans, who did not resist. In no more than a minute his wrists had been tied, and tethers looped over his head. He was led past the teahouse to the street. A number of people were standing there, among them the carpenter, who looked more than sober now, looked shocked and concerned.

The prison was simply a part of the police station, and had withstood the typhoon when most other buildings had not. When Hans was brought in, one of the men's cells had five occupants: accused looters. The other was empty. After the *yoriki* had questioned him and taken his statement, he had him put in the empty cell. Because he was an unknown quantity arrested for attacking a samurai, they also chained him by an ankle.

The prison was a holding facility, its prisoners kept there only while awaiting trial. Imprisonment wasn't used as punishment. Punishments could be a fine, or flogging, or restriction to job and home; more severe crimes could result in exile, or mutilation such as cutting off an ear or even a nose or hand; and sometimes execution. Sentences were passed by the magistrate, after a hearing. Sentences of mutilation or execution were reviewed by the *daimyo* before being carried out. Lord Matsumura rarely approved severe mutilation; a criminal was much likelier to have his head cut off than his hand.

Hans knew none of this, but assumed something not entirely unlike it, because the Neoviking system was not so dissimilar. They too didn't punish by imprisonment. Mostly they used fines, and for more severe offenses, sentences of outlawry which amounted to exile, for an outlaw could be killed by anyone unless he left the country within a given period. Now and then, blood feuds were approved, and occasionally there was an execution, a beheading.

Hans had nothing with which to pay a fine. And as alien as he felt here, as unconnected and friendless, it seemed to him he'd never come out of this alive, unless he was found guiltless.

And he wasn't even sure what his crime had been.

He hadn't been in his cell very long when another prisoner was brought in—the *ronin*. His head had been bandaged, and his eyes seemed unfocused. The *doshin* had him put in the same cell as Hans, but because the two prisoners had fought, so to speak, the *ronin* too was chained, where they couldn't get at one another.

The *ronin* was conscious now, enough that he knew what he was there for. In Lord Matsumura's district, it was illegal to attack anyone with an edged weapon except in a formal duel, with a public challenge. And these required seconds, and approval, and a waiting period of at least twelve hours. When the requirements were ignored, as they typically were, the duel was customarily fought away from town in some more or less secluded place. Not in a tea house on Bridge Street.

He scowled vaguely at Hans but said nothing. After a bit, both went to sleep.

There was an important part of the night that Hans didn't know about. At the end of his shift, the *yoriki* had sat down to write his shift report. When he'd finished, he added a brief note to the new magistrate: Matsumura-sama placed great value on the giant barbarian, and this new prisoner might well be the foreigner's kinsman or countryman. Both were remarkably tall and had strangely colored hair, and both spoke with similar accents, using a mixture of archaic words and phrases. Perhaps his lordship would want to see this prisoner too.

Considering what had happened to Magistrate Fujigawa, it would be wise to assume it, but the *yoriki*, of course, was not so ill-mannered as to say so in his report.

The pinnace wasn't at the landing place this time either. And hadn't been since the typhoon; that was clear by the lack of imprints of the landing legs and force shield. Briefly, Hans stood with his head tipped back as if expecting it to show up overhead, settling toward the ground. Then they turned and started back toward Momiji Castle.

TWELVE

Lord Matsumura's apartment had its personal bath, but in a nearby room was a larger one, what might almost be called a conference bath. There the *daimyo* could relax with as many as a dozen guests, to discuss whatever they chose.

On this evening, Matsumura had requested Iwatoku, Nils, Hans, and Akira to share it with him. When they'd stripped, it was the *daimyo* who, per protocol, first eased himself into the steaming water, looking up at Nils who followed him. "Naked," he said, "Inrinu-san appears even larger than with clothes on." He laughed as the Northman sat down. "Women must find you more impressive than swordsmen do. Here, let me see your burn."

Nils held out his right hand for inspection. Matsumura shook his head at it. "I had not imagined that hands could be so large. All the sword callus will peel off, after a burn like that. You will have to start over again; the new skin will be soft as a baby's."

He peered curiously at the Northman. "That will be no problem for you though. You do what is necessary, without stint or quibble. That is the kind of man you are. I can tell." His gaze was direct but relaxed.

Hans had been the last seated in the tub. When he'd first put a foot in the water, he'd very nearly hissed at how hot it was. *You could cook potatoes in it*, he'd told himself. But the others had gotten in and sat down; he'd decided he could too. Now, up to his neck in it, he felt all the unrecognized tension, all the kinks, going slack, and decided he liked it.

Matsumura turned his gaze to him. "And you, Hansu, you have already been very useful to me. With the help of your report, I am rid of a treacherous bailiff."

Hans remembered his manners. "Thank you, Matsumura-sama, but I am not worthy of your praise."

Matsumura ignored the formal disclaimer. "You were most resourceful, too, in escaping him. Otherwise it would be you who lay dead now, instead of Akawashi Kata. I only wish we'd caught one or more of his men." He pursed his wide mouth, frowning. "Even without them, though . . ."

Instead of finishing, he looked again at Nils. "You say you wish to find Ojiisan Tattobu. You will have to travel to do that. And in these times, travel can be dangerous in Yamato, even for so excellent a swordsman. There are numerous men today who have little regard for the law, or for lives, including their own. Bandits prey on travelers in the mountains. Groups of *ronin* wander, many of them unruly, some little better than the bandits. Especially when they drink too much *sake*, which many do whenever they can. In fact, they are more likely to attack a swordsman than they are a peasant."

"Please excuse me, Matsumura-sama," Iwatoku put in, "but there would be many fewer ruffians on the roads and in the towns if Tenshi-Kawai[15] had not required the *daimyo* to reduce, and reduce again, the number of samurai they keep. For two reasons: First, the bandits are mostly *ronin*. And second, with more samurai, the *daimyo* could mount more patrols to hunt the bandits down."

Matsumura grunted. "Yamato can better abide bandits and lawless *ronin* than continuing wars. Bandits may be more indiscriminate, but wars are more destructive of both the empire and the people, and crops are destroyed or neglected. No, the reduction of armies is good. We should not complain of its side effects."

For a long minute he seemed to brood on this, then shook free of his mood. "Inrinu-san, do you have a living father?"

"When last I was at home. He is a smith, and a very strong man. He is likely to live for many more years."

"But he is far away."

"Very far."

The *daimyo* looked appraisingly at Nils for a moment, then

---

[15] Beloved emperor.

continued. "It would be very useful for you to have a family in Yamato. A fighting man is expected to belong to a family; he then carries with him its honor and strength. Possible ill-wishers know that there are those who will avenge him if he is wrongly killed. This is always useful, but especially when one travels."

Nils nodded. "Matsumura-sama is correct, of course."

Again Matsumura sat silent for a few moments, then went on. "I have called you Inrinu-san, but that is very formal. It is more a title, I believe, than a name. Is that right?"

"That is right."

"Would it be impolite of me to call you Nissa? It has a nice sound, even if it is foreign."

Again Nils nodded. "I would be honored if Matsumura-sama chose to call me Nissa. As I was when you called me Inrinu-san."

"Good." Matsumura said nothing more for a long half minute, but no one filled the gap. It was clear to all of them that he wasn't done talking yet, though only Nils knew what he was thinking. Finally he spoke again. "I'm considering adopting you, Nissa, making you my son. What would you think of that?"

Iwatoku was so surprised, his mouth fell open.

Nils looked long at Matsumura, not keeping his eyes averted as good manners would have him do. "I am honored that you are considering it," he said. "But are you sure I am worthy? As a foreigner susceptible to errors of behavior, I might easily bring embarrassment on you. Also, excuse me for asking, but what might your son say to this, the son of your flesh?"

"I am his father. My son does not question my decisions, nor is he unhappy with them."

"Your son is very dutiful. You may find me less so, if you decide to do this. I am a chief among my people, and while they are not numerous or wealthy, they are notable. Before I completed my twentieth year, I had led them successfully in battle, and afterward I was the speaker of law to them. I tell you this not to boast, for I disdain boasting, but so you may know and understand my thoughts on your so generous offer. I would be greatly honored to be your son, but I must also be what else I am: the master of my life, to use it wisely or foolishly, and eventually lay it down."

Matsumura sat without answering, submerged to the chin, his black eyes fixed on the Northman. Finally his gaze shifted to Hans, and he spoke, changing the subject. "Nissa says you are a poet. Recite poetry to me."

Hans had been puzzled by Matsumura's talk of adopting Nils as his son. That night, before they went to sleep, he raised himself on an elbow and looked at Nils by the dim light of their lantern.[16] "Why is this Yamatske chief thinking of adopting you when he already has a son?" He spoke Swedish for privacy, not using names which Akira might recognize.

Nils turned his head toward Hans and grinned, answering in the same tongue. "He asked himself that, earlier today. And decided we must have been comrades at arms in some earlier life. Also, he likes men who are bold and honest, and he considers me both. And he finds our foreignness attractive.

"But what weighs most heavily with him is the status and influence of his family. And therefore my size and strength, and sword skill; he would like to have large strong grandsons by me, preferably with wizard talents. If he adopts me, he'll try to get me married."

Hans lay back down and gazed at the ceiling. Such thinking was really not so unlike that of his own people. Though among the Northmen, attention was not on family but clan. And as for having children by Nils Järnhann— Normally, girls who became pregnant before marriage were married by whoever was the father, if he was available and willing. If he wasn't, the girl was laughed at, and usually had to settle for a poor match. But if she had a child by the Yngling, especially a son, she was honored by her clan, and could expect proposals by good men.

"Nils," he murmured, "would you marry here?"

"Probably. I can give my foster father good grandsons, and they would belong to a good family. And he would be a very good grandfather."

Hans tried to visualize Matsumura-sama as a grandfather, and decided Nils was right about that. Then another thought

---

[16] Usually, in Yamato, lanterns contain candles made by processing the fruiting heads of the lac tree, *Rhus vernicifera*.

drifted into his mental field. "Where do you think the sky boat went?" he asked. "I never thought the star people would abandon us. Especially Ted Baver, after traveling across the world with us on foot and horseback, sometimes in danger, sometimes going hungry. He even fought beside us."

"Perhaps they didn't abandon us," Nils suggested. "Perhaps something happened to them."

"What could happen to *them*? They have their weapons of power, and the sky boat, and its invisible shield that nothing can break through."

Nils made no answer, and Hans could think of none for himself. Yet surely Ted—Ted at least—wouldn't simply abandon them. He wondered then what had happened to their trail companions—to Achikh as well as Ted.

Kamoshika Akira lay listening to the two foreigners murmuring in the lantern light. It was easy to forget that Tetsu-te Nissa was a wizard, even given his eyes. Mostly he didn't seem like one.

They didn't often speak their own language. It seemed to him they must be discussing Matsumura's offer. It was intriguing to listen to. He'd long heard that people in other lands didn't know human speech, but he'd never believed it until he'd been with these two. Still they seemed to get by well enough with their substitute.

Then another thought occurred to Akira. *Does Nissa know what I'm thinking?* He examined first the question, then himself. Did it matter, really? After all, what kinds of thoughts did he have? Surely nothing terribly discreditable, compared to some he must have heard. And besides, he could hardly listen to all the thoughts around him. He'd live in a virtual mental cacophony.

It was nothing to be concerned about, he decided, and closing his eyes, invited sleep.

In Yamato, samurai were mostly the sons of samurai. But a *daimyo* had long had authority to appoint someone a samurai, to serve him. After the great battle at Gifu, however, the then young Emperor Junichi, father of the present Emperor Hikari, had set a limit on the number of samurai a *daimyo* could employ.

Also, the appointment of a samurai was provisional at first. Permanance depended on the appointee being interviewed and approved by the Emperor or his representative.

Later, with two reductions in the force a *daimyo* could keep, and the abundance of masterless samurai who resulted, appointments became rare.

As a *tehon daimyo*, however, Matsumura was allowed five times the number of samurai an ordinary *daimyo* could keep—one company assigned to the inherited family estate, and four, a full battalion, to the liege estate assigned him as a *tehon daimyo*. Furthermore, Matsumura had been made an Emperor's representative for the approval of such appointments.

Thus, on the day after their talk in the bath, Lord Matsumura Shinji announced the appointment of Tetsu-te Nissa and Utayomi[17] Hansu as samurai. Their hair was tonsured in the samurai style, they were provided appropriate clothing, and they began training in Yamatoan courtesy and the Shosen doctrine of the sword.

And a notice was sent to the Emperor of the formal adoption of Tetsu-te Nissa by Lord Matsumura Shinji, as his son. And also of Utayomi Hansu by Tetsu-te Nissa. Both to be effective in ten days.

When they had sufficiently mastered Yamatoan courtesy, the two would be ready to go out and seek the old master, Ojiisan Tattobu.

---

[17] "Utayomi" is Yamatoan for *poet*.

THIRTEEN

The thunder crack was nearly simultaneous with the blinding flash, the combination stunning Matthew Kumalo for a moment. *One of the trees by the road*, he thought. *Probably shattered to the stump.*

The wind snarled around the air intake on the back of the pinnace. He'd turned off the force shield when the storm arrived; it would attract lightning. He'd have lifted above the storm, except for the thought that Nils, or Hans or Achikh, might come back and find the pinnace gone. Hopefully it would blow over shortly, a squall, but the thought was unavoidable that this could be more. As a planetologist, he was aware that typhoons could visit these islands in this season.

The pinnace, heavy as it was and as low as it sat to the ground, shuddered at a gust, and the lightning's irregular strobing showed him Nikko's silhouette beside him.

"Maybe we ought to lift," Ted said from behind him. "It's getting worse, and I don't think anyone's going to come back till it's over. I don't think anyone could even find us, the way it is out there."

"What do you think, Nikk?" Matthew asked.

"I think— Suppose this turns into a typhoon. Could a typhoon wind damage us?"

"Strictly speaking, no. But typhoons spawn tornadoes, and if . . ."

He paused. The voice of the storm had changed, the sound now like nothing they'd heard before, like some pre-plague express train approaching. "Shit!" One hand reached, touched the glowing light switch in front of him, illuminating the control panel, and a finger jabbed the AG switch. He couldn't hear its hum through the storm noise, but after a moment, a red light turned green. Again the finger jabbed. The *Alpha* lifted, abruptly enough that they felt the acceleration sharply. As they lifted, he touched the commast retract key. Then the twister gripped the pinnace, jerked it tilting and spinning off its gravitic vector. Matthew kept his seat with an effort, grabbing the manual flight control, which fortunately hadn't been activated.

"Hold on!" he shouted. The pinnace whirled as if gripped in some enormous centrifuge, and something hard struck them multiple blows, perhaps a building timber or piece of tree trunk. Seconds later the twister spit them out.

Alpha continued accelerating upward, lifting into clouds that pulsed with light and made their hair stand up. A long minute later, they were above them and still climbing. A winking red light on the screen called attention to an accompanying readout: the portside landing legs had been damaged. As had the commast, and in trying to retract it, the motor had burned itself out. On top of that, they'd lost hull integrity. Matt parked close above the storm clouds. Even at 14,000 meters, the rate of air loss seemed insignificant. The possibility of repairs was uncertain, and at any rate would have to be done on the ground.

All three expedition members slumped in their seats, feeling drained and saying little. Mostly they sat napping and waking intermittently until, at 0417 hours, an alarm began to blare: internal air pressure was down to 700 milli-bars. Muzzy-headed, Matthew generated the force shield to reduce the pressure gradient, and bled in some air from the backup tanks. Then he sat back and dipped in and out of sleep again until the limb of the sun broke the horizon, and morning lit the clouds below them. Which weren't as high as before; the typhoon had passed.

With the hull on transparent, they examined their landing gear from inside. It was apparent now to Matthew that the legs wouldn't support the pinnace's weight, and belatedly he saw another problem. Switching the force shield off, he lowered the pinnace to 8,000 meters, then read the remaining power charge.

"We're up that legendary creek without oars," he said grimly. Ted stared at him. "What do you mean?"

"I mean we can't land. The AG grid has to be clear of the ground. If we sit down on it, we'll damage it, and then we can't take off again."

"Do we really need to land again? Can't we hover at thirty centimeters—something like that?"

Matthew shook his head. "The power reticulum only recharges with our weight on the ground."

Ted stared at him uncertainly.

"Think, man! You had basic pilot's training!" Matthew's uncharacteristic flash of anger surprised both of them, and he continued more moderately. "We can't recharge if we can't land. And the AG generator draws more heavily when hovering within the interface zone, right? With the drain increasing exponentially downward. Even at two meters, hovering uses a lot more power than flying." He paused, shaking his head. "The force shield eats it up pretty heavily, too, and besides all that, we depend on the reticulum to recharge the power slugs for every tool we have."

He asked the computer for the charge remaining. When it answered, his lips thinned to a slash. "We don't even have the option of abandoning Nils and company and flying back to Varjby. We couldn't even reach the Caspian with the charge we have left."

"So what do we do?" Ted asked.

Matthew didn't answer at once. Finally he said, "First we find a remote mountain meadow. Then Nikk lets you and me out without landing. We fell a couple of trees, cut a pair of logs out of them, and pry them around so I can land on them and still have the generator clear of the ground. Then we sit there long enough to recharge the reticulum; twenty minutes ought to do it. After that we do what we talked about doing before, but this time we do it. We go back to Varjby. The Northmen are the nearest thing we have to a reliable and friendly supply base. We fly to Varjby, let you off without sitting her on the ground, and you'll have them lay down a pair of logs to land on there. So I can do what's necessary to strengthen the landing legs. We've got a welding torch, and Varjby's got a smithy with odds and ends of steel. The result won't be pretty, but it'll serve and won't take long. At the same time we'll refill the water tanks and replenish the food locker."

"We're going down and check the contact site here before we leave, aren't we?" Ted asked. "In case Nils or the others are there?"

"We'll check, but we can't wait around. We'll check, then leave, with or without him. Or them. And come back later."

They stopped six meters above the landing site. Though the storm was past, it was still raining. No one was in sight— not even the residents of the demolished farmhouse. Ted wondered if they'd fled or been killed.

For a moment, none of the expedition said anything. Then Matthew raised the *Alpha* to 2,000 meters, and they flew northwest over mountains, watching on the screen for a meadow that was level enough, and away from any sign of human activity. Before very long, Matthew was circling one surrounded by old pine forest, at the head of a little draw. The trees seemed mostly about forty to eighty centimeters in diameter; sixty would be plenty.

He chose a spot near an upper corner of the meadow, then settled to about ten meters—effectively above the interface zone. "Here's what we'll do," he said pointing. "We'll cut two trees along that side, felling them crossways of the slope. After we cut the branches off, we'll cut a log out of each and roll them where we want them. We can cut a couple of stout pry poles to roll them with. Then we'll jimmy them around till the spacing's right, and set down on them. Shouldn't take long."

Ted nodded. He'd already gotten the pinnace's laser saw from the tool locker and checked the power slug. Nikko lowered the *Alpha* to half a meter, and the two men hopped out. The rain had dwindled, and the wind had fallen to a moderate breeze, only occasionally gusting more strongly.

Matthew wielded the saw. He'd grown up a farm boy, and had felled trees before, though he wasn't any expert. He chose an old veteran pine about eighty centimeters in diameter, cut a neat notch in the direction he wanted it to fall, then began the backcut. About three-quarters of the way through, he stopped and swore.

"What's the matter?"

"Its weight is wrong, or actually the breeze is. It wants to fall downhill instead of out where we want it. The cut's closed, and I don't have any wedges."

"What do we do?"

"Cut a different tree."

He chose another, which fell nicely where intended, and then another. Wading through the wet grass, he cut a stout, five-meter log from each trunk, careful to stand on the uphill side in case it rolled when it fell free. There was enough slope that the logs did roll downhill a short distance on their own, to where the slope flattened a bit. He cut two pry-poles then, and with considerable effort, they got the logs positioned suitably to land the *Alpha* on.

Matthew straightened, grinning with satisfaction. *Nothing to it!* he told himself. *More slope than I wanted, but we're not going to be here more than half an hour.* He turned and waved for Nikko to bring the pinnace down. At a meter's height she stopped, and with hand signals, he guided her until the *Alpha* sat nicely on the two logs, the AG generator safely clear of the ground.

"Nice work!" Nikko said as the two men climbed aboard. "I hadn't realized I'd married a logger." She spoke instructions to the computer then, and the reticulum began recharging. A readout started to roll on the screen. Looking at the two men, she added, "You're soaked to the hips from the wet grass. You ought to change clothes and throw those in the drier. Your boots too."

Matthew grinned. "Yes, mom." He sat down, and had just begun removing a boot when something struck the pinnace violently from above. The vessel lurched, sliding along the logs and partly off, coming to a halt canted about ten degrees to one side.

"*What the hell!*" Ted swore, picking himself off the deck. "What happened?"

Matthew didn't have to look; he'd realized as soon as it happened. "It's the tree I cut mostly off the stump," he said. "The wind gusted, and pushed it hard enough to break it off. And it was tall enough that the top reached us."

All three got out to look. The treetop, where it had struck the pinnace, was only twelve or fifteen centimeters in diameter, but it had had a lot of momentum, a lot of force. The ship-metal hull had resisted caving in or even denting, but two landing legs had collapsed. The AG grid had hung up on a log, jammed there by the combined weight of the tree and the pinnace. They stared without speaking, almost without breathing. Then Matthew climbed back aboard and asked the computer for a status report, glowering at what it gave him.

"Shit!"

Nikko, just climbing in the door, knew it was bad without asking; Matthew rarely swore. "What?" she asked.

"The AG's inop; we can't fly. And structural integrity's further reduced, not that that makes much difference now. And the commast not only won't retract; it's smashed. We don't have radio, except for our commsets. No good for monitoring broad wave bands. The good news is, the reticulum's still charging."

Ted peered over his shoulder at the screen. And remembered his winter with Nils and Achikh, and Hans, north of the Altai Range in Siberia. They'd lived in a lean-to in the autumn snow, while with axes they'd built a crude and drafty log hut. This wasn't half as bad. Here they had shelter and heat and even a kitchen, and didn't have to breathe smoke from a fire pit.

"Well," he said, "in the meantime maybe we ought to get that tree off our roof."

They spent the next forty minutes cutting up the windfallen tree, rolling the upper trunk off the pinnace, and lopping down the tops of all three pines. Every time Matthew looked at the *Alpha*, his guts knotted; they really were stranded. *Come on* Phaeacia, he thought. *Get here!*

When they'd finished, they climbed back into the pinnace and changed into dry clothes. Nikko prepared brunch, splurging a bit. *Matt needs it*, she told herself. *As the in-charge, he worries more than Ted and I. Not that he needs to.*

When they'd eaten, they sat back and relaxed over a mug of hot spruce tea, from buds obtained from the Northmen—a little bitter, but relaxing. "Nice lunch," said Ted. "Let me volunteer to go to market."

Matthew looked at him wryly.

"We can hunt, I suppose," Ted continued. "But I saw fields, farm fields I mean, in the valley on this side of the mountain, before we put down here."

Matt's expression changed. He'd known the new Ted Baver was different, but even so, he hadn't expected this level of observation and initiative from him. "You used to be afraid of getting lost," he said. "Are you sure you want to do this?"

"I'm still leary of getting lost. I certainly don't have the built-in homing system that Nils and Hans have, and Achikh. But I can handle a short-range trip like this. And someone needs to go. If you'd rather?" he finished.

Matthew shook his head. "You'll probably do better than I would, and I'm sure you're in better shape for mountain hiking than I am."

Ted nodded. "We need to scout the area anyway. I'll follow the draw; it grows into a sort of shallow ravine farther down, as I recall. There's probably a brook in it we can get water from. It's bound to come to a valley before too far. Then I'll go downstream till I come to some farms, and see what the possibilities are for buying food." He looked around. "What can we spare that I can use to trade with?"

"Gold and silver," Nikko said promptly. "Danish coins we had for buying supplies in Denmark and Germany. I can't imagine anyone objecting to King Jørgen's face on them." She turned to her husband. "What's the matter, Matt?"

After a moment he answered. "These—Yamatoans can be a violent people, judging from the castles we've seen. And" — he looked at Ted, who sat intent but calm— "you'll be going down there alone. With nothing we can do to bail you out, if anything happens. So you'll go prepared. And I want you to be careful."

"Sure, Matt. I'm no Nils; I'll be as careful as I can. And I'll be armed. Just the sound of a slug thrower should be enough to stop these people. If not—" He shrugged. "I can always shoot someone in the leg or shoulder, I suppose. But nothing's going to happen. Even the Kazakhs could be talked to, bargained with. And this—" He gestured at his jumpsuit. "They've never seen anything like it. What they'll be is curious, maybe a little awed. Probably the way I talk will help, too."

Half an hour later, Ted was ready. He'd declined to take a sleeping bag; it would cut down on the amount of food he could bring back. He'd sleep in some farmhouse or hay shed. They'd agreed he wouldn't tell anyone about the pinnace, and wouldn't bring anyone back with him. If he could, he'd avoid being followed, even if he had to ambush a follower and lay him low with the stunner on his belt. His commset was in a pocket, along with extra magazines for the pistol. And for extreme emergencies, he had one of the *Alpha's* few grenades clipped on his belt, a concussion grenade made in the *Phaeacia's* machine shop, after the Northmen had pre-empted their supply of fragmentation grenades for the Orc war. For producing casualties, it was inferior to a fragmentation grenade, but it could kill, especially up close. And just as important, it seemed to him it would scare hell out of people. In the unlikely event he needed it.

On his back, covered by a poncho, was a willow pack frame with a large, woven willow basket lashed on it, provided by the Northmen two years earlier, and used by Matthew for bringing supplies to the pinnace on research trips. Ted climbed out, then turned to them and waved—grinning!—before he strode off downhill, and out of sight into the forest.

"Well," said Matthew, "the new Ted! I'd pretty much given up on him ever being worth much, back before he took off with Nils last year."

Nikko nodded. "And we haven't adjusted to the changes yet. You know, before we came down this morning, you talked to him as if he was a fool. You almost never speak to anyone like that."

He sipped his tea ruefully. "I suppose it was partly because of the magnitude of the situation. And partly because I hadn't realized what it meant till just then; I should have known right away. So I took it out on him. Apparently it didn't bruise him though."

Matt shifted mental gears, putting the subject aside. "Meanwhile we're stranded in the mountains a long way from Varjby and the Northmen. We'll just have to sit tight until the *Phaeacia* arrives back from New Home, whenever that is. It could easily be a year or more. Even two or three."

"It shouldn't take them long to find us when they do," Nikko said. "As long as the electrical system functions and we can keep the reticulum charged. I realize the commast is inop, but it's not as if we have to monitor for them. The first thing they'll do is scan for us, and their instruments can pick up our beam, commast or no."

Matthew pursed his lips thoughtfully. "They'll find us all right. If we stay with the *Alpha*."

Nikko's eyebrows raised. "Why would we leave it?"

"Good question. Probably we won't. But I can think of two or three scenarios, more or less unlikely, that could force us to leave." *And there are probably others*, he added to himself, *that wouldn't occur to me*.

He wished then that he hadn't said anything about it. Nikko's expression had turned troubled, and there'd been no point in worrying her, when it was all hypothetical and there was nothing they could do about any of it.

FOURTEEN

Not fifty meters below the meadow was a large seep, giving birth to a rivulet. Ted wasn't sure whether it ran constantly, or only when there'd been a lot of rain. Within the next hundred meters, however, more seeps enlarged the rivulet to a small brook, which surely, he thought, must run all the time, though no doubt it would shrink somewhat with a week or two of clear weather. After a little, the draw became a small ravine, which eventually fed into a larger, with a full-fledged creek three meters wide. It must have been swollen by the typhoon, but its water was clear nonetheless. Using his pocket comm, he informed Matthew, then made a small cairn, actually a stack of three rocks, so he'd recognize the junction when he came back. When he'd finished, he started downstream. Travel was slowed by tangled patches of fresh blowdown, but not as much as he thought it might be. It was as if the structural integrity of the stand, along with protection by the terrain, had saved it from severe wind damage. He saw several ancient trees that had been riven by lightning, freshly scarred from crown to bottom and with pieces of top scattered about, attesting to the electrical violence that had come with the wind.

After several kilometers, the ravine opened into the valley. He paused to mark the place with five pieces of dead wood, set up like a miniature teepee frame and tied at the top with a length of snowberry vine. Then he checked in with the pinnace to update them. The valley bottom was forested there, and a swollen and powerful stream surged through it; Ted hoped he wouldn't have to cross it. Paralleling the stream was a wide trail, or perhaps a rough and narrow road; he wasn't sure which concept applied best here, in a land where there seemed to be almost no wheeled traffic. Along the trail or road, blowdown

121

had been severe. It was as if the stream gap had served as an entry point, funneling the wind, which had reaped the streamside forest like a scythe, windrowing the trees.

Ted paralleled the road, keeping well back from the river to avoid the worst of the blowdown. After four or five laborious kilometers, he came to a hayfield. Again he informed the *Alpha*.

In the forest, the trees had been dripping. It wasn't till now that he realized the rain had stopped entirely. Perhaps for the day, because the clouds had thinned enough that dimly he could see his shadow. The hay had been cut, and cocked over racks that looked like segments of tall rail fences, but much of it had blown away. What remained stuck like soggy green-gray mats on the windward side of the few surviving racks. About a kilometer ahead, he could see the remains of a hamlet, with people moving around amidst the debris. As he walked toward it, keeping to the road now, he came to what he recognized as a potato field, its plants flattened by wind and beating rain. Presumably they were mature enough that the potatoes themselves could be harvested. He wondered how things had gone with their other crops. It occurred to him that the people here might not have any surplus they'd care to sell him.

No one noticed him till he was about a hundred and fifty meters from the hamlet. By that time he'd distinguished two sorts of people ahead. Some were working; others were sitting or squatting, talking. It was the latter who reacted to him. They got to their feet, and he saw they were armed, holding bows, stringing them. Soldiers, he thought, then revised his impression to bandits, because they weren't uniformed. And it struck him with a jolt that they could easily reach him with a flight of arrows, leave him dead. His slug thrower, on the other hand, had a practical range of perhaps forty meters. He'd had some training with it, and some time on a target range, but beyond forty meters, to hit something man-sized would be luck, not skill. Taking them all out with it, before being skewered with arrows, seemed impossible beyond a dozen meters.

He threw the poncho back off his shoulders.

Half a dozen of the armed men walked partway out to meet him. *Close the gap to a dozen meters*, he told himself, and kept walking, his right hand reaching across to his pistol and loosening the holster flap, then finding the grenade. *A dozen meters*, he repeated, *then stop and talk, see what develops*. Somehow, though, he doubted they'd be interested in conversation, and wished he'd thought this through before he'd started out. He should, it seemed to him now, have skirted the fields through the forest fringe, where they wouldn't have seen him. Scouted the place before he showed himself.

But on the other hand, there'd been no reason to expect bandits.

He took his commset out of its pocket, switched it on, and clipped it to the front of his jumpsuit. "*Alpha, Alpha*, this is Ted," he said. "I've encountered what looks like either bandits or local militia. About fifty meters away. They've strung their bows and have arrows nocked. Wish me luck. Ted out."

It seemed obvious now that his greeting party had no intention of shooting him out of hand. They stood eyeing him, talking amongst themselves, seemingly not worried but watchful. A little nervous, perhaps, because of his jumpsuit and poncho. Their clothes were rough and dirty, and they wore short rain capes made of straw. At twenty meters, one of them called out to him.

"Stop!"

He took two more strides and stopped, pistol in one hand, grenade in the other. The grenade could be activated by thumb pressure; an impact then would set it off.

"Who are you?" the man asked. "What are you doing here?"

Ted raised his arms as if blessing them, each hand holding a weapon. His bowels felt as if he had diarrhea, as if he could soil his shorts right there, but his mind was clear. "I come from Heaven," he said. "I am sent by Amaterasu-omikami.[18] She has a demand to make of this village, and I will speak with its headman. Take me to him. Now!"

---

[18] "Heaven-shining Great Deity," or Sun Goddess, who in the religion of present-day Yamato, shares the central godhood with the Buddha Amida.

No one had raised their bow yet. The jumpsuit had stopped them, Ted thought, that and his brazen claim. After an uncertain moment, the man who'd spoken bowed, just a little; others followed his example, some more deeply. "Please be so kind as to follow me," the man said. As he turned away, Ted felt an urge to shoot him, then empty his magazine into the others, now, when they were off guard. But he didn't. There were others watching, some on their feet, and besides, if they were militia instead of bandits, it would be an act of murder, a canker on his conscience, and make enemies of the people here.

And then it was too late, for some of the group fell in behind him as he followed their spokesman into the demolished hamlet. Bandits, definitely, he decided now, and there were at least twenty of them. They seemed to be samurai, though they looked shaggy and unkempt; most wore two swords scabbarded in their sashes. The people who worked carried no weapons; those who didn't were armed. He wondered if, given a chance, the farmers would fight.

Ted had assumed the man he'd spoken with was the leader. Now it was clear he wasn't, for he stopped and bowed before an open-sided, straw-mat shelter. Its occupant sat on a log like a scowling bullfrog, while the other reprised what had been said out in the field.

The bandit leader turned his gaze to Ted, eyes like obsidian marbles, and seemed to turn him inside out for inspection. Then, "Make him captive!" the man barked.

Ted surprised himself perhaps as much as he did the bandits: He shot the leader in the middle of the forehead, then turning, dropped to one knee and continued pulling the trigger, nearly emptying the magazine before he stopped. Six bandits lay wounded or dead, while the others had prostrated themselves or knelt with their faces in the dirt, hands beside their heads.

"Which of you is the leader now?" Ted asked. "Let him receive my orders!"

One answered, his forehead on the ground. "I am that unworthy person," he said. "It is clear that you are what you claim to be. It is yours to order, ours to obey."

"Good. What is your name?"

"I am called Yorigifu, your holiness."

Ted grunted. "Get up," he said, and gestured at the others with his pistol. "Have these pig-like non-humans pile their bows and swords on the ground in front of me. Now!" They got up, milled around briefly getting into a line, then filed past him, eyes on his slug thrower, to pile their weapons, each man bowing when he'd done so. It seemed to Ted they wouldn't have been so docile, even in the face of the slug thrower, if they hadn't bought his claim now to having come from the goddess.

"Stand over there," he said when they were done, gesturing with the pistol again. They gathered in a watchful clump.

"Now get on your knees, all of you. Or the power of Amaterasu-omikami will destroy you as it did those others."

They knelt. *I could kill them all with the grenade now*, he told himself, but didn't. Instead he turned to the farmers, who had also prostrated themselves. "You! Farmers! Which of you is the leader? Come to me now!"

An aging farmer got to his feet and started over, hat in his hands, eyes on the ground. About four meters in front of Ted, he got down on his knees again and bowed his forehead to the dirt.

"You are the leader of these people?" Ted asked.

"Excuse me, yes, your reverence. I am not worthy of it, but they insist."

"Good. Stand up."

Hesitantly the man stood, his eyes on his work-gnarled hands.

"Tell me what these others, these bandits, have been doing here."

The farmer told a story of plundering, vandalism, rape and murder—told it not only to Ted but to the commset clipped to the jumpsuit, though he didn't know it.

"Thank you. Have some of your men come to me. Have them bring strong ropes, and—" Not knowing the word for machete, he groped, then improvised. "And chopping knives."

The farmer turned without hesitating, calling names and an order. Within a few minutes, the bandits' hands were tied. Then Ted had them roped together by the neck and walked to the nearby forest edge, where he supervised tying them to windbroken tree stubs. When he returned to the hamlet, someone had cut the heads off the wounded and dead bandits. Ted looked at the results distastefully.

"Now," he told the old man, "have the bodies disposed of. I must go apart from you and speak with the goddess. Later I'll tell you something else to do."

He walked about fifty meters back up the road then, and squatted. He'd gotten good at squatting, during his year with the Northmen. "*Alpha*," he said, "this is Ted. *Alpha*, this is Ted. I guess you heard it all."

"We heard, Ted. How many people did you shoot?"

"Six."

Matthew didn't say anything for several seconds, then asked, "What's being done for the wounded?"

"The locals hacked their heads off with machetes, while I was having the captives tied to trees."

There was another long pause, then a sigh that Ted could hear over the radio. "Well, I guess I can understand that."

Ted took over the conversation. "It's too late to start back," he said. "It was slow hiking, even downhill, with the blowdown in the woods, especially here in the valley. And going back, I hope to be carrying a load of food. Mostly uphill. I'll spend the night in the hamlet. They've got some log sheds here they've been more or less roofing. I'll get food from them in the morning— grain if I can, otherwise probably potatoes—and start back."

He felt suddenly all used up, and began to shake. A response to the killing, he realized. He stayed where he was till it stopped, then went back to the hamlet.

Fires had been made, and bedding hung on makeshift racks to dry. *Makeshift*. It occurred to Ted that primitive people were good at makeshift—clever and resourceful. They fed him, and while he ate, his commset came to life. The voice was Nikko's, speaking Anglic. The people near him backed away, alarmed and awed.

"Ted, this is *Alpha*. Ted this is *Alpha*. We have a tiger outside. Repeat, a tiger outside. A great big thing. Matthew saw it, and switched on the force shield. It just bumped its nose on it, and didn't like it.... Now it's trying to climb the— It slid off." There was a pause. "Now it's circling. Ted's loading an assault rifle; we can't have it hanging around here."

There was nothing then for a long minute. *She's getting ready to switch off the shield,* Ted thought, and raised his bowl to his mouth again, shoving mush in with chopsticks. A shot banged, then a short burst of them, and another, sounding strange over the commset. He put down his bowl in alarm. Had Matt missed? Half a minute later, Nikko spoke again.

"The tiger jumped when the shield switched off, as if it felt it, and Matt missed his first shot. Then it took off running. Another shot made it's hindquarters go down, then it was up and running again. The third one sent it down entirely, but it got away into the forest. He's going out now to see if he can find it and finish it off."

"Which way did it run?"

"Downhill."

Oh great. A wounded tiger between here and there. "Tell him to be careful."

"He will be. I'll let you know whether he kills it or not. It must be pretty badly hit though, to have gone down."

We'll hope.

An hour later, Matthew called. "Ted, I didn't find him. I'm really sorry about this. Apparently he took off and kept going. I expect he'll be very cautious about humans now, but be alert coming back. Alert as you can be."

"You can bet on it." Ted paused, thinking, remembering the wild bull he'd shot, back in the Balkans. A slug thrower didn't have a lot of authority against large animals. "What do you think of a stunner, against a tiger? On full strength and close up, it might work better than a slug thrower, don't you think?"

Matthew's reply came slowly. "You may be right about that. Stunner on full, with a semi-broad beam. That way you're sure to hit it, and any kind of hit should put it down, out to maybe six or eight meters."

The planetologist had sounded worried, unhappy. "Okay," Ted answered. "Sounds right to me."

When they were finished, Ted considered taking a local along with him, to watch to the rear. But that would jeopardize the pinnace; the man would go back and tell what he saw. No, he'd have to go alone. And Matt was right: the tiger would probably steer clear of humans now.

Or if it didn't, surely it would be gun-shy. *Pistol first*, Ted told himself, *if I have time. Then the stunner if it keeps coming. Then a bullet in the brain, to finalize things*.

He wasn't very happy with the situation, though.

FIFTEEN

When Ted lay down in the shed to sleep, that evening, he kept his web belt on, with his holstered pistol attached. His stunner and commset he laid under the edge of the woven straw mat he'd been given to sleep on, where his hands could find them easily in the dark. The stunner was set on medium-beam low—sufficient to stun, to paralyze someone at close range. For convenience, the commset was on crisscross.

He hadn't been asleep long when someone, two someones, came into the shed and grabbed him, jerking him to his feet, their strength surprising. A torch flickered weakly from the doorway. He struggled, kicking, throwing his weight around. A blow in the belly drove the wind from him, and a fist struck his face twice, hard, like being kicked by a horse. The world went black.

Kirisaki Hoshin had arrived with his men not long after dark. Arrived tired and surly and late. They'd hoped to arrive the evening before, but the ambush had gone sour. He'd lost several men and most of his horses, and made off with little more than one captive, a high-born girl, daughter of a lord.

Then the *taifu* had struck, and they'd spent a wet and utterly miserable night huddled in the forest. In spite of the storm, that stupid Mitsuya had tried to rape the girl in the night, and he'd had to cut his head off. What kind of human would try to rape a samurai's daughter? Disgraceful! Some of these *ronin*! With dawnlight they'd set out up the road, on foot in the rain, leading the few horses they had left, struggling around blowdown all the way. At one point they'd seen human bodies in the river—headless bodies!—caught in the branches of a fallen tree. It had made him more cautious than he might otherwise have been. It seemed to Kirisaki one of the worst days he'd ever lived through.

The farmers, not knowing of them, had posted no sentries. Hoshin had expected sentries—Ono-san's sentries—and not being challenged as he approached the hamlet, he'd stopped before entering. What could be wrong? He'd sent men to scout the hamlet's perimeter, and they'd found some of Ono-san's men tied to trees! They'd cut them loose and brought them to him. One of them had been Yorigifu, who told him all that had happened. It explained the headless bodies.

Kirisaki slapped the peasant woman on the rump and sent her back out of the shelter with her clothes in her hands. She hadn't been much good, but in a place like this, after a day like his had been . . . He pulled on his clothes, and by the light of a candle fastened the web belt around his waist.

Yorigifu insisted that the small iron club scabbarded on it was a terribly deadly weapon. Kirisaki found it hard to believe. Certainly it hadn't produced thunder and lightning for him. It didn't even have a sharp edge! *In the morning*, he told himself, *the foreigner will have recovered from the beating Setichi gave him. I will question him about it then.* Meanwhile the belt and its appendages looked and felt good on his waist.

The peasants gave them breakfast, and loaded the horses with barley, beans, and sweet potatoes. The barley was somewhat wet, but he'd take a couple of village boys and they could spread it on a canvas in the sun, when they stopped for rest.

While preparations were being made, Kirisaki had the foreigner brought to him, and looked him up and down. The foreigner's clothing was very strange; he'd never seen so many pockets, nor any pocket at all that opened and closed in such a marvelous way. It almost made one believe the man's story. But surely no one from the Goddess would stand before him with his hands tied and his face swollen and discolored.

Kirisaki began to unzip pockets, till he found in one of them a purse with gold and silver coins. The bandit put it inside his shirt, under his sash, then drew the iron club from its scabbard.

"What is this?" he asked.

"My *teppo*," said the foreigner.

"*Teppo*? What is *teppo*?"

"A magic weapon given to me by Amaterasu-omikami."

Kirisaki slapped the man's face, hard, rocking his head to one side. It irritated him that a foreigner would claim such a thing. Besides, there was a certain fear that the man might be speaking the truth. "Tell me how it works," he ordered.

The foreigner stretched forth a hand, as if Kirisaki was to hand it to him. Again Kirisaki slapped the swollen face, even harder this time, to teach him respect, so the man settled for telling him: one pressed back on the little lever. (He didn't mention the safety.) When nothing happened, no thunder and lightning, Kirisaki slapped the foreigner again, leaving the imprint of his palm on the man's face.

The foreigner then explained that the *kami* had given it only a limited blessing, sufficient only for himself. Perhaps prayer by some sufficiently exalted personage—the emperor for example—might exalt it sufficiently that it would work for him. Otherwise it was only an ordinary club.

When they left the hamlet, the foreigner left with them, a leather rope around his neck, a tether. They also took several of the hamlet's women to cook for and entertain them. They'd send them back before they left the valley. Kashira would want to examine the foreigner and his iron club. Perhaps he could even make it roar.

Shortly after the bandits left, one of the farm wives heard a muffled voice coming from the shed the foreigner had slept in. She looked inside timidly and saw no one, but the voice continued.

She hurried off to tell the headman. Hesitantly he went to the shed and looked inside. Just as he looked, the voice spoke again. Frowning he stepped in, then raised the straw mat the foreigner had slept on. There beneath it was a magic amulet, which spoke in some unintelligible tongue, perhaps that of the gods.

He stepped back, suppressing his fright, and watched the amulet until it stopped.

There was another object with it, but it said nothing.

He sent the woman, his daughter, for a piece of silk that had been salvaged from his demolished house. When she'd brought it, he carefully wrapped the commset and stunner in it and buried them reverently next to the little chapel where the hamlet worshiped Amida, marking the spot with a round stone the size of his head. When there was time, he'd have a more suitable marker made.

Matt and Nikko had been getting ready for bed, the evening before, when the ship's comm had picked up sounds of angry voices, one of them certainly Ted's, muffled and unintelligible. Matthew's first impulse had been to call and ask what was going on. Then the noise had stopped, and he'd decided to leave well enough alone. There was nothing he could do to help, if help was needed. It seemed best to remain unknown, and let Ted call him when he had the chance.

But when the sun was well up and he'd heard nothing further, he decided to call and see if Ted answered. He didn't, and it seemed to Matt that something bad had happened. He tried again from time to time, without much hope. It seemed to him the bandits must have gotten loose and captured Ted. And considering what Ted had done to six of them earlier, Matt didn't expect to see the young ethnologist alive again.

Prove me wrong, Ted, and I'll be the happiest man on Earth, he told himself.

Meanwhile they had about three day's food for the two of them. He supposed he'd have to go to the village sooner or later and try to get some. Hopefully the bandits weren't settling in there for the winter. For now, though, he'd stay with the *Alpha*, just in case Ted called after all, laying his fears to rest.

They stretched their three days' food for five. On the sixth, Matthew rose early, and with an assault rifle in his hands, and pistol and stunner on his belt, hiked to the valley. There he skirted the field, staying within the forest edge, and approaching the village, heard screams. His heart almost spasmed in his chest, and he hurried forward, rifle ready.

He only had to go partway. The tiger came trotting from the hamlet with a child in its jaws, feet dragging. Matthew aimed, squeezed the trigger, and this time the cat collapsed, while the gunshot echoed through the valley. He ran to it then, ready to shoot again, and to his surprise found the child alive, her eyes wide and vague, chest and shoulder pierced by the big cat's fangs. The tiger was dead; the bullet had struck it behind the shoulder, piercing the heart. There were two older bullet wounds, one through the hips, the other scoring the tail hump.

Two women came running and crying. They paid almost no attention to Matthew, but helped the child to her feet. When her legs wouldn't hold her, the younger of the women hoisted her in strong arms and began to carry her back toward the hamlet. Several other women and men had come running after, and it was these who descended on Matt, dropping to their knees before him, thanking him.

By midday he was on his way back to the pinnace with the pack basket Ted had left, full of barley, potatoes, and a jar of something the locals called "miso."

And with the story of what had happened to Ted Baver. So far as he could see, there was nothing he could do about it, nothing at all.

SIXTEEN

Achikh had spent perhaps fifteen percent of his total living hours on horseback, but never before lying across one on his belly, tied in place and gagged, the gag threatening to dislocate his jaw. The saddle was simply a straw mat. Rain beat on him— not cold, as rains go, but it soaked the heat from his body nonetheless, and he had spells of violent shivering.

At one point, early on, he knew by the splashing that they were crossing a stream. If it was the same one he'd noticed from the pinnace, it had been a braided set of small and shallow watercourses sharing an otherwise dry riverbed. Now it was already receiving the beginnings of storm runoff.

Wind blasted and howled; thunder rumbled and banged and crackled. Having the usual Mongol fear of electrical storms, he kept his eyes tightly shut, but the almost constant lightning flickered through his lids.

Soon after the river crossing, they began to climb. The road passed through forest now, Achikh knew, for the wind only plucked at them now and then, though it roared through the treetops. Too, the rain no longer slashed. It simply poured.

The sound of trees falling became an increasing counterpoint to the wind and thunder. After the time it takes to ride a league on level ground—half a league or less, climbing the mountain road—they stopped, perhaps to rest the horses. Then he heard the one called Takada talking to the others, shouting to be heard above the storm, and sounding impossibly cheerful: "It is the *taifu*," he said. "There is no doubt of it. Very soon the river will be impassable behind us; there can be no pursuit. We will shelter at the inn on Hibari Pass, and continue in the morning."

Moments later they went on. Achikh hoped that Hibari Pass was not too far away.

It was far enough. In places the road was blocked by fallen trees. Some of these they dragged out of the way, men and horses straining. Mostly, though, they picked their way around them, on treacherous side slopes through pitch-black forest, the riders on foot, groping, swearing, leading their horses. Achikh was sure it was midnight when they rode into the open. There the wind struck like the fists of God, buffeting and grabbing at him, while the rain was like a whip, threatening to flay the skin off his exposed neck. His horse staggered at a gust.

Finally they stopped, and he opened his eyes, twisting his head in an effort to see. Little enough was visible; the wind had long since snatched the torch flames into oblivion. But the almost constant lightning let him glimpse a building of logs, as a sort of after-image. Then someone untied him from the horse, and hands set him on his feet. They let go too soon, and he fell. Someone kicked him. Someone else hauled him to his feet again—two someones—and held him upright till he could stand alone, then led him through a door.

It was a large stable they entered, lit by several oil lamps. Besides horses, it sheltered more than a dozen people, not including Achikh and his captors. They lay on pads of woven straw, or squatted on the dirt floor. The innkeeper hurried over and talked with Takada Chiu. The stable was his strongest building. The inn itself had been losing panels to the wind well before the storm hit its stride. By now, who knew what was left? Surely not the roof, on this exposed saddle and with wall panels gone.

With nine new travelers, the inn-keeper sent most of his staff to sleep in a shed. The logs of its walls were not wind-tight, and rain could blow in, but clients must have priority, certainly samurai clients. The stable roof too had developed numerous leaks through which water trickled to muddy the floor. A small wood fire, now little more than coals, glowed between two mud patches; above it, a pot steamed on a tripod. Elsewhere, a brazier held burning charcoal. A new fire, located away from major leaks, was built for Takada's company, and they sat around it, their clothes steaming. Achikh lay on the floor behind Takada. Quickly enough, they were eating barley noodles with *miso* and shavings of fish, and pickled giant radish, all but Achikh, whose gag was still in his mouth. *Sake* had been warmed on the brazier, and bowls were poured for them.

Four *ronin* were sheltered there, uncouth looking, long unshaven and with their hair wild, not at all in proper samurai style. Their clothing looked as if they hadn't taken it off for a month or more, let alone washed it. Takada's lieutenant murmured in his leader's ear: "Excuse me for bringing it up, Takada-san, but I don't like the look of those *ronin*. Would you like me to question them?"

Takada Chiu lowered his head and looked at them briefly from beneath his brows. "Ignore them," he murmured. "It is true they look like malcontents, but four are too few to make trouble for us. And in the long run, malcontents are likelier to be on our side than on that of the Emperor."

After a little, the innkeeper asked if Takada wanted his captive to be given food or water. The samurai looked coldly at the man. "Do not trouble about him. He is my concern, not yours. He is a foreigner, and without caste."

The innkeeper bowed deeply and went back to the brazier. Servants unrolled pads on the floor for the newcomers, all but Achikh, and soon they were asleep, even the Buriat, though he woke often, once with leg cramps that almost made him cry out around his gag. Being bound and gagged as he was, was worse than the cangue.

At daylight, Takada and his lieutenant stepped to the door and looked outside. The great wind had passed, and the rain had diminished to a light but steady fall. Nothing was left of the inn itself but the floor posts, as someone had guessed. The roofs were gone from most of the log outbuildings.

Takada said the obvious: "Every stream is in flood; even creeks must be impassable. We will wait here. If the rain stops soon, tomorrow the smaller streams may be fordable." He stepped back in, closing the door. "Take the foreigner outside to relieve himself," he murmured, "then give him food and drink and gag him again. We cannot have him talking in here."

The day passed slowly. Most of the travelers spent it drinking and napping. By midmorning the rain had stopped and the sun shone sporadically. Soon the leaks stopped dripping.

The next day dawned clear and bright. When Takada awoke, the four *ronin* had already left. It was a good sign as well as a welcome departure; they'd apparently decided the road was passable. If they were going southeastward toward Momiji-joka, Takada had no doubt they were wrong. But northwestward— He sent two men ahead to the next stream; they were to come back and tell him if it was passable. Less than an hour later they were back. It was passable; one of them had crossed it to make sure.

An hour later they'd eaten, and servants of the inn had saddled the horses. This time they put Achikh upright on his, though his hands were still tied and he wore a rope around his neck. When they were away from the stable, the gag was removed from his mouth.

They crossed the first stream, and not much later reached the second. While they were fording it, arrows flashed out of the forest. The targets had been deliberately chosen. All of Takada's party were wounded or killed except himself and his prisoner. Takada, his sword gripped in both hands, refused to surrender, so he was beaten down by lance shafts, and bound. His wounded men were killed. Then their assailants led them off the road and up a shallow draw to a trail along the ridge crest.

SEVENTEEN

The line of bandits rode their horses through the forest. Mostly not following what had been the trail, because mostly the trail had run along the crest. And the crest, exposed to the full force of the typhoon, was a chaos of heaped and tangled blowdowns. So they picked their slow way along the leeside, where windfalls were far fewer. Occasionally the blowdown pattern allowed them to follow a hoofworn road.

They'd untied Achikh. It was, he thought, as if having been Chiu's prisoner had given him a certain status. He rode freely, though he was kept in the middle of the string of horsemen.

If he didn't know who his new captors were, at least he knew from things they said to each other that they were bandits. Among them were the four *ronin* who'd been at the inn on the pass. The others were the same sort of men, wearing worn and dirty clothes, their beards wild and unkempt, their hair grown out. In their sashes, however, they wore the paired swords of samurai.

He might quite possibly have escaped, and he considered it. His horse was as good as theirs, and the country was wild. Had he picked his time and place well—a place where speed was possible, and a situation in which he couldn't readily be cut off—it was questionable whether they could have caught him or even shot him. Yamatoans were good horsemen, by most standards, as good as the Polish and German knights he'd fought half a world away, but it seemed clear to him that they weren't as good on horseback as his own people, nor were they as good in the wilderness as he. True the Buriats were basically a steppe tribe, but they also hunted and traveled and raided in forested mountains—the Jablonovyj Chrebet, the Altai Shan, and lesser ranges that interrupted the Mongolian steppe.

So escape seemed possible, with a little luck. But escape to where? He decided to remain with the bandits, travel with them, learning more about these Yamatoans, and something of the geography here.

On one occassion, when a deer watched them from across a small meadow, Achikh borrowed a bow and two arrows from one of bandits. It was a considerably longer bow than he was used to, though not as stiff, and he didn't expect a hit. It was simply an opportunity to evaluate the weapon. His first arrow took the deer in the throat at some hundred paces, and the second wasn't necessary. Achikh concealed his surprise. After that they spoke to him now and then, beyond simple orders, as if his foreignness was no longer such a barrier.

They rode for three and a half days, more or less northwestward, zigzagging as necessary to accommodate the terrain, or to seek a crossing of some still-dangerous mountain stream. On the fourth day they reached the main bandit camp, in a high meadow where the bandits grazed their horse herd. Near the upper end were two longhouses, low-roofed and made of crudely chinked logs. At that elevation, it seemed to Achikh that in winter, deep snows would build up, and the bandits would hardly overwinter there. Especially since their horses had already overgrazed the meadow; the animals would surely starve.

Most of each longhouse was one long narrow common room with many pallets for sleeping—thirty or more, Achikh reckoned. Together, the longhouses would easily sleep sixty, a hundred with crowding, but until the raiding party arrived, there were only fifteen or twenty there. The chief, called simply Kashira, had a separate room at one end of a longhouse, next to the storeroom. One of his men had reported the raiding party's approach, and Kashira was waiting for them in the common room. Achikh and Chiu were taken to him there.

Kashira sat upright on a keg, legs splayed, hands on knees, a husky man all angles in his sitting posture, and watched them enter. He scarcely noticed Achikh; his attention was on Chiu. Chiu's hands were tied, and his face swollen and discolored worse than Achikh's. The sergeant who'd led the party bowed low.

"So, Fujishige," Kashira said, "what have you brought me?"

"Twelve packhorses of goods, and two prisoners. One is a foreigner, and the other an emperor's courier."

"Indeed!" He indicated Chiu with a hand. "How do you know he is an emperor's courier?"

"Watanabe heard him talking."

"Mm-m. Watanabe, please step forward!"

Watanabe stepped up without enthusiasm. He sensed that something was wrong here. "How did you know this man was an imperial courier?" Kashira asked.

"During the *taifu*," Watanabe said, "we stayed in the stable on Hibari Pass. This man" —he indicated Chiu— "entered with his party. I positioned myself near him, and overheard what he said to the innkeeper. It was clear to me then that he was an imperial courier who might have valuable information."

Chiu said nothing, but his eyes glittered with cold passion. Kashira stood up and punched Watanabe in the face, knocking him down. "Tie him!" he said to Fujishige. Fujishige positioned himself above Watanabe, sword in hand, and barked an order to one of his men. The man hurried into the supply room and came out with a length of leather thong. Fujishige then personally bound Watanabe.

"I have distrusted you for some time," Kashira said to the bound man. "Now I know you for a liar." He gestured toward Chiu. "Untie him. He is Takada Chiu, a friend of mine, and a younger brother of Lord Takada Keizo. Certainly no friend or courier of the emperor." He looked again at Fujishige. "What person struck my friend, that his face is swollen?"

Fujishige bowed low. "That too was Watanabe."

"Hmm. Well. We must see him properly punished." He looked at Achikh now. "And this one?"

Fujishige looked worriedly at the Buriat. "He was a prisoner of Takada-sama."

Kashira turned to Chiu, questioningly. Chiu nodded. "He was caught trespassing in the compound of Akawashi Kata, and was unable to explain himself convincingly. Akawashi wished to kill him. I decided instead to take him with me, and question him at my leisure." He shrugged. "I have since seen enough of him to know he is no agent of the emperor, nor of Matsumura,

Kata's lord. He is a simple barbarian, just as he appears to be. He is tough, though. Perhaps he has the skills necessary to serve you here."

Fujishige then described Achikh's archery. Kashira looked the Buriat over more thoroughly. "Let us go outdoors," the bandit chief said. "I will examine his swordsmanship."

Outside, Achikh was handed a wooden practice sword, and ordered to demonstrate his drill. He obliged, the sword whirling and hissing. When he was done, Kashira grunted. "Interesting. Wherever he comes from, they do not teach the Shosen School. But he will do." His hard eyes fixed the Buriat. "Will you swear to serve me loyally?"

"I swear it," Achikh lied, and his face, his eyes, showed no sign of it. He'd stay with these men a while and learn what he could, then pick his way back to where the sky boat had been, and see if he could find his *anda*.

That evening, Watanabe was executed. Chiu had the privilege of deciding the means. The bandit was tied to a length of pole, and fed into a campfire feet first, a little at a time. His screams could be heard for the better part of a kilometer. The bandits stood by and watched, some laughing and joking, some thoughtfully, and some with concealed distaste. Achikh, hardened though he was by his years under Kazi the Undying, considered the spectacle one of the most disgusting he'd ever seen.

As he watched, one of the bandits sidled up to him, a tall, rough-looking man. When the screaming had stopped, and the victim was pushed the rest of the way into the fire, the bandits turned back to the longhouses. Then the tall man spoke to Achikh. "Excuse me if I am intruding," he said. "You are a newcomer and a foreigner. Perhaps you could use a friend here. My name is Hidaka Satoru. What is yours?"

Achikh looked at him neutrally. "Achikh," he answered.

Satoru repeated it, mispronouncing. "Achika. Where do you come from, Achika?"

This Hidaka Satoru seemed friendly, but there was something about him that roused Achikh's distrust. "From the Buriat lands," he answered tersely, "across the sea. Broad grasslands."

"That's very interesting. How did you come to Yamato?"

"On a boat."

The man chuckled. "Excuse me for asking such a foolish question. Of course you came by boat. There is no other way. Have you chosen a sleeping place? There is one unoccupied beside mine, and I am interested in the stories a foreigner can tell."

Achikh eyed him without replying. The Yamatoan went on: "You and I have something in common: Both of us became bandits by chance, not intent. I was in a caravan which they attacked and robbed, and volunteered to join them." He shrugged. "It was better than being left without food or money, in a place far from any village. And we are both from distant places: I'm from Hokkaido, myself. We are more natural there than people on Honshu—not so formal."

Still Achikh made no comment, and the Hokkaido "wizard born into a family of wizards" spoke no more just then. He was listening to Achikh's thoughts, and learning. Interesting, interesting! A sky boat! It was hard to believe, but the texture of the foreigner's memories compelled it. Satoru had already eavesdropped on the thoughts of Kashira and Chiu. Elements of a possible plan moved in his mind as he and Achikh strolled with the others toward the longhouses.

They arrived at the longhouse where Fujishige's section was housed. The crippled samurai who cooked for the longhouse served them barley and boiled meat with bean paste. Most of the men took their food outside, away from the trapped smoke, to eat sitting on logs that served as benches. A few stayed inside, and when they'd eaten, played knucklebones beside the fire pit. Outside, some talked, while others practiced their sword drills. Achikh watched the swordwork, analysing.

Shortly afterward, Satoru came out and squatted beside him. He looked intently at the Buriat. "Tell me about your trip across the sea," he said. "Were there storms?"

Achikh shook his head. "No storms. Nothing like the *taifu*." And said no more about it. He didn't trust Hidaka Satoru, and Satoru didn't pursue the conversation. Shortly, as the September evening cooled, Achikh got up and went inside, going to the sleeping place he'd chosen, well apart from where he'd seen

Satoru go. He unrolled the pallet he'd been issued and lay down on it, covering himself with the tattered quilt he'd been given.

If they have nothing warmer than this, he told himself, *then clearly they don't plan to stay here till winter.* Meanwhile he wasn't sleepy at all, and lay staring up toward the dark-shrouded roof, reviewing the span of a week or more since arriving in Yamato, and considering the future. Being a bandit was agreeable enough to his venturesome nature. He'd been worse. And when they left the mountains, he'd find his *anda*, Nils, if he hadn't flown away by then. Also, he'd find the man called Akawashi, and shorten him by the length of his head.

For now though . . . *I'm feeling sleepy after all. Sleepy. So sleepy. Surprising, when only a few minutes ago . . . Light and sleepy. It's as if this pallet was a cloud, soft cloud, and I'm sinking down into it. Down. Down. Sinking deeper—and deeper—and deeper. So restful. Very very restful. And my lids are heavy, heavy. . . . They're sliding shut. They're closed, and I don't want to open them. Can't open them. Couldn't open them if I wanted to, and I don't want to. It feels so comfortable to lie here, sinking into the cloud. Sinking deeper, deeper and deeper. Deeeper. Deeeper. . . .*

That Hidaka's not so bad, really. Not bad at all. Not at all. I'm getting to like him. I like him. Yes. And he knows how things are done here. I'll do whatever he tells me, and everything will work out right. I can trust him. Just do what Hidaka tells me. . . .

After some minutes, Hidaka Satoru instructed Achikh to waken on a count of five, remembering none of it, then whispered the count into the Buriat's hypnotized mind. On the count, he withdrew from it and lay grinning. He had him now; the man was his. He'd be able to trance him with a brief command, almost at will, and by skillful questioning, learn anything he knew.

Hidaka chuckled softly in the darkness, and an expansive optimism swelled him. He could be what he wished, do what he wished, have what he wished. He need only decide.

Despite his characteristic impatience, he would not rush.

Take a step at a time, he told himself. *Wealth, power, possibly an empire is there for you. A step at a time.*

Then he sat on his feet in the Yamatoan style, and began to create in the other world, through the window to the spirits. He needed to be prepared in advance. He'd make his move the next evening, if the weather was suitable.

EIGHTEEN

Hidaka Satoru's grandfather was a village shaman and herbalist. In Yamato, a shaman traditionally restricts his powers to curing. In fact, among peasants, especially on Hokkaido, to practice wizardry outside of curing, or to be thought to, was risky for any but a priest; one could be murdered for it. That Satoru's grandfather went well beyond curing, therefore, was his closely guarded secret.

At age seven, Satoru went to work for the old man as errand boy and herb collector. Eventually his grandfather made him his apprentice, and taught him hypnotism, useful both to shamans and wizards. He'd been fourteen then, a precocious fourteen, and had promptly used his new skill to get under the skirts of the prettiest girl in the village. Fortunately it wasn't her father or brother that caught them, but his own grandfather, who proceeded to thrash him. Hypnotism was not to be used in ways that exposed its non-curative potentials. The family was prosperous, and therefore widely envied, and if the villagers became aware of the family's powers, bad things would surely happen. The example his grandfather used was, their house might be burned—with them inside it, bound hand and foot.

Young though he was, Satoru had recognized the truth of that, but it was a hard lesson to heed, for someone young and willful and often impatient.

Now, in a bandit camp on Honshu, he lay too pleased with himself to sleep. Lay thinking of the old man, and his apprenticeship. When he'd matured somewhat, his grandfather had worked with him to open his telepathy, unscreen it. Telepathy was one of their three major secrets—their most useful secret, the old man had told him. Through it and covert

145

hypnosis, his grandfather had become the district's richest peasant.

Actually, neither the old man nor his apprentice developed deep telepathy. They sensed emotions activated and impulses felt, and "read" the flow of thought. But were not sensitive to what lay beneath and gave birth to those thoughts—the latent emotions and impulses, and the unexpressed body of concept and image.

Hypnotism was the old man's principal tool—along with his wits—but telepathy made it far more effective than it would otherwise have been. Generally, people could be hypnotized only with their cooperation. But a telepath could eavesdrop on a person's mind, and with experience could rather easily slip his own thoughts in with theirs without discovery. Thus cooperation wasn't necessary. By no means was everyone susceptible—you had to have at least some latent telepathic sensitivity to receive hypnotic commands telepathically—but many were susceptible. Probably most.

Unlike the rest of Yamato, on Hokkaido, village militias still were legal, and as a son of a free-holding family, Satoru had been enrolled at age fifteen, and trained as a spearman. Large and strong, he quickly thought of himself as a grown man. At age nineteen, his troop marched with Lord Yoshite to the Congress of Western Hokkaido, at Sapporo, and there he'd gotten a sense of the world outside his own district.

So at age twenty, he left the village of Nikawa. His grandfather, for all his skills, had been content to live there all his life. Nikawa was large and relatively prosperous, for a Hokkaido village, but to Satoru it had come to seem dull and generally inadequate. Taking with him little more than his skills, he hiked to the market and port town of Tomakomai, where he worked for a cloth merchant, testing his wizard skills while concealing them. He prospered.

Besides teaching him the "useful secrets," his grandfather had made him aware of the alpha-matrix, which the old man thought of as the window to the spirits. Satoru had been left to find a use for it himself. It was something they sensed only vaguely, like movement seen through a screen of oiled paper, and although it had seemed to Satoru that there must be some use he could make of it, there'd been no psychic fulcrum with which to pry it open for study.

In Nikawa, the priest had taught the young children of freeholders to "meditate." Mostly this served to keep them quiet for a little, now and then. Nothing more. But Satoru's grandfather had told him it was a means to power, and worked with him on technique.

In Tomakomai, he'd done more than work in the dry goods business. On days off, he took a lunch and walked into the countryside, where he concealed himself in a thick woods to sit in meditation, contemplating the window to the spirits, and experimenting. Gradually he began to perceive it more clearly and sense it more deeply. At length he learned to manipulate some of what he found there, though his understanding was very limited and distorted.

Meanwhile, using telepathy and covert hypnosis, he got money from merchants, had covert affairs with their daughters, and had slept with his employer's pretty young wife, after bewitching both her and her husband.

Finally, as a personal challenge, he'd bedded the bailiff's youngest daughter, and been caught in the act by her mother. Pursued by the woman's shrieks and the father's guardsmen, he'd fled Tomakomai with only the clothes he'd worn that evening—carrying them under his arm—and the money in his purse. Hiding in a canebrake, he discovered that, despite the nearly fatal experience, he was enormously pleased with himself: he'd been stimulated by the excitement, and would like more of it. He decided it was time to go to Honshu and undertake bigger things.

From Tomakomai, he'd hiked and worked his way to Muroran. There he'd gotten employment as a seaman and cargo handler on a junk which crossed Sugaru Strait and traded its slow way down Honshu's west coast. The sea agreed with him, though the labor didn't. Sometimes they spent the night tied to a quay at some small port, but more often they spent it at sea. Mostly the weather was fair, and at night, he was given to sitting on his feet beneath stars or moon or overcast, learning to do what had daunted his grandfather: learning to communicate through the window to the spirits, and create in it.

It was a window, and there were spirits on the other side. And more than spirits. There was "stuff" there, ethereal stuff. He perceived it as a difficult clay, and his intentions as hands; with sufficient care, sufficient concentration, he could mold it, and will it into the reality he lived in. Thus the helmsman, more than once, saw a lovely woman ahead, floating above the water, beckoning, a woman who appeared definitely to be there, but in fact was not.

As for spirits—most paid him no heed, as if he were some innocuous moth and they had esoteric affairs of their own to deal with. But there were those that did pay him heed. He'd first come to know them and test their nature in the forest outside Tomakomai. Of these, only one kind interested Satoru: the kind that could be used. Though he didn't realize it, these were souls who'd greatly degraded themselves during their last previous life on Earth, degraded themselves with evil, to the point that even in the "astral" zone, they had not yet confronted their karma. Thus they had not yet entered life again to pay their debts, and in their degradation they could be ordered, though their reliability was poor.

He quit ship at Toyama, and attached himself to a cloth merchant planning to travel cross-country to Miyako. It was on that trip he met with the bandits and joined them.

NINETEEN

Early the next day, Achikh went out as part of a detail sent hunting; another raiding party was expected back soon, and more meat was needed. About midday they spotted a band of *maral*[19] in a mountain meadow, and killed two of them. Achikh's skill and quickness in field dressing the carcasses impressed the Yamatoans, especially the sergeant who led the detail. They were back in camp well before dusk. The meat was cut into strips, and hung on racks used for drying and smoking it. After dark, most of the men, well fed on fresh venison, sat on their feet or squatted, gazing at the drying fires. From the upwind side, to avoid getting smoke in their eyes.

Hidaka Satoru stood up before them then, Achikh beside him, and got their attention. "When I joined you," Satoru said loudly, "I told Kashira-san I was a wizard. Some of you heard me, and did not believe. Some of you have ridiculed me for it. Now I will show you some wizardry that all of you can see.

"Look! Above the fire! Do you see the demon?"

More than two dozen pairs of eyes squinted into the thin smoke. It seemed perhaps that something might be there, but— Then one of the bandits laughed loudly, artificially, in scorn. "Ha ha ha ha ha! There is nothing there but smoke!" he called. "You are a fraud!"

"Fraud!" others echoed, and "we should beat him for that!"

---

[19] A very large deer native to central Asia, introduced into wildlife parks in pre-plague Japan and naturalized there. Mature bulls average more than 300 kilograms, and occasionally large bulls exceed 400.

Most of the *ronin*-turned-bandits resented the few who were not of the samurai class.

Satoru barked a return laugh, and his voice, when he spoke, was commanding, compelling. "I see it is necessary to make it more solid! Look again!"

Now, without doubt, above the fire stood—something. Something that appeared very real, very solid. Something four meters tall and vaguely anthropoid, with a giant baboon-like face, great jaws with curved, boar-like fangs, and four spidery arms ending in great hooked claws. Its torso was bright green, its limbs and face turquoise, its eyes like ruby beacons. From its shoulders spread rubbery black wings that seemed far too small to keep it aloft. As it looked at them, Satoru laughed again, a loud and thoroughly sham laugh: "Ha ha ha ha ha ha!"

The wings thrust, and it launched itself across the fire and the drying racks. The bandits broke and ran, most of them toward the longhouses. Only four stayed behind, two of them dead. One was the man who'd taunted Satoru; the flesh on his face and torso was deeply furrowed, torn and bloody, as if by great claws. Another had had a coronary seizure. The other two were Satoru and Achikh. They watched the demon fly to the longhouses, where it alternately hopped and flew back and forth in front of their doors, its wing-beats small thunders. It glowed with a light of its own. Achikh took a scabbarded sword from one of the dead samurai, along with the man's sash to wear it in. Satoru looted the other, then led to the edge of the woods. He'd stashed two bows and two quivers of arrows there, and handed one of each to Achikh while keeping the others. Then they trotted to the paddock, which made up most of the meadow.

The horses were milling wild-eyed; they too saw the monster, which was no illusion. So Satoru, with a thought, sent it flying out of sight beyond the trees. Achikh had not been frightened by it, nor had he wondered why not. Satoru had prepared him subliminally. He went into the tack shed and got bridles, then went among the horses, speaking to them in Mongol. They calmed as if they understood, and he bridled four of them, tying the reins to a hitching rail. Then he and Satoru saddled them, and with two trailing behind on tethers, they rode off down the trail toward the road, half a dozen kilometers away. The last thing Satoru did before they left was to return the monster to its beat in front of the longhouses.

"How long will it stay there?" Achikh asked.

"As long as I will it to."

Like most wizards and other primitive technologists, Satoru had little notion of the physics behind his practices, but he knew more than he told Achikh. The creation would soon disintegrate, cease to be. It required his continuous attention, or an input of intense fear from onlookers. And at any rate, when the demon ensouling it felt sufficiently gratified, it would withdraw into the window to the spirits.

Nor did he tell Achikh that it wasn't truly physical, although as close to physical as he could manage. He'd created the quasi-physical aspect of it the night before, the precursor, the object matrix, then had brought it to the verge of visibility, there by the fire. It had needed only to be occupied by a demon to give it the semblance of physical reality. The ravaged bandit's wounds had not been produced by physical claws. They were akin to the spontaneous stigmata of some religious fanatics, only more extreme. In this case they were inspired not by religious fervor, but by sight of the monster, by the "astral wind" of its beating wings, and by old superstitions that few in Yamato truly believed, but which most had not entirely rejected, either.

TWENTY

On the second day after Satoru and Achikh had deserted, a raiding party returned to camp somewhat fewer than it had left. Kashira was not pleased at the casualties.

It brought with it two captives, one a strangely dressed foreigner responsible for half a dozen of the deaths. The other was a young woman of rank and wealth; that was evident from her clothing, despite its being rumpled and dirty. Kirisaki, in command of the detachment, had considered her worth Kashira's attention: she might be a means of leverage, or if her father was wealthy enough, of sufficient ransom to make her worthwhile.

She was of noble family, obviously, and a female of the samurai class, whether noble or not, was not to be raped. It was, if not unthinkable, at least not something a samurai of any honor at all would actually do. So aside from being tired and saddle sore, she was not in poor condition.

Ransom. Kirisaki couldn't know that the wealth gained by these raids was secondary. All the men realized, of course, that this banditry was in some way political, though they hadn't been told just how. But they assumed that money was at least as important as whatever the political motive might be. And it was not unimportant; simply incidental. It made the operation possible, feeding and paying the *ronin* and others who filled its ranks, holding their interest and loyalty.

Actually, having the woman there was a nuisance. But there she was. Kashira had his room in one of the longhouses; he took her there and questioned her brusquely but not harshly. Her father, he discovered, was Lord Iwato, an indifferent supporter of the Emperor. He would send a courier to Takada, he decided, with a sealed message to be forwarded to Lord Arakawa, who would decide what to do with her.

When he'd finished questioning her, he sent her to the storeroom, which would be her bedroom, and had the foreigner brought in. He looked him over intently; the man was tall, like the departed Hokkaido wizard. Just now his face looked lopsided, his eyes were discolored, and his lips purple-black, swollen and split. Several teeth had been broken or knocked out, and he held himself as if he had broken ribs. Clearly, Kirisaki had been angry with him for the men he'd killed.

Roughly, Kashira gripped the man's chin with his left hand and shook the damaged face. "Who are you?" he asked. The foreigner barely winced.

"I am called Ted," he mumbled. His damaged mouth made enunciation difficult.

"Tedu." Kashira tasted the strange name, and wondered if the man had selected it because he was foreign.[20] "Where are you from?"

Peering through swollen slits, Ted tried to evaluate his new captor. He'd prepared for this questioning, had thought it out. Kirisaki had given him his worse beating when he'd claimed to come from Amaterasu-omikami. "From across the sea," he said, "from the land of the Hokkitami."[21] He didn't mention the pinnace. When the *Phaeacia* had first arrived, with the full expedition, the orcs had taken several of its members hostage, in an attempt to get control of the pinnaces. He would not subject Matthew and Nikko to that kind of pressure.

Kashira frowned, and turned the foreigner's face from side to side. His speech reminded him somewhat of the other foreigner's, the one who'd run away with the wizard from Hokkaido. It wasn't the pronunciation—his mouth was too damaged to evaluate that—but already he'd used archaic words. *He doesn't look like him though,* Kashira told himself. *Not at all. Perhaps all foreigners speak like that.* He pursed his lips thoughtfully. *Hmm. A foreigner might say "Hokkitami" to refer to someone from Hokkaido. Could there be a connection?* "Why did you come to Yamato?" he asked.

"My people are peaceful," the foreigner mumbled. "They

---

[20] *Tedu* is Yamatoan for "distant."

[21] Yamatoan for men from the north.

do not believe in killing. When I killed a man, they declared me an outlaw, and drove me away."

Kirisaki had given Kashira the foreigner's weapon. He examined it again. It didn't look like much—an iron club, short and crooked—but according to Yorigifu and his squad, it struck men down with thunder and lightning. Kirisaki had been unable to make it repeat its performance. "Tell me how it is used," Kashira said.

Put the small end in your mouth and pull the trigger, Ted thought. But better this man in charge than Kirisaki, so instead he said, "Point the small end at a breastplate or cuirass. That will show you what it can do."

Frowning, Kashira looked at his own cuirass, hanging from a peg on the wall, but left it there and herded Ted out into the large common room. The crippled cook had a breastplate, hanging on a peg above his pallet. Kashira walked over to it, Ted following, and at a range of about a meter, pointed the slug thrower at it. "Now what?" Kashira asked.

"There is a ring with a small lever inside. You make the weapon—do what it does—by putting your finger inside the ring and squeezing the lever. But first there is a small object beside the ring. You must push it forward before you squeeze the lever."

Kashira examined the weapon carefully, then released the safety. "Now," Ted said, "point it at the breastplate and squeeze."

Despite what he'd been told, the noise and recoil surprised Kashira. And the other bandits inside at the time; their conversations stilled abruptly, and all eyes were on him. He stared first at the pistol in his hand, then at the breastplate, which now had a sizeable hole in it. He swung it aside and looked at the wall behind it; there was a hole of indeterminate depth in the log. On an impulse he turned and pointed the gun at Ted; Ted closed his eyes. *Click!* the hammer snapped. Ted opened them again. Kashira was frowning at the pistol; he checked the safety and tried again. *Click*.

"Will it not harm you?"

Empty, Ted thought, and shook his head. The beginning of a plan was beginning to form in his mind. "That's not it," he said. "The god who gave it to me provided only a limited blessing.

It seems to be used up now, and won't work again until it's re-blessed."

"Can you bless it?"

"Excuse me, but I'm not able to. I'm only a human being."

Kashira scowled first at Ted, then at the pistol, and moved as if to throw it into the embers of the nearly dead cooking fire. Ted held his breath. But Kashira changed his mind, and tucked it into his sash. *Perhaps Lord Arakawa will wish to see it*, he told himself, *or Prince Terasu*.

Over the next quarter hour, he satisfied his curiosity about the foreigner's fighting skills. The man was so inept with the bow that he succeeded in taking the skin off his left wrist when he released the bowstring. The bandits laughed uproariously. Next he was given a practice sword and told to show them his drill. For a long several seconds he stood silent, looking chagrined, then began to hack and chop. For a moment the men stared at the spectacle unbelieving, then fell apart with mirth, laughing with tears in their eyes, slapping their thighs and each other.

"Are you completely worthless, then?" Kashira asked. He looked around. "Atsushi!"

The smallest of the samurai, hiccuping from laughter, straightened abruptly. "Yes, Kashira-san!"

Kashira had drawn his shortsword. With a casual twitch, he freed the captive's wrists without marking the skin. *I will keep him alive*, he decided. *Lord Arakawa may want to see him.* "Fight him!" he said to Atsushi, "but do not kill him!"

Atsushi, not an accomplished karateka, stared uncertainly at the foreigner, who was much larger than himself. Then he pushed the uncertainty away. "Yes, Kashira-san!"

Ted was a decent boxer, but the strategy he'd decided on was to seem completely harmless. He raised his arms as if to fend off an attack. The bandit moved toward him, hands raised. It occurred to Ted that he could be truly injured here. His attention was fixed on Atsushi's hands when the bandit's left foot struck him. Fortunately, Atsushi hadn't practiced for some time, and his flexibility and precision were less than he thought. His heel struck Ted a somewhat glancing blow on the upper thigh. Having intended a groin kick, Atsushi's following punch missed the nose and struck Ted under the chin instead, hard, snapping his head backward. He fell like a stone, partly from the effect of the punch and partly deliberately. Atsushi stepped back, and turning, bowed to Kashira.

Again the bandit spectators howled with laughter. Kashira gave orders, and one of the men trotted into the longhouse. Before Ted had gotten to his feet, the man was back with leg shackles on the ends of a 50-centimeter length of chain. It would allow the captive to walk with short steps, but running was impossible, and crosscountry travel in the forest impractical. He could be of use around the camp until it was time to leave for the coast.

One spectator hadn't laughed at Ted's performances. Emiko, the female captive, had peered from her storeroom refuge after the gunshot, then moved to the doorway when the last of the bandits had gone outside to watch. The doorway didn't provide a good view, but she saw enough. She'd seen the foreigner beaten before, and had winced at his injuries. Now she winced again. And when she saw him get to his knees, then his feet, and walk with his chain, she promised herself to help him in every way she could.

TWENTY-ONE

The Gara-gara River ran eastward past Omugi to join its waters with the Momiji, some kilometers east of Momiji-joka. After two weeks of pleasant weather, it still carried somewhat more water than before the typhoon, but it was tame, easily forded on foot or horseback.

The village of Omugi existed again, and promised to look much as it had. Its peasants had known disaster before, had a tradition of disasters, of persistence and rebuilding. When Satoru and Achikh rode through it on an early autumn afternoon, few people were about. Most were in the fields, or busy indoors. Achikh paid little attention to the bailiff's house, except to loosen his longsword in its scabbard.

Satoru had told him what he wanted. They left the road through a gap between two ravaged poplars—and the sky boat wasn't there. Achikh wasn't surprised. He wasn't even disappointed; his memories of Nils had been hidden from him hypnotically by Satoru, almost as if they had never been. The Hokkaidoan questioned the farm wife, who said the Heaven Boat hadn't been there for weeks; she thought it must have gone back to be with Amida again.

They rode to the landing site anyway, where Satoru sat in the saddle staring upward, considering. The Heaven Boat had been his object of preference; if he could travel in it through the heavens, and use its weapons . . . But it seemed it was not to be. He would settle for joining the conspiracy he'd learned of by eavesdropping on Kashira, and make himself indispensible to the new Emperor as his personal wizard. Then he'd enslave the Emperor, as he had this foreigner, and rule from behind the throne. Do and have whatever he wanted.

It was as well that the sky boat had left, he decided, and

157

turned to Achikh. The Buriat was thinking about it, and wondering, which was undesirable. When they stopped for their midday nap, he'd hide all memory of it, too. It was no longer useful to him. "Come," he said. "We will ride to Miyako, sell our horses, and buy comfortable passage on a ship to Osaka. My fortune awaits me there."

TWENTY-TWO

... *höj å vålsam växte åskmoln,*
brej å svart d' stod i himmlen.
Atjikk glodde på kolosen,
pekte på å sa d' rätta,
"d' ä ikke vanli sjybrott,
ja' har hört om såna förre,
finns en mäkti jodspök hos att
slå Stenklivare, sin hammar."

Pålt vi rask vår häster därom,
spredde brej att stormen ikke
skulle döjdslå allihopa
mä en enkel vålsam blixhugg.

Då vi läggde oss på marken,
platt som möjli därför att vi
ikke bli så goa måler
för jodspökens brakne blixslag.
Läggd vi oss mä näs' i gräset.
Alla utom Yngling' läggd sej.
Rakt stod han å såg på stormen,
å förente sej mä jodspök',
höll jodspök' mä milda sinnen,
kjennte ham i annen därför
att vi skulle släppa döjdslag ...

> . . . the thunderhead grew tall and mighty,
> broad and dark stood in the heavens.
> Achikh stared at the colossus,
> pointed and observed correctly,
> "That is not a common storm cloud,
> I have known of others like it,
> dwells therein an elemental,
> bursting hammer poised to strike us.
>
> Quickly picketed our horses,
> scattered broadly so the storm-soul
> could not kill them all together
> with a single stroke of lightning.
>
> Then we lay down on the prairie,
> low and flat so that we wouldn't
> be good targets for the lightning,
> for the ax blows of the storm-soul.
> Embraced the ground as close as lovers.
> All lay flat except the Youngling.
> Straight he stood and watched the storm
> approach, joined spirits with the storm-soul,
> embraced in love the elemental,
> that we might be spared its death strokes.
>   From— The Järnhann Saga
>   Kumalo translation

Matsumura Shinji had sent a courier to his son, Matsumura Harujo, who occupied and managed the family's hereditary estate. The message was a long one, but basically it told Harujo of his father's plan to adopt a foreigner, Tetsu-te Nissa, as his *basshi*, his youngest son. At the same time, Nissa would adopt a son of his own people, providing Harujo with a new nephew, and Matsumura Shinji with another grandson.

It pointed out that as the eldest son, Harujo would inherit the estate, of course, and the title of *daimyo*. And that his sister was well provided for: Eight years past, the family had married her to another *tehon daimyo*, Lord Ibaraki, sending her to him with an outstanding dowry. Tetsu-te Nissa would receive from the family a *basshi*'s income, which it could very easily afford, and enjoy the status and protection of family membership.

He gave the date of Nissa's formal reception into the family, to be held before the *tehon daimyo*'s court at Momiji Castle. Harujo was requested to attend, a request which filial respect and duty did not, of course, allow him to decline.

Harujo would not have considered refusing. He was not particularly given to jealousy, and there were no bad feelings between father and son to be aggravated by the appointment of this unexpected younger brother. But on the other hand, it was something of a shock. It was not at all uncommon for a man of property to adopt a son, but this was usually because he had produced no son of his own, or had lost an only son, or had a nephew orphaned.

The letter hadn't mentioned wizardry. They would draw their own conclusions when they saw his eyes. It simply described Tetsu-te Nissa as a great swordsman and a man of outstanding character, who had no family in Yamato, and who might well prove a credit to the Matsumuras.

Harujo could only hope his father had become neither bewitched nor prematurely senile. Probably, he thought, this decision of his father's was due partly to the death of Kenji, the second son. Kenji, an outstanding warrior, had died when a flux had spread through the fleet four years earlier, in a campaign against pirates.

The reception was a success. Harujo was impressed as much with the open and honest nature of his new brother, as with his size. They parted, if not close friends, friends at least. His brother-in-law, Lord Ibaraki, had been more restrained in his approval—Tetsu-te Nissa was *very* foreign—but had expressed no disapproval, either openly or in private. If Matsumura Shinji wanted this giant as his *basshi*, Ibaraki would support his decision.

It had been agreed between Matsumura and Nils that three days after the ceremony, Nils and Hans would travel to Miyako, to be introduced to the Emperor and spend some time at court there. It was politic for the son of a *tehon daimyo* to do this. Besides, the Emperor was interested in things new and different, and nothing was more different than these two tall young foreigners.

Kamoshika Akira would go with them. Matsumura's new son and grandson had both adapted readily to Yamatoan ways, and had learned well their lessons in proper beliefs and behavior. But not all contingencies could be foreseen, and Akira had grown up in a proper samurai household; his father was a member of Lord Shimano's household guard. He could provide useful guidance.

Nils enjoyed the movement of the horse beneath him. The day was perfect—warm but not hot, the air dry, the sun bright but not oppressive. In the hills of northeastern China, and even more in the Buriat land around Urga, the leaves had been changing color a month earlier. Here, along the road to Miyako, he saw only the first tinges of autumn color.

They'd reached the heart of the Kanto Plain here—broad fertile fields dotted with hamlets, with villages at intervals along the highway—and a graveled road with wheel tracks! Along the south side was the usual row of trees—poplars and *sugi*, mostly, with occasional chestnuts—to shade travelers in summer. Here woods grew mainly along watercourses, coppice woods cut frequently, furnishing little more than fuelwood and small posts.

The villages they came to invariably had a roadside teahouse, or even two, catering to travelers; Hans saw one now, not far ahead. "Nils," he called pointing, "I'm hungry! Let's stop there!"

Nils laughed. Hans was usually hungry. As hungry here, where food was readily available, as he'd been on the long trail across the steppes of central Asia, where on some days there'd been nothing to eat but some curdled mare's milk, and perhaps what was left of yesterday's marmot, grown pungent from the heat.

Akira knew little of that, and not much more of their experience in China and Mongolia. And he took his job of behavioral guide quite seriously. "How can you be hungry so soon?" he said. "You have a sweet-tooth, that's all. You like the taste of *manju* and *yokan*. But remember, you're a samurai now. Exercise restraint!"

Hans tossed his head. "There is time enough to do without when there is nothing. Besides, I exercised restraint at the last three villages. Now I'm hungry."

Akira looked at Nils for support. The big Northman only grinned. *Nissa is too lax with him,* Akira thought, but decided to say nothing more about it. He was not the boy's father.

As they approached the tea house from the west, another party had just arrived from the east, with a priest, judging by his robe, and by the priestly scarf draped over a shoulder. But whereas most went bare-headed, he wore a hat like a porter's, like some broad inverted bowl. There was also a small retinue of samurai. Akira recognized the samurai as imperial guardsmen, recognized them by their helmets and cuirasses, lustrous laquer and bright steel, instead of ordinary traveling clothes. Their presence indicated that the priest had been the Emperor's honored guest in Miyako; clearly he was someone very important. A Zenist in all likelihood, Akira decided, for despite the man's obvious importance, he had only one priestly attendant and no banner.

One of the guardsmen helped the senior priest from his horse, though he seemed agile enough to have gotten down by himself. His feet were hardly on the ground when he looked up sharply toward the travelers from Momiji Castle. His face trapped Hans's gaze, for his skin was whiter than any Hans had seen before, as white as chalk. Straightening, the priest gestured the guardsman aside, and watched the three of them ride up.

Unlike Hans, Akira knew what priest this was, had to be—Juji Shiro—and only with difficulty avoided staring. *A truly holy monk!* Juji Shiro was the abbot of Yama-wo-Mammoru, the temple on the midslope of Osoroshii-yama, the Terrible Mountain. It was his duty to commune with the *kami* in the mountain, and inform the Emperor when it was unhappy or restless. At least that's what people said.

And it seemed to Akira that the priest's pink eyes were on Nissa. The attendant priest murmured something, and the elder shook his head. They stood waiting then, while the newcomers dismounted, the imperial guardsmen alert, distrusting the strange-looking trio.

"Hold these for me," Nissa murmured, handing his reins to Hansu, and walked toward the senior priest. He stopped scarcely two meters from him, and bowed.

"I hope that we may talk together," Nissa said. He'd neither averted his eyes, nor used the speech form appropriate in addressing so holy a man.

But clearly this did not disturb Juji Shiro. The priest laughed, a sound light as wind chimes. "I would like that," he answered. Nissa stepped up to him and held out a thick forearm, which the old man took without hesitation, and they walked together to the tea house like old friends. With effort, the sergeant of the guard detail shook off his astonishment, and marched his men after the two.

It was the sort of tea house where you walk inside, instead of sitting on the edge of the raised floor with your feet on the ground. Thus it was necessary to remove one's sandals. The old man did this without difficulty, standing on one foot at a time, then went with Nissa to a corner table which seated only two. Akira, with Hansu, moved quickly to another as near as possible, to listen and watch, for the meeting of Nissa and the priest seemed very strange, and he wondered what their conversation would be like.

"So you have come from China to speak with Ojiisan Tattobu," the priest said to Nissa. Akira frowned; he hadn't heard Nissa tell the man that. "Ojiisan came to spend last autumn with me," the priest went on, "and ended by staying all winter. I told him he only stayed because he was afraid to walk out through the snow." Juji Shiro crowed with laughter. "Actually, he has walked much farther in snow than I have. He answered that he wanted to be there when the mountain tired of our presence. He wanted to see it eat us up, he said.

"When he left, he told me he was going to visit the monastery on Komoru-san, high in the Hida Range; a teaching monastery. But it seems unlikely that he is still there."

"I am interested in more than Ojiisan," said Nissa. "Please tell me about the mountain."

Juji Shiro glanced at Akira, who further averted his eyes, then grinned and looked back at Nissa. "The way to know the mountain," Juji answered, "is to know the mountain. You are welcome to spend the winter with me, if you'd like. Meanwhile I will tell you what I can." Again he looked at Akira, and this time spoke to him. "It won't take long, but you will not be able to hear. Perhaps your large friend will tell you something of it later."

Then he turned back to Nissa, and for some time they sat facing each other without speaking a word. A serving girl brought tea, and asked the others if they wished to eat. For a moment it seemed she would also ask Nissa and Juji, but simply poured tea for them. Occasionally, absently, they sipped it. Finally Juji Shiro laughed. Nissa was grinning.

"You will be welcome," Juji said.

By that time, Hansu had finished his plate of *manju*, and the others their tea. Nissa and the holy man stood up and bowed to each other. Then the priest and his retinue returned to their lunch, while the three from Momiji Castle left. It seemed to Akira that he had witnessed something highly uncanny, although in a way, it also seemed very ordinary.

That night, in the inn where they'd taken a room, it was Akira who questioned Nils. "Had you ever met Juji Shiro before?"

"I hadn't even known he existed."

"Then how . . . ?"

"Those who can speak together through the mind, recognize each other."

To speak through the mind! "What did he tell you about the mountain?"

"It is beyond me to tell you. It was not in words. Through his mind, I perceived it much as he had."

Akira lay still for a time, wondering what that would be like. "And—does he speak to the mountain?"

"No. He listens to it. Not to the mountain itself, but to the soul of the mountain—Osoroshii-kami."

It was Hans who asked the next question. "Does the mountain eat people up, as Ojiisan Tattobu said?"

"Ojiisan was joking. The mountain doesn't eat people. But if it bursts, it will destroy the priests who live on its slope, and anyone else who is too near."

"Is it likely to do that?"

Nils didn't answer at once. Then he said, "The mountain is not now threatening, but there has been a change in the *kami* recently. An anticipation. Perhaps the mountain will explode, as it did long ago, and cause great destruction. Or perhaps Osoroshii-kami will leave the mountain, and rejoin itself with the Tao."

"And then the mountain will be safe?"

"No. The mountain is a thing of its own, with great power. Do you remember the hail storm on the steppe?"

Hans remembered. He would never forget. He'd even made a poem about it, a kanto for the Järnhann Saga.

"There are many hail storms," Nils went on. "Some do great harm to living things that get in their way. But rarely does one have a soul—or rather an elemental, which functions somewhat like a soul. An elemental, like a soul, provides volition, but on the steppe, an elemental isn't necessary for a hailstorm to batter men or horses to death. Or in Yamato for a mountain to explode. But Osoroshii-kami, knowing the detailed working of the mountain, can create an explosion, if the mountain is able."

Hans looked worried now. "Are we going to spend the winter with him on the mountain?"

The Northman grinned. "Possibly, but I doubt it. It would be very interesting, but it's Ojiisan I want to commune with, not Osoroshii-kami."

Akira lay awake for quite a while, thinking. Matsumura Shinji had acquired more foster son than he perhaps realized. And more wizard. This Tetsu-te Nissa was here for a higher reason, whether he knew it or not. Perhaps the Buddha Amida had a hand in the coming of the Heaven Boat after all.

TWENTY-THREE

Kodoka, d' burrjat' jätten,
skrätte på d' milda Yngling',
stod mä hännerna i sidan,
skrätte hån å glodde hatfullt.
"Vågar Du att brottas?" sa han,
"du som står så långt i kroppen,
du så brej som ja' på axeln.
D' finns ingen a di annra
som törs brottas mej," han skrätte.

Då sa till Nils sin själsvänn Atjikk
att Kodoka hade dräpit
varje man som brottas mot ham.
Ty var han så stark i kroppen,
brottsknep hans så fasli döjdsam,
ingen kunne överleva.
Log ännå d' mäkti Järnhann,
frågte vilka häst Kodoka
tykkte bäst om sina ridjur.

Bröllte, Kodoka då pekte
på en hingst stån höj som älje
bland di småa burrjat häster.
"Där d' finns," sa han, å gapte
då Järnhann slog d' helt på näsan,
så d' föll ju döjd på marken.
Då vennde Ynglingen å sade,
"Brottas ikke mot dej, jäkla,
slås vi oss mä näver bara,
t' d' ena ligger asen.

_____

Kuduka the giant Buriat
laughed aloud at the mild Youngling,
stood there with his arms akimbo
laughing scorn, his black eyes eager.
"Wrestle with me, if you dare to,
thou so large, so tall of body,
broad as I am in the shoulders.
There is none of all these others
who dare wrestle me," he boasted.

Achikh warned his friend the Youngling
that every man Kuduka wrestled
died with neck or backbone broken.
So terrible his strength of body,
the deadly clever holds he levered,
no one ever had survived them.
Nonetheless the Youngling laughed and
asked which horse the prideful Buriat
liked the best of all his horses.

Puzzled, Kuduka then gestured
at a mighty stallion standing
tall among the Buriat ponies.
"That's the one," he said, then gasping,
saw the Youngling strike the creature
on the nose. It fell down lifeless.

Then the Youngling turned and told him,
"Wrestling you would be a fool's game.
We'll fight instead with fists and see
which one of us will live to tell it."
                From— *The Järnhann Saga*
                        Kumalo translation

The three travelers approached Miyako on the morning of
the fourth day, having kept a leisurely pace.

The typhoon had damaged Miyako far less than it had

the much smaller Momiji-joka; it had been farther from the eye.

The city covered an area several kilometers on a side, much the largest town in Yamato, with canals running through it to the river, to take away storm runoff. It didn't occur to the two Neovikings to wonder, and Akira hadn't heard, but the most recent imperial tax census credited Miyako with more than 84,000 people—two percent of the empire's 4 million. That was a very large city for an isolated and mountainous agrarian empire whose commerce was almost entirely internal. And dependent on primitive single-masted ships, beating their slow way up and down treacherous coasts, ambushed by squalls and storms, and sometimes by pirates.

Miyako had been built on nearly flat terrain, and the imperial palace was the dominant feature in its landscape. The palace walls enclosed a much larger area than a *daimyo*'s castle, that was plain to see as they approached the town. But once inside the city, although their road ran straight as a rule to the palace wall, streetside buildings cut off most of it from their sight. Then they reached the perimeter street, and there it was, close before them, tall and broad, with a moat around it.

The gate guards' uniforms were far more decorative than at Matsumura's castle. They wore scarlet tunics with gold brocade, and golden breeches with small chrysanthemums stitched in red. Their helmets bore stylized horns of lustrous black lacquer, resembling in form, and somewhat in detail, the sweeping horns of water buffalo. Hans wondered briefly how one might come by such a helmet, and determined to take one back with him to Varjby, if at all possible.

The guards were large men, for Yamatoans, and business-like. Those that stopped the three travelers from Momiji Castle stood with knees slightly bent, hands on sword hilts, while behind them were several halberdmen, and behind them, narrow-eyed bowmen with arrows nocked. Hans wondered if such care was truly needed.

Actually they were always careful, but the sight of Nils, with his 198 centimeters, 118 kilos, and alarming eyes, had intensified their caution. A page was sent running to the marshal, with a message from Lord Matsumura to the Emperor, brought by the foreign giant. The strangers had also presented identification provided by Matsumura, wore Matsumura's colors, and their message to the Emperor had been sealed with wax, stamped by Matsumura's seal. But their foreignness, and the appearance of the largest, dictated extraordinary procedures.

It was as if the trio had been prepared for this, for they sat their horses patiently, quietly as they waited. Within ten minutes, one of the marshal's aides arrived with a squad of guards, who impounded the trio's swords. Then the aide led them through the gate, chatting easily as if to put them at their ease. Lord Matsumura was, after all, both a *tehon daimyo* and a *tenshi-no-kobun*. Besides, he had sent an advance message about them. But even so, the aide kept glancing at Nils as if not quite believing. The path they followed was a broad gravelled walkway, through marvelous sculpted gardens unlike anything they'd seen even in the Tibeto-Chinese emperor's compound in the Dzong at Miyun.

They were led through halls walled by burnished wood, and delivered to the marshal, who accepted their bows with a nod. The nod was all the bow they'd get from him; he was representing Emperor Hikari. He looked them over briefly, comparing them with the description given by Lord Matsumura. Satisfied, he spoke briefly with Matsumura's new son, meanwhile wondering what had caused the burly *tehon daimyo* to adopt such an extremely foreign person. His description had included the foreigner's excellent character and swordsmanship, as well as his size and eyes, but even so . . . Well. It seemed he was well-spoken, too, although his voice was oddly accented and some of his words archaic.

The marshal called a steward, who took them through further halls and up flights of stairs to an apartment that would be theirs, with a bath of their own in a side room, and a *chozuba* in another. The *chozuba* had almost no odor of human wastes, and it was not simply that a fragrant candle burned there on a shelf. Also, there was a lever at the side of the seat. Akira explained that in the palace, the smells of urine and excrement were unacceptable. The sumps were limed several times a day and emptied late each night, as at Momiji Castle, the contents taken as fertilizer to farms belonging to the Emperor. The lever was to be held down while relieving oneself, opening a shield which otherwise shut off the sump from this particular *chozuba*. A non-human, a *hinin*, would come around when they weren't there, to clean the chute above the shield, and in this apartment, it had probably not been used since it was cleaned. Hans was impressed.

Warm water was brought, and soap. They'd hardly finished washing when a secretary came; they were to be received by the Emperor personally, at the ninth hour after sunup. The secretary asked questions: a few about Matsumura, and about typhoon damage in the Momiji District, and some about Nils and Hans, and the land they came from. Their time would be limited, he explained, and with this advance information, the Emperor could better decide what he wished to explore with them.

A page notified them when the time had come. They changed into clean kimonos they'd brought with them carefully folded, and followed him down more corridors, accompanied by guards. At the door to the private, or lesser audience chamber, other guards stopped them. Another functionary instructed them in the required courtesies, a reprise of coaching they'd been given by Matsumura. Finally the door opened, and the functionary motioned them in.

They entered, knelt on both knees, put their hands on the floor and bowed till their foreheads touched it. It occurred to Hans that this was ridiculous, but if Nils could do it, he could. Then a mild voice said, "Rise and come forward."

They got up, not looking directly at the Emperor, though Hans stole a glance. The room was not large—about ten meters by six. The Emperor Hikari sat near the far end, with a guard on each side of him, long swords bared and held at shoulder arms. One wall had almost continuous large windows, open to the outside, and a pleasant breeze entered.

They were led forward to about four meters' distance, then their guide stopped them.

"Closer," the Emperor said. "I'm sure they do not bite. I'd like to look at them more closely."

Their guide took them ahead two more short steps, and they stopped again.

"You may look at me. You are, after all, a son and grandson of Matsumura Shinji, and I can know you better if I see your eyes."

They looked. Hans saw a man of a bit more than medium height, for a samurai, with his hair in the samurai style. He was clean-shaven, and his eyes were direct and clear.

Just now they were looking at Nils, seemingly giving most attention to his eyes, but he didn't mention them. "You are Matsumura Nissa, called Tetsu-te?"

"Yes, Your Imperial Majesty."

"Lord Matsumura writes that you are a splendid swordsman, but he did not explain how you acquired the name Tetsu-te. Please describe it to me."

"If Your Majesty wishes, I will be greatly honored to do so. I received the name for something that happened when I was seventeen. A gray-bearded warrior of my clan was accosted by a warrior of another clan, a larger and much younger man, who wished to force a fight. This was during an annual meeting of the clans, and swords were not to be drawn, so they fought with knives. Even that was illegal, but less serious. My clansman was killed. I then told the other warrior that in a year, when my sword-apprenticeship was completed, I would fight him, unless he was afraid.

"By implying that he might be afraid, I offended him. Deliberately. But without more serious provocation than that, a warrior may not attack someone who is not a warrior. As a crime, that is most serious if the attack is with a weapon, and least with the bare hand, so in his anger, he struck at me with his fist. I dodged and struck back, and killed him; a possibility I had failed to foresee.

"For this blow I was given the warrior name Järnhann, which in our language means Tetsu-te.[22]

"Now for a non-warrior who kills a warrior, the usual penalty is beheading, as in fact can also be true for a warrior who kills a non-warrior. However, Kalle Blåtann was well-known as a trouble-maker and bully; had even been threatened with loss of warriorhood. So I was simply exiled. Later I was accepted

----

[22] In English, Ironhand.

back, to become an advisor to the war chief, the *taisho* in your language. Later I would be named *lagmannen*, the reader and judge of the law."

The Emperor raised an eyebrow elegantly. "Ah." A slight smile played on his lips. "It seems to me there was a great deal you left out between being exiled and becoming advisor to your *taisho*. Your people are war-like then?"

"Within limits, Your Majesty."

"Hmm. An answer that can cover a great deal. Matsumura says you are mighty as well as large, that he'd never seen another man with such muscles. Remove your kimono, and let Fujioka hold it for you."

Many men might have been discomfited by the order, like a slave displayed on the block, but the Yngling removed his kimono calmly, and then his shirt, handed them to their guide, and turned slowly and completely, his muscles relaxed but thick and sinewy.

"Very interesting," the Emperor said. "I did not doubt Lord Matsumura's word, but I wished to see for myself. You may put your shirt and kimono back on."

He turned his gaze to Hans then. "And you are Matsumura Nissa's adopted son. I presume you were also a samurai in your homeland."

"Excuse me, Your Imperial Majesty, but I regret to say I was not. I was too young. We are not born samurai there." He didn't elaborate. Let His Majesty assume he would have been made a warrior when he was old enough.

The Emperor went on: "Lord Matsumura says you have been trained in poetry, in your land. Perhaps someday when I have time, I will ask you to recite some of it to me."

"Please excuse me, Your Majesty, but I have not made poetry in your language. My knowledge of Yamatoan is not adequate."

"Then I will hear it in yours, and you can tell me what it means. But for now, I will end this audience. I have pressing business. I will want to speak with both of you another time, at much greater length. I will send a young man to be your personal host, that you will not feel bored or confined while you are with us." He looked at Fujioka then. "Kobo, please have these samurai returned to their apartment."

❊   ❊   ❊

In the women's garden, a very lovely young woman, Shibata Toko, was being teased by two others, scarcely less pretty. "You were funny when you cried out," one of them said.

Half a dozen young women had been allowed to watch the audience with the foreigners, through peep holes in the wall behind and to one side of the Emperor's throne. It was a privilege allowed on special occasions, and this had been one. It was very rare that a foreigner was brought before the Emperor. In fact, foreigners were seldom seen anywhere in Yamato. Most who did land there were Korean or Chinese smugglers, or seamen forced ashore by storms, and never on the east coast. Furthermore, the report had been that these foreigners looked much more foreign than any foreigners seen before in Yamato.

"I did not cry out!" Toko objected.

"Yes you did!" The other two girls giggled. "And they heard you, too. I'm sure of it. His Majesty will not be happy about that."

"If they heard anything, it was you, giggling!"

They giggled again. "And those eyes!" the third girl said. "I believe he saw you when you cried out. He looked right toward you! Those are eyes that can see through walls!"

"And through clothing!" said the other. "They are surely wizard eyes!"

"Really though," Toko said, "I wonder what kind of man he is. I hope we'll get to watch when His Majesty questions him again. He did not seem fierce, for all his size and the story he told."

"You know what they say: big man has a big . . ." They giggled some more.

"Oh! You are shameless!"

"Us shameless? We didn't cry out when the foreigner took off his kimono. I wonder if it's true, what they say of foreigners as lovers."

"What do they say?"

Renewed giggling. "Oh, nothing."

Toko walked away from them, realizing she'd been baited. She wondered, though, what if anything was said about foreigners as lovers. She knew quite well what was said about the size of large men's penises. She simply didn't know if it was true. And the foreigner was very, very large, and she was an imaginative and very bored young woman.

When Nils and the others were back in their apartment, they changed their kimonos for silk tunics, light and cool. Twenty minutes later, a young man presented himself at their door. He introduced himself as Sugitani Katsumi, a young samurai assigned to the Emperor's staff. With him was a guard, who returned their scabbarded swords, as if the marshal had decided it was safe for them to be armed within the palace.

Katsumi was a bit reserved at first, ill at ease with such foreign-looking persons as Nissa and Hansu. He particularly avoided looking at Nissa's eyes, and as carefully avoided mentioning them. But he was young—twenty-five—and basically high-spirited, and quickly warmed to them. First he took them to the small temple on the palace grounds, where the rector spoke with them about Ojiisan, who had stayed with him for a time, a few years earlier. The rector had studied in a Zen monastery. "After fourteen years of meditation," he said, "and of beating my poor thick head on the koans given me by my master, it seemed to me that satori was not to be mine.

"And when my master told me I should leave and be of use somewhere—" He shrugged, but his eyes were lively and his lips bowed in a smile. "I left, and for some years served in one and another temple to the Buddha Amida. Invariably my people liked me, unworthy though I was. Finally I was brought here to the palace." His smile grew to a grin. "Zen masters often stop at the palace when passing through Miyako, and somehow that's when I am happiest. For then they stay at the temple, and we talk, and invariably they are amiable. Certainly more amiable to the rector who does what he knows how, than they were to the student struggling to do what he could not.

"I have not experienced satori, but I believe what I was told. And for me, belief serves well enough."

"And what belief is that?" Katsumi asked.

The rector looked at him, then at Nils. "Would you care to guess, Matsumura Nissa? For I believe you are a wizard."

Nils grinned back at him. "What you were told is that he who experiences satori, finds himself exactly where he started. For he was already complete."

The rector clapped his hands. "And therefore, it is all right to seek, and it is all right to fail to find; it is all the same. For I am already complete." His smile became rueful then. "But still I wish I'd experienced satori. It would be nice to know, and not simply believe."

As they left the temple, Katsumi asked Nils how he'd been able to answer the rector's question.

"It is a skill some wizards have," Nils answered, and left it at that.

From the temple, they visited the *dojo*, where they watched young men of the court drill with swords under the tutelage of the highly reputed instructor, Shibata Saburo, a young nephew of Lord Shibata. The famous master, Hyogo Musashi, was elderly, Katsumi told them, and worked only with a few special students. Especially he worked with Shibata Saburo, preparing him to follow as master when Musashi retired.

That evening before supper, Katsumi asked if the three young men from Momiji would care to visit a geisha house, a house of dance. There was a large and very fine one, The House of April Leaves, not far from the palace. It was reserved for samurai members of the imperial staff, and the Emperor's guests. Those who could afford it. The Emperor's secretary had told him that the two Matsumuras, their companion, and Katsumi as their appointed guide, could attend at the Emperor's expense.

They agreed, of course. Akira was particularly eager. He'd been to geisha houses before, but nothing with a reputation like The House of April Leaves for beauty and refinement. Led by Katsumi, who was in high spirits now, they strode down the street to the house. It was large and ell-shaped, and two stories high, with graceful, pagoda-like tile roofs, set amidst fenced gardens lit softly by candles in colorful paper lanterns. Storm-ravaged trees and shrubs had been removed or pruned, and the damage was not conspicuous. Representative, Katsumi said, of the quality of management.

The proprietor had been told they were coming, and met the imperial guests personally in the waiting room, bowing low. Only for a moment did the foreign appearance of the Northmen rattle him, and he addressed them in terms of high respect. Then he led them to a spacious room with comfortable cushions to sit on. Four of his loveliest girls would arrive shortly to entertain them. There would be a brief wait, he said apologetically. He'd had only two minutes warning. He was sending Shinshiro Chiyoko, he told them. As if Chiyoko was very special.

Then he bowed again and left them.

"Chiyoko?" Akira said. "Is that the name of the number one girl here?"

Katsumi nodded. "She came here from Aichi, two years ago. She is the most beautiful girl in Miyako; probably in all the world. The most graceful and accomplished dancer, and the best conversationalist. Every man in the palace wishes she would invite him to her room, but if any has ever gotten there—and surely some must have—he hasn't talked about it. As he wouldn't, of course. For unlike most geisha, her father was a well-known samurai, who died heroically at the battle of Gifu."

Hans looked puzzled; he sensed only vaguely what went on here. Katsumi, misinterpreting his expression, elaborated. "Very important men come here, some of them *daimyo*. And some, if the girl doesn't invite them, will try to invite themselves. And if the girl never agrees, there are some who will complain to the proprietor. If too many complain, she's at risk of being beaten. Or in the case of a girl of samurai family, her contract might be cancelled, and her family would have to repay the unearned portion plus a penalty. The prettiest and most famous can be quite selective, but even they must please the clients, one way or another."

Hans frowned. Among the Northmen, to beat a woman or girl for anything short of adultery brought one scorn as a coward, and she could take the matter to the chief. Even to the *lagman*, if necessary for satisfaction. He said nothing though. He'd seen enough of the world, these past sixteen months, to realize how different folkways could be.

But if he asked a geisha, he told himself, and she refused him, he'd say nothing about it.

Akira's eyebrows had raised at the description of Chiyoko. "How did a daughter of a well-known samurai come to be employed as a geisha?" he asked.

"The family was not well-to-do, and with the father dead, her elder brother went to Osaka and wasted what property they had on high living—the theater, silk kimonos, gambling, and addiction to expensive brothels. Soon the family was bankrupt—there wasn't even a dowry left for Chiyoko—and the mother had to hire out her only daughter, a terrible disgrace. Lord Aichi arranged the contract with The House of April Leaves, the most reputable house in Yamato."

Akira grunted. "What of the brother?"

"As you'd expect. *Seppuku*. He botched that too; he crawled out to the street, howling and holding his guts in with one hand, and expired in the dust."

Akira shook his head in disgust. Then a small bell sounded delicately in the hall outside their door. A serving girl opened it and lowered herself gracefully to her knees. Four young women came into the room then and made a sort of curtsy, all grace and loveliness. All were exceptionally pretty, and fair skinned—not only their faces, which were artificially whitened, but their hands and wrists. It was as if they never saw the sun. Their lips were reddened, and their plucked eyebrows replaced by a high curved brush stroke.[23] Their beautifully embroidered kimonos were white silk. Each girl carried a musical instrument, three with strings, one a sort of flute. And they walked very differently than Neoviking girls did, their steps short, their bodies swaying.

Smiling, they curtsied again, then each knelt by one of the guests without apparent selection. The one who knelt by Hans was close enough to make him squirm. One whom he thought must be Chiyoko, knelt by Nils, but that was to be expected.

---

[23] The women of Yamato do not blacken their teeth as women of pretechnological Japan did; Hans might not have thought them so pretty if they had. Rather, Yamatoans tend to take meticulous care of their teeth from early childhood.

The serving girl came in carrying a vase of hot *sake* and a nested stack of porcelain bowls. She knelt, set them on the floor, turned and slid the door closed behind her, picked them up again, rose, and distributed the bowls among the guests and geisha. Then, kneeling repeatedly but always graceful, she poured, first for the guests, then for the geisha, serving the geisha just a little. When she'd served them all, she put the vase—a seeming work of art—on a stand above a small, fragrant oil lamp, then bowed her way gracefully backward to the door. Hans watched the whole procedure with a look of disbelief.

Katsumi named the guests to the hostesses, and Chiyoko named the girls. Hans's was Mariko, who smiled at him and asked his age. "Sixteen," he told her, and somehow managed to blush.

"Oh!" she said. "Sixteen and already so tall!" Then she laughed, a tinkling laugh of pleasure. The blush intensified, but Hans did not wish himself elsewhere.

Mostly they did not talk one on one; it was a group conversation, led mainly by Chiyoko, who knew how to draw people out of themselves. The porcelain *sake* bowls were small, and from time to time, one of the hostesses would pour from the vase, the women drinking very little.

Then the girls got into a poetry-reciting contest with Katsumi and Akira, taking turns. "You have not spoken a poem yet, Nissa-san," Chiyoko said, tipping her head to one side like a lovely bird. Hans thought she was incredibly pretty when she did that, even prettier than Mariko, whose nearness had given him an erection.

"I know no poems," Nils said grinning.

"Not even one?"

"Not even one. But Hans knows enough for both of us. He is a poet who both composes and recites; he is already famous in our clan."

"Oh!" said Mariko, and touched Hans's arm lightly with one hand. It tingled, and his breath stuck in his chest. "Hansu-san! You didn't say anything about that!"

Actually he'd said little about anything, feeling out of his depth here.

"Perhaps Hansu-san will honor us with one of his poems," Chiyoko said gently.

"I— They are in my own language. The words would mean nothing to you."

"Please excuse us for that. But we would like to hear one anyway."

Hans looked at Nils for rescue, but Nils only grinned.

"Yes," said Katsumi, "let us hear one." Akira was nodding energetically. Hans took another sip of the *sake*, cleared his throat, and began with one he'd been playing with in his mind recently, starting in the middle, for he was dissatisfied with the beginning.

> *Kodoka d' burrjat' jätten*
> *skrätte på d' milda Yngling',*
> *stod mä hännerna i sidan.*
> *Skrätte hån å glodde hatfullt . . .*

he began. Quickly his voice took on the rich, sonorous quality of the trained Northman poet. The bardic meter sounded nothing like what the others had recited, but once started, he felt confident.

When he'd finished, the hostesses clapped delightedly, their hands like the wings of delicate birds. The men applauded too, but them he scarcely noticed. He took another sip of *sake*, and obliged their request for more, reciting not another of his own, but one by his mentor, Algott Skalden, his favorite kanto to date in the *Järnhann Saga*, richer in alliteration than almost anything he'd done himself yet.

And as he recited, became aware of new respect in the eyes of Akira and Katsumi.

After Hans had finished, Katsumi asked the girls to play. They did, the music much like that their ancestors had played in the days before either the plague or technology. Nor was it altogether unlike some Neoviking music, which had changed markedly from that of pre-plague Europe.

Next Katsumi asked the girls to dance. Chiyoko, who clearly had rank among them, requested that the others dance first, saying she would play for them. The other three girls got to their feet, while the men moved to the wall and sat down again.

Chiyoko raised her flute and began. The dance was slow and subtle, its movements subdued, but as it progressed, it became more sensuous, the sensuosity as much in the movements of hands and eyes as in feet and hips. When they had finished, the men applauded. Then Chiyoko laid down the flute and rose gracefully to her feet. Katsumi caught the other men's eyes with his, meaningfully.

She hitched her kimono up under her *obi*, baring her lean legs to the loin cloth, and performed a dance very unlike the one just finished, indeed unlike any seen by the ancients. None of the girls had picked up the flute; they played the stringed instruments. The dance began somewhat like a slow martial arts drill choreographed for aesthetics, with high leg movements, precise and graceful sweeps and kicks, marvelously balanced, marvelously flexible, coordinated with sinuous movements of arms and hands. Gradually she speeded, till her legs flashed ivory and her hands and feet blurred. Then gradually she slowed again, the movements becoming more sensual. The men stared, transfixed.

When she was done, her face glowed with sweat and exertion, and they applauded softly, eyes warm. When the applause was finished, she stepped to Nils and knelt in front of him, face averted. "If it would please you, Nissa-san, I hope you will do me the favor of accompanying me to my room."

For a long moment, the only sound was of breathing. Then, without speaking, Nils stood, bent, and helped her to her feet, and they left. Katsumi stared after them, then at Akira, as if not knowing what to say. Mariko got up and knelt before Hans. "If it would please you . . ."

When she'd finished, Hans sat dumbly for a moment before rising to his feet. Following Nils's example, he too helped the girl up and went with her down the corridor to the lodgings wing.

Mariko's room was dark, except for the light that spilled in from the hall. She lit the candle in a lantern, and by its flickering light, closed the door, then turned to Hans, and stepping up to him, put her arms around his waist and raised her face.

He'd never been with a girl before. He'd been fifteen when he'd left his clan and village to go adventuring, and at fifteen, most girls at home had crushes on sword apprentices, of which he had not been one. But neither was he stupid, nor unobservant. He lowered his face to hers, bending at the knees to make up for the large height difference, and they kissed. Then she began undressing him.

It was much later when Nils came to get him. Neither of them spoke. Hans knew he'd come back though, as often as he could. He was sure he was in love.

TWENTY-FOUR

Stor tidragen han t' flikkor,
ofta kjikt i ham på sölstig,
blikkor fölte ham i midda,
nog dröjd när en mö i sjymning,
viskte bjääli t' vä ellen.

Fascinating he to women,
often glanced at him by morning,
followed him their eyes at midday,
lingered near sometimes at twilight,
whispered to him in the firelight.
>   From—*The Järnhann Saga,*
>   Kumalo translation

   Shibata Toko had awakened feeling—all right but not *good*. She'd dreamt of the giant foreigner, but he hadn't made love to her. She didn't remember the details, but he hadn't made love to her.
   Life as a lady of the court, attending one or another of the Emperor's three wives when it was her turn, was not very satisfying. This morning she'd been assigned to take a calligraphy lesson with Masayo, which she might have found agreeable enough, had not the junior empress been given to snide remarks about her brush-work. "You form your *kanji*," she'd once said, "like some common clerk in a hurry to visit his mistress."
   Toko would have been happy, she thought, to be someone's mistress. Not some common clerk's, of course, but a well-placed samurai's. Her main problem, as she saw it, was that she had neither husband nor lover. Men were plentiful enough at court,

but attendants like herself had little opportunity to speak with them, certainly not in private.

Toko was a notably lovely woman of eighteen years. Her father, the fifth son of a minor western *daimyo*, had stretched his budget to afford advantages for her—*competent* instruction in poetry and painting, calligraphy and flower arrangement, and the dance—all the graces desirable in the daughter of a lordling. In fact, a lovely and accomplished daughter of proper behavior could be the making of a minor family. There'd been instruction in sexual technique, too, from a book, of course, with lectures from an experienced courtesan. This was usual for young women of samurai families. It reduced the risk of divorce, which was simple for men, and any tendency to waste money on prostitutes.

Despite the phlegmatic, deliberately technical treatment of the subject, it had inspired Toko's imagination.

At age sixteen, it had been arranged that she serve at the imperial court. That had been a great honor for her family, for as a young woman of the court, she would be a ward of the Emperor. Hopefully her beauty would attract an important husband there, perhaps even one of the numerous young men of the imperial family—cousins of the Emperor. At any rate it got her out of her mother's hair.

It was her eldest brother, Saburo, who'd arranged the appointment for her, therewith putting his own and his family's honor on the line. So far he'd been the bright star of their father's household, a swordsman of wide reputation, who'd been invited to a tourney at the imperial palace, and then to stay as principal instructor under the old master, Hyogo Musashi.

(In fact, Musashi had told the Emperor that he planned to retire as soon as he'd guided Saburo to spiritual maturation. "He is still passionate," the old man had said. "And while passion is not entirely inappropriate in a young master, complete mastery is approached only after passion has been extinguished—when the master views matters from outside those matters, and from outside himself.")

So far, almost all of the court's eligible young men had seen Shibata Toko, but none had sent a go-between to the Emperor to propose marriage. Part of the problem was that her father was only a minor lordling, and her dowry would be trivial by the standards here. Also, most of the young ladies of the court were beautiful, even if mostly less than herself. While she'd been there, three of them had wed, though none to a member of the imperial family.

Actually, in the absence of marriage, Toko would have settled for a night, regardless of risk, for she combined strong sexuality with impatience and an active imagination. Her family had considered her willful and hot-blooded. At age fifteen, she'd been caught in a compromising situation with her poetry instructor. The young man had been flogged, and exiled from the district, while her family had heaped shame on her for a month, and severely restricted her freedom until she'd gone away to Miyako.

Unfortunately the women's court, with its noble but often spoiled daughters, its boredom and jealousies, could be a kettle of rumor and gossip, and sometimes of malice. So word soon reached Saburo of his sister's supposed emotional reaction to the giant foreigner. Naturally this embarrassed him, so he arranged a private meeting with her, and arriving upset, told her accusingly what he'd heard. She'd denied it angrily, and had he accepted her denial, which was true, nothing might have happened. But he considered that there must be at least some truth in what he'd heard, and reminded her of her duty to her family. And to the Emperor while she was his ward.

"No man wants a wife who exposes herself to gossip," he finished.

She bit back the retorts that arose in her.

As he marched stiffly from the room, he thought with indignation that she lacked even the grace to weep.

The men of the court were less bored and far less constrained in their behavior, and as a matter of samurai honor didn't gossip freely. Still, the novelty of the giant foreigner, and Chiyoko's uncharacteristic invitation to him, caused Katsumi to mention it, in confidence, to the young man he shared a room with. He, in turn, mentioned it to his partner in *dojo*, confidentially of course. Within two days, the story had spread throughout the court. The young ladies, perhaps jealous of geisha glamour and relative freedom, professed to hold geishas in scorn, as little better than prostitutes. So they buzzed about the story with pleasure. The consensus was that someone as ill-bred as Chiyoko was well-suited to the barbarian, whose equipment was no doubt as outsized as the rest of him. "Like a donkey," one of them said. "He probably beset her like an army storming a castle," another added. "Probably," said a third, "she is sending him messages to visit her every night."

This was followed by a gale of giggling. Most of them would fantasize about the foreigner after this; Chiyoko's resented glamor enhanced his sex appeal.

It was the comment about messages that inspired Toko, and she sent one of her own to Chiyoko, via a serving girl. After all, a ward of the court and the granddaughter of a *daimyo* was as far above the daughter of a country samurai as the samurai's daughter was above a peasant girl. And a geisha lost any formal status in class while employed as an entertainer. A proposition by some noble she might decline, but an order from a noble woman should be complied with.

Two nights later, Katsumi again took the guests from Momiji Castle to The House of April Leaves, after arranging in advance to have the same four girls assigned to them. Shortly before going to meet the guests, Chiyoko did two things: She sent a servant of the house to the palace, with a note to Shibata Toko. And she informed the doorman that a young woman would arrive that evening, dressed as a boy, with a message for her, probably an oral message. He was to send the girl to Chiyoko's room, and a serving girl to let her know that the messenger had arrived.

The conversation between the four geisha and their visitors was not quite as enjoyable as before. The girls had bedded them the first time, which altered the chemistry. But the music was as good, and the dancing, and the men all felt that surely the girls would invite them to their rooms again, so they were more horny than before, in anticipation.

After dancing, Chiyoko excused herself from the party, saying she'd be back very soon. A few minutes after returning, she invited Nils to her room again. This time she did not light a lantern. Instead she undressed him in the unlit room, slowly, kissing his skin as she uncovered it.

Again she excused herself for a moment, and went to her wardrobe. A moment later, Shibata Toko came out of it, thinking to be mistaken in the darkness for Shinshiro Chiyoko. She beset the Northman avidly, wriggling around on top of him, fondling and kissing with startling passion. Anticipation had aroused her before he'd ever entered the room; soon she climbed astraddle of him, and they began to have sex. She was in the midst of intense orgasm when the hall door was slid violently open on its rollers, much more widely than need be. Light flooded in. Toko didn't stop, wasn't aware that her brother, Saburo, was standing aghast in the doorway, the distraught proprietor beside him, with one of his *ronin* guards.

Toko had dropped Chiyoko's message. Wakaumi, one of the court ladies had picked it up, read it, and with perverse pleasure, had sent it to Saburo with a quick message of her own.

Now, staring from the doorway, Saburo's initial horror was replaced by outrage. He'd thought perhaps to catch his sister in the act, yet remarkably, somehow hadn't foreseen what he might find. He'd thought totally in terms of concept, of principle, of righteous wrath, not of her frenzied bobbing, her passionate nasal whimpering.

"Toko!" he bellowed. *"Toko!"* This jerked her to awareness, and with an effort she stood up, hands covering herself as if that could help. He drew his sword then, and screaming, she placed herself in his way as he advanced to kill the Northman. He pushed her aside, but she threw herself on him, grabbing him around the head. He had to resheath his sword to free himself, cursing her as he did so.

Meanwhile Nils had rolled to his feet and gotten his swords, long and short, from the pile of clothing by the wall. But made no further hostile move.

Along with Saburo's shouting and Toko's screams, the proprietor had been calling for more guards. Two samurai patrons from nearby rooms peered in grinning at the brother-sister wrestling match, while the hall filled with men and girls running up from the entertainment wing. Soon it would be abuzz with reports passed along.

Disentangling himself from his nude sister had broken Saburo's blood fixation. He became aware of what was happening outside the open door, and realized what he'd done: In trying to protect his sister's reputation, he'd destroyed it by drawing attention to her indiscretion. Nor could he claim she was being raped, for she'd been on top, riding the foreigner like a jockey. The proprietor and his guard had watched, and no *ronin* could keep such a story to himself. It would spread; there was no avoiding it. His family's honor would be severely damaged, and the fault was as much his as hers.

With an iron grip he seized her wrist and ordered her to dress, then let her go and did his best to clear the door of watchers. Now Toko too realized the seriousness of what had happened, and the disaster that would surely result. Swiftly and contritely she dressed in her boy's costume, then Saburo hustled her past grinning onlookers and out a back way.

Chiyoko would have been better off if she'd stayed in the wardrobe. But when more guards had come and pushed the spectators and would-be spectators out of the hall, she came timidly forth, wearing a kimono. The proprietor was as upset as Saburo: A hullabaloo like this would severely disgrace the reputation of his house, and surely result in it being made off-limits to the imperial court. It would probably be shut down entirely.

So when the proprietor saw Chiyoko emerge from the wardrobe, his eyes bulged with anger. Clearly she was behind this! It was undoubtedly her fault! With an oath, he strode into the room and slapped her with a fat hand. "You!" he hissed. "What have you done? I am ruined, and you are to blame!"

She cowered, and that encouraged him. "I'll fix you!" he said. "I own your contract! I'll send you to my brothel on the waterfront! With your reputation for refinement and beauty, every rough hoodlum in Miyako will be standing in line to crowd himself between your legs! Then we'll see how . . ."

He stopped, because Nils had grabbed his hair and held his sword to his neck. The man's guards stopped in their tracks. "Do not harm or humiliate this lady!" Nils said calmly. "She is the daughter of a samurai. If you harm her, I will claim her dead father's right to vengeance."

The proprietor's rage deflated. His guards could hardly save him. They probably wouldn't even avenge him, for he was only a merchant, and in the entertainment profession at that, while they were samurai. But if his rage had evaporated, his indignation remained. "She has ruined me!" he said. "I must have restitution!" Then changed his tone to wheedling. "I did not really mean I would let riffraff abuse her; I only wanted to frighten her, so she would realize all the trouble she caused me. I have a geisha house in the pleasure district, that caters to prosperous merchants. I have customers there who would pay a hundred *chogin* to spend the evening with her; men who have heard of her beauty and grace, but have not been eligible to enter here. They would not mistreat her; they would feel privileged to hear her play and sing, and watch her dance."

Nils looked into the proprietor's mind, scowled, and shook the man's head by the hair. "I see revenge in your thoughts," he growled. "But it was not this girl who injured you; it was the young man who just left with his sister. He is Shibata Saburo; threaten him if you dare." He stared hard into the man's face, and his blank eyes seemed surely to have life. "Beware," Nils went on, "for I intend to marry this lady. If the law requires it, I will buy her contract from you. But if you name an unreasonable price, I will flay you and keep your skin to decorate my wall."

The proprietor's round face went slack. This barbarian giant must somehow be noble, he thought, to have standing at the imperial court. And a merchant had few rights in contract dealings with nobility. Especially a merchant in the entertainment business, for they were regarded as the lowest of merchants, regardless of whatever wealth they might have, facing prejudice in legal conflicts even within their class.

Nils read him like a notice on a wall. "Meanwhile," the Northman went on, "I can use such influence as I have at court toward keeping this house from being permanently closed. It may be that your injury will be less than you imagine."

Hope began to glimmer in the proprietor's eyes, although the giant still held him by the hair.

"Now you will go," Nils said, "and leave us alone, Chiyoko

and me. She is afraid of you, and needs someone to assure her." He let go the man's hair. "And when I have gone, you will not trouble her, because you depend on my good will. And because otherwise I will kill you."

Nils spent the night there, leaving when dawn began to thin the darkness. They did not talk much together. She'd heard all that he said to the proprietor, and there was not much more he could say to reassure her until he'd looked into the possibilities. He was content to hold her, and she to be held. Her fear of the brothel dwindled, and her thoughts of suicide were gone; Futori was afraid of Nils, and at the same time at least a little hopeful that he could help. But worry for her future remained. She did not know the legalities of her situation, nor of the foreigner's, and neither of course did he.

TWENTY-FIVE

Katsumi had told Nils that his query should go to the Emperor's marshal. And at any rate, the Emperor was away; this was the day he spent practicing mounted battle, at a place called Jariheichi, outside the city.

Thus Nils stood before Lord Tsuyama Shisha, who looked at him appraisingly. "You wish to marry this geisha?"

"Excuse me, yes. She is the daughter of a samurai."

"I'm aware of that," Tsuyama answered drily. "There are no legal objections to such a marriage. I am also aware of the events in her room, the night before last. Do you appreciate their full significance?"

"I realize that they have placed the Matsumura and Shibata families in a position of—mutually abraded honor."

This foreigner uses the language well, considering, Tsuyama told himself, and shook his head. "To marry another involved person will worsen the situation."

"Sugitani Katsumi has kindly pointed that out to me. He also agrees that my involvement was incidental, while that of Shinshiro Chiyoko—"

Lord Tsuyama cut him short. "Incidental? In what way was it incidental? You were caught in an act of *kogo* with Shibata Toko, an act arranged by Shinshiro Chiyoko. This act was witnessed not only by Toko's brother, but by other persons, greatly aggravating the situation."

"Excuse me, Your Lordship, but I had not gone to Shinshiro Chiyoko's room to have *kogo* with Shibata Toko. I went there to be with Chiyoko; I had never seen nor heard of Shibata Toko. But it seems that somehow, unaccountably, Shibata Toko had become enamored of me. Also, Shinshiro Chiyoko claims that she received a message, a demand from Shibata Toko.

191

Telling her to arrange for us to meet in her darkened room, under circumstances in which I would suppose Toko to be Chiyoko."

Lord Tsuyama's expression turned thoughtful. "Does Shinshiro Chiyoko have this message now?"

"She looked for it before I left her, but unfortunately could not find it."

"Umm. If it exists and she finds it, it will throw a very different light on the matter." Lord Tsuyama paused, frowning thoughtfully, then spoke again. "I have a letter from Shibata Saburo to the Emperor. I haven't shown it to His Majesty yet; I am not obliged to. In it, Shibata asks that His Majesty arrange an exhibition of arms between himself and you, an exhibition before the Emperor and Hyogo Musashi, and His Majesty's court. The stated purpose of the exhibition would be to compare the Shosen style of swordsmanship with that of your people. What would you think of taking part in such a match?"

"I would be willing. Against so renowned a swordsman as Saburo, of course, the result will be in part a matter of personal ability. Perhaps more so than of styles."

Lord Tsuyama examined the foreigner's mild features. *He appears remarkably dispassionate, this Matsumura Nissa. Or supremely confident. I wish he had eyes I could read.* "I will give the request to the Emperor, then," Tsuyama said, adding silently: *and hope that Shibata is honest in this.*

Shibata Saburo sat on his feet in his small room, his back ramrod straight, in the Zen meditation posture. But he only appeared to be meditating. In fact, thoughts were cycling through his mind in futile circles. Despite his efforts, he'd seen no alternative to his plan, a plan which distressed him. It seemed to him the odds were heavily in his favor. He was reputedly the best swordsman in Yamato—better even than Hyogo Musashi, since Musashi had grown old and slow. But he found little satisfaction in the odds, for what he planned seemed basically dishonorable. A dishonorable way of retrieving, somewhat, his family's honor.

He ground his teeth.

He'd have challenged the foreigner to duel, but duelling

was forbidden to members of the court. The punishment was death, and more humiliating, public exposure of the corpse—an extreme dishonor. So Saburo had come up with an alternative: murder in the guise of accident. As an accident, it would not be entirely convincing; he did not delude himself in that. But no one could prove it wasn't, and it seemed to him that the Emperor would let it pass. For given the state of the Empire, it would not do to have two of his supporters at war with one another. Matsumura was a *tehon daimyo*, while the Shibata family was a firm imperial supporter in a part of the island where the Emperor didn't have many.

And it seemed to Saburo that Lord Matsumura, pressed by the Emperor, might also let it be. For the foreigner was not a son of his flesh; was not even Yamatoan. No one would severely fault Matsumura Shinji in such a case, though his enemies would make disparaging noises.

He himself, of course, would be dismissed from his position, along with that shameless Toko. The grounds would be that his carelessness, his failure to control his sword with sufficient precision, had caused the death of Matsumura Nissa. The Emperor would have no choice, and hopefully that, along with imperial pressure, would be enough to placate Matsumura-sama.

On the other hand, there was the possibility that the Emperor would anticipate his true intention and refuse to sanction the match. That would leave the matter unresolved. And surely His Majesty had foreseen possible treachery.

"Excuse me, Shibata-san." Someone had spoken quietly outside his door. After a moment the voice repeated, slightly louder. "Excuse me, Shibata-san. Are you there?"

Saburo got to his feet. "Who is it?"

"Sugitani Katsumi. Excuse me, but I have a message for you, from Matsumura Nissa."

A vacuum formed in Saburo's belly, a sick emptiness. What could this mean? "Wait a minute," he said, and going to the door, slid it open. Katsumi stood in his best kimono, holding a roll of rice paper in his hand. He extended it to Saburo.

"Matsumura Nissa does not know how to write our language. He told me what to write, and I wrote it for him in his own words."

Saburo took the message and turned away, leaving Katsumi standing where he was. Mind numb, breath frozen in his chest, the swordsmanship instructor crossed to the window to read the message in better light. *Honorable Shibata Saburo*, it began. *I wish to apologize for my unwitting involvement in a situation that caused you distress. I deeply regret that such an unfortunate thing happened. I had gone to the room expecting to make love with the young geisha, Shinshiro Chiyoko, with whom I am enamored, and in the darkness did not realize the identity of the young woman with whom you found me. If there were some way of undoing what happened, I would gladly do it. Written for me, Matsumura Nissa, by my friend, Sugitani Katsumi.*

Saburo's hands trembled with the desire to accept the apology, but he fought it off. The apology was not abject. More importantly, it did not accept the blame. It was honest, he felt sure, but it was not adequate to the Shibata honor. Now *he* would have to be *dis*honest. He ground his teeth again. Turning, he faced Katsumi across the room and bowed, his calm and quiet voice belying his agitation. "It was generous of Matsumura Nissa to apologize, and of you to write and bring it to me. However, it is not possible to accept at this time. I will contemplate the matter, and let you know my decision when I've made it. Meanwhile, I thank you very much for coming here."

Katsumi bowed in return, then turned and walked away down the hall, his thoughts hopeful. *Clearly the situation has eased*, he told himself. *Saburo has always been known as a man of reason, as well as honor. He will surely accept the apology.*

It was at noon of the next day that Shibata Saburo was called to the marshal's office. Lord Tsuyama's eyes examined him mildly enough, but he delivered the Emperor's answer without courteous preamble. "His Majesty has decided on your request for an exhibition match with Matsumura Nissa. He has approved, and Matsumura Nissa has agreed to it. You will fight on the fifth day from today, at the fifth hour. With wooden swords, to lessen the chance of—serious accidental injury. I will referee the match. This has the further advantage that neither of you need withhold your strokes. It will more closely approximate a deadly fight."

The answer left Saburo numb. Wooden swords. He bowed. "Thank you, Tsuyama-sama. The Emperor and yourself are very kind to so unworthy a servant. Please convey my deepest gratitude to His Majesty."

Saburo was not clear how he got out of the building. In the courtyard, the mellow autumn sun brought him back to himself. *Of course wooden swords are unusual between masters,* he told himself, *but I should have foreseen it.* And he could hardly kill so large a man, skilled and hard and massive, with a wooden sword. Be awarded a "fatal stroke," yes—a fatal stroke as judged by the referee, Lord Tsuyama. He quite expected that. But the only fatal stroke that mattered was one that left the giant foreigner truly dead, redeeming his family's honor. And with wooden swords, if anyone was killed, it would be himself.

With a clack of teeth, he cut short that line of thought. It *was* possible to kill so large a man as Matsumura Nissa with a wooden sword. He himself was considered exceptionally strong, and the foreigner's very size could be used against him, for surely he'd be somewhat slow. *While of my natural gifts,* Saburo reminded himself, *the most outstanding is my quickness. A hard thrust—very hard— into the solar plexus, rupturing the belly sac[24] and gut, or in the throat, crushing the voice box, or . . .*

He rehearsed the possibilities. *Difficult, yes,* he told himself, *but possible.* Without a doubt possible. And returned to the *dojo* and his students.

---

[24] The peritoneum.

TWENTY-SIX

The population of Miyako, its porters and smiths, its housewives and woodworkers, its mat makers and shopkeepers, was a world away from the imperial court. Thus while Nils Järnhann was known now to everyone at the palace, the people he passed on the street, this early evening, had never heard of him or imagined anything like him. He strode past them as unexpectedly and alarmingly as some giant out of mythology, and they drew back, staring with varying degrees of awe and fear. He seemed too strange and large, and quite possibly dangerous, even to be curious about. Only a few small children followed him, and they at a little distance.

The sleeves of his light cotton tunic ended at his elbows, baring his forearms, which were disproportionately long by Yamatoan standards, even for his height. At the same time, they were thick and corded, ending in huge, long-fingered hands. It was such proportions and disproportions that fixed their attention; hardly any who saw him that evening even noticed his eyes, let alone his smile.

For the first time, he was going to visit Chiyoko in her new lodgings.

Through a go-between, Nils had arranged living quarters for her with the widowed grandmother of a palace serving girl. He'd met the widow a few nights earlier, when he, together with Katsumi and the granddaughter, escorted Chiyoko to the old woman's home. The house was well built and comfortable—the widow's husband had been a prominent sword-polisher[25] and notable character, who'd counted court officials and other

---

[25] Sword-polishers do more than polish swords. They remove rust and even pitting, and sharpen them to a razor edge. Samurai

noblemen among his clients. He'd invested money in a shipping company, so his widow was not in actual need, but the income was irregular, and having an aggressive attitude toward finances, she'd decided to take in a renter.

The widow was a notable character in her own right, fearless even of the foreign giant who'd stood in her living room. She was quite capable, her granddaughter had insisted, of running off unwanted suitors who might be attracted by Chiyoko's beauty.

Nils had intended to pay Chiyoko's rent, and indeed had paid the first ten days of it, because the money she'd saved as a geisha, which was considerable, had gone toward buying out her contract. She, however, intended to find employment at some local shop, and pay her own rent. Besides, she pointed out, she "needed" income to repay Nils, who'd paid off the rest of her contract price. As a younger son of the Matsumura family, he'd been sent off with a well-filled purse that would be refilled from time to time. He could also ask for financial help as needed, and meanwhile had already borrowed against future moneys, from Katsumi.

The widow's house was set in a small yard planted mostly with vegetables. Surrounding it all was a two-meter bamboo fence overgrown with squash vines. No gate blocked the entry. The tall Northman turned in and rapped strongly on the door, for the old woman was hard of hearing.

She bustled to answer, and invited him in. Stepping into the beaten-earth hallway, he asked for Chiyoko. "Chiyoko!" the widow shouted, "It is the foreign lord! Matsumura Nissa!" Then, turning to Nils she said, "Come! Come into my living room! I'm afraid it isn't worthy of a Matsumura, but it will be an honor if you choose to sit in it."

"Thank you," Nils said, not particularly loudly despite her deafness, and took off his straw sandals before stepping up onto the polished wood floor. "That is very kind of you. To invite me into the living room of Toganatoki Tora is to honor me unduly. I am only Matsumura-sama's youngest son, while

---

do not ordinarily sharpen their own swords, except on campaign. Even *ronin* prefer to have the job done professionally, when they can afford it.

Toganatoki Tora still is widely regarded as the greatest of his noble profession."

Surprisingly the widow simpered. Chiyoko entered the room and bowed to Nils. "It is kind of you to come," the young woman said quietly. "I am unworthy of your kindness. I feel guilty for the trouble and expense I have brought on you."

Nils reached out and raised her averted face. "You are a person of quality. I am privileged to be your friend."

He looked at the widow then. "I would like to speak privately with Shinshiro Chiyoko."

The old woman laughed, a sort of squawk resembling the crowing of a young pheasant. "That should be easy, I am so deaf." She raised her eyebrows, then grinned. "You are young and full of juices, and Chiyoko is beautiful. It isn't seemly that I leave you by yourselves. I'll sit in the corner there and continue my embroidering. If you speak quietly, I'll hear none of it."

He nodded. He'd come primarily to talk with Chiyoko, and though he'd have preferred talking in bed, he hadn't expected to. He turned to her and spoke softly.

"I've come to repeat my request that you marry me. I am of good family, and not given to abusing women or children. I have already shown I can protect you. And I feel great affection for you, as I believe you do for me."

"Oh yes, Nissa-san, I feel very great affection for you. But I am not worthy. You are a son—a chosen son—of a *tehon daimyo*."

"I have discussed this matter with Tsuyama Shisha, who is the Emperor's marshal, one of the three most elevated personages in the palace; only the Emperor himself, and *kubo-sama*, rank higher. He says there is no legal barrier to a marriage between you and me."

"You have not asked the approval of your father. That is important, especially in noble families. And it would be an embarrassment to Lord Matsumura to have a daughter-in-law who'd been a geisha."

"Matsumura-sama wishes me married. He told me this. I answered that I wasn't yet ready to take a wife. He said that when I changed my mind on the matter, it would cause him great pleasure. That he knew I would be traveling much of the time, but if I found a bride, he would be glad to take her into his home and honor her."

Chiyoko sat as silent and motionless as autumn sunlight on a pool. Finally she said, "There are other barriers!"

Nils said nothing, so she continued. "What happened at The House of April Leaves, between you and— I know well the noble name Shibata. It is why I agreed to—do what I did. Lord Shibata is an important personage, and the young man who—found you there with . . . he must be Lord Shibata's son."

"The young man, whose name is Shibata Saburo, is Lord Shibata's grandson, by his lordship's fifth son. I've been assured that that degree of remove from Lord Shibata himself, somewhat lessens the impact of the disgrace on the Shibata name."

Chiyoko didn't answer at once. Finally she said, "Still there remains considerable disgrace on the Shibatas. They must consider you the instrument of that disgrace, and me an accomplice to it. If you and I should marry, after what happened, they will consider it a further offense."

She had not met his eyes as she spoke; it would not be fitting. He sat on his cushion facing her, looking into her mind: a quiet, responsible mind. And despite her socially imprinted self-deprecation, a mind that included a strong and reasoned will.

"My answer," he said, "is to repeat: I wish to marry you. It is not simply a matter of having cost you your position as Yamato's most admired geisha. On that first evening, although I'd never heard of you before, I sat with the others, listening to you speak and play, and felt something that went beyond admiration. I wanted then to reach out, to touch your cheek, stroke your hair, and cherish you. Will you marry me, Chiyoko?"

She did look at him now, her eyes steady, and said nothing for perhaps a minute. "Despite the possibility of trouble between the Shibatas and the Matsumuras?"

"Despite that. But I must tell you, an important part of my duties, among my own people, was keeping peace between offended families."

Again she looked long at him. "Why did you not approach

me through a go-between? Which you must know is customary in these matters."

He saw the thought beneath that question, too. She assumed he'd asked someone, and they'd refused because of the potential conflict between two noble families. "I could have," he answered. "Kamoshika Akira offered his services. But I knew the delicacy of your feelings in this, and wished to ask you myself, believing that I could ease your misgivings.

"I prefer that your answer grow out of an affection for me, a trust in me, and a feeling that I will make you happier than you might otherwise be. I realize that you consider your happiness less important than peace between noble families. But I know Lord Matsumura's mind and character intimately, and I assure you he will prize you as his daughter-in-law. As for peace, I do not believe our marriage will cause enmity between the Shibatas and the Matsumuras."

She sat quietly for a long time, perhaps five minutes. Finally she spoke, wondering at herself as she did so, for her misgivings were by no means stilled. "Yes," she said, "I will marry you, Matsumura Nissa."

Each got on their knees and bowed to the other, lowering their foreheads to the floor, then rose to their feet and bowed once more. "I will return to see you again very soon," he said. "I can ask questions and advice of my friends at court. Then I'll be better able to discuss when the marriage should be performed."

When he'd left, the widow of Toganatoki Tora poured tea for herself and Shinshiro Chiyoko, talking as she poured. "I thought you would never tell him yes! When you are as old as I am, you no longer worry so much about what other people disapprove of. That Matsumura Nissa is a prize not to be given up lightly."

Chiyoko blushed. The old woman cackled. "Sometimes old women lie. It is allowed them. I am hard of hearing, but not as deaf as I let on."

A night bird of some unfamiliar species was talking to itself in a garden tree outside their room, when Hans raised himself on an elbow and looked at the dimly seen bulk of Nils.

"Do you love her, then?" he asked.

"Yes."

"As much as Ilse?"

"As unconditionally as Ilse, and as much. But it is different."

Hans considered that. By Neoviking law, a warrior could have three wives, if he wished, and most did. But Nils had had only one, and somehow Hans had never expected him to take a second. Of course, Chiyoko was much prettier than Ilse, and more—sexually appealing. But the German witch was much bigger and stronger, and smarter, it seemed to him.

"Love is different things," Nils went on. "In one way I love you, Achikh, Matsumura . . .Shakir the Kazakh . . . I have felt moments of love for many others."

Hans shifted uncomfortably. It was not the way among Northmen to speak of love for other men. Nils went on.

"But the love between man and woman is different, in a way that includes but goes beyond having sex with them. I loved Nephthys, a daughter of Kazi, partly because of her love for me, partly because of her psi power, and partly for her great courage. And also because of her beauty, which is greater than any other woman's, even Chiyoko's. And partly for reasons I do not know. While Ilse— We have things in common with each other which we have with no one else. Our powers are similar, and we share with each other things impossible to share with anyone else. We understand each other almost perfectly. When I am with her, I am somehow more complete; I am wiser and stronger then. And it is the same for her."

Hans pursed his lips unseen in the darkness, thinking. *Yet Ilse left you. She left you to go with the Star Folk to their home above the sky*. And wondered if that was why Nils was going to marry Chiyoko.

"No," Nils said, answering Hans's unspoken thought. "I would marry Chiyoko even if Ilse was still in Varjby. These are two different worlds, and Ilse and I agreed that we should each be free to follow our muse. Hers led her to go away with the Star Folk. Mine brought me here.

"While Chiyoko— She is beautiful, of course, but so is Shibata Toko. And we have strong sexual attraction for each other, Chiyoko and I. But also— I see her thoughts, and what lies beneath them. She is someone with goodness far beyond most people, and great inner strength.

"And as with Ilse and Nephthys, there is a love and trust that lie deeper than admiration and desire."

Both lay silent awhile before Hans spoke again. "If you marry Chiyoko, does that mean we'll stay here in Yamato?"

"Do you want to stay here?"

"No. I mean, I could. But— I'm a Northman. And I have a responsibility to write your saga for our people. I like Mariko, of course. Very much. She—does very nice things, and seems to like me very much, too. But there are plenty of girls at home, and when we get there again, they will pay more attention to me."

"I expect to go home, too," Nils said. "Assuming I am not killed first. But meanwhile I will marry Chiyoko. This is a very different people than ours. When Chiyoko's father died and her brother wasted their inheritance, including Chiyoko's dowry, and her mother sold her to The House of April Leaves, many barriers were erected between Chiyoko and happiness. Still, she fashioned a life for herself that brought her great admiration. Even respect. Now she has lost that life, and it is doubtful that she could regain it in another geisha house, for the story of that night is spreading.

"As for happiness, married to some other man— As beautiful as she is, she has no dowry. Many samurai would be overjoyed to have her as a mistress or concubine, but she would not care for such a life, and he could cast her out honorless when she grew older. Some wealthy merchant would be happy to marry her, dowry or not, but probably it would be because of her beauty, and her fame as a geisha. He would wear her like a jewelled ring, show her off. Perhaps even making harsh demands on her, undertaking to profit from his good fortune.

"I, on the other hand, love her. And admire her person, her character, her beingness.

"Another thing: I cost her her position in The House of April Leaves. Because I knew that the woman who came to me in her room was not Chiyoko. The darkness did not hide her soul. But I didn't look deeply enough to see what the situation was. I was only interested in enjoying the moment.

"I have had Akira write down much of what happened that night, and that I will marry Chiyoko; he has written it in my words. He will leave tomorrow, to deliver them for me to Matsumura-sama.

"So I will make Chiyoko Matsumura-sama's daughter-in-law, and together we will give him a grandchild. Perhaps more than one. That will please him."

Hans's laughter took even Hans by surprise; he almost choked, stifling it. "It just occurred to me!" he said. "Chiyoko will be my foster mother! I will have the most beautiful mother in the world!"

Then he added with a sense of wonder: "And Ilse is already my foster mother; I hadn't thought of that before. And I already have a mother of my own. With Chiyoko I will have three mothers!" He paused. "Will we take her home with us, when we go back?"

"Could she be happy, living among the Wolf Clan? Working hides in a log hut with a dirt floor, her hair smelling of wood smoke? Her hands greasy, and stained with dirt and blood?"

Hans shook his head; he couldn't imagine it. Yamato was the world Chiyoko was meant for.

"Unless something happens that causes me to change my mind, I will leave her here when we return to our people. Leave her with Matsumura-sama. I know the kind of man he is better than anyone. Better than he does. He will care for her. Probably find another husband for her, one she likes, someone who will respect her."

The serenity in Nils's voice as he said this made Hans uncomfortable. Yet he could see it made sense. It was as if, given a bad situation, Nils had worked out the best long-term solution he could.

"Do you think Ilse will come back from the world of the Star Folk?" he asked.

"If she wishes to. If she chooses. It's possible."

TWENTY-SEVEN

Initially, Shibata Saburo had wanted their sword match held outdoors, in the sandy ring occasionally used for such contests. It would have permitted and produced a sizeable audience, before which even a refereed victory would have helped his damaged image. Matsumura Nissa, however, had accepted on condition that the match be private. This was generally perceived by the court as a fear of being humiliated by his much smaller Yamatoan opponent, and gave rise to a certain satisfaction, for Saburo was theirs, and well liked.

The Emperor, however, had selected his main audience room for the match, with a major part of it marked off by silk ribbon to accommodate the contest. Those gathered to watch included the Emperor, his marshal, his *kubo-sama*,[26] his personal adviser, and several other ranking officials, as well as Hyogo Musashi and his two other advanced students. And Hans, as Nils's son, and the court physician, in case of severe injury. Of course, the Emperor's bodyguards were also there, but not to watch the contest.

None of the young ladies of the court were allowed at the peep holes; this was not for their eyes and gossiping tongues. Even the empresses were excluded.

Saburo wasn't sure what to expect. He'd watched the foreigner's drill, but that didn't tell him how quick the man's reflexes might be, or how deft. The two contestants wore no protection, and would fight stripped to the waist, that the referee could better score the blows landed. Seen shirtless, the foreigner

---

[26] In the imperial government of Yamato, *kubo-sama* is the operations officer, the most important figure in Yamatoan government short of the Emperor.

looked even more impressive than with a tunic on. But if one imagined what shrunken old Musashi would look like shirtless, yet how dangerous he still was with a sword, it was easy to discount the importance of those remarkable muscles. Besides, Saburo himself looked strong and athletic. And almost the entire audience was noble samurai, men who'd had intensive training with the sword. While impressed by strength, they accepted skill and quickness as senior to it.

With the approval of both contestants, one part of the agreement had been changed: Hyogo Musashi would referee, instead of Lord Tsuyama. No one could judge as well as Musashi what a given stroke would mean, had it been delivered with steel instead of oak. Actually, Saburo wasn't happy with the old master as referee, for when he tried a true death stroke— one that could kill even with a wooden sword—when he tried such a stroke, if it failed, Musashi-sama would surely see what he was up to. And as referee would no doubt stop the bout, probably even give it to the foreigner. But to object to the change was inconceivable. He would simply have to succeed on his first attempt.

Per dueling protocol, the two principles positioned themselves at opposite ends of the square, and the match began when Musashi called out: "Please begin!" Their swords hissed from the scabbards, and they stepped toward the center. In the Shosen school, one often allows one's opponent to make the first move, basing one's own attack on one's counter move. Thus Nils moved first, his extended sword tip describing a small circle, then thrusting abruptly. Deflecting it, Saburo's blade struck strongly at the Northman's forearm, and the fight grew quickly into *Tensetsu-Ransetsu*, a furious exchange without pause.

Their styles were very different. Saburo wielded his sword with both hands, the blade slashing and spinning, while Nils held his with one, depending on skill and strength of wrist to parry Saburo's swift strokes. The spectators, as well as Saburo, were quickly disillusioned that the foreigner might be slow. He was less nimble on his feet, but his hand and wrist were lightning quick, quicker than in his exhibition drills, and his one-handed style allowed more and better use of thrusts. Within the first minute, he'd reached Saburo twice, the rounded end of the weapon leaving a darkening spot on Saburo's naked torso.

Saburo redoubled his efforts then. Both touches had been hard enough to bruise, and Musashi, as referee, would now be reckoning in a theoretical loss of blood. Saburo also began to fear, for when their swords met squarely, a shock ran through his arms; the giant was incredibly strong. He felt a momentary rush when his blade struck the foreigner on his sword arm, a meaningful though glancing blow, but the man leaped back—*and quick as light changed his weapon to his left hand without apparent loss of dexterity!* For just an instant, Saburo was disconcerted by this, and the foreigner's sword end struck his belly hard enough that pain flashed through the anaesthesia of combat excitement. From an intensity born of desperation, Saburo's weapon spun hissing, in a display of virtuosity that none there would forget. But the Northman fended every stroke. It sounded like a half dozen quarter-staff fighters in a melee. Then Musashi called, "Please stop!", and the two samurai separated, already oily with sweat, wooden swords lowered.

"The match is over!" Musashi said. "Shibata Saburo has fainted from the deep thrust into his belly, and a consequent heavy loss of blood. His life cannot be saved."

Saburo lowered his head. He had not come near to winning, let alone actually killing the foreigner. He scarcely heard the applause.

It was the Emperor's voice that brought his attention out of himself. "A marvelous match!" he said. "The greatest bout I've ever witnessed! Saburo! I've never seen such speed! And you, Nissa! You not only gave the winning stroke; you survived the most amazing assault I've ever witnessed, and without being touched by it! Your style is as awesome as your strength. I do not doubt that this court holds the three greatest swordsmen in Yamato."

"I am deeply honored by your words, Your Majesty," the foreigner said, "though unworthy of them. I was fortunate to win. In three years of wars and blood-fights, I have not before fought a swordsman as skilled as Shibata-san. I would much rather have him fighting beside me than against me, and I hope we will be friends."

Saburo's jaw clamped with pain at the praise. It was not unusual for a victor to praise the loser in a match, but usually it was praise with condescension. From Matsumura Nissa's lips, it somehow seemed sincere.

For the next several minutes, men circulated, gesturing, talking excitedly, stepping on each other's words, in a scene as disorganized as any that one might hope to see in the imperial court. Somehow, Saburo found himself in the hallway, accompanied by Musashi's other two advanced students, who jabbered excitedly about the exhibition. Somehow he made it to the privacy of his small room above the *dojo*. The foreigner's words still echoing in his mind: "I hope we will be friends." Saburo's eyes burned with inexplicable grief.

Nils intended to visit Chiyoko often. The reassurance would be good for her.

Thus he visited her on the evening after the match with Saburo. She was employed now, she reported. Knowing many *kanji*, and capable with both ink brush and abacus, she was keeping records for a grain merchant. The wage was much better than she could make as a sales clerk, or as a waitress in a tea shop. Even better than at an inn, where attractive serving girls made good money but were under pressure to provide sexual favors to prosperous travelers.

There were two drawbacks to her clerical job: Her employer was interested in services beyond those agreed to; and the warehouse was on the waterfront, a neighborhood frequented by criminals, some of them without honor. She'd taken care of the first drawback by telling her employer that her suitor, a samurai in the imperial court, would not approve.

As for the second drawback— Like many samurai daughters, she'd been drilled with both sword and *naginata*, a long-bladed, short-handled halberd third only to the sword and bow as a sporting weapon. Such training for daughters was not taken as seriously as it was for samurai sons, but a respectable competence was nonetheless common. And Toganatoki Masayo, her landlady, had given her a short sword to carry, one left with her late husband for reconditioning, and never reclaimed. The sight of its hilt, protruding conspicuously from her *obi*, would give a would-be attacker pause.

This did not guarantee her safety, of course. It simply improved her odds. It was growing dusk when she left her work, and already on the first day, her passing had drawn lewd offers from rough men. In a few weeks it would be dark when she left for home, and she might be ambushed—grabbed before she could draw her sword.

Again Nils offered to pay her rent. He could borrow money again if he had to, and pay it back when he'd gotten more from Matsumura-sama. But she declined; she wanted to pay her own way, and not as his mistress. In two weeks, perhaps she'd quit the job she had—she'd have some money then— and find employment as a waitress after all.

He'd compromised. Whenever he could, he'd meet her after work and walk her home. And surely in two weeks he'd have word and money from Matsumura. They could plan then, and be married.

Things were much simpler among the Northmen. First came the agreement. Over the next few days, the village joined to cut and peel and drag up logs, split out boards for roofing, and build a cabin. When the chimney was done and tested, and the roof was on, the marriage vows were made before the village headman or clan chieftain, and the thing was done. Then everyone, or almost everyone, got drunk to consecrate it.

At the end of Nils's visit, Chiyoko went with him to the front door, and outside into the shadowed night. And there, though it wasn't proper, they kissed, long and lingeringly. "You must go now," she whispered, and he did. She'd thought he might prove resistive to leaving, but he whispered his love, then turned and disappeared through the opening in the fence.

On the street, he paused, looking down it in the direction of the palace, then began walking. Not far ahead was a thicket of tall bamboo, and as he approached it, a dark figure moved in its shadows.

"Good evening, Shibata Saburo," Nils said.

"You know me!"

"My eyes are not like yours. I can see in the dark."

Nils could feel the man's glare. "I have come to kill you." Saburo's voice was hoarse, as if he'd been shouting all day.

"I wish you would not. I am not your enemy. I do not even dislike you."

"You have dishonored my sister," Saburo husked. "In front of witnesses. You have brought dishonor on the entire Shibata family!"

"Excuse me for seeing it differently. I am only a foreigner, and do not always understand the way people of my new country look at things. Among my tribesmen, though honor is dear to us, people can do foolish things, as Shibata Toko did, without considering the family's honor harmed. Mostly we let such matters pass, saying that youth is a time of errors. Must you and I try to kill each other because of your sister's brief passion? Her mistake? I'm sure she was mortified enough that she has learned her lesson."

"It was not her alone! She did not rape you! And that geisha was the go-between! Chiyoko, whom you now have made your mistress! It is intolerable!" Saburo drew his sword. "You must defend yourself, or I will cut you down like a dog!"

"I will not draw my sword against you."

Saburo quivered like a plucked bowstring. "You must! Otherwise you will have no chance, for one of us will die here."

Nils's mind probed Saburo's agitation, and he answered: "You have seen the note Chiyoko sent to your sister. The one Wakaumi sent you."

The breath died in Saburo's chest as he stared. "How did you know about that?"

"I know."

What *was* this! Someone had told him: either Toko or Wakaumi. Or possibly one of those other loose-tongued girls. "It makes no difference," he said. "The act was yours, and the geisha was the go-between."

"There was another note. Have you seen it, too?"

Saburo stared.

"It was the note your sister sent Chiyoko, telling her what she was to do. She was to conceal Toko in her wardrobe, then take me to her room but not light a lantern. When she had disrobed and aroused me, Chiyoko would excuse herself and go to the wardrobe. Toko would come out pretending to be Chiyoko, and have *kogo* with me. No one was to know except Toko and Chiyoko."

Nils read the bleak pain Saburo felt at his words. And the belief. He continued. "It seems that Toko, with other young women, had secretly watched my first audience with the Emperor, and become enamored of me. Because I am a giant and have yellow hair, it seems I am attractive to some women despite my being unworthy of such feelings. And by having *kogo* in secret—even I was to think it was Chiyoko—she thought no harm would be done.

"Chiyoko had left the note folded on her dressing table. Later she could not find it. I believe that when she left Toko there, and went to the room where she and other geisha were entertaining some of us, Toko came out of the wardrobe, saw the note, and took it. Ask her for it. Then, if you still want to kill me—you must do what you must do."

Saburo took three steps backward, almost staggering, with a ragged oath sheathed his sword, and turning, left at a trot that would grow to a run. Nils waited a minute, then followed at an easy walk.

Saburo sat at the table in his room, ink block at hand. Mostly his brush moved slowly. At times it stopped. Now and then he looked at a piece of rice paper on the table close to the one he wrote on. It had been folded small; now it lay open. Toko had given it to him without argument.

All argument had gone out of her when he told her what he "knew," and what he wanted. Already the dowager empress had suspended her from duty. She'd been confined to a room in disgrace, and would remain so until their father wrote, telling what he wanted done with her. It would probably be a month before the message arrived.

Saburo knew by looking at her that she'd been weeping, and for the first time since her childhood, he'd felt sympathy for his difficult and headstrong sister.

Nor could he ignore the fact that harm need not have come of her act. Wouldn't have, had he not arrived steaming with indignation, the proprietor and his guard at his side, and thrown the door open. And even then, had he not lost his head, had he slid the door shut again as if not knowing the young woman involved . . .

Writing, he no longer ground his teeth. He knew exactly what he had to do.

TWENTY-EIGHT

Early the next afternoon, Nils was in the *dojo*, demonstrating aspects of his sword style within a half-ring of students. A shaft of autumn sunlight shone through a window, illuminating the bare brown skull of Hyogo Musashi, who sat on his high stool watching. A page ran in, slowed, and approached the old master respectfully, stopping at three meters to bow very deeply.

"Musashi-san," he said apologetically, "please excuse me for interrupting. I have come from Lord Tsuyama. He wishes to see Matsumura Nissa as soon as possible."

The old man nodded curtly without looking away from the demonstration. As soon as Nils finished the *kata*, the form he'd been demonstrating, Musashi called out. "Matsumura-san! Lord Tsuyama wishes to speak with you. The rest of you will now practice your own forms. *Your* forms, not Matsumura-san's. I will digest what he has demonstrated, before I decide how to apply the lessons they contain for us."

He clambered carefully down from his stool to exchange bows with the giant foreigner. "Thank you for your thought-provoking demonstration," he said.

"Thank you for your kindness in inviting me," Nils replied, and they bowed again. Then the Northman left with the page, out into warm sunlight and through gardens, to enter the administrative wing of the palace.

The fine sheen of perspiration hadn't yet dried on Nils's face when they reached Tsuyama's office. The page stepped into the doorway and bowed low. "Excuse me, Tsuyama-sama. Matsumura Nissa is here to see you."

He stepped back out and Nils entered, also bowing. "I have come as you directed," he said.

Lord Tsuyama beckoned. "Come nearer."

Nils approached to two meters and stopped, eyes properly averted.

"Is it true you do not read?" Tsuyama asked.

"I read the language of the Northmen. Unfortunately I have only begun to learn yours. The *kana* are very different from the homely symbols used by my people."

"Hm." Tsuyama wondered what those symbols looked like, and whether they were actually homely. Without looking at the sheets of paper in his hand, he spoke. "Shibata Saburo committed *seppuku* last night, leaving a letter for the Emperor. In it he writes that he also sent one like it to his grandfather, Lord Shibata, before taking his own life."

Nils said nothing. Lord Tsuyama continued, re-scanning the letter and summarizing. "In it he presents certain facts, as well as a note written by his sister to the geisha, Shinshiro Chiyoko. He absolves you and the geisha, and also the proprietor, of any substantive blame in the unfortunate event in The House of April Leaves. Further, he states that because of his own ill-considered impulsiveness, the major blame is his. He wishes his grandfather and father to forgive, so far as possible, the culpability of his sister, and asks them to hold no grudge against the house of Matsumura."

Tsuyama looked back up at the Northman. "Writing this letter was a remarkable act that does honor both to Saburo and the Shibata family. His Majesty is composing a message to that effect to Lord Shibata. It occurred to me that you would like to know these things. Now I must direct myself to other business." He gestured dismissal.

Nils bowed deeply this time. "Thank you, Tsuyama-sama. It was very kind of you to inform me." He bowed again, turned and left.

It was less than an hour later that Nils was interrupted again by a page, while he and Hans practiced the Yamatoan syllabary under the guidance of Sugitani Katsumi. An ability to read Yamatoan was important, for literacy was common among all classes, and the use of signs, posters, and written messages was general.

This time the page informed him that he was to meet with

the Emperor in the lesser audience room at the ninth hour—
midafternoon.[27] Nils took advantage of the wait to bathe at a
basin, and to put on clean underclothes and kimono. Again a
page came, to make certain he wouldn't be late.

During his previous audience, the Emperor had sat alone
with his guards. This time he waited with his personal aide,
Okaya Yari, a tall, well-built, and very handsome Yamatoan.
Nils knew of Okaya, had heard him mentioned; he was believed
by some to be a wizard. Okaya didn't sit next to the Emperor,
but behind him, and enough to one side that when someone
addressed His Majesty, Okaya was not in his immediate field
of vision.

Briefly the Emperor examined Nils, frankly but not rudely,
his gaze finally coming to rest on the strong face with its peculiar
eyes.

"Matsumura Nissa, you have walked through gossip and
controversy, as well as admiration, both here and in Momiji.
And all of it, I am told, with great equanimity. As perhaps you
know, you were preceded to Miyako by a long letter concerning
you, sent to me by your father, my noble servant, Lord
Matsumura. A warrior much admired not only by myself but
by my father.

"Also, the honorable Shibata Saburo, before his *seppuku*,
wrote something of you: That he followed you last night with
the intention of provoking a fight to the death. And that instead
of fighting, you spoke to him of certain things, which caused
him to rethink his position regarding the honor of himself, his
sister, and his family. That was most remarkable of you.
Throughout my reign I have tried to reduce dueling and killing,
and to increase peaceful solutions to problems of honor."

Nils bowed. "Thank you, Your Majesty. However, Saburo-
san gives me more credit than I deserve, and himself not
enough."

The Emperor gazed at him quizzically for a moment, then

---

[27] The Yamatoan system of specifying time is unlike earlier systems,
in Japan or elsewhere. Though using twenty-four equal hours, it
counts from sunrise. Thus, for example, meridional noon comes
at different hours as the season changes.

stated dryly: "I am quite aware of his exceptional honor in this, though I could wish he hadn't fallen on his sword. But now: I am interested in your people—how they live, how they are ruled. Are they all as large as you?"

"No, Your Majesty. In height they are variable, a few no taller than this".—he gestured at the height of his ribs— "others, an occasional one, as tall as myself. You have seen my companion Hans, my adopted son. He is somewhat taller than most grown men among us, but his height is not uncommon."

"Um. And how do you feed yourselves? What crops do you raise in your country?"

"My people are not great farmers, Your Majesty. Where they dwell now, they raise a little wheat, as well as root crops of several sorts. Mostly, however, they herd cattle on the broad grasslands there, and eat much meat."

"Where they *now* dwell, you say. Have they changed their land of occupancy?"

"Only four summers ago they left a land far to the north, which we still call the Homeland. In living memory, the winters there had grown longer, the summers seriously colder and shorter. Until even rye could not be depended on to mature. Finally, one spring, snow covered the ground so long that it seemed they'd need to feed hay to the horses and cattle for most of the summer. And the summers had become so cold and wet, we could no longer cure adequate quantities of it.

"So the chiefs of the clans, and of the tribes, met in council and decided to take their people and leave. And almost all the people agreed; only a relative few stayed behind."

"Indeed! And how numerous are your people?"

"Not nearly so numerous as yours. We had no towns, dwelling only here and there, the land between settled places being wilderness in which we hunted. Our warrior class numbered only some twenty-two hundred. Of course, they were a very small part of the total, rigorously selected from all boy children at puberty, from those with the greatest aptitude in spirit and body, in strength and quickness and agility. And of those, some were later pruned away by the sword masters, typically because they would not or could not take instruction well. And certain others were pruned away because of certain misbehaviors, or because they were excessively arrogant."

The emperor's elegant eyebrows rose at this. "For excessive arrogance! Interesting! And your samurai are selected, you say? It is not inheritance?"

"Except so far as warrior qualities are inherited. My own father is a smith, whose main business with swords is their forging."

"Remarkable! But mostly you have spoken in the past tense: 'Was.' 'Were.'"

"In our new land, things have been done differently. Because of many enemies, all youths have been weapons-trained. Even most grown men who were not warriors have been drilled with the sword. But when I left, the old system was being taken up again. All youths will continue to be trained, but less intensively than the sword apprentices, who will become warriors."

"Ah. Those who would take someone else's land must live by the sword. It can easily become a self-perpetuating problem. And what of the people you displaced?"

"They call themselves orcs. They had previously conquered the land and suppressed the inhabitants; killed very many of them and enslaved most of the rest—women, mostly. When we drove the conquerors out, they killed almost all their slaves, rather than see them freed. Those who were not enslaved still live in the mountains. We have told them they are free to return to the plains and till the soil, for we are more interested in herding than in farming. Our new land is mostly grassland, and we are becoming horsemen."

The Emperor's gaze was steady, his expression thoughtful. "In our first meeting," he said, "you described yourself as a chief. Tell me more about that chieftaincy."

"I did not head a tribe, or even a clan. And when I was proposed as war chief, after Björn Ärrbuk was killed in battle, I refused it, remaining the adviser of chiefs. Later, in our new land, after we'd driven out the Orcs, I was named the speaker of law, deciding disputes between tribes and clans, and assigning penalties. Subject, of course, to reversal by the council."

The Emperor's brow wrinkled thoughtfully. "How old are you?"

"I was born in the Rutting Moon. I have probably fulfilled my twenty-third year."

Twenty-three years old! Apparently strenuous and violent years, the Emperor told himself. Not impossibly young for the face he looked at, though the man gave a somewhat older impression. He changed direction then. "According to Matsumura-sama's message, you came to Yamato in a boat from Heaven."

"In a manner of speaking, Your Majesty. But that heaven is not Amida's Heaven, It is simply the sky."

"The sky? Please elaborate!"

"The people who fly the sky boat, we call Star Folk. They tell us that the stars, most of them, are like the sun, but so distant, they appear as points of light. Indeed, they say that there are many more which are so far away, we cannot see them at all. And most stars have, as associates, smaller objects circling them, invisible from here. Those smaller objects are worlds, many of them more or less like ours, this one we walk upon in life.

"The Star Folk came from one of them in a great starship. What in Momiji has been called the heaven boat, and by my people the sky boat, is a small boat carried here inside the starship, which itself has not landed on our world. People come down from it in sky boats, and I have been taken up to visit it."

The Emperor looked long at Nils then, his face carefully manifesting neither doubt nor belief. "And what are these Star Folk like?"

"Much like you and I. But they know much that we don't. It is thus they can fly between the stars. And they are peaceful, having no wars among themselves. When our enemies, the Orcs, attacked them without provocation, the Star Folk were dismayed; such behavior seemed beyond belief. But having little choice, they struck back at the Orcs, using as little force as they could, and still punished them the way the hail storm batters down grain."

"Hm-m. A peaceful world. One might envy such a people.

Do you suppose people of this world might be peaceful someday?"

"I have no doubt of it. The Star Folk are descendants of the Ancients of Earth, who had learned to fly through the heavens. Before the Great Death, they sent people to settle on the world the Star Folk would come to call New Home. Now the people there have sent the starship to see what has become of us."

"Interesting. Interesting indeed." The emperor said nothing for a bit, and Nils waited. "And you, I am told, are not only a chief, but a wizard," the emperor said at last.

"That is true, Your Majesty."

"What magics do you make?"

"I do not make magics, Your Majesty. I have the sight. I see not with these eyes, but with the spirit. And with the spirit, I also see into the souls of men."

The Emperor contemplated that answer for a long moment, then asked, "And do you find those souls distasteful? Perhaps disgusting?"

"I find them human, Your Majesty, with all that that includes. I seek a fuller appreciation of them—of them and what my old teacher, and also Jampa Lodro, called the Tao. That is why I have come to Yamato. Jampa Lodro is a seer, a very wise old man in China. He told me I might seek out another seer in Yamato, a man he considered wiser than himself. Shisho-san, he called him. Also called Ojiisan Tattobu. And the Star Folk kindly brought me here. If you could help me find Ojiisan, I would be very grateful."

The Emperor chuckled. "Ojiisan comes and goes as he pleases, reporting to no one. It is hard to know where he might be. I will notify the rector here, and have him send a message to all the great temples and monasteries of Honshu that a foreigner is here who came across the sea just to speak with him. A foreigner who has ridden in a Heaven Boat. Perhaps he will come. No one orders Ojiisan, though, not even his Emperor."

The Emperor glanced at Okaya then, his eyes inviting the aide to ask a question of his own. With a slight head shake, the man declined. The Emperor looked again at Nils Järnhann. "Thank you for talking with me, Matsumura Nissa. You have given me food for thought. Perhaps we shall speak together again."

When Nils had left, the Emperor and his handsome, well-dressed aide also left, going to a room where they could be free of bodyguards. Removing their stiff overjackets, they gave them to a valet, who left the room and did not return. Together the two men went to a wall where armor hung, and began to lace one another into it, speaking from time to time as they worked.

"What do you think of our barbarian, Yari?" the Emperor asked.

"He is much as described, much as he said. I do not think he lied in anything."

"Is he dangerous?"

"Dangerous to those who attack him, and perhaps those who attack others near to him. But he is not generally dangerous. Beyond that—there is a purity about his mind and soul that someone like myself, an empath, especially appreciates. If most men even approached him in that, I'd be less reclusive.

"Also, I have no doubt that he is a seer, as Matsumura Shinji claims. One more sensitive than I."

"And a better swordsmen than the two of us together."

"True. He is like a giant Musashi."

The Emperor laughed. "There are those who'd call that blasphemy, that no other swordsman should be mentioned in the same breath as old Hyogo."

They strapped helmets on, then went to a wall where a pair of beautifully carved practice swords hung, made of teak heartwood, polished to a deep and lustrous brown. But bruised, indented from much use. Each man took one down, and they faced each other. "Are you ready, Yari?" Hikari asked.

Okaya Yari nodded. "Yes, Your Majesty."

From their posts in the corridor, the Emperor's guards could hear the familiar clashing.

After Nils had returned from escorting Chiyoko home, Nils and Hans walked the road on which they'd entered the city. Tea shops and *sake* shops were open, as well as small establishments, their doors open to the street, where readers could be heard reading aloud from popular dramas and comedies, dramatizing with voice and face as they read. But the two Northmen weren't out to be entertained. Autumn was still early enough that evenings were comfortable, and it was pleasant to walk while conversing.

"Is Musashi-san as good with the sword as Matts Sväädkunni?" Hans asked. Sväädkunni was the chief trainer of sword apprentices back home in Varjby.

"Musashi is better in the skills of single combat, beyond a doubt, but I think not in battle skills. He hasn't particularly troubled himself with the techniques used in war—in mass combat—which differ in part from those used in dueling."

"Was Saburo as good as Musashi?"

"Saburo was quicker, but as good as he was, Musashi is more skilled than Saburo would ever have become. Skill can go beyond technique, and Saburo did not have the sort of mind which could fully comprehend that, let alone learn it. Even though he believed it. Old as Musashi was, when Saburo first came to the palace and won a tournament held here, the two contested privately before the Emperor, and Musashi won easily. But he was happy to let Saburo take over the teaching of all but the most advanced students. Saburo was very good at teaching technique, which is all most people can learn."

Hans grinned slyly, and asked: "Is Musashi better than you?"

Nils laughed: "I am much younger and quicker. But his skill is greater; I had never fully appreciated that such skill could be. He has taken me as a special student now, partly because he wants to further observe my techniques, and partly because I too have that which is beyond technique, and learn very quickly."

"And you are much stronger!"

"True. But he is much stronger than he looks, for strength springs partly from the spirit. And with sufficient skill, the importance of strength and even quickness become much less. I have little doubt that, even at his age, Musashi could have beaten Kuduka, who was as strong as any human, and almost too quick to believe. And Kuduka was as skilled—as tricky, at least—as anyone I ever fought, until Saburo."

"What about Leif Trollsverd? Was Saburo more skilled than Leif?"

"I've never fought with Leif, but I've watched him. No one I've seen is more skilled than he, except Musashi; Leif is more skilled than Saburo or Kuduka, beyond a doubt. He was *born* with skills that most warriors are never able to learn."

"And what of the Emperor? What did you think of him?"

"He is a good man, not like the other emperors I've known. Not depraved and cruel, like mad Kazi, nor sly and ruthless like Songtsan Gampo. Like every human, this Emperor has weaknesses, but his have nothing to do with cruelty or harshness."

"Tell me one of them," Hans said expectantly.

Nils looked at him and smiled. "Would you want me to tell others your weaknesses? Or things that I've seen in your mind?"

Hans blushed.

"I've seen nothing there to discredit you," Nils continued, "but even so, usually a person wishes to keep certain things to themselves."

Hans shook his head. "If you've looked very often, surely you've seen discreditable thoughts in my mind."

"Ah! But what we think of as good and bad in people is much less what thoughts pass through their minds than what they do about them. When I'm with other people and open myself to them, I am washed over by various thoughts, and also see that which lies beneath the thoughts. Unjust thoughts, ill wishes, selfishness and envy and jealousy, the desire to force another wrongfully to one's will—these sometimes afflict even the minds of people who are mostly kind and loving to others. It does not make their kindness less, nor does it lessen them."

Looking at what Nils had said, Hans nodded. He was sure it was true; it *felt* true, anyway. But still it would be interesting to know what weaknesses Nils had seen in the Emperor. They'd be more interesting because he *was* the Emperor.

TWENTY-NINE

It was late the next morning that Kamoshika Akira returned
with Matsumura Shinji's reply to Nils's message. He reported
to Nils at midday, over lunch with Sugitani Katsumi and Hans.

On arriving at Momiji Castle, Akira said, he'd reported at
once to Matsumura-sama. The old *daimyo* had read the letter
"with quick darting movements of his eyes," then had sat
motionless for a long moment, frozen-faced, as if two sides of
him were locked in conflict on the matter. Finally he'd nodded
curtly, and dismissed Akira without comment.

That evening, though, he'd invited Akira and Captain
Iwatoku to share a bath with him. There, relaxing in the
near-scalding water, he'd spoken his thoughts quite amiably.
No *daimyo* would actually rejoice at having an ex-entertainer
for a daughter-in-law, he'd said. But she was of a samurai
family, and he'd heard of the beautiful and refined Shinshiro
Chiyoko when he'd visited the palace last. Someone had
even suggested that so beautiful a geisha might well become
the concubine of some member of the imperial family; this
had happened to famous geishas before. Yes, the old *daimyo*
said, men would envy Matsumura Nissa his bride, even if
they were critical of the marriage.

Also, it was known at the palace that she was the daughter
of Shinshiro Yumi, a bona fide hero at the three-day Battle of
Gifu, where Matsumura himself had so enlarged his reputation.
Two stories were told of how Yumi had gotten his name, which
it seemed was not the one he'd been given on his Seventh
Day. He was known for both his power and accuracy with the
bow; and he was as direct as an arrow.

"She is of such quality," Matsumura had decided, "because
her father was such an excellent man. In announcing the

marriage, I will point out his identity." He'd nodded slightly, as if approving the thought. "Besides," he added, "my son is a foreigner. Allowances will be made for that."

Evidently the *daimyo* was not entirely thrilled at the prospect, but he'd approved the marriage, and was busily rationalizing, accommodating himself to it. He'd also sent along another purse of silver, to pay off the loan Nils had taken to buy out her contract. The wedding was to take place at Momiji Castle, and he'd named the date—on the day of the next full moon, which gave them twenty days.

The nearness of the date meant that the ceremony would not be large by noble standards. *Daimyo* would not be traveling considerable distances to attend. But neither was Nissa-san an elder son, so the small size of the wedding, according to Katsumi, was no sign of displeasure.

After they'd eaten, Hans asked Nils if they could speak privately. They climbed stairs to the top of the palace wall, where they leaned on the battlement and looked out across the roofs of Miyako to the waters of Omori Bay. Hans began the conversation. "Nils, I too want to marry."

"Have you talked with her about it?"

"No. I haven't had a chance. When The House of April Leaves closed, she was sent to Futori's other geisha house, The Thrush Garden, in the upper entertainment district. But— the last time we were together, the night when you and Saburo's sister . . . I told her then that I loved her, and she said she loved me."

He stopped there, less than happy. "Yes?" Nils nudged. He knew the answer, but wanted Hans to say it.

"I—don't know whether she says that to other men."

"Ah. Ask Katsumi to take you to The Thrush Garden. I'll give you some money. When you get there, tell Futori that tomorrow I will ask Lord Tsuyama again what can be done to reopen The House of April Leaves. And to allow men from the palace to attend there. I'll point out to his lordship that what happened there was no fault of Futori's. Tell him the Emperor has already praised me for preventing a feud between *daimyo* from growing out of it. Then tell him you wish to speak with Mariko. If you don't have sufficient money for entertainment, ask just to speak with her briefly.

"If he says you can't do that, thank him courteously, and say you'll be back again soon. He'll be impressed with courtesy from a samurai, in spite of himself."

He straightened. "Now it's time to go to the *dojo*. I've promised Musashi to give instructions to his advanced students." He nudged Hans with an elbow. "You need to spend more time there. I know your muse is poetry, not war, but if you're going to wear a samurai's swords, you need to be skilled with them. Someone may challenge you someday."

That evening, walking Chiyoko home, Nils told her Matsumura-sama's response to their marriage, and the date he'd set. "We should leave here in ten days, allowing three days on horseback for the trip, or more if you're not familiar with riding. Katsumi tells me you need not concern yourself with wedding clothes until we get there."

She didn't answer at once, but he felt her unhappiness, and peered beneath it. "You are unhappy because you have no dowry," he said.

She nodded. "It is shameful for me to marry without bringing a dowry into the house of my husband's family."

"Ah! It's not for a dowry that I wish to marry you, but for love."

They walked on for a time without either saying more. Then Nils spoke again. "You have told me that you truly love me."

She looked straight ahead. "And it is the truth. I had never expected to truly love a man, until I met you."

He said nothing more just then, leaving it to her to break the silence. Shortly she did. "You are unlike other men. You are gentle and kind. You undertake to set my mind at ease, and lay my fears to rest. I am not worthy to be your wife, yet I feel that we can be more happy together than any other man and woman. I will always be ashamed to have brought no dowry to your father's house, but if you truly want me as your wife, I will undertake to forget my shame."

He squeezed her hand gently. When they reached the widow's house, they sat in the living room and discussed Hans's interest in Mariko and what the possibilities were. For Mariko's father was no samurai, but the owner of a fishing boat.

Futori would not allow Hans to simply speak with Mariko, but he welcomed them as paying customers, and sent Mariko in as one of the two girls. Katsumi paid; Hans could repay him later. After a while, Hans went with her to her room, and between love making, they discussed marriage. Her contract had helped her father buy his boat, and she could not leave for two more years unless it was bought out. When she told Hans how much it would cost, he was dismayed. How could people be bought and sold like that? He told her perhaps he'd kill Futori.

"Oh no!" she said. "Futori-san paid my father in good faith! It would be dishonest not to honor the contract, and even worse to bring Futori harm. And anyway, at his death, his contracts would no doubt become the property of his wife, who likes none of us geisha. She says we are spoiled. She might send us all to the brothel!"

"Not you! I'd take you away with me!"

"Please do not talk like that, beloved Hans! I would have to kill myself for shame!"

He stared at her in the lantern light. She began to nibble on his neck then, his shoulder, his chest, while her small fingers ran gently across his skin. He sighed a ragged breath. He'd just have to find a way to buy her contract from Futori.

THIRTY

Katsumi had told the two Northmen that most samurai would strongly disapprove of their son marrying a fisherman's daughter, but that it wasn't illegal, and such things were not unheard of. In fact, a very popular play told the supposedly true story of a *daimyo's* son who fell in love with and married a woodcutter's daughter. Katsumi didn't mention the play's tragic ending. In this context, the point was that they'd married, and that playgoers sympathized, considering the story beautiful, if sad.

Of course, Nils had no objection at all to Hans marrying Mariko. The question, Katsumi said, was what Lord Matsumura would think.

There would hardly be a problem with Mariko's parents. Before he left with Nils for Momiji Castle, Hans had gone home with Mariko on a local festival day, and met them. They were awed by this very tall, very young samurai with red hair and round, gray-blue eyes. Also they were impressed with Hans's manners—the general belief was that foreigners were all barbarians who didn't know how to act—and even more impressed that he was Lord Matsumura's grandson. When the subject of Mariko's contract was brought up, the parents excused themselves and went to the kitchen to talk privately. The upshot was that they would contribute to the buy-out of their daughter's contract, for as owner of his own boat, her father was beginning to know prosperity.

Nils began formally to work in the *dojo* with Hyogo Musashi, teaching single-hand techniques with the longsword, with and without a shortsword in the other hand. This duty provided a modest stipend, enough to help buy out Mariko's contract. Meanwhile, Nils had convinced Lord Tsuyama to allow the probationary reopening of The House of April Leaves. On condition that Futori discount the unearned value of Mariko's contract by sixty percent.

Two days later, Nils and Chiyoko, Hans, Akira and Katsumi, rode together out of the city, westward toward Momiji Castle.

Matsumura received Nils and Chiyoko in his large, simply-appointed living room, and in minutes she'd charmed the burly *daimyo* with her beauty, her perfect manners, her conversation. His eldest son arrived with his wife two days in advance of the ceremony. At first the wife showed some jealousy of Chiyoko's beauty, and disapproval of her background, but by the day of the ceremony was able to talk pleasantly enough with her soon-to-be sister-in-law.

Chiyoko's brother-in-law to be, Matsumura Harujo, was polite and even friendly, while Matsumura Shinji was perfectly affable.

The ceremony was led by the rector of Momiji Temple, the same rector that once had planned to have the bridegroom executed by strangling. He did his best now to avoid meeting those blank glass eyes.

When it was over, the principals and guests went to the banquet hall, where servants had set out food and drink. There were musicians and dancing, the steps unfamiliar to Nils and Hans. As bowls were emptied and refilled, the guests became freer and freer, in step and tongue. Matsumura came over to the couple and whispered in Nils's ear. The groom and bride drifted back to a wall, and along it. When they were near the door, Matsumura drew the party's attention with a tribute to the musicians. The couple slipped out then, hurried down the hall and up a guarded stairway. They'd been abstinent since that night in The House of April Leaves. Now they need abstain no further.

THIRTY-ONE

After more than a month in the bandit camp, Ted Baver looked worse than wretched. His beard was a wiry mat, his hair a filthy tangle, and even with the food Emiko smuggled to him in the evenings, he was gaunt from chronic hunger. But at least the bandits hadn't been punching and kicking him lately, and his ribs were pretty much healed.

His biggest concerns were two. The most pressing was shelter, for high in the mountains, autumn was advancing, and he wasn't allowed to sleep in either longhouse or tack shed. The other, and actually most serious was, what would be done with him when the bandits broke camp for winter, for this was not a winter camp. They'd put up no hay for their horses, nor any large stock of firewood. Presumably they'd soon disperse to their home villages and towns. And when they didn't need a camp flunky anymore, it seemed to him they'd probably kill him.

He'd given thought to both concerns. One of his main chores was to cut firewood with a short-handled ax—fell deadwood and drag it to the longhouses, then chop it into suitable lengths. While he'd worked, the first days, he'd also cut stout green saplings and leaned them against a very large, windfallen tree trunk for rafters, weaving in slimmer saplings to form a lattice. He'd also stripped the dried bark from old rotting snags, for roofing, weighting them in place with additional stout saplings.

He didn't delude himself that it wouldn't leak, but since the typhoon, there'd been only one brief shower. What it did do was reduce radiation cooling at night. And to insulate himself from the ground, he'd pulled up dead bracken around the fringe of the meadow, stuffing it into his crude lean-to as a bed. Also, Emiko had brought him a ragged quilt to cover

228

himself with. He'd grown used to sleeping cold, waking from it in the night, then shivering himself back into a semi-sleep filled with mostly unpleasant dreams.

Hunger was his constant companion. One of the bandits, not a *ronin*, had been told off to feed him each evening, his one official daily meal: boiled barley and *miso*. Sometimes bits of meat had been boiled with the barley. It was brought to him in a wooden bowl, and in the morning he'd take the empty bowl back to the longhouse.

The main problem with that arrangement was that often the man didn't bring it. The bandits had casks of captured *sake* in the longhouses, and he could hear them laughing more or less drunkenly at night. Presumably on the nights he wasn't fed, the man was drunk, and either forgot or didn't give a damn. Whichever, his meal was skipped nearly as often as not. What kept Ted functioning was food brought to him almost daily by Emiko—usually barley cakes and pickled radish. She did this at dusk; she'd told him she was afraid to come out later, when the bandits were getting drunk. Sometimes the two of them talked briefly. She was, she told him, the daughter of a *daimyo*, Lord Iwato, in Tochigi State.

As autumn progressed and cooled, his thoughts went more and more to getting away before the bandits broke camp and killed him. And so far as he could see, he had but one resource: Emiko. One evening when she brought his barley cakes, he asked her help. "Can you bring me a shortsword tomorrow night?" he murmured.

Her eyes stared, unreadable in the twilight. "I have no shortsword," she said.

"Steal one. Late at night. Sooner or later they'll all be asleep. You can steal one then."

"I'm afraid to leave the storeroom when they're drunk. They might—do something to me."

"Do they let the fire burn down at night?"

She nodded.

"They won't see you. If they do see someone moving around in the dark, they'll think it's one of them. When you go back in, this evening, look around. See where there are swords, and decide which one you'll take."

Emiko thought for a minute. "What will you do with a sword? If you commit *seppuku*, that will be the end for you."

"I'm not going to commit *seppuku*. I'm going to escape. You know the one they call Kuso, that brings me food sometimes. He has the key to my leg irons. He was drunk when he fed me last night, and showed it to me. He laughed and told me he was going to drop it in the latrine; that I'd have to jump in and get it, or wear these irons forever. Then he laughed again and said that for me, forever won't be very long. That winter will come soon, and I'll die.

"Usually he comes out late. If I have a shortsword then, I'll kill him, use the key to take my leg irons off, and run away."

"They will catch you, bring you back and kill you most unpleasantly."

"They'll kill me soon anyway. There's only one raiding party out now. When it comes back, they'll break camp and go home. That's when they'll kill me, unless I escape first.

"And they won't miss him when he doesn't come back. The ones that aren't asleep are usually at least half drunk by then; at least he is. And the moon will come up not long after it gets dark. I'll follow the trail by moonlight, then leave it and travel through the woods when daylight comes.

"And if you could steal a bow and arrows, too, put them in the weeds by the near corner of the longhouse, I'll have at least a chance to kill some food. I'm not as poor an archer as I pretended."

She didn't answer for a long moment. Then: "Take me with you," she said.

Now it was his turn to stare and hers to beseech. "Emiko," he said, "it wouldn't work. We . . ."

"Please! My father will never pay ransom for me, or do anything else they wanted. It would compromise his honor. And when he refuses, they will be angry with him. I'm terrified at what they might do to me then. These bandits are not honorable."

In planning, he'd considered various possibilities, and had settled on one that required the least from Emiko, for her cooperation was the necessary element in everything he'd thought of. Her request put him in a position to ask for more difficult help. "I had a weapon," he said. "My wizard weapon. Do you know where it is?"

"It lies on the table in Kashira's room. I have seen it; he has no door in his doorway. But I heard him say its magic has been used up."

Ted grinned through broken teeth, and patted the zipperless side pocket that held two spare magazines. "I lied to him. I know how to give it life. If you can get it for me, instead of the bow, we'll run away together." His mind raced. "Bring me a shortsword late tonight, after the men are asleep. I'll hide it in my bedding. Then, when Kuso comes to feed me tomorrow night, I'll kill him with it. Or the next night, if he doesn't feed me tomorrow. Then I'll make a noise outside the storeroom, so you'll know it's time. You can sneak into Kashira's room and get my *teppo*, my wizard weapon."

She agreed. Fearfully, but she agreed. There were gaps in the chinking between the storeroom's log walls. She'd put a stick through one of them, sticking out. He could move it around, rattle it, and she'd know it was time. Then he'd return to his shelter, and she'd bring the pistol to him there.

Two brothers, Iboji and K'waiken, lay still awake in the longhouse, watching the dying embers in the fire pit and talking in murmurs. There was no chimney. The smoke spread, most of it finding its slow way out the vent holes beneath each end of the roof pole. The brothers had been a bit manic with drink, but were sagging now, their smoke-irritated eyes half shut.

Snores arose here and there, mostly not distinctive. Kashira's, however, were easily recognizable, even from his separate room: strong, jerky, and spastic, a bit like a boar driving sows. It was K'waiken who first saw the woman standing in the storeroom doorway. He hissed a low hiss, and gestured toward her with his head. Iboji turned over to look. She scanned the room, failed to see them awake, and stepped furtively into the common room, then entered Kashira's. K'waiken's chuckle was like small grunts back in his throat. The brothers grinned at each other.

"I wonder what he promised her?" Iboji whispered.

"Who knows? Maybe she's just man-crazy. I'll bet they've done this before, and we didn't know."

"Ah! Maybe we should tell her we're available."

More breathy chuckles. A long minute later, Kashira's snoring stopped. K'waiken snickered. "I wonder what she does to waken him? Maybe we should go and watch through the door."

"If he saw us, he'd kill us."

"Do you suppose she's good?"

"Good enough. Kashira said her father is a *daimyo*. He no doubt hired a good teacher for her."

"I'd like to be her teacher. Maybe he does *nanshoku* with her, so she will still have her maidenhead when she goes back to her father."

Iboji grunted and let his eyes close. "I don't want to think about it. Not when we don't get any. I'm going to sleep."

K'waiken closed his eyes, too. Not to sleep, he thought, but to ease them. He imagined himself slipping into the storeroom and grabbing her when she came back in. Then the drift of thought took a course of its own and became dream.

Emiko shook like a leaf. She laid Kashira's bloody short sword on the sleeping pad beside him, and stood up. She'd been terrified that he might waken. That danger was over now, but she shook anyway, and hugged herself in an effort to stop. Blood had sprayed on her; she'd felt it. It would be impossible now to deny she'd killed him.

She dared not leave yet. Someone might be awake out there, might have seen her come in. Let them think she was having *kogo* with their chief. Her eyes were used to the dark, and some light still was being given off by the dying fire in the longhouse. She could see the wizard weapon still on the crude table built against a wall. She'd leave it there for now, otherwise she might be seen through the doorway, which had no door in it. If someone *had* seen her come in, she'd give them time to go to sleep.

When she left, she wore a pair of Kashira's breeches and a shirt beneath her kimono. *If anyone sees*, she told herself, *they will think I'm going out to the latrine.*

❀   ❀   ❀

After meeting Ted at his shelter, Emiko took off the bloody kimono and stuffed it beneath his bedding. He thought they should keep it—it could provide a little extra warmth—but she couldn't bear to wear it any longer.

They skirted the meadow, to take advantage of the moonlight in the opening, while staying in the shadows of the forest's edge, for there were guards watching the horses. At the lower end of the meadow, he found the well-worn trail he'd been brought there on. They followed it downhill, going as fast as they could, which wasn't fast, because very little moonlight found its way through the evergreens. Shortly they came to a mountain brook, and left the path to follow it, not downstream toward the valley, which was predictable, but upstream. They found the head of the brook in a small wet meadow, where they stopped in the moonlight and shared barley cakes she'd brought inside her shirt. Kashira's shirt.

Then they pushed on, uphill now to the ridgecrest, where they stopped. Some of the climbing had been steep. Emiko was trembling with exhaustion, while Ted was weak from malnutrition. The best shelter they could find was a huge old fallen tree. They lay down close to it, arms about each other for warmth; there wasn't much.

Ted felt hopeful nonetheless. He didn't believe their trail would be found. By daylight, Nils could have tracked them, he thought, and probably Achikh or Hans, but the bandits weren't barbarians in the same sense as the Northmen and the Buriat were. It seemed to him unlikely they'd be recaptured, as long as they stayed away from the road the first two or three days. The trick would be to find their way to civilization without starving or playing out. Preferably to the Kanto Plain, which it seemed to him must be off to the southeast somewhere. The most critical factor was the weather: if it held fair, they had a decent chance.

Inwardly, grimly, he chuckled. *And you're the guy that was scared spitless, a year and a half ago, afraid of getting separated from Nils and Hans. Afraid if they got out of your sight, you'd be lost and die.*

THIRTY-TWO

The cargo ship *Hokushin* had not tied up at Osaka itself, which was a largely military and administrative town sharing an island with the Black Castle. Rather, like most shipping, it had docked at Isomachi, the commercial town on the adjacent river shore, and the second largest in Yamato.

Achikh was grateful to be ashore. Not that sea-sickness had been a problem; the weather had been congenial all the way from Miyako, and his stomach hadn't been seriously tested. What had troubled him was the confinement. The ship resembled somewhat a Chinese junk, perhaps twenty-five meters long, with a high poop and forecastle and a single sail.

Hidaka Satoru was glad to be ashore for a different reason: Osaka was his city of destiny, he had no doubt. Just being there raised his native optimism to a new high.

His plan was bold beyond the limits of arrogance, but he felt no anxiety over it, nor any urgency. While sailing, he'd played with various possible scenarios for dealing with Arakawa or his agent. His favorite was forthright: He would explain that he'd been with Kashira, then had left. That he'd learned of the conspiracy by his wizardry, and decided he could contribute much more to it as a wizard than as a bandit.

He'd concluded, however, that that was a bit reckless, even for him, and had decided simply to react to the situation as he found it. He'd lived his whole life like that, after all, and it seemed to him that things had gone quite well.

Appearances were important, so once ashore, they went first to a public bath, where they scrubbed, then luxuriated in a hot tub. Next they left their swords with a sword-polisher, from whom they rented a pair to carry while theirs were being reconditioned. Only after that did they take a room at an inn, eat a proper meal, and arrange laundering for their filthy travel clothes. That evening they visited a brothel.

They drank little, however. Satoru wanted to be clearheaded when they crossed the bridge to Osaka.

The next morning they had their hair tonsured in the samurai style, telling the barber it had grown out on a long sea voyage. The barber doubted the claim but said nothing, for samurai or not, their money was good. Besides, they looked dangerous. With their hair in the samurai style, Satoru then spent almost all their remaining money on a pair of longswords to go with their rented shortswords, and silk sashes to hold their scabbarded weapons.

Finally he was ready, and they crossed to Osaka itself on a stone bridge with a timber draw-span.

A guard stopped them at the castle's great gate, and asked their names and business. For the first time in his life, Satoru experienced nervous stomach, appreciating suddenly how brazen his plan was, brazen and dangerous. But he didn't show it. "I am Hidaka Satoru," he said, "a wizard of exceptional power, who wishes to serve Lord Arakawa Hideo. This is Buryatu Achika, my retainer. I would like an appointment with someone in authority, who will be able to evaluate my ability."

The gate guard was all business, a samurai well suited to his position, his hard face looking neither impressed nor scornful. He barked an order to a runner, who left at a trot. He was not without an opinion, however: This so-called wizard, who was clearly no noble, had presented himself boastfully and without proper courtesy. Five to one that Sugimori-sama would have the arrogant bastard thrown out.

Satoru read his thoughts. *I must present myself more nobly*, he told himself, *and at the same time more humbly. These are very highly placed persons I'll be dealing with. There'll be time enough later to speak plainly.*

The gate guard had them stand out of the way while they waited, a wait of more than half an hour. Finally two guards arrived, who escorted them through the gate and courtyard into a tall, pagoda-like building with black roofs. In the entrance hall, business-like guards took their swords and knives, giving chits for each of them, then their escorts led them on. They followed a splendid hallway, climbed two flights of stairs, and at length were seated on a bench in a guarded room. Satoru fine-tuned his senses, and reached. Beyond a guarded door, he found an interrogation taking place. The official—Lord Arakawa's marshal, no less!—was questioning a captain of the guard, who described for him a case of attempted bribery. These were, it seemed, people who took the law seriously, at least when it affected them.

In a few minutes the interrogation was over. The guard captain strode out, hard-faced and straight-backed, and left. The sergeant in charge of the waiting room looked at Satoru. "Please stand up!" he ordered. "Lord Sugimori will soon call for you!"

They stood. And waited on their feet for several long minutes, Satoru eavesdropping again on the minds in the marshal's office, sorting among them. Two were guards, their thoughts of no consequence. The others were the marshal and an adviser, now discussing appropriate punishment for the would-be briber. And—*the adviser was either an empath or telepath, it wasn't clear which!* This was something Satoru hadn't foreseen, and his guts knotted. The adviser would look on him as a rival! And if he was a telepath, the man could read his thoughts. He'd have to screen them as his grandfather had taught him, and hope for the best. Satoru took several breaths, rather as one did to begin meditation, but without blocking a nostril with a thumb. It eased his tension markedly.

Finally another guard appeared in the door. "Please enter!" he ordered.

They stepped in, Achikh following Satoru's lead, bowing when he bowed, and as deeply. "Your names!" the marshal demanded. The *kami-shima* he wore emphasized his authority and power; a word from this man could lose them their heads.

"I am Hidaka Satoru. This is my retainer, Buryatu Achika."

"You claim to be a wizard!"

"Excuse me, your lordship, if I seem to be boasting, but it is true that I have wizard skills which might be of value to the *takai daimyo* and yourself."

"Where are you from?" The marshal's voice was milder now, but his mind was like the eyes of a snake, intent. He'd have to lie carefully, Satoru decided, and hope the adviser was not a jealous man.

"From Hokkaido, your lordship."

"I take it your retainer is from Hokkaido also?"

"Excuse me, your lordship, but my retainer is a foreigner."

"Indeed. He looks the part. Only samurai are permitted to wear two swords. How did this foreigner become a samurai?"

"He was appointed one by my father."

"Ah! Then you are the son of a *daimyo*?"

"Indeed yes, your lordship. My father is Hidaka Eiji," he answered. Surely in southern Honshu, the officials wouldn't know the noble houses of distant Hokkaido.

"Excuse me, Sugimori-sama," the adviser interrupted. "May I question this noble wizard?"

"Please do."

Satoru's telepathic focus had been entirely on Sugimori. Now he turned it to the adviser—and went cold with fear. The man had screened his thoughts, but one could not screen feelings. And the adviser's feeling toward him was malignant. "What form does your wizardry take?" the man asked in a tone of simple interest.

Satoru told himself he should have gone to Miyako and become a spy for wealthy merchants, as he'd planned back on Hokkaido. "I read the thoughts of others," he said, his voice suddenly hoarse.

"Read mine then!"

Satoru knew that whatever he said, this man would discredit him. There would be punishment.

"We are waiting."

"I, I . . . There is nothing."

The adviser nodded to the marshal. "He is a fraud, Sugimori-sama. He is trying to cheat Lord Arakawa through you. His powers, if any, are slight, and he lied when he said he is the son of a *daimyo*. He is not even a samurai!"

The marshal didn't waste a moment. *"Guards arrest them!"* he barked.

Satoru didn't struggle, and following his lead, Achikh didn't either. "Take them to the dungeon. Have them stripped and flogged, then chain them in a cell. I will have them questioned later, to make sure they are not part of some plan against us. Who knows who may have sent them."

Achikh discovered then what Nils and Hans had learned in Momiji-joka: Yamatoan police, or in this case guards, are skilled with rope. In the antechamber, their wrists were quickly tied, then they were manhandled into the corridor, and walked—in part dragged—to the dungeon.

There their shirts were removed, and they were raised by ropes till only the balls of their feet rested on the stone floor. Then each was flogged with a thick, somewhat stiff strap, thirty strokes each. Achikh made no sound other than grunts, but after the first dozen or so, Satoru couldn't hold back his cries. When the flogging was over, an assistant jailer threw a bucket of salt water on each back, drawing another cry from Satoru. Then they were let down and dragged by the feet to a cell, their bloody backs scraping over the rough stone floor. Ankle irons were bolted on, and they were left without water or food.

Even now, Satoru's optimism reasserted itself in the reduced form of hope: perhaps there would be no further punishment. He'd answer everything truthfully, and leave his mind wide open during the interrogation. The adviser would see that he was not part of any conspiracy, and have them released. Yes, that was it. There'd be no further punishment.

The next day, after questioning the prisoners, the adviser reported to the marshal. "Excuse me, my lord, but I have questioned the criminal who claimed to be a wizard and a *daimyo*'s son."

"Ah! And what did you learn?"

"His name actually is Satoru, and he is from the Hidaka District. He is no samurai though, let alone a *daimyo*'s son; his father is a farmer. It is the grandfather who was the bad influence—a village shaman and seller of herbs, who taught him some illusions as a boy. Also, it seems he actually can read emotions somewhat as I do. What he lacks is honor. And the skill in questioning, and in reading eyes and face, that permit me to determine answers from the resulting emotions."

"Ah. And is there a conspiracy?"

"No. He came here on his own volition. He is simply a criminal with great ambition and no respect for his betters."

"And the foreigner? What is his name again?"

"Buryata Achiku. He is retarded. He does not think for himself, can only do what his master tells him. At least the foreigner is honorable. He is like a dog—unintelligent but loyal."

"Umm. What do you suggest be done with them?"

"I suggest we brand this Hidaka's forehead with the *kanji* for criminal,[28] put out his eyes, and free him. Let his dog go with him, undamaged. Perhaps the foreigner will keep him alive long enough to contemplate the wages of villainy.

Achikh had been interrogated first, and when they'd brought him back to the cell, he'd seemed undamaged. This had relieved Satoru, who assumed he'd fare no worse. He was wrong. When his answers were not as expected, a fingernail was torn off, and his shriek reached every part of the dungeon. Within a few minutes he lost two more the same way. Finally a stone from the fire was laid on his right palm, and with another shriek he passed out. When he awakened, he was back in his cell, in shock.

The next day, when he was taken from his cell again, Satoru was in a far more pitiable state than he'd been after the flogging. Fear had shut down his psionic powers entirely, and his reasoning power wasn't much better off. Two guards strapped him into a chair. When he saw the cherry-red branding iron, he began pleading, then shrieked when the grinning jailer pressed it to his forehead. The man revived him, then showed him the small knife and told him what he was going to do with it.

Satoru came apart utterly. *"Oh please!"* he cried. *"In the name of Blessed Amida, please do not blind me! I will never again trouble their lordships! I promise they will never see me again!"*

---

[28] Yamatoan is written very largely with phonetic symbols. However, symbols called *kanji* still are used for convenience, dating from pre-technological time. A *kanji* represents an entire concept, in this case the concept of criminal.

The jailer laughed. "Excuse me, but you are mistaken. It is you who will never see again." He shook his head mockingly. "Too bad I have no choice. I am only a poor jailer, unclean, a non-human." His own eyes gleamed in the lantern light. "Consider yourself blessed that you need no longer see the cruelties in this world." An assistant gripped Satoru by the hair then, holding his rocking head still.

"I am merely an instrument," he added chuckling. "Merely an instrument. Think of my hand as Sugimori-sama's, for it was Lord Sugimori Michio himself who ordered me to do this."

Those were the last words Satoru heard before the knife moved forward and he passed out.

THIRTY-THREE

Nils and Chiyoko stayed at Momiji Castle for only three days after their wedding. Then, with Hans, they returned to Miyako, and Nils's position as an instructor in the imperial *dojo*. Leaving Akira behind; a position was available for him now in Lord Matsumura's household guard, and the *daimyo* considered that Nils no longer needed Akira to help him through Yamatoan etiquette.

Chiyoko quickly found a job as a salesgirl for Miyako's largest cloth merchant.

With Katsumi's guidance, Nils had already rented a small house in the neighborhood of the palace, a neighborhood occupied very largely by palace staff. Hans, on the other hand, had no job and no income. He could live with Nils and Chiyoko, sleeping in their living room, but when he married Mariko, such accommodations would not be satisfactory, if for no other reason than no place to put things.

So Hans was interested in getting a job. Katsumi, serving as go-between, looked into possibilities. Hans had continued to grow, particularly in weight. He stood 189 centimeters tall now, and weighed 80 kilos, bone and sinew. His frame seemed hostile to fat, and he'd been training semi-regularly at the *dojo*, prior to their trip. Thus it seemed to Lord Tsuyama that he'd make an impressive doorguard for the Emperor.

Hans, on the other hand, couldn't imagine himself standing in one place for hours at a time. He was afraid, he told Nils, that he'd die of boredom and inactivity. So he was hired as a courier, instead, mostly outside the palace. His long, lean legs seemed ideal for carrying messages and occasional packages to and from the mercantile district, two kilometers away, while his size and swords would give serious pause to would-be robbers.

And with the modest wage it paid, he could marry Mariko. They set a date, and between her parents and Nils, and her own savings, she bought out her contract from Futori and moved in with Nils, Chiyoko, and Hans until they could rent a house of their own.

Six days later they were married. Three days after that, on the day of rest, they moved into a house less than half a kilometer away. Nils rented a large, two-wheeled pushcart, and he and Hans moved the newlyweds' possessions in two trips. When they'd taken all of it into the house or onto the small porch, the two young women began to arrange things. There was not a lot of it—in an ordinary Yamatoan household there never would be—but it was necessary that it be arranged just so. So the two husbands left, hiking to the riverbank, where they sat down on the ground and watched the water flow slowly past.

For two or three minutes, neither spoke. Then Hans turned to his friend. "Nils, why is life here so—complicated?"

"What do you mean?"

"You know."

"I do?"

"You can read my mind."

"If I wanted to. Suppose you tell me."

"At home, people are not hired out as slaves, then have to pay to get free. And if you want to have a house, you get some friends and you build one."

"Ah, but this is a town, in a different country, with a different people."

Hans's expression remained glum. "I wish we were traveling across the world again," he said, "as we did last year, camping at a different place each night. If we wanted to eat, we shot a marmot and built a fire, drank some mare's milk . . ."

"What of Mariko and Chiyoko?"

"They would be with us, of course."

Nils didn't answer. After another minute, Hans spoke again. "They wouldn't like it very much."

"Probably not. Certainly not at first."

More silence, longer this time. "I don't know if I'll be able to leave Mariko when the time comes to go back."

"Perhaps you'll decide not to. Perhaps you'll stay here. You may be a father by then, and at any rate you'll be used to the differences."

"Will you stay too?"

"I won't worry about it now. When the time comes, the decision will be clear enough."

Hans didn't answer that at all. Perhaps it would be clear for Nils. But for him . . . He decided to write down the verses he'd composed for the Järnhann Saga. Then, if he wanted to stay in Yamato, perhaps Nils would take them back with him.

THIRTY-FOUR

From—"*Sketches of Some Post-Plague Terran Religious Figures: Ojiisan Tattobu*," by Joao Tusi. Pages 357-383, in *Modern Perspectives on the Psyche and the Mind*, Viljo Tabayoyon, ed.

Ojiisan was born at Horuoka Tochigi, and as an infant was named Jobu because of his size and behavior. In modern Yamatoan, *jobu* means strong and vigorous, but also carries an implication of boisterous. This child-name carried over into early adulthood, because of his size and his notably free and uninhibited behavior. In the (Amidic) Buddhist school of his village, he is said to have been caned repeatedly by his teacher for rowdiness and irreverence. Nonetheless, Buddhists in Yamato generally believe that he had previously completed the life-times, and the accompanying life lessons, necessary for blissful reunion with the Tao. And that he had reincarnated again to help advanced souls clarify for themselves the nature of man relative to the Tao.

From childhood, he is said to have worked with his father, a wood-cutter and sometime stone-cutter. The heavy labor, no doubt in conjunction with decent nutrition and a suitable genotype, resulted in a relatively large and very strong body. Tales are told of his youthful prowess in contests of strength, particularly hand strength. His hands are said to have been exceptionally large.

At that time—Junichi was not yet Emperor—militias still were legal on Honshu and the southern islands. And beginning at age 15, Jobu was required to train weekly in his local company, with the *naginata* and bow—the standard militia weapons.

(Formal training with the sword had already been legally restricted to the samurai class, though others could be licensed to carry a short sword, and legally be familiarized with its use through brief training by the local magistrate's office.) At age 17, however, Jobu was accepted as a student by the Zen monastery at Warabiyama, in Tochigi State. The abbot there was a famous master, Oyomei, best known for his somewhat controversial views. There too, Jobu earned a reputation for his unrestrained spirit, but seems to have had the favor of Oyomei.

After three years, however, the abbot sent him away, commenting, "I can no longer guide him." Some, it is said, took this to mean that Jobu was too willful to learn, while others considered that he'd outgrown the monastery, and could best learn on the stage of the world, as Oyomei himself had done three decades earlier.

For the next three years, according to Ojiisan's own account, he lived in the wilderness during the warm half of the year, alternately roaming, and living in rude shelters. He communed with the peaks and clouds, the moon and the "River of Heaven" (the Milky Way), and as best he could, with the Tao. His ex-brothers at the monastery might have blanched at how he fed himself during that interval, with his bow, or by setting snares like some disreputable mountain outlaw, killing animals like a common butcher, and sometimes even eating them without benefit of fire. (The butcher's trade is looked down on as unclean.)

With the approach of cold weather, however, he served as hired man at the inn on Tsuga Pass, at that time owned and operated by four ex-nuns who'd been ejected from their temple for prostitution. At the inn, they served not only the usual food and *sake*, but sexual favors to travelers they liked and who could afford it. Jobu's duties consisted of general repairs, cutting and dragging up fuelwood, manhandling barrels and baskets, waiting on customers, and occasionally enforcing order. (And providing his female employers with male company on occasion? In winter, the road could be impassable for weeks at a time.)

Large and rough though he seemed, it is said that guests frequently felt impelled to talk to him. It is claimed that he always listened without censure or unasked-for advice, nodding as appropriate, and no doubt responding vocally on occasion. He heard and absorbed their tales, and the stories of their fathers, neighbors, and communities.

And seemingly garnering wisdom therefrom. For afterward, lying on his pallet in the storeroom, or beside some fallen tree on the mountainside, he would contemplate what he'd heard and seen and experienced. And observe, as he said, the feelings, emotions, and thoughts that such rememberings generated in his mind, tracing them to the events and beliefs from which they arose. Sifting those beliefs, and discarding those he considered unsuited to his goals. Which were, at different levels, total humanity; total admiration for all persons; and a sense of the Tao.

After three such years, he went on to the capital, where he spent an autumn at the market square, speaking to passersby from a small wooden stand he carried on his back. As tall as he was, commonly the tallest person present, even in a crowd, this stool made him easy to see. His high-pitched, resonant voice made him equally easy to hear, and the things he said sometimes stopped people in their tracks. His begging bowl invariably received enough copper *zeni* to keep him fed. And although the public clergy did not approve of him, or of all that he said, the rector at a local temple allowed him to sleep in the shed where the gardening tools were kept, even providing him a pallet and quilts.

But before the first serious snowstorm, Jobu moved out of the toolshed. An officer in the employ of the *daimyo* in a neighboring district had listened to his preaching in the market on two or three occasions, and suggested to his lord that the unconventional monk might prove worth keeping at the castle for a while. His messages were interesting.

He stayed there for two winters and a summer, and whenever a traveling monk asked for lodging, he'd be invited by the *daimyo* to hold private or public discourse with Jobu at the castle. Such monks tended to leave thoughtful, and he rapidly developed a reputation as a wise man. He also taught the *daimyo* and some of his retainers. But after a year and a half of this, he left, saying only that his own growth must be continued elsewhere.

Perhaps it was simply a matter of getting away. He's been quoted as saying that people tended to make too much of him, that he was simply a human being with certain characteristics of thought. Perhaps he got tired of what he considered excessive admiration. At any rate, after that year and a half, he seldom stayed longer than a single winter at a time at any one place.

It may have been during the subsequent few years that he developed his psionic powers. There is no evidence that he had developed or discovered them prior to that. But on the other hand, though various dubious powers were later ascribed to him—for example, an ability to walk for days without food or water, to speak with birds and animals, and to walk dry through rain storms—there seems to have been no special awareness of his ability to read minds . . ..

THIRTY-FIVE

At midday, between the morning students and those of the afternoon, Nils had a free hour in which to rest. At that time he would visit a cart allowed inside the gate, from which was sold bean curds, pickled giant radish, and barley noodles with beef. He would buy and eat two bowls of noodles, then take a short nap. Hyogo Musashi had questioned his eating so much at midday—he himself ate only in the morning and evening, and then sparingly—but Nils said it was the way of his people to do so. "There are times of want, when we have little. It was that way for Hans and me, traveling across the world. But in times of plenty, we do not stint ourselves."

The old master didn't mention it again. This youth was already a master, and besides, there was that about him . . .

One drizzly autumn noon, when Musashi whirled his rachet to signal the end of morning class, a boy from the temple came in with a message to Nils from the rector: Ojiisan Tattobu had arrived. He planned to spend only a few days, resting after the slow, weeks-long walk from Komoru-san.

"Thank you for bringing me good news," Nils said. "Will you take me to him?"

The boy nodded soberly. He was overawed by this giant with the yellow hair and blank eyes.

"Good. Let's go."

The small palace temple had a modest apartment for its rector and his assistant, and two rooms for guests. It was to the rector's quarters that the boy took Nils. In it he found the rector and a considerably taller figure, still straight but with the large frame gaunt, the strong-boned face well lined, the once muscular neck like a turkey's. His monk's tonsure had grown out somewhat, as if readying his head for winter, and

248

scattered black hairs persisted among the white. Ojiisan was looking expectantly at the door when Nils entered, as if he'd heard his straw shoes, or perceived his approach by subtler means.

Nils paused and bowed; the old man laughed, a strong laugh. "So you have been looking for me," he said.

"I have. A friend of mine, named Jampa Lodro, said I would find you most interesting."

"Jampa Lodro! No doubt you found him interesting, too." The old man paused, then grinned. "And he you."

"He found me unusual."

The rector peered quizzically from one to the other, not really surprised at their manner of speaking to each other, like friends of long standing. Again Ojiisan laughed, then turned to the rector. "Excuse me," he said, "but I wish to commune with this large young man silently, and perhaps at length. Not as a discourtesy to you—you and I will no doubt chat again this evening—but because he and I can come to know each other more thoroughly and deeply if we dispense with speech. We will now go to the room you so kindly made available to me."

The rector bowed. "Of course, Shisho-san. It is entirely understandable that two such as yourselves would wish privacy. I will consider it a privilege to speak with you later, should it be convenient to you."

He bowed them from the apartment, and in the hallway, Ojiisan spoke to Nils through the mind, grinning. <<Now you see why I prefer staying at Zen monasteries. It can be pleasant with people who look at me as just another old man, and not as some superior species.>> He led the Northman to his guest room, where they sat on facing straw mats on the floor for most of an hour, coming to know each other in a sense that few others could. Finally, also silently, they made certain arrangements. Then Nils returned to the *dojo* without having had his usual lunch.

Chiyoko was already at home when Nils arrived at day's end, and came from the kitchen to embrace him. After kissing, he sat, folding his legs into a lotus. "Ojiisan arrived today," he said. "He will rest a few days and then leave, to stay with the priests on Osoroshii-yama. He will live in a small guest house near the temple, perhaps remaining the rest of his life. He's invited me to spend the winter with him there, or whatever part of it I wish."

"And you wish to do it."

Nils nodded. "Perhaps you would care to come with us as far as Momiji Castle. We will stay there awhile, while Ojiisan rests again, and you could live there while I'm gone. It would be a good and safe place for you, especially if you're pregnant."

She nodded, not meeting his eyes. "I will go to Momiji Castle with you, as you wish. But you must know that I am sad. We have been husband and wife so briefly, and now you will go to the mountain to live with celibate priests. It will be for all winter then?"

"I can't be sure yet. I sense in Ojiisan, things I greatly wish to learn. But whether it will take a winter or a month, or less, remains to be seen."

The next day at work, she requested time off. When her employer refused, she asked his pardon and left anyway, a truly remarkable act that would probably lose her her job. Half an hour later she was at the palace gate. The guards recognized her as the wife of Matsumura Nissa, and let her enter without question; at her request, they directed her to the temple.

The rector was reluctant to let her disturb the old holy man, saying he was meditating. At that moment, however, Ojiisan himself looked in the rector's door. "You are Chiyoko," he said. "I am pleased to meet the wife of Matsumura Nissa." He gestured at the rector. "This good rector, Kawakami Hiro, wishes to spare me any disturbance, but as it happens, you are someone I especially hoped to meet. Please come with me. We can talk in my room."

She bowed low, first to Ojiisan, then to the rector. "Thank you, Kawakami-san," she said, then followed the old man into the hallway, the bemused rector looking after them.

In Ojiisan's quarters she bowed again. "Please sit down," he said, gesturing to a mat, and when she'd settled herself, he sat down facing her, his back straight, thinking that she was as beautiful as Nils considered her to be, physically and spiritually. "You have come to ask me something. Please tell me what it is."

Stories were told of Ojiisan's powers, mostly untrue, while his actual powers were more or less unsuspected. The tales she'd heard, she'd neither especially believed nor disbelieved, but if Nils regarded him so highly that he wished to study with him . . .

Still she was not intimidated. "Excuse me, revered Ojiisan," she said softly, "but it is my unworthy wish to accompany my husband when he goes with you to the mountain. We have not been married long, and he may be there all winter. I will be pleased to cook and clean for you while remaining very quiet. I can sleep in a place apart—some outbuilding perhaps—to avoid distracting my husband from his meditations and study."

Ojiisan barked a laugh. "Your husband is not someone who needs isolation from physical joy in order to expand in the spirit. He could meditate if he held you in his arms every night! Ask *him* if it is all right to accompany us. Tell him it is all right with me. If he does not grow in the spirit, it will not be because you are there."

Thus Nils, Ojiisan, and Chiyoko rode together to Momiji Castle, slowly, for Ojiisan was unused to riding. And because it drizzled and rained almost continuously, they stopped early to dry out and warm up. On the second day, Chiyoko woke up with morning sickness and was unobtrusively miserable. By the time they reached Momiji Castle, Ojiisan was coming down with a bad cold.

They decided to wait with Matsumura-sama until Ojiisan was well. Chiyoko became his attentive nurse, though Matsumura assigned a servant to take care of him. Nonetheless, the cold became pneumonia, and the old man hovered near death. An early snow fell, covering the ground with twenty-five centimeters of white, and although it melted quickly in the sunshine that followed, Nils began to carve himself a pair of skis.

After several days, it was clear that Ojiisan was recovering, but he was very weak, and at his age, his strength would no doubt take a month or more to return. At the urging of his own body and Lord Matsumura, Ojiisan agreed to spend the winter at Momiji Castle.

THIRTY-SIX

For hours after his blinding, Hidaka Satoru lay delirious and incoherent in his cell. All Achikh could put together from his babbling was that he'd been blinded by the hand of Lord Sugimori Michio.

Two days later, Lord Sugimori had them put out of the castle. Nor did he return their swords. He simply sent them off in the charge of an officer, with instructions to put them on the next ship out of Isomachi. The officer was to pay the ship's master for their passage, at the cheapest rate, to anywhere far away from Osaka.

It so happened that the next ship out was eastbound. It wasn't actually headed for anywhere: It would trade its way along, and probably get to Miyako. The cheapest fare provided no place beneath an awning or other cover, but Achikh was large and dangerous-looking, and thus at night was able to shelter his master beneath a bench against the forecastle, somewhat protected from radiation cooling. He himself slept close against Satoru, providing the blind and almost comatose Hokkaidoan with his body heat.

Food wasn't a severe problem, for anyone willing to live on an unbroken diet of hardtack and *miso*. Achikh's greater problem was getting Satoru to eat at all, at first, and to keep down what he ate.

By the third day out, however, Satoru was a little stronger, if still in psychological shock. The weather had been clear, and he sat gray-faced in the sun, his mouth no longer slack as an idiot's. He did not talk, except, mumbling, to ask for the latrine bucket, which Achikh emptied over the side for him.

No one spoke to them. The *kanji* for "criminal," branded on Satoru's forehead, and the barbaric mien of his servant, discouraged anyone from even looking at them directly. On the night before they reached Shingu, Achikh stole a loose-fitting cap from another passenger and hid it in his pants. A few days later, the same passenger got off at Hamamatsu, and Achikh was able to put the cap on Satoru, who endured it without apparent notice. It not only gave protection from the autumn chill, but hid the incriminating brand.

Satoru's psychological shock was deeper than it might have been in another man. Because he'd lost more than his eyesight; his psi power had turned off completely, as completely as his vision, and it seemed to the Hokkaidoan that his life had been destroyed, left without hope.

The captain put them off at Shimoda, saying that that was as far as he'd been paid for. Achikh had no idea of the local or regional geography, but southward and eastward lay the ocean, and they had come from the west. Thus, if they would leave Shimoda, only north was available to them.

They had neither food nor money, and now necessity brought Satoru's mind to life. "There must be a temple here," he muttered. "Take us there. They will feed us at least for a day." That was more words than he'd spoken in any day since his mutilation. Achikh took him to the temple, and when they'd been fed, he asked a priest how they could go northward.

"There is no road," the priest told him. "No one travels north by land. But there is an old trace, a road of the ancients that can still be discerned. It is overgrown by trees, and I'm told that in places it has been washed out by mountain torrents. But if you stay on it long enough, it should eventually take you somewhere. Perhaps to the Imperial Highway that goes east to the capital."

The cook fed them again in the morning, and gave them a straw bag containing cooked barley to sustain them. They set out under a clear, early morning sky, without bedding or even a straw raincape to protect them, hiking slowly because Satoru could not see, and because his legs, strong two weeks before, were somehow weak and shaky now. Quickly they were into wild and jumbled volcanic terrain, overgrown with forest and scrub. The only indications that humans had ever been there were the weathered cuts and fills of a road almost eight hundred years abandoned. The pavement had long since disintegrated.

In mid-afternoon, after they'd drunk at a rivulet, Achikh put Satoru beneath the root disk of a tree tipped partly over by the wind, to hang up in the crown of a nearby oak. Then he told him his plan, and trotted back down the trace toward town. He was back next midday, with a knife on his belt, a bow and quiver, and a bundle wrapped in quilts. In one hand he carried an ax. He helped his master from his den, helped him to drink, gave him some cold barley, and they set out again. For supper they had rice cakes and cold potatoes, baked by a man who now, unfortunately, lay dead in his own blood.

Fifteen kilometers a day was good progress. Achikh took one morning off to hunt, and killed an animal rather like a dog with a black-masked face. On another day he shot a partridge sitting on the road, a bird too ignorant of humans even to fly from them.

Despite the severe circumstances, the walking and isolation improved Satoru's condition. His powers had begun to return, and he scanned psionically again, paid attention to sounds, and occasionally asked a question or made a comment. On the seventh day, during their midday break, he said, "There is a *kami* near here; a very powerful *kami*." Standing up, he turned in a slow circle. "It is all around us, but mostly— Its center is this way." He pointed to the west, which was uphill. "Take me to it."

It seemed to Achikh that he could sense it too; there'd been at least one shaman in his recent ancestry, and among the Buriat, such sensings were considered respectable. They set out, struggling, and in Satoru's case stumbling, for hours up a long rough slope, forested and with much rock. Finally they denned up for the night in a hole among a jumble of great basaltic boulders.

Near the following midday, they reached the rim of a great volcanic crater containing a marvelous blue lake. Nearly circular and some four kilometers across, it held two small lava cones, each an island. From one of them issued either steam or smoke, Achikh couldn't tell which. He stopped, holding Satoru back.

"What is it?" Satoru asked.

Achikh stared, then said: "Master, you can read my mind. See it through my eyes. It is beautiful!"

Satoru stood open-mouthed with concentration. Then, "Gracious gods!" he said. "I see! I see!"

He turned to Achikh, embracing him, and began to weep. When he'd wept himself out, he said, "Look again, Achiku, that I may see it once more."

When he had looked his fill, he said, "I wish to stay near here, where the *kami* is strong."

"We can camp by the old trace, master. It is not nearly so high up. Here the snow will pile deep, and the game will be driven to the lower lands. Here we would die, of hunger and cold."

Satoru gripped Achikh's wrist hard; his strength had been returning. "By the trace then," he said.

Going back downhill was considerably faster than going uphill, even with Satoru blind. They spent the night in a lean-to Achikh made against a great old fallen tree. The next day they came to a slump bench, deeply shaded by large cedars, not thirty paces above the trace.

"Here is the place, master," Achikh said. "The thick trees will hold off much of the snow, and the rain will not fall hard beneath them."

Over the following days, he built a log hut on the slump bench, made with the trunks of young pine that he chopped, and dragged or carried there. The work went slowly, for it was hard, hunger-producing work, and he took time out to hunt. He wondered that he knew how to build it, for this was not something his people did. It was not as well built as the one, unrecallable, that he'd helped Nils build at the foot of the Altai, with Hans and Ted. This one had no window, and the entrance had no door to close it. Also he was unsuccessful in trying to split out planks from larger logs, for he had only one ax, and it didn't occur to him to carve out splitting wedges from hardwood. Thus he roofed it as best he could with great slabs of bark stripped from blowdowns.

It went better when he'd killed a maral, while it drank from the stream that paralleled the trace. The maral provided abundant immediate food, and meat to smoke for winter, and a large hide to fend the rain from their sleeping place, for the roof leaked. Later he killed a deer, its hide providing a flap for the doorway to help retain warmth. All in all it was a miserable, smoky hovel, but it meant survival. The forest protected it from even strong winds, and a fire in the evening provided a bed of coals and hot rocks for heat at night.

While Achikh labored, Satoru spent the nicer days sitting on a rocky point below the trace, overlooking the stream. Near midday, and briefly at other times, the sun shone through to warm him. There he communed with the *kami* in the mountain, a *kami* whom he quickly realized was Osoroshii-kami. When the weather of deepening autumn was too cold for sitting outside, he sat in the hut, huddled in the growing robe of rabbit and other furs that Achikh's snares and deadfalls were gradually providing.

Hunting and exploring took the Buriat farther and farther from the hut. One day he smelled smoke, and turning aside, followed his nose northwestward. Eventually coming to a monastery.

THIRTY-SEVEN

In Osaka, 320 kilometers west of the hovel where Satoru meditated, Lord Arakawa sat in his office. Cold rain blew in off the Inland Sea,[29] rattling against the storm shutters. Lord Sugimori sat with him, with him and one other. Neither of the two lords was happy. A project they'd taken for granted—the bandit depredations on the trans-mountain roads of central Honshu—had seemingly gone at least somewhat wrong, and it was necessary to find out what had happened.

They'd never expected major results from the project. Its rationale had been to increase the perception, among the *daimyo*, of a breakdown of order in the empire, but the decisive reason had been Prince Terasu. The prince had poor judgement, pushed impractical ideas, and sulked when he didn't get his way. Thus, the more he was gone when major decisions were being discussed, the better.

When Terasu had suggested the bandit project, Arakawa had embraced the proposal, seeing in it a way of pleasing Terasu while getting him out from underfoot. And all with what seemed minimal risk. He'd put the prince in charge of recruitment and management. Terasu had easily and happily accepted the

---

[29] The Inland Sea is the broad strait lying between the islands of Honshu and Shikoku, connecting the Pacific Ocean, lying to the east, with the southern end of the Sea of Yamato to the west. Three hundred kilometers long, its much indented coasts and numerous islands provide many obscure anchorages used by fishermen and pirates. A number of small villages have their own shipbuilding facilities, producing their own hemp and tar, and having their own saw pits for sawing out ship's planks and timbers.

need for secrecy and disguise; it appealed to his sense of the dramatic. Komokoro Tadashi— "Kashira" —had been put in charge of operations on the ground, because of his innate toughness and practicality; his experience, in his youth, as a hunter of bandits; his demonstrated skill in command; and because he knew the region well. But now—

In front of Arakawa sat Kirisaki Hoshin, with word of Kashira's death—his murder.

"You say it was a foreigner who killed him?"

"Either the foreigner or the girl; I believe you have been informed about her. She is Iwata Emiko, a noble girl who was with a caravan we attacked."

"Ah yes! Iwata Emiko! She could not have killed him. I know her family well; she is a refined and delicate young girl. I did not inform her father of her unfortunate capture. We have brought him around to our point of view; it would not do now to plant questions in his mind. Let him think she was lost to ordinary bandits.

"Now, about this foreigner: what was he like?"

"He was tall, and wore very peculiar clothing: a single garment covered him from ankles to throat. Initially he claimed that Amaterasu-omikami had sent him. It was clear that he had never used a bow, or learned to fight with his hands and feet; he was completely inept. Kashira had shackles locked to his ankles, and he was used to perform camp chores."

"Hmh! And how did such a person, shackled, succeed in killing Komokoro Tadashi?"

"Apparently the girl somehow got the key to the shackles, and took it to the foreigner in the night. He removed his chain, came to the longhouse, and killed Kashira in his sleep. Then they fled on foot."

"I suppose you killed them when you caught them?"

Kirisaki's face was rigid when he answered. "Excuse me, your lordship, but we did not catch them. They escaped."

Arakawa looked thunderstruck at this. "You did not catch them?!"

"Their absence was not discovered till morning. I sent a search party on horseback then, to follow the only path out and overtake them, but they could not find them. Then I had men on foot seek along the path for where they might have left it, but they found no tracks. The path, of course, had been heavily trampled by horses, and at the time there was no mud. Finally I had nearly the whole company searching the forest, looking for signs of them, but—" He stared intently at the floor. "Nothing."

Arakawa's expression was thoughtful now. "Did they have any reason to consider you as other than an ordinary band of robbers?"

"I'm sure they didn't, your lordship. The men had been warned not to talk to her. Only Kashira talked to her. And the men didn't like the foreigner; I myself once beat him badly for his insolence. They spoke to him only to give him orders; he'd killed several of them before he was captured. Killed them with his wizard weapon. Finally we caught him in his sleep."

Arakawa frowned. "Wizard weapon? What sort of wizard weapon? I have never heard of such a thing!"

Kirisaki looked apolgetic. "It was an iron club, Arakawa-sama, short and crooked, that made a sound like small thunder. When he pointed it at some men, it made the sound repeatedly, and six of them fell dead or dying."

"Where is this wizard weapon? Why wasn't I told of it earlier?"

"Kashira tested it once, pointing it at a steel breastplate on the wall. It made a hole through the breastplate, and deep into the log behind it. But after that, the weapon would not work any more. The foreigner explained that it had been blessed by a god, and apparently the blessing had been used up. Perhaps that is the reason Kashira did not send word of it to you."

"Hmh! I should like to see it." The *takai daimyo* looked narrowly at Kirisaki. "I suppose you brought it with you?"

"Excuse me, your lordship, but unfortunately I haven't seen it since some time before Kashira was killed. I don't know where he kept it. Perhaps it is in his gear, which we brought here with us. I didn't look through it."

Arakawa pressed his lips together. "I will examine it myself. Tell me more about this foreigner."

"He was tall, as I said, and wore a single garment that covered him from throat to ankles. His hair was brown and considerably curly, and his skin somewhat pale. Also he'd lost most of his front teeth from a beating. And of course, he'd become quite thin by the time he escaped."

Arakawa shook his head, unable to conjure much of an image from the description. "So," he said, "and one of Lord Takada's men brought you here. You must have known that Takada knew who was behind this banditry. Yet Kashira was to tell no one of Takada's connection or my own. How did you find out?"

Kirisaki told him what he knew of the capture of Takada Chiu. And that Kashira, a personal friend of the nobleman, had released him, sending him on to Takada Keizo. He also told him of Watanabe's execution for lying about Chiu, lies which had resulted in Chiu's capture and abuse. "Kashira executed Watanabe for that by burning him alive, feet-first in a campfire. At Takada Chiu's request. It was natural, therefore, to guess that the Takada brothers might know to whom Kashira's murder should be reported. And who might arrange for the men to be paid, for we are owed considerable money."

By the time Kirisaki had finished, Arakawa was scowling. "What did the men make of the business with Takada Chiu?"

"Excuse me, your lordship, but I was not there at the time. I know only what Kashira told me when I returned from a raid. I never heard the men speak of it. All they could talk about was the desertion by a wizard from Hokkaido, and a foreigner. A different foreigner than the one we've talked about."

"Another foreigner?!" Again Arakawa seemed thunderstruck. "And a wizard? Tell me about this!"

Kirisaki was surprised by the sharpness of Arakawa's interest, and by the vehemence of his demand. He described all he'd heard about the two, and the circumstances of their leaving, including of course the monster. "Even Kashira saw it," he finished apologetically. "He described it to me himself."

Arakawa glanced accusingly at Sugimori, whose mouth had tightened, then looked back at Kirisaki. "This Hokkaido wizard: What was his name?"

"Excuse me, my lord, but all I know is Satoru. Something Satoru. A tall rough man, I'm told, a peasant who thought himself better than his station."

"And the foreigner with him?"

"It is said he was somewhat large and very strongly built. Who was himself a wizard with the bow."

Arakawa's voice was thoughtful now. "And what of this foreigner's speech?"

His speech? "I have heard that—that he spoke somewhat like the other foreigner, the one who escaped with the girl. He used many old-fashioned words, some so old that no one was sure what they meant."

Arakawa sat contemplating for a long minute. Finally he spoke again. "You have done well, Kirisaki Hoshin," he said, and turned to an aide. "Ichiro, have this *ronin* quartered with the household troops for now. Also, tell Captain Tottori to assign him a post that will make proper use of his excellent initiative and sense of responsibility." He looked at Kirisaki again. "You will no longer be a *ronin*. I will make you one of my sworn men."

Kirisaki bowed deeply, and left just as deeply relieved and grateful.

Arakawa and his marshal discussed what they'd learned. Typically, years passed without even hearing of a foreigner. Now these two had come upon the bandit project, two foreigners with a similar manner of speech. One of them with very strange clothing, and a weapon that sounded like something from ancient myth.

And there were not only those two: He'd heard report of a boat that had come down from the sky to land near Momiji Castle. And a story of two foreigners in the imperial court, rumored to have come from heaven in the boat; they too were said to use old words and forms of speech. One had been adopted as his son by that old opportunist and imperial sycophant, Matsumura Shinji.

And the one who'd escaped after murdering Kashira, taking with him Iwata Emiko— They might well have gotten lost and died in the mountains. It would be easy enough to do. But suppose they'd reached a village. *Suppose they'd reached Lord Iwata!* What might the girl have overheard, living among the men in the camp? Had she heard the Takada name used?

Arakawa scowled at Sugimori. "And what of the Hokkaido wizard? Something Satoru. Surely the man you had blinded and turned out! Branded and blinded! What might he have learned while one of Kashira's men? Especially being a wizard—seemingly a powerful one after all. Your treatment of him may have been a serious mistake. Where might he have gone when he left here? Undoubtedly thinking of vengeance! Straight to the Emperor, with whatever he knew!" He turned to Ichiro, who'd come back from his earlier errand. "Get Ayabe! I have some questions for him!"

Ichiro bowed, and hurried off to bring the empath. Arakawa questioned Ayabe sharply without telling him what he'd already learned. Ayabe insisted that the Hokkaido wizard was a man of no real powers. Finally Arakawa dismissed him curtly, waiting for him to be gone before saying anything more.

"Ichiro, follow him. Make sure he does not leave the castle. Arrest him if necessary." Again Ichiro bowed and hurried off. "Michio," Arakawa said when he'd gone, "we have put too much trust in Ayabe Iki. He is not truthful. Unless you have some good reason not too, I believe I will have him killed. But we should question him first, under torture if necessary.

"What Kirisaki has told us puts everything in a different light. I had hoped to turn a number of additional *daimyo* to our cause before acting. To include a fourth *takai daimyo* in addition to myself, Kyushu, and Miyagi. With such strength, I'd hoped that a palace coup might serve to bring Hikari down without the costs and destruction of war. But these . . ." He gestured at the air, or perhaps the ceiling. "They form a whole set of new factors, of unknown but threatening significance. Iwato's daughter might turn him against us, and he in turn, turn others. Takada might be exposed, and with him his allies.

"And what is the significance of these foreigners? How might they be connected with each other? What other wizard weapons might they have, and what purpose might they have in Yamato?"

He shook his head. "With this Hokkaido wizard free, the Emperor will soon know what we are doing, if he doesn't already. Certainly he's known of the widespread disapproval, and must suspect that someone would be plotting to take advantage of it. But to *know* what we are doing! That would certainly bring about preparations against us. He might even preempt the initiative.

"Michio," he said with sudden decision, "we must move without further waiting—strike in the spring, and be victorious before the monsoon rains begin in June. Final plans must be made, and preparations completed swiftly. Numerous *daimyo* must be notified before the passes are blocked with snow."

THIRTY-EIGHT

While Ojiisan recuperated from his pneumonia, Nils and Akira took horses, and Nils's new skis, and rode to the terrible mountain to visit Juji Shiro. At Momiji Castle, the second snowstorm had come and gone, and the snow had melted. But at the temple, even though it was not high on the slope, the snow was still knee deep in the forest.

The two travelers arrived there on a midafternoon. Juji Shiro bowed to his guests. "I am pleased that you have come, Matsumura Nissa and Kamoshika Akira. I have news you will be glad to hear." The albino rector beamed. "One of my priests has recently returned from Nagano. While there, he spoke with Ojiisan Tattobu, who told him he planned to spend the winter with us again. If in fact he does, he should arrive before the snow gets much deeper."

"Ah." Nils grinned back. "I have just come from Momiji Castle, and . . ."

Juji saw his thought, and burst into laughter. "Your information is fresher than mine, I see. But ill? Pneumonia? That is not a matter for laughter. Still, as he is recovering, I suppose I might be forgiven.

"It is unusual for serious snowfall to come so early," Juji continued. "We have neighbors who will suffer for it."

Nils stared psionically at the rector, and at the image which lay below the statement.

"You know him!" said Juji.

Nils nodded. "But I had not imagined he was here. I'd heard he'd been . . ." He left the statement unfinished, Juji having perceived the rest of it.

"Yes," Juji said, "he is with someone. A blind man he referred to as his master."

"A term I'd never thought he'd use," Nils said, and turning to Akira, told him briefly about Achikh. When he'd finished, Juji continued.

"He said his master would not care to shelter in the monastery—that he preferred to contemplate in solitude. And I believe I know what it is he contemplates. There is a human presence besides our own that is in touch with Osoroshii-kami; it seems very probable that he is the master of your friend. He is in deeper, fuller contact than we are. Our purpose is solely to monitor; his seems to be to know the *kami* intimately. We have avoided that, not knowing what the effect on the *kami* might be. Or whether it can be done safely. In the early years of the temple, certain priests attained closeness with the *kami*, and entered trances from which they could not be roused. Even snow on their genitals failed to rouse them. The *kami*, on the other hand, became restless until finally the priests died.

"Happily, the presence of Achiku's master has been innocuous. So far at least. In fact, the *kami* seems more stable than usual." The rector cocked a white eyebrow. "We will see what develops. If later the *kami* becomes unhappy, we will have a decision to make. We prefer, however, not to interfere."

Akira looked interested. "Then the mountain is unlikely to cause trouble?"

Juji Shiro shook his head. "It is not possible to know that. The mountain may erupt with or without the *kami* acting. The mountain is itself. But the *kami*, we know, can influence it—calm it, seemingly *direct* its activity, make it more violent or less. We can sense the *kami*, and we can sense the mountain itself. Or the mountains. People believe that Osoroshii-kami rules all the mountains of Yamato. That is not true. His sphere embraces this mountain" —he gestured with a hand— "and Hakone-san, and lesser volcanoes nearby. Some other districts also have *kami* in their volcanoes, but none so powerful as Osoroshii-kami."

His pink eyes were intent now. "We believe that the mountain will erupt—the great one or Hakone-san—within the next year. We hope that the *kami* will see fit to make it less severe, less damaging, than it might otherwise be. And certainly that he will not make it worse."

Nils spoke then. "I would like to visit Achikh, see what has happened to make him some man's servant. And to learn what manner of man his master is."

Juji Shiro looked long at the Northman, then said: "We do not know where they are. To the southeast somewhere. If you can find them, I hope you will not upset his master. Surely not if he happens to be communing with the *kami*."

Nils nodded. "I wish to see. As for finding them—finding is something I do well."

"Then I wish you success. Perhaps you will consent to eat the evening meal with us, and spend the night here. You can start in the morning and have all day to find him."

Nils told Akira that it was best he go alone.

He was up before dawn, to eat with the priest who stood the morning watch. Then, with food packed by the cook, the Northman started on horseback through the snowy woods, following his intuition. For three hours there were no tracks, no sign of any other human. Then he saw snowshoe tracks, made when the last snow was fresh, and followed them. In another hour he sensed a human mind, but did not recognize it as Achikh's. Minutes later he saw the hut, scarcely taller at the ridgepole than his shoulder. He dismounted and led his horse, speaking aloud to it, not for the horse's sake, but to make some innocuous noise so that no one would be startled at his arrival.

One of them wouldn't be, for he was in a deep trance. The other heard Nils's voice, and pushing the deer-hide aside, showed his face through the door. Achikh's face. For just a moment, Nils paused. Achikh's mind! His soul was his own, but his mind was so changed!

Achikh slipped outside, and straightening, came to meet the Northman. There was no sign of recognition, nor of surprise at a stranger, or at the stranger's size, coloring, or eyes. "Are you lost?" was all he said.

"No. I had heard that a man was here. Perhaps a wizard, or a holy man."

Achikh chuckled. "My master. He no longer calls himself wizard, and I have never heard him called holy man. He sits inside the hut, and contemplates the spirit of the mountain. I make sure he has food and water, and fire."

"You are a good servant. Perhaps I might be allowed to contemplate your master. I have no wish to interfere with him. Only to observe his spirit."

Achikh looked long at his *anda*, his eyes slightly troubled, then nodded. "If you can do so from outside the hut. It might disturb him if you go inside. He has become strange lately. Often he seems hardly to know me, as if his spirit goes away and only partly comes back."

"As you wish," Nils said, and walked to the hut, where he squatted outside the door. Achikh squatted beside him, and they stayed like that for nearly an hour. Briefly and as unobtrusively as possible, Nils observed Satoru's totally focused but quiescent mind, learning little. Then, very gently, he entered Achikh's mind and became a seeming part of it, muttering introspective questions as if they were Achikh's own, reading what they brought to view, and learning a great deal. Though much of it seemed irrelevent.

Finally he disengaged and got to his feet, murmuring softly: "Thank you, my friend. It is best I be gone before your master wakens." In half a trance, Achikh nodded.

Backtracking, Nils reached the monastery before dark. <<The man is my friend,>> he thought to Juji after supper, <<but he doesn't know me now. His master has entered his mind, and hidden or changed many things. Achikh knows little of his past now, except that with his master.>>

<<Ah! And you chose not to disturb them. That seems well to me. Although . . . if the mountain erupts next year, yet Achikh still lives, you might choose to come again, and remind him of that past.>>

Nils nodded. <<Achikh made a decision, a series of decisions, and eventually they led him to the hut on the mountain. Thus although he is a slave, he is not a victim. But next summer, or perhaps fall, it may be time to free him.>>

After supper, Nils too contemplated the *kami*, though not too closely. In the morning, he and Akira started back to Momiji Castle.

THIRTY-NINE

Nils and Akira returned to Momiji Castle in weather pretending to be spring. While they'd been gone, Hans had arrived with Mariko, and Nils, striding down the corridor to his own apartment, sensed the young poet's mind. Locating it, he stopped outside Hans's door and knocked. It was Hans who opened. "Nils! Chiyoko told me where you were. I didn't think you'd be back so soon."

"But I am. Are you here to stay?"

Hans shrugged, frowning. "I'm not sure. I didn't like being a courier. It was all right the first couple of weeks, but after that, I thought I'd die of boredom."

Nils laughed. "Earlier you were afraid you'd die of boredom as a guard. Being a courier was supposed to be better."

"It probably was." Inside, Mariko had gotten up and was putting a teapot on a small charcoal brazier. She smiled at Nils but didn't interrupt.

"Yet you're not sure you'll stay," Nils observed.

"Matsumura-sama is angry with me. And he doesn't like Mariko!"

He turned and looked at his wife, who had lowered her eyes. Nils detected disagreement between them, though not conflict.

"Can you imagine?" Hans went on. "Disliking someone because her father is a fisherman? I'll bet he wouldn't hesitate to eat her father's fish!"

It was Mariko who responded. "Excuse me please, honorable husband. I do not wish to disagree, but Matsumura-sama cannot help feeling as he does. It's the way he's supposed to feel. Any lord would feel that way if his grandson married a fisherman's daughter. And he has not even been cruel! He simply does not speak to me."

269

"Or to me, hardly. I asked him what was wrong, and he told me. Since then, he hasn't said a dozen words to me, and none at all that he could avoid."

Nils nodded. "I'm not surprised."

"You're not?" Hans stared. "Do you think he's mad at you, too, now that he knows?"

"Perhaps."

"What will you do?"

Nils grinned. "Perhaps let him be mad. Or maybe I'll say something. Nothing angry though." He glanced toward the door. "I need to see Chiyoko now. She's pregnant, you know."

Hans nodded glumly. "She told us. She's really happy about it. We wish Mariko was pregnant, but she's not. Almost two months, and she's not pregnant yet!"

"Two months isn't long. It's not rare to go two years without getting pregnant."

The comment didn't cheer Hans. Mariko looked concerned, not because she wasn't pregnant, but because her husband was unhappy.

"You think it's because you're inadequate as a man," Nils observed.

Again Hans nodded, still glum.

"There are heroes who have no sons. Or daughters. Leif Trollsverd is childless by all three of his wives, despite years of earnest efforts, and there is no greater fighting man among the tribes. While some men of no reputation and little quality have had many. Children are not the measure of a man."

Hans shrugged, resisting assurance. Nils let him be. "I'll go and see Chiyoko now," he said. "You and I can talk about things later."

After Chiyoko's welcome, Nils went to the office of his adoptive father, and had a servant tell the old *daimyo* he was outside the door. He heard Matsumura-sama's voice rumble an answer—Nils didn't need telepathy to recognize grumpiness—and the servant returned. "Lord Matsumura requests that you come in please," the man said, and Nils entered.

"Good afternoon, father. Please excuse me if I have come at a poor time."

"It is as good a time as any." He sat like a rock on his chair, knees spread, palms on thighs, elbows out—the epitomal *daimyo*. "So. What did you find at the mountain?"

"Snow. And Juji Shiro. Each as white as the other. Juji believes the mountain will erupt within a year. The *kami* is calm, but the bowels of Osoroshii-yama are restless. Also, there is another person of power communing with the *kami*, a stranger with no eyes, like myself. He lives in a hut, low on the mountain's east side. It is little better than a cave, but he has a servant tending his needs. Juji Shiro believes the *kami* is actually more calm because of the stranger, but whether it will stay calm, no one knows. Perhaps it will become excited when the time approaches."

Nils paused and changed the subject. "When coming down the corridor, I ran into Hans."

The old man grunted. "And his fisherman's daughter; you had not told me what she is."

"I told you she is a lovely woman. Lovely and loving."

"And you do not care that she is common."

"The father of my flesh is a smith. A maker of ax blades, of shovels and plowshares. As well as swords."

"But you are a warrior. A samurai among your people. And your wife is the daughter of a samurai hero."

"True. But I married her because I love her."

Matsumura's mouth was like a snapping turtle's. Like a bulldog's. "Matsumura Hansu has embarrassed me. And brought shame on you, if you but knew it."

"I am very sorry that you are offended with us. Such embarrassments can be the price of bringing foreigners into your family, as I once mentioned. But please allow me to make one additional comment. Two comments. Then I will stop bothering you with my unworthy presence. Hans is upset that you so dislike his wife, but she has told him in my hearing that you are right to disapprove. She takes your side in this."

He paused. "The second comment is this: I sometimes see the future, though seldom clearly or in detail. However, I see Hans someday doing for you more than you might ever hope. And I see you honoring him for it."

He then bowed to Matsumura Shinji more deeply than he

ever had before. "Please excuse me, father, for my boldness in saying these things to you. With your permission, I will go now, and visit Ojiisan Tattobu."

The *daimyo* grunted surly approval, and Nils left. But it seemed to Matsumura-sama that he'd left an unspoken whisper behind: "*Ojiisan Tattobu, the stone cutter's son from Tochigi.*" The old man snorted, and turned back to the records of harvests and taxes piled on his work table.

When Nils arrived at Ojiisan's door, the old man was asleep; it was evident from his mental processes. So he returned after supper, and Ojiisan greeted him more than amiably. He was sitting up on a comfortable chair, with a *kotatsu* over his lap.[30] Their exchange was more of concepts, images, and emotions, perceived directly, than of words. Here we can only present them as language.

<<Well! What did you see and learn on the mountain?>>

Nils showed him the trip, the more significant exchanges with Juji, and the visit with Achikh.

<<And your homecoming? How was that? (Sense of laughter.) Not with Chiyoko, but with Matsumura-sama.>>

<<He and Hans will probably come to an accommodation; both are men of good will. But it may take a while.>> Nils changed the subject. <<What have you concealed from me? Something you feel I should know but aren't eager to expose.>>

<<Ah! You not only perceive superbly, but you analyze nicely as well! So. I have long had a policy of not sharing what I learn from people's minds, regardless of what it is. But this, it seems, I must show you.>>

Nils had never known a psi before who could screen selectively. The story the old man began was one which Nils previously had hardly an inkling of, yet found not surprising at all.

---

[30] Yamatoan homes, including castles, tend to be cold in winter. A *kotatsu* is a frame covered with a quilt, and has a small charcoal burner beneath it. One sits with the quilt over their lap, to warm the legs and hips. And the hands, if one puts them under the quilt.

During the summer prior to wintering with Juji Shiro, Ojiisan had spent four weeks in Osaka, as Lord Arakawa Hideo's guest at the Black Castle. Arakawa was always curious about the world around him, especially its more interesting people, and having never before met the holy monk, twice had a long private talk with him. Ojiisan had also been a guest at several long and leisurely suppers with the *takai daimyo* and his court, where he eavesdropped on their thoughts. And perceived what lay at the roots of those thoughts, for like Nils, Ojiisan read more deeply than most psis.

Thus he knew of the conspiracy, though not how it stood at present, for that had been a year and a half earlier. Also, he knew well the Emperor and his court, for roads tended to lead the traveler to Miyako. And whenever Ojiisan was there, he was an honored guest at the palace, talking privately with Hikari.

He found much to admire in Arakawa Hideo, but even more in the Emperor. Arakawa was a strong, energetic man, with many good qualities, but he felt love for none outside his own family. The Emperor, on the other hand, felt love readily and widely. Thus Ojiisan, not overjoyed at the prospect of civil war, had been tempted to tell the Emperor what he'd learned in Osaka. But he hadn't.

The reason lay as much in practicality as in his policy of not divulging people's secrets: He doubted that Hikari could long continue to rule in any event. The Emperor had been inconsistent in the enforcement of imperial laws, and his tendency to tolerance was often seen as laxity. This had cost him respect. But more serious was the growing rumor that he practiced sodomy with his aide, Okaya Yari. Their closeness had long been obvious, and now and then, someone unhappy with the Emperor had dared to suggest that it went beyond nature. Since the Great Death, homosexuality was generally disapproved of in Yamato, children being valued, and for a samurai to play the female role was considered highly degenerate.

But for years, few of the *daimyo* had taken the suspicion seriously; in fact, many had never heard it. Arakawa himself had rejected it as impossible for a son of the late Emperor

Junichi, and had frowned severely on his court speaking ill of the Emperor in any way, although the Emperor's policies could be criticized.

What had changed his view was his future son-in-law, Prince Terasu, telling him that he'd encountered the two having *nanshoku*, with Hikari playing the female role.

Arakawa's acceptance of Terasu's story had been catalyzed by the *takai daimyo*'s disapproval of the way Hikari ruled: He considered tolerance a weakness, as in fact it sometimes was, in a country whose local and regional rulers were autocrats, and sometimes greedy and arrogant to a fault. While inconsistency, of course, was an invitation to resentment.

Beyond that, Hikari had inherited resentment by the *daimyo*, for his strong and soldierly father, the Emperor Junichi, had much reduced the number of troops they were allowed to keep. When Junichi died, virtually all the *daimyo* had begun, covertly but substantially, to rebuild their military strength. And when Hikari had finally responded, ordering them to trim their ranks under pain of confiscation and exile, many had resented it deeply. Even though he'd allowed them four years, with three reduction stages, to carry it out.

Arakawa had willingly enforced the order in his domain. As all the *takai daimyo* had, for it strengthened their own authority, and made their subordinate *daimyo* easier to control. But by that time, the master at Osaka had decided that Hikari must fall. And that he was the one who must lead. Under most circumstances, to unseat an emperor would be nearly unthinkable, for only a descendant of the Sun Goddess could rule Yamato. But now Hikari's only brother was available[31] and eager, while the disaffected *daimyo* were susceptible to agitation.

---

[31]Junichi, though he'd sired seventeen children by his three wives, had fathered only two sons, while all seven of Hikari's children to date had been daughters. If this record reflects a new genetic tendency, rather than a statistical aberration, it endangers Yamato's basic political stability. For if the numerous cousins and other collateral relatives were to become eligible for the throne, succession might routinely be decided by wars.

There was another factor, too—Danna-no-Kyushu Tadaki, who was both Terasu's uncle, and a *takai daimyo* of particular power. It was Kyushu and Arakawa who, between them, held responsibility for suppressing piracy around the southern islands and from Korea. Thus they had naval forces much stronger than were allowed other *takai daimyo*. Old Kyushu was surly, and sometimes seemed less than intelligent, but he disliked—even hated—the Emperor.

Arakawa was not without occasional qualms, for he was a rational man, and found no joy in war. Prince Terasu, on the other hand, was selfish, irresponsible, and immature; he believed his own lies, and could be vindictively cruel. But Arakawa had no intention of letting the young man rule, in spite of having become his father-in-law. He planned to arrange Terasu's death before the prince could actually take the throne, then rule himself, as regent, until his infant grandsons, Terasu's twin boys, were old enough that the eldest, by minutes, could be enthroned.

In fact, Arakawa might have been a supporter of Hikari's, had he not believed the story about the Emperor and Okaya. As it was, that belief, and the widespread resentment of Hikari by the nobles, weakened the empire. Of the nine *takai daimyo*, not more than four, if that many, would actively support Hikari in a showdown. The core of the Emperor's support was rather the *tehon daimyo*, whose strength was less in military power than in geographic position. And they provided only defense of the Imperial Home State, the Kanto Plain, not control of the empire at large.

Sooner or later, it seemed to Arakawa, the Emperor would surely fall, to civil war or an assassin. And when he fell, if he was not succeeded promptly by someone who could hold the empire together, it was likely to break up into its nine constituent states. A period of *daimyo* wars, including wars between *takai daimyo*, would almost surely follow. The destruction and suffering would be terrible.

When Ojiisan had shown him all this, Nils gazed calmly at him: <<You seem to feel that Yamato might be better off with Hikari gone, and Arakawa ruling as regent.>>

<<And so it might. For Arakawa is strong and able, and is

driven not by greed for power, but by a desire to see the empire
well ruled. Yet he has drawbacks. A regent cannnot claim descent
from Amaterasu-omikami, and will therefore be resented by
the *daimyo*. Factions will arise. Thus ruling would pose serious
difficulties for him. Also he has little regard for the law, when
it stands in his way. And although he does not take pleasure in
cruelty, he is ruthless with opposition. Thus he has the potential
to become a tyrant.>>

  <<When do you expect civil war to begin?>>

  <<I do not know. Arakawa is a deliberate man. But I suspect
it will be within three years. The longer he waits, the greater
the risk that the Emperor will learn of his plans. But I believe
he will not act until he has the committed support he feels is
important to success.>>

Nils regarded the old sage. <<You have shown me this in
confidence. Yet you know Lord Matsumura is my father, and
will surely be involved in the war on the Emperor's side. What
was your reason for letting me know this?>>

  <<I have shown you these things because you are a new factor,
not only in the question of who can rule, but of who can best
rule. True you are but one man, without an army or political
power, but you can play a decisive role, if you decide to. Though
what that role may be, the Tao has not shown me.>>

Ojiisan's body had sagged as they'd communed, for physically
he was old, and weakened by illness. But he wasn't done yet.
<<Your father already knows the weakness of Hikari's support
among the *daimyo*, and the whys of it. As you were well aware
when you sat down with me here. What he does not know is
that a conspiracy is active. If he knew, he could guess who the
conspirators are, because Terasu is the key. And Arakawa is
Terasu's father-in-law, and Kyushu his uncle. Tell Matsumura-
sama that you anticipate a rebellion against the Emperor. He
considers you a wizard, which you are, and will believe you.
Then he will take whatever steps he sees fit.>>

That evening, Nils went to the small chapel within the castle,
and meditated at length. And came away believing that the
rebellion would be sooner than Ojiisan believed, though he
had no notion why.

FORTY

In the morning, Nils went again to his adoptive father. After the opening courtesies, he said, "You advised me to have myself measured for armor. But I thought, if there is no war, I will not need armor, and armor is costly. Last night while meditating, however, it came to me that there will indeed be war, a civil war, probably in the spring."

Matsumura Shinji looked with consternation at the Northman.

"I wish to have armor of the sort I'm used to," Nils went on, "and a sword and shield of the Northman kind. I will fight more effectively with them. Also, such armor looks much different than yours, and along with my size, and my use of a shield, it will make me recognized and feared. Do not doubt I will be feared; feared and marked. I will have Hans equipped as I am. I intend to train both of us very hard this winter, as hard as Hans can stand. I intend that we be at your side in battle, and make the enemy pay in blood."

The old *daimyo*'s face was sober now, and deeply concerned. He did not doubt for a minute. "Who will make such war?"

"Excuse me, father, but I have no evidence. Only wizard sight, which is often fragmentary. Also, the future is subject to change at the will of men. As to who the Emperor's enemies are—you know the politics of Yamato much better than I. It may be that you can name the principal enemies yourself. Almost certainly the Emperor can."

By the time they'd finished talking, Matsumura-sama had given Nils permission to go to the castle's armorers. The Northman went first to the carpentry shop, and himself made two practice shields of stout pine boards. Then he ordered four bull's-eye shields, seventy and sixty centimeters in diameter, built of the hardest oak available, covered with a layer of boiled

277

bullhide shrunken on, and rims and spokes of steel. He also got two pieces of oak, and set to work on the spot, with chisel and mallet, drawshave and knife, making heavy practice swords of Neoviking design.

Finally he went to the smith and gave him specifications for two Neoviking swords, to be made of the best quality steel. He also asked the smith if he could get wrought-iron wire about one and a half millimeters in diameter.

"There is a place near Miyako where steel wire is made," the smith replied. "If strength is important, steel is better than wrought iron."

"How much would forty kilos of it cost?"

"Forty kilos?! At least five *koban*, I would think. It is slow and costly to make, and that is a very great quantity of it. Forty kilos of steel is expensive before ever being made into wire. And such fine wire! Yes, surely at least five *koban*."

"Ask Matsumura first then," Nils said. "If he permits it, I will myself ride to Miyako and make the arrangements. I can show the foundryman exactly what I want."

Two days later, Nils was on horseback to Miyako, trailing two remounts and wasting no time. A week later he was back. Forty kilos of steel wire was to be delivered as soon as possible— within two weeks. The delivered cost was to be six *koban*. Meanwhile he brought with him two meters of cheaper wire, to show the armorer what he wanted done with it. Nils had watched chain mail being made by the Magyars, when he'd been a teen-aged mercenary among them. Had watched closely and asked questions.

From that point on, through the winter and well into spring, Nils spent the mornings with Hans, and with Matsumura's best trainer and other good men, learning to fight on horseback with sword and shield, against samurai swordsmen, and archers firing blunt-tipped arrows. Alternating, he rode the three largest warhorses the Momiji District could provide. After a midday nap, he and Hans practiced fighting on foot, again with trainers, learning to fight Northman style against skilled and seasoned samurai, not as duelists but in battle. They sweated in the cold like summer's stevedores, and before midwinter came, worked burdened with heavy chain mail, dealing blows that confounded and chagrined their armored trainers.

The intensity and violence of their training became a leading subject of conversation around the castle, and drew spectators from its samurai, including, eventually, Matsumura-sama himself. Matsumura became almost friendly toward Hans, and toward Nils both friendly and admiring.

Despite their letting their hair grow out. For Nils had decided they'd wear it in Neoviking warrior braids, instead of samurai style.

Daily they returned to their apartments with new aches and bruises, and the old *daimyo* ordered that a scalding bath be ready for them. Before they relaxed in the bath, however, they saw to the proper disposition of their horses, then oiled their hauberks against rust. After their hot soak, they collapsed for a brief nap, before eating more voraciously than anyone the Yamatoans had seen before.

Nonetheless, on many evenings Nils meditated for a time with Ojiisan. One evening, Ojiisan said archly that the Northman, with his inherent psychic calm, could no doubt reunite with the Tao while still in that life, if he dedicated himself to meditation.

Nils laughed. <<I was born to this life to live it. Which is what I'm doing, and will do. I meditate, when I meditate, to help me live it with greater satisfaction, not to escape it before my time.>>

Eyes crinkling, Ojiisan laughed back. <<If I'd had any doubt of your wisdom, that answer would have dissolved it.>>

As for celestial wisdom—Nils saw no more deeply than before into human minds, nor did he penetrate, or try to, the nature of the Tao. But under Ojiisan's guidance, he began to see, more and more clearly, the schematic which underlay human variation and desires, the schematic which guided Ojiisan's understanding and tolerance, the understanding from which grew his extraordinary amiability, and his love for his fellow humans. He also appreciated more fully, Jampa Lodro's advice to seek out the old sage.

FORTY-ONE

At the pinnace, Nikko and Matthew had watched the early first snowstorm pile up thigh deep on their meadow. Within a week, though, it had melted in the open, even on the moderate north slope where the *Alpha* lay disabled. Only on forested north and east slopes did significant snow remain, fifteen to twenty centimeters of it.

Matthew had taken advantage of the thaw to cut a block from the trunk of one of the pines he'd felled earlier. Using the laser saw, he'd then ripped four, three-foot-long slabs from the block, and from them made crude, heavy snowshoes. Testing them in the forest, he found them treacherous; they slid on the slopes like unmanageable skis. So he'd glued wooden strips on their bottoms for traction, and they'd practiced on them. He'd also gone hunting on them, but to no avail, for the wild game had largely left the high slopes.

Despite eating frugally enough to give them food dreams, they'd gotten critically low on supplies, and he'd been ready to make another trip to the hamlet. Instead, the next snowstorm arrived, or rather a series of them—three storm pulses spaced a day or two apart. When they were over, the pinnace lay half buried by 170 centimeters of white. And now the Kumalos felt fear: another storm could blow in next week or tomorrow, and they had no reason to believe the snow they had now would melt before spring. They could imagine themselves buried here without food.

The computer data on Yamato's climate dated from before the plague, and its validity for their time was uncertain. In south-central Honshu, it said, winters were not long, and were marked by moderate temperatures and lots of moisture. Snowfalls, however, were often heavy.

It also told them that the gravitic vector on which the pinnace sat intersected the ground at 1,463 meters above mean sea level. Presumably snowfalls would be heavier than on the coast, and wouldn't melt nearly as quickly, while winter rains on the Kanto Plain would mostly be snowstorms up here on the mountain.

Their total food supply consisted of several potatoes sprouting in a cabinet.

Matt and Nikko discussed the pros and cons of staying or leaving, then agreed to sleep on it before deciding. But both of them knew, before they lay down, what their decision would be.

In the morning, neither had changed their mind. Certainly it was desirable to stay with the pinnace, which provided them shelter and heat, safety with comfort against the winter. Not to mention locatability, should the *Phaeacia* return to Earth.

But the risk of starving seemed too great. While the computer printed out contour maps of Honshu for them at different scales, Nikko baked their potatoes. Then they packed everything they could think of that was both desirable and readily carried, including two assault rifles and two full shoulder bags of loaded magazines for them. They both remained conditional pacifists, but were prepared to defend themselves, particularly after the rape of the hamlet, and Ted's violent capture and probable murder by bandits.

Finally, Matthew dictated their situation and intentions to the computer, and instructed it to broadcast, at one-hour intervals, a short-range beacon—a "finder signal." Long range message pulses would be broadcast at longer intervals. They would go to the hamlet and ask to be taken in temporarily. When travel conditions were suitable, perhaps not till spring, they'd either return to the pinnace or possibly try to find their way to Miyako, the imperial capital.

Getting down the steep timbered slopes on their crude snowshoes was a virtual and exhausting hell. Even with traction strips, they slid and fell repeatedly. And in soft snow on steep slopes, getting up was difficult in the extreme, especially if one's head was downhill. It took them almost all day to reach the hamlet.

Even there the snow was 120 centimeters deep. And because of bandit pillaging, the previous September, food supplies were short there, too. But the villagers remembered well Ted's efforts to save them, and Matthew's rescue of the child from the tiger. Thus they took the foreigners in and fed them without reluctance.

When most of the valley-bottom snow had been melted by a thaw and winter rain, Matthew went hunting with the men of the hamlet. And with his rifle killed not only a deer, but a maral bull. The locals were enormously impressed, and urged their guests to stay all winter.

FORTY-TWO

In the Yamatoan "Second Month," approximately February by the European calendar, official word from the palace reached Matsumura Shinji of expected rebellion. Among other things, His Majesty's spies had come into possession of certain messages. Some had witnessed unquestionable preparations for war, including the renovation and building of warships on Kyushu and Shikoku, and on islands and the Honshu coast of the Inland Sea. Hostilities were expected in spring, or possibly July. Lords Arakawa and Kyushu were the principals in the conspiracy. Arakawa's military forces already controlled traffic on roads west of Hondoro Pass, while units of his fleet were said to be based near Cape Daio, patrolling the sea whenever weather permitted.

Lord Matsumura held a meeting of his officers, including Nils now. Hans also sat in unobtrusively. Matsumura told them what the palace had learned, and answered questions. Gifu State, ruled by Lord Nagoya, another *takai daimyo* like Arakawa, lay between Arakawa's State of Kyoto and the Imperial Home State, known also as Kanto. Lord Nagoya was loyal to the Emperor, and would prevent Arakawa from moving his army cross-country. Thus they need be concerned only with invasion by sea.

Unfortunately, the combined fleets of Arakawa and Kyushu were as large as that of the Emperor, for they'd long had the principal day-to-day responsibility of suppressing fleets of pirates marauding not only from their own coasts and islands, but from the Ryukyus and Korea.

In fact, the two rebel fleets combined were probably larger than the Emperor's, because of illegal shipbuilding.

Someone asked if Lord Tokuyama would attack Kyoto State from the west, after Arakawa's main army had left to attack the Emperor. Matsumura-sama looked as if something tasted bad, but avoided saying that Tokuyama's loyalty was luke-warm at best. "Lord Tokuyama is in a difficult situation," he answered, "with Chugoku State lying between two rebels, Arakawa and Kyushu. Also, his naval force is insignificant, compared to either of theirs."

He went on: "His Majesty has ordered that all *tehon daimyo* around the periphery of Kanto bring their forces to full readiness, and that all *takai daimyo* in southern and central Honshu prepare not only to enforce loyalty among the lesser *daimyo* in their states, but to provide forces for the defense of Kanto.

"Here in Momiji," Matsumura added, "we are already prepared, due to the premonition of my adopted son, Matsumura Nissa."

Nils stood and bowed to his adoptive father. "Excuse me, I am undeserving of your praise. It was my *shisho*, Ojiisan Tattobu, who turned my attention to the future of the empire. Without him, I would hardly have foreseen as I did."

Then an officer asked, "Besides Arakawa and Kyushu, what *daimyo*, and especially *takai daimyo*, are disloyal?"

Matsumura scowled. "Nothing has been said about other *daimyo* being disloyal. All *daimyo* can be assumed loyal, in the absence of evidence that they are not. But realism dictates that in some instances, that assumption may prove wrong. I myself can ensure the loyalty of my subject *daimyo*, because I am as strong as any four of them,[32] and because they know I am entirely loyal to the Emperor, and will not tolerate disloyalty."

Shortly afterward, the meeting broke up. The officers were neither very optimistic nor very pessimistic. But that there would be war, they had no doubt. Couriers were sent to those

---

[32] Under regulations then applying, a *daimyo* could maintain one company of samurai—100 men. A *tehon daimyo*, by contrast, was required to keep a full batallion— 400 men—on his liege land. A *tehon daimyo*'s liege holding had approximately four times the *hektaro* of land, and could support so large a force.

(One *hektaro* is a unit of land somewhat variable in size, according to fertility. Borrowed from the term *hectare*, it supposedly will produce 100 *hiyo* of barley in a normal year.)

lesser *daimyo* subject to Matsumura's military authority, calling them to a strategy conference.

That evening, Chiyoko looked at Nils and asked, "Who will win this war it seems we are destined to have?"

Nils looked up at her from his practice reading. "The Emperor will win," he said.

"Do you say that to reassure me? Or do you truly believe it?"

He laughed. "Reassure? My people say a warrior should consider himself dead when he enters battle, and therefore not worry about being killed. And if he is not killed, he should not rejoice at being spared, for there will be another battle. And if there is not another battle, or if he survives it, there will be a blizzard or famine or sickness, or a wounded bear or angry bull, or the ice will break when he crosses it. Or at any rate, he will die of something.

"The principle applies also to those who do not fight. It is true for the careful as well as the reckless. Death is where all lives go, and death, we say, brings the beginning of another life, after a short rest in the other world. According to Jampa Lodro, the Buddha Sakyamuni has said that all this will end for a person when the soul reunites with the Tao, and Ojiisan has no doubt of it. But whatever the truth may be, we Northmen live our lives, fight our battles, raise our cattle and crops and children, and do not worry greatly about victories. Life is to enjoy or suffer, and we enjoy as greatly as we can, so far as possible within the bounds of justice."

Chiyoko looked at her husband without visible reaction for a moment, then said: "Life is also to live with honor and kindness. This too is the teaching of the Buddhas, and it is what I believe. It is also what I have seen in you. It is at the heart of my love for you."

She paused, then asked: "And Hans: is he skilled enough to fight in such a battle? Mariko has come to love him very much, and is afraid for him."

"Hans is strong and quick, and savage in his attack. As for technique—he would be in serious trouble, facing a skilled samurai in a formal duel. But in a melee, with his shield on his arm— He may well live to be old."

FORTY-THREE

By Mongol standards, it had been a short winter. The forest still was snow-covered, but the snow was shrunken and hard. Achikh sat on a fallen tree near the hut, gnawing the remains of a hare, and breathing the clean spring air after a night in the smoky hut.

He couldn't recall how he'd learned to make such a hut. His own people, with great pastures and many cattle and sheep, lived in large and comfortable *gert* made of felt, and had no structures of logs.

He'd wondered about this occasionally. Idly. It seemed peculiar that he could remember so much of his childhood, and so little of what came after. The missing years had been numerous; he could sense them but not recall them. He couldn't even remember how he'd come to this strange land, couldn't remember anything since Europe, nor much of that. But he knew this wasn't Europe.

Satoru sat inside the hut now; it was still too cold for him to sit long in the open. He said little to his servant any longer. His spirit and mind dwelt mostly with the being known as Osoroshii-kami, inside the mountain. He knew the *kami* intimately now, more intimately than he'd known his father, or his grandfather, and it was with the *kami* that his destiny lay. He was certain of this, though he didn't understand it. The rest of the world scarcely existed for him.

FORTY-FOUR

April was fading, preparing to hand down her fresh-smelling kingdom to May.

The army had left the mountains two hours' march behind it, and was drawn up in battle order across fields washed with the delicate green of young barley; with potato hills not long planted, their ground hoe-loosened, dark brown and moist; with fresh green pasture growing faster now than the horses and cattle could graze it down. A land in contrast to Hondoro Pass, where the remains of winter's snow, harsh and granular in its final weeks, had crunched beneath their feet the day before.

By Yamatoan terms it was a large army, march-hardened, mostly infantry but with strong cavalry units. Facing them was another of similar size. Between the two were met the two commanders with their staffs. They'd been parleying for the better part of an hour.

"What it comes down to," said Arakawa, "is who you would have on the throne. What son of the Imperial Family." His eyes left Lord Nagoya, the *takai daimyo* of Gifu State, to scan briefly the lesser *daimyo* who'd ridden out with Nagoya. "Do you prefer a degenerate? Or his noble and upright brother?" He turned with stiff respect to the handsome, still-young man beside him, and bowed. Prince Terasu had shaved his beard so that he looked again like the young man they'd seen on their visits to the palace. His blaze-faced black stallion was magnificent, and his red-lacquered armor the most beautiful in all the army. His face wore a blend of nobility and hauteur, tinged with latent ferocity, a convincing expression well rehearsed before a mirror. He was able now to assume it without conscious decision, whenever the circumstances seemed appropriate.

Arakawa continued. "Do you prefer an effeminate man who listens to Okaya Yari whispering in his ear? Or one who counsels with a bold old warrior like Kyushu Tadaki. One who lounges indolently in his palace with another man, who has fathered only daughters, and can scarcely bring himself to service his wives? Or a man who, between siring sons, has ridden the mountain roads with a small band of samurai, living like the heroes of old."

Nagoya Kobushi looked around at his own *daimyo* and scowled sourly. "I have pledged my loyalty and my honor," he growled. "Therefore I will not take arms against my Emperor, regardless of what is said of him by those who would profit by it." He paused, then added, "But it is clear that civil war has begun. It began when you crossed the pass. And no one can say how it will end, or which brother will sit on the throne a few months from now."

He paused long, creating a silence broken only by the stamp of a random hoof, the buzz of an occasional, premature fly. "I will take my regiment back to Nagoya," he said at last. "As for these others—they may do as they please."

Arakawa released a silent sigh of relief. For a moment there . . .

Thus freed by Nagoya's decision, three of his lesser *daimyo* joined with Arakawa. The others marched off to their home districts, their separate baronies, to wait and see who won. Nagoya's son, who managed the family's traditional lands and ruled its traditional district, took his company and his grim face southward with his father, his mien a statement that he'd rather have fought these rebels here and now.

Arakawa wondered how much of it was pose, and how much principle. "Nagoya Kobushi says he has pledged his honor," he muttered, more to himself than to Terasu. "But a man of honor takes a stand, and I would think better of him had he fought us. Though I didn't expect him to, and we are very fortunate he didn't."

I wonder what Nagoya would think if he knew about Lord Miyagi's regiments, he added silently. *But those we will keep secret if we can. In any event, they will greatly improve our prospects, but kept secret, they ensure our success.*

FORTY-FIVE

Almost a month had passed since Arakawa Hideo had marched his army over Hondoro Pass. A month of slow progress through mountains—of short marches, and frequent negotiations with *daimyo* along the route. Of painful delays while newly-joined companies gathered supplies for the march. A month of swift political developments, galloping couriers and alarming messages. May would soon give way to June and its monsoon rains, and it seemed that the waiting was all but past.

Matsumura had been preparing for him. His battalion had assembled outside its township not far west of Momiji-joka, the town which lay spread beneath his castle. Four subject *daimyo* had arrived with their companies, bivouacking them nearby. Matsumura-sama had had a canopy erected, its sides open to the sweet weather of high spring. There he had gathered his senior officers and those of his allies, along with Lord Maebashi Satsuma, the Emperor's liaison chief. Now Matsumura stood jut-jawed before them, elbows slightly forward, fists clenched against the skirt of his jointed cuirass, the stance a stylized expression of *daimyo* attitude.

"The army of the traitor dog Arakawa should be only a day's march west," he reported. "It is said to include more than five thousand samurai." He didn't say that it's swollen size resulted from unexpected successes in the recruitment of *daimyo* in the region through which it had passed. A moment's consideration would make that obvious, even if they hadn't already heard the reports, and to state it could serve only to dishearten.

"I expect it to attack on the day after next, a belief shared by Lord Maebashi. But we must be prepared to fight tomorrow, in case Arakawa decides to force his march and strike early. Just now we number only eight hundred, but Lords Fujimoto and Hamaoka should arrive with their companies near midday, and three regiments of imperial troops are expected later today, along with my eldest son, Matsumura Harujo, and his company. This will bring our forces to about forty-six hundred, a satisfactory number. We will make our stand four kilometers west of here, where the plain has narrowed and become the valley. It is only a kilometer wide there, and the valley walls are steep. We will be able to prevent them from passing."

He paused, and Lord Ashibaya spoke. "Why has the Emperor not sent more regiments than three?"

Matsumura looked distastefully in the man's direction. Ashibaya's lack of fortitude was as apparent as his lack of confidence, an offense before the gods. "Have you forgotten that Arakawa's and Kyushu's fleets are expected, with strong forces of marines and other troops? These could attempt to force Omori Bay, and attack Miyako directly, or simply land on the Sagami Coast and strike northward. Imperial forces must be prepared and positioned for both eventualities." He paused, then his words became more measured, almost a challenge. "We will have as many as we need here. Assuming we strike boldly, and not like women amusing themselves with the *naginata*."

He reviewed assignments then, including the order of march westward that morning, and positions on the chosen field. When he'd finished, there was a sense of determination among the *daimyo* and their captains. Even Ashibaya seemed committed to stopping the invading army.

But their mood was not entirely focused. For days the earth had trembled from time to time, and a steam plume rose from an island within Osoroshii-yama's great crater, sometimes climbing high, sometimes scarcely showing itself above the rim. Rumor had spread that the priests on the mountain believed it would erupt soon, perhaps before summer. No one knew what form the eruption would take, whether lava flows or explosion, and if explosion, whether it would be one mighty blast or continuous small ones.

The bigger question was, had the *kami* taken sides? Were

these omens favorable, or did they presage an imperial defeat?

Nils had not been invited to the briefing. He and Hans sat their horses with the rest of the household troops. Hans, recently turned seventeen, had grown very confident of his fighting skills, and proud of his thickened muscles, his newly grown strength. And Osoroshii-yama meant little to a foreigner from a part of the world where the very word for volcano had been lost.

But the apprentice poet-become-warrior was nervous nonetheless, at the imminent prospect of battle and its possible consequences. "What will happen to Mariko and Chiyoko if we are killed?" he asked Nils, speaking Swedish for privacy.

Nils smiled at him. "They are samurai wives, and unlikely to be harmed. Also they are members of the Matsumura family; they will hardly be left poor and homeless."

Hans examined the answer. It was no more than he'd told himself before. But if the rebels won, would they respect the Matsumura family? And suppose the enemy soldiers got drunk? Would they remember the difference between the family of a defeated noble, and those of common farmers? And perhaps more to the point, could traitors be expected to act honorably?

Then Matsumura came from the tent with the other lords, hoisted himself into the saddle, and looked around. After a moment he waved an arm, and with his household troops, rode to join his battalion.

At about the same time, other men prepared for combat, men some 190 kilometers northeast. Among the cluster of mounted samurai, one man wore no armor. Ted Baver still wore his jumpsuit with its remarkably durable fabric. It was clean now, though, with a red sash about the waist to hold his pistol.

He was staring toward the northeast, his head tipped back. There was no question about it, despite the brisk breeze; a signal fire had been kindled atop the tall hill he looked at, its thickening smoke dispersing eastward. Lord Miyagi's fleet had been seen headed south, and a series of signal fires lit to carry the word.

Iwato-sama barked an order, and a trumpet blared. Heels nudged horses into rough ranks. Infantrymen got to their feet and formed up. Another order was voiced, and the trumpet spoke again. The column began to move southward.

Lord Iwato Shoji, father of Emiko, was in charge of the force, the senior *daimyo* of the three whose companies had assembled there, and Ted stayed by him as his bodyguard. His pistol had made a powerful impression on the old warrior.

Now Ted Baver was riding to war, someone else's war, a civil war, something he didn't really care to do. But it was one way to reach the capital, and there was a lot to be said for arriving in the retinue of a victorious noble. Besides, this was not a major strike force. It was a feint, as much as anything, a diversion designed to draw northward and engage the loyalist forces under Lord Ibaraki, before Lord Miyagi's fleet landed his much larger army on the coast a few day's march northeast of the capital. Hopefully things wouldn't get too wild and dangerous here.

Matthew Kumalo had seen battle only from the air before, never from ground level, and never where he might become actively involved. Though he'd come close during the raid on Kazi's palace, half a world away. Back on New Home, Gus Fong had insisted the expedition's ground team learn basic combat skills. They'd argued, never imagining they'd need them, and from anyone else might have united in refusal. Now . . .

Nikko was on his left, each of them on one knee in the waiting position. Ranked cavalry waited two paces behind them. About three hundred meters in front stretched a rank of mounted invaders perhaps fifty meters long, backed by others.

For the moment, the two sides faced each other nearly motionless. Matt shrugged his left shoulder, a release of nerves. From the handsome dappled gray gelding behind him to his right, Captain Makimori seemed to growl, then called out to his men, reminding them not to draw their bowstrings without his order, regardless of what the enemy did. On both wings, other officers repeated the command down the line. A movement on Matt's left was Nikko tapping the magazine in her rifle, as if to ensure it was properly seated. She'd tapped it half a dozen times already.

Now the enemy ranks moved, began to approach at a brisk walk, almost knee to knee, bows raised, no doubt with arrows nocked. Matthew raised his assault rifle to the firing position, the sling snug, shoulders and elbows locked against anticipated recoil, following a selected horse with his sights. At what he judged was a hundred and fifty meters, he squeezed, briefly holding down the trigger, sweeping from his right toward the center. Unheard beside him, Nikko's rifle racketed as well. In the enemy's lead rank, several horses and men plunged to the ground. He squeezed off another burst, and another, and the enemy charge dissolved, the remaining riders wheeling, galloping back toward their commanders, who stood in their stirrups, watching dumbfounded. Matthew slapped another magazine into place and squeezed off three more bursts. Left behind were fallen horses, fallen men, three rudderless horses circling without riders, and one armored figure on his feet, staring across the field at the loyalist ranks from which had come such seemingly sorcerous death.

Makimori shouted, and to both right and left, men on horseback surged forward to take advantage of enemy confusion and disarray. Hooves thudded, men shouted, and for just a moment, Nikko and Matthew watched the driving haunches of samurai steeds galloping northward in a cloud of dust. Then Makimori's infantry ran past in two ranks, the first with spears at a thirty-degree angle, the second with ready swords in hand. Matthew engaged his safety and turned, hand reaching to Nikko's elbow. They went to their horses, mounting up beside Makimori and his aide and couriers. Makimori's intent gaze followed the men he'd sent charging off.

To the north, the whole enemy force had turned and was fleeing. Makimori looked at Matthew and spoke, a certain distaste in his tone, reflecting his unhappiness with these new, though admittedly effective weapons. "It happened as you said it would. We will follow, in case they re-form and try again.

It may be they will need a second dose of the medicine you serve."

The rebel flight didn't stop for nearly a kilometer—until the pursuing cavalry had overrun the fleeing infantry and begun to cut them up. Then the invader horsemen rallied, turned about still disorganized, and charged tentatively, pulling up to let fly a swarm of arrows at near maximum range. These hissed down to cause more damage among the unfortunate rebel foot troops than among their loyalist attackers. The loyalist cavalry backed off, reforming ranks as if to charge again, while the surviving rebel infantry stumbled on toward their own lines.

A wide-eyed Ted Baver watched from the saddle. *Assault rifles! The* Phaeacia *is back! It has to be! That's the only explanation! And Ram, or whoever is in command, is supporting the Emperor.*

He turned to Lord Iwata. "Excuse me, Iwata-sama," he said, "but it is clear that Heaven has sided with the Emperor, sending down personages with much greater power than was given me. I recommend that you return home. Meanwhile, if you will send me to them with a flag of truce, perhaps I can prevent worse misfortune. Otherwise Heaven Boats may come and destroy you from the sky."

Matthew stared wide-eyed at the man riding toward them in a jumpsuit. *Ted! It has to be!*

As the rider neared, no doubt remained. He pulled up a dozen meters away, waving back the nervous escort who carried the white banner of truce. "So the *Phaeacia* is back," he said in Anglic. "Thank God! I was afraid I'd never see you two again!"

"It's not back," Matthew said. "Not as far as we know. But thank God anyway. We're together again."

Briefly they talked further, then Ted turned to his escort. "These are my friends from Heaven," he said. "They have promised me they will not send Heaven Boats to punish Lord Iwato and his allies, if he will return to his own district. They have also ordered me to stay here with them. Please convey my thanks to Lord Iwata for his esteemed friendship. He is a most noble *daimyo*, and I wish him well in all things except this ill-chosen war, which I hope he will abandon."

The man nodded and galloped off. Ted turned back to Matt and Nikko, speaking Anglic again. "I'm pretty sure they'll leave. But listen. Tell your guy these people are just a diversion. There's to be a major landing from the sea, by a Lord Miyagi, a *takai daimyo*. Near a place called Mito."

Matthew turned and began to speak to the stern-faced Makimori. Ted listened, hoping this was going to work out all right.

FORTY-SIX

Yesterday's sunshine had been replaced by dirty clouds, and from a low prominence in the Momiji Valley, Matsumura Shinji watched the invaders position themselves. He had more than his samurai drawn up. He'd called up the old militia archers of his districts, who'd been disbanded and disarmed in his boyhood. More than a hundred grayheads were still able-bodied enough to draw a longbow and send one arrow after another more than a hundred meters to a target. He'd had them practicing again for the past two weeks.

Speaking Swedish, Hans asked Nils why the enemy had come right down the valley, instead of dispersing, infiltrating through the forests on the steep valley sides to bypass Matsumura's army. "That's what I'd have done," he said.

"Matsumura has pickets watching in the forest, in case they try that. But in Yamato, it is considered far more honorable to meet your enemy in the open, and win by weapon skills. Stealth and cunning are less honored here than at home. Perhaps if they were fighting a foreign enemy, it would be different.

"Also, in Yamato it is considered that one should use his samurai in a manner that permits the commander hopefully to control their movements. It is not usual, nor are men trained, to maneuver and fight independently in small groups, as would be the case with men infiltrating."

Hans examined all this thoughtfully. His concern over Mariko's safety had slipped to the back of his mind now, out of sight, and his nervousness had abated somewhat. He was ready, semi-focused, his range of attention narrowed to the situation. He and Nils sat their horses close to Matsumura.

Both commands were behind their main forces and flanked by their reserves; Matsumura had fewer reserves than he'd

296

have liked. His trumpeter sent a short series of notes ringing across the valley, and his bowmen, both samurai and old militia, sent their first flight of arrows toward the rebels, following them with others. From the rebel lines, answering flights began, and Hans and Nils held up their shields, angled for deflection.

The exchange continued for about a minute, men falling, horses bucking or wheeling from arrow hits. Then, from the rebel center, a cavalry charge erupted toward the center of Matsumura's lines. Matsumura's trumpeter spoke again through his instrument, and loyalist cavalry rode to meet the attack, followed by infantry. The situation wasn't conducive to defense by massed ranks of pikemen, nor did either army have them.

Neither side had a great wealth of war horses, either, so the ratio of infantry to cavalry was roughly three or four to one. Arakawa's cavalry substantially outnumbered Matsumura's, but during their approach, they were subject to archery from the entire loyalist center.

A Yamatoan cavalry charge seldom involved lances; the horsemen rode at each other shooting arrows, then closed with the sword. It was considered dishonorable deliberately to kill horses, but many were hit regardless, both accidentally and on purpose.

The horsemen met in a cloud of dust, and as they fought, Arakawa's infantry advanced, finally breaking into a trot as they got close. From that point on, tactics consisted mainly of trying to dispatch reserves to the right place at the right time. And in Matsumura's case, of having his old peasant archers direct their fire toward rebel reserves approaching the fight.

It started to rain.

As the fighting continued, order began to break down among the units. Matsumura's defensive line broke here and there, but for a while, the enemy who fought through it were individuals and small groups, engaged and mostly swallowed up by reserves. When the breakthroughs increased, Matsumura turned to signal in the rest of his reserves—and discovered that most of them, the companies of Lords Hamaoka and Tsudagawa, were withdrawing from their ready positions. Deserting! There was nothing to do about it but swear, and he wasted little energy on that.

As if the desertion was a signal, Matsumura's left flank began to give way and break apart. Nils spoke to Hans then, telling him to stay by Matsumura, and alone he charged into the breach, where he surged about on his big horse, conspicuous by his size and strange armor, and by the shield he used not only in defense but as a weapon. He struck savagely, laying men low, clearing a space around himself wherever he went. Confounded, the invaders who'd broken through drew back, while the defense reformed.

But the reversal was brief. Invader reserves charged in, and Nils's horse went down. For some seconds, Hans could still see him, by his size and the eddies of movement around him. Then he became busy in fighting of his own: The household cavalry platoon charged out, to meet a force of rebel cavalry striking toward the old *daimyo*, intending to behead the loyalist army. The defensive line was collapsing now. The two cavalry forces crashed, and for several minutes, Hans was in the thick of it, chopping, thrusting, striking men both in the saddle and on the ground. Nor unlike most samurai, was he reluctant to strike horses.

A trumpet bleated, an officer bellowed. Matsumura himself was withdrawing now, as the rebels overran his infantry. When it was able to disengage, the scraps of Hans's platoon followed in headlong flight eastward.

The Battle of Momiji was over, except for the rebel mop-up of loyalists afoot, who unable to run away, and not allowed by the enemy to surrender, stayed and fought, and died.

From his vantage, Arakawa had witnessed the two tall foreigners fighting on horseback, and was impressed. He'd also seen the largest unhorsed, and had ordered an aide to have the man found. Alive if possible, and save him from the massacre that would surely follow. He hoped to question him.

The surviving loyalist cavalry didn't stop to reorganize till they'd reached the confluence of the Gara-gara and Momiji Rivers, some kilometers east of Momiji-joka. There, by Matsumura's grim estimate, only six or eight hundred formed up, including imperials. He didn't expect to see any of his own infantry again, ever. Nor of Hamaoka's and Tsudagawa's companies; their desertion had tipped the balance, and they'd no doubt joined the rebels.

Except for them, his men had fought well and strongly, doggedly, and given the invaders many casualties. But with certain exceptions, they'd lacked the fire, the spirit, the expectation of victory that the enemy had had. The exceptions had included Nissa, who'd been a giant of ferocity and strength. And Hansu, who'd fought like a hero.

Jaw clamped, Matsumura looked toward his grandson, who seemed unwounded. Nissa was dead, he was sure. When the *Inrinu's* horse had gone down, his chances of survival had become virtually zero. The rebels would not allow men afoot to escape alive; certainly not one so conspicuous.

FORTY-SEVEN

On the ridge's lower slope, Nils stood behind a stout-boled pine, watching, soaked more with sweat than with the light rain that fell. The fighting had thinned to patches here and there, as rebel infantry and squads of horsemen finished off the surviving loyalist samurai on foot. Never before had he found himself in a worse situation in battle, yet it was the first time he'd come through such a fight without a wound.

After he'd gotten his breath sufficiently, he turned and hiked diagonally up the steep ridge through the forest. Reaching the crest, he turned eastward, following it.

After three kilometers, he could see Momiji Castle ahead, on the end of a short spur ridge, a little lower than his own position. Stopping within the edge of a group of young pines, he settled down to wait and watch. Already the castle had been occupied by rebels, and from his vantage he could see the road that ran up to it from the town. Men rode on it in both directions, but mostly uphill. There'd been no fighting there. In this war, the castle had no strategic value, and hadn't been worth leaving a force to defend it.

For a while, the rain continued intermittently, never hard. Evening came late in that season, but after a while dusk arrived, and gradually dark, a darkness thickened by clouds. But to the Yngling's senses, though he perceived it as darkness, it was a darkness transparent as noon. Taking off his hauberk, he hid it, along with his shield, beneath a prostrate sprawl of ground juniper. Then he started down to the narrow backbone that led to the prominence on which the castle stood. The rain again had stopped, perhaps for the night, perhaps only for the moment; the darkness hadn't thinned at all.

The castle wall loomed concave before him, its upward curve

nearly vertical near the top, its massive, squared stone blocks uncemented. On a night as dark as this, anyone standing guard above would fail to see him. He followed its base until, above him, he saw the building in which he lived with Chiyoko. There he took his sword from his belt and lay it on the ground, then began to climb. His length of arm and leg helped, and even more his psi vision.

The building overhung the wall a bit. He stopped close below it, where an irregularity allowed him to rest, both feet on a projection eight or ten centimeters wide, while he leaned against the block in front of him, fingers hooked around its ends. Leaned and rested, and scanned psionically.

He found Chiyoko's mind; she was all right. He tried to catch her attention, to tell her he was all right too, but she was not significantly telepathic, and failed to perceive his thought. Along with Mariko, and supervised by one of Arakawa's regimental surgeons, she'd volunteered to help tend the wounded—rebel wounded—who'd been brought in. But being seven and a half months pregnant, she'd tired and gone to her room after a time.

Both women had been courteously treated.

He scanned farther then, and found the castle's new commander. The man was relaxing in Matsumura's large hot tub, taking oral reports from officers. Their victory had been complete, and while rebel casualties had been fairly heavy, Matsumura's army no longer existed.

Nils eavesdropped for perhaps twenty minutes, then heard something that made things click within his mind. *The rebel fleet was led by a lord named Sugimori Michio!* A name he'd learned from Achikh's mind, on the lower slope of Osoroshii-yama. And now he did something he hadn't succeeded in doing since Ilse had left for the stars. Ilse who'd demonstrated to him that it could be done, and how. He left his body, not relocating instantaneously this time, but soaring high and swift over nightbound mountains and forest until he saw the sea ahead.

Below him was a volcano, not Osoroshii-yama, but another not so large. It too held a lake in its crater, with a plume of steam from an island within it, rising pale beneath the clouds.

Then he was past it, and in front of him lay ships, scores of them, perhaps a hundred, riding stone anchors in the lea of a forested shore.

He homed on one unhesitatingly, ignoring the lookouts, ignoring the marines sleeping beneath awnings and almost covering the deck. He stationed his viewpoint in a cabin beneath the poop, never wondering how he'd known to come to just that place. A man slept there, his thoughts just now amorphous, useless to his visitor, so Nils shifted to the marine sentry squatted outside the cabin door, thinking of tomorrow.

Would Lord Kyushu arrive? the samurai wondered. If he didn't, would they go ashore and march north without waiting? He looked forward to being on firm ground again, and wished that Sugimori-sama had let them land and bivouac, instead of staying here on the ships, many not a bowshot from the beach.

To go ashore! Mostly they'd sailed far from land, so as not to be seen, with only mountaintops showing above the horizon. The rumor was, though, that Lord Sugimori had said they'd sail northward to the head of the broad open bay, before they landed.

Lord Sugimori had definitely said it might be a day or two, or even longer before Kyushu-sama arrived, and who knew, for sure, how strong the Emperor's army was they'd have to fight? It would certainly be best to wait. To be defeated here, so far from home, would be terrible. Fatal.

Time would tell. At least they had sufficient food, and they'd replenished their water casks from the nearby mountain stream that flowed into the bay.

Nils withdrew to his body, where it clung to the castle wall like some great, thick-limbed spider, and climbed back down to his waiting sword. Then he hiked down the ridgeside to Matsumura's military township west of the civilian town. A rebel cavalry battalion had occupied it, its horses picketed by squads in the adjacent pasture.

Sentries were posted at intervals. Nils moved carefully among them in the cloud-thickened darkness, homing on the largest horse he saw. A sentry stood nearby, as good as blind this night, but it was doubtful that anything was wrong with his hearing.

Silent as a shadow, Nils slipped up behind him, and with a single quick move, clapped a large hand over the man's mouth, then broke his neck.

The horse wore its bridle but not its saddle. Calming its mind with his, Nils put the bit in its mouth, mounted bareback, and rode quietly out of the pasture unnoticed.

FORTY-EIGHT

Prince Terasu and his battlefield retinue rode up the winding approach to the castle, glad that the rain had stopped, but wishing the darkness was less dense. Guards halted them at the gate, peering into their faces by the light of a lantern. Terasu was recognized at once, and they were led inside, where the prince turned over his horse to his groom. One of the guards then showed him to the command room, where at that late hour, a sergeant was in charge.

The castle's new commander had finished a hot soak, and was lounging in a fresh kimono with an aide, two local women, and a jar of *sake*, when the prince came in without announcement. The commander was momentarily angered at the interruption, then recognized who had entered, and promptly stood to bow.

The prince asked for and got a report, then asked to see the hospital. Still in his kimono, the commander took him there. Actually the hospital was several rooms, each with its floor largely occupied by wounded men on pads. In the largest room were three women, working under the supervision of an army surgeon. The surgeon recognized the prince, and bowed deeply to him. The women, though not knowing who the newcomer was, followed the surgeon's lead. Terasu gestured them to continue what they'd been doing. Then, while pretending to observe the wounded, he sized up the women. Two seemed clearly to be servants. The other was very young and very lovely, probably a member of Matsumura's household.

Terasu had participated in running down stragglers after the battle, and had killed several. Killing, he'd discovered, had aroused him sexually, and sidling up to the surgeon, asked in a quiet voice who the lovely young woman was.

"Your Majesty," the man murmured, "she is the wife of Matsumura's grandson, son of the adopted foreigner we've heard about."

"Yet she works here?"

"Excuse me, but I believe she is here in case her husband is brought in wounded."

"Ah! And what is her name?"

"Her adoptive mother called her Mariko."

Terasu nodded curtly, and sauntered over to where she was holding a bowl to help a soldier drink. When she'd finished, she straightened, and saw a handsome, noble-looking officer watching her from behind. Despite her noble husband and doubly noble grandfather-in-law, she felt intimidated by this stranger, and bowed deeply.

"I see you know me," Terasu said. "It is late now, and you are a noble woman. These others can do what is necessary here. Go to your room and rest."

She didn't move. "Excuse me for my poor ignorance, but I'm afraid I do *not* know you."

His eyebrows rose. "I am Prince Terasu, who soon will be Emperor. Now. Go to your room and rest."

She bowed again, even lower this time, and hurried out. When she'd gone, Terasu went to one of the other women. "In what room does Matsumura Mariko live?" he asked.

She'd overheard his conversation with Mariko, and knowing who this man was, was unable to squeak out a word to him.

"Show me!" he ordered. She bowed as deeply as she could, and almost scurried out; Terasu had to hurry to keep up. They went up a level, and reversed down a corridor. There the woman stood with eyes averted, and gesturing, whispered "Here."

His nod was curt again. "Leave!" he said, the word preemptory but quiet. When she'd gone, he waited a moment, then rapped on the door.

"Who is it?"

"I have news about your husband."

He waited. After a long moment the door slid aside a dozen centimeters, and Mariko peered out. He put his foot in the opening. "Invite me in, that I may talk without standing in the hall."

Reluctantly she slid it further aside, and stepped away. He entered, and turning, pushed it shut. Looking at her, he could almost see her pulse speed with fear. Delicious fear, it seemed to him.

"News?" she asked.

"It is not what you had hoped for. Your husband is—dead."

A small cry leaped from her mouth, and she raised her hand to it.

"I had heard it in the field, and after you left, I spoke to the man I'd heard say it. To be sure I hadn't misunderstood. Your husband was fleeing the battle, and was shot from the saddle by an arrow. He tried to surrender then, but was cut down by a sword. Because of his singular appearance, my man went to examine him, and found him quite dead."

She began to weep, and Terasu went to her, wrapping his arms around her as if to comfort her in her grief. She had appeared small, but in his arms was excitingly rounded, and his pulse quickened. One hand began to stroke the small of her back, and suddenly she pushed away from him. "No!" she said, looking up at him. "He would never try to surrender, and he is not dead!"

She didn't say what else had occurred to her: that he'd told her what he had to take advantage of her.

"I do not lie!" he said stiffly. "But I will forgive you for saying it, this time. You are naturally upset. I will leave you now, and hope you feel better tomorrow."

He turned and left, she staring after him. When he'd gone, she began to cry again, silently. After a few minutes, she went into the hall, and down it to the room of Chiyoko and Nils, where she knocked. Chiyoko let her in.

"What is wrong, Mariko? You have been crying!"

Mariko told her what Prince Terasu had said, and what he'd done. "And when he held me, he began to stroke me," she said. "It was then I realized he'd lied, that he only wanted to have *kogo* with me."

Chiyoko nodded. "It seems probable."

"Do you think Hansu is dead?"

"It is possible. Thousands must have died. Nissa may also have been killed."

"I am afraid of Prince Terasu. He is not an honorable man."

"That is true. I have heard stories told about him; he has a reputation. When he wanted some woman, he did not stop until she gave in. He would not only lie to her; he would lie about her if she continued to refuse."

Mariko paled, hand to mouth. Chiyoko went to a small chest standing closed on a table, and unlocked it. Inside she sought beneath some things, and came out with a—something. She pressed a stud on the side of it, and a knife blade snapped out, driven by a spring. Mariko stared at it, partly fascinated, partly horrified.

"Take it," Chiyoko said, and her eyes were like the knife. "Keep it with you. And if Prince Terasu molests you, do not struggle, but afterward, use this. Not for *jigai*; there is no vengeance in dying yourself. Use it to kill him."

Chiyoko snapped the blade shut and held it out. "You are a samurai's wife," she added.

Mariko stared first at the knife, then at Chiyoko. She'd heard that the other was a hero's daughter; now she began to realize what that could mean. Hesitantly she took it, then bowed. "Thank you, beloved Chiyoko," she said, "you have given me heart."

Mariko returned to her room then and prepared for bed, tucking the switchblade beneath her futon. After she'd lain down, her mind returned to Hans, and for a while she shivered uncontrollably. Prince Terasu may have lied, but still—was Hans alive or dead?

The next morning, someone knocked on her door, and she opened it. A soldier, a sergeant stood there. "Lady Matsumura Mariko," he said, "you are to pack some things at once. Not more than your maidservant can carry by herself. As a member of Matsumura Shinji's immediate family, you are to be taken in the retinue of Prince Terasu, as a hostage."

The world seemed to spin around her, and she gripped the edge of the door. "But— Excuse me, but I am of little value as a hostage. Lord Matsumura does not approve of me. He would let me be killed without a thought!"

"Nonetheless I am to take you with us. Prince Terasu has

ordered it. Quickly now! Have your maidservant pack some clothes for you, and some for herself. Otherwise you will have nothing in which to change when these become soiled. There is no place to launder them on bivouac."

He started to say more, hesitated, then spoke on. "And if the prince wishes you to have *kogo* with him, it will be well to agree. He can be unpleasant if you frustrate him. And he will soon be Emperor. You could become a royal concubine, with servants and everything you want. You might even become an empress!"

He bowed slightly, then turned and left, sliding the door closed behind him.

FORTY-NINE

Nils rode through the night and the next day, at length to leave the hoof-beaten dirt of the imperial "highway." From time to time he dismounted to rest his horse, but even afoot he trotted, reins in his hand, to lose as little time as possible.

He was going to the hut at the east foot of Osoroshii-yama. Rather than take the long route via the monastery, he rode mostly southward now, shortening the distance considerably. He guided by intuition, for this far north, the old road trace had been in the path of heavy volcanic ash fall, five centuries earlier, and been buried meters deep in ash. It was necessary to stop from time to time, to let the horse graze in some meadow or glen, while its rider napped in the sun.

Some time afterward, he reached far enough south to find the old trace again. Over one stretch, his way took him over raw lava, where sharp rocks lamed the horse. Nils left the animal then, continuing on afoot.

Achikh had built his cooking fire outside, and was roasting a shoulder of venison, when Nils came in sight of the hut. The sun had lowered behind the mountain, but it was still daylight. The Mongol watched him stolidly as he approached. Nearby, Satoru sat on his feet, watching through Achikh's mind, seeing what Achikh saw.

After a first glance, it was at Satoru, not Achikh, that the Northman looked. <<Hello, Hidaka Satoru,>> the Northman thought at him. <<I have news for you, of someone you know. Lord Sugimori Michio.>> He watched recognition flare, and intent interest. Now would come the real challenge. <<Would you like to see where he is? What he is doing? He is nearer than you might think. What would you be willing to do to destroy him?>>

Satoru's interest took an edge, an avidity.

<<Come with me then, in the spirit.>>

He didn't wait for doubts or questions. Still in intimate psionic contact with the Hokkaido wizard, he left his body again—and Satoru found himself with him, doing what he had never done before. Nils traveled less swiftly this time, in case Satoru needed to orient himself. They passed over jumbled volcanic terrain, old lava flows weathered and overgrown, others relatively young, mostly barren, dark and rugged. By dusk they passed over the other, lesser volcano, its steam plume pink in the sunset, blowing eastward, losing itself in the air above the anchored fleet.

They didn't pause, but went straight to the flagship, where Lord Sugimori Michio sat on the quarterdeck with his aide and his admiral, taking the evening meal. Sugimori was examining alternative landing scenarios. The two spirits eavesdropped for long minutes, then withdrew, snapping back to the hut as if on some celestial rubberband, to hover above their seated bodies. And to ease back into them, for Satoru was new to this.

Briefly then, they communed with each other, the Neoviking chieftain and the Hokkaido wizard, exchanging concepts and thoughts. Finally Nils got to his feet. <<I will go now,>> he thought. <<I have my own battles to fight.>>

He turned to Achikh, who looked at him with mild curiosity. "Do you have something I can eat?" Nils asked. "I have far to travel, as fast as I can."

Without speaking, Achikh carved off a two-kilo chunk of the shoulder he was roasting, and gave it to him.

"Thank you, my *anda*," Nils said aloud. "Perhaps we will meet again."

He strode out of sight then, eating as he walked. He had a long hike north and east to rejoin Matsumura. But the need for haste was over now. The decisive battle, it seemed to him, would be over before he could get there. Meanwhile he'd done what he could.

Giving no further thought to the giant foreigner, Hidaka Satoru sank slowly into communion with the powerful, far-reaching entity he'd become so familiar with, so intimate with through the winter. The *kami* had at first regarded him as a curiosity, then as an amusement, later as a teachable student interested in the workings of the mountain, and finally as a sort of human protege.

Now Satoru would test the relationship and his skills.

FIFTY

Ordinarily, patience was one of Arakawa's virtues. Ordinarily.

After the battle of Momiji, he'd marched his army east, and at the end of the second day, made camp near a small village known as Nabemura, in the midst of the Kanto Plain. He was prepared to stay there till Sugimori and Kyushu had landed their troops on Sagami Bay, forty kilometers south.

There was no hurry, and Arakawa knew it, but he was impatient. Sugimori was at anchor south of Odawara, and couriers had traveled back and forth between them. The holdup was Kyushu; the difficult old fool hadn't arrived yet. Meanwhile, here at Nabemura, a strong imperial army was drawn up opposite his own.

He looked around at the officers gathered in his large command tent. "Kyushu still had not arrived at midday," he said, saw the expressions of irritation and disgust, then continued. "Tomorrow at midday, Sugimori will move up the shore to Chigasaki, and unload his troops there regardless. Then they will march northward. Also" —he paused— "tomorrow after midday, we will attack the imperial army."

There were looks of concern at this. Arakawa saw them and went on. "We arrived at Momiji stronger than I expected, due to our successful recruitment of *daimyo* in the country between there and Osaka. And our victory at Momiji was decisive. Matsumura's allies did not perform well there. Two companies of them, and three others from farther north, have joined us here since then. It seems clear that even unaided, we can drive back the imperial forces facing us.

"Meanwhile, the Emperor surely knows of Sugimori's fleet, and must suspect that it waits for Kyushu. What he does not know is where it will land. Will it land on Sagami Bay and

312

strike north? Or will it attempt to force the Omori Narrows? Or with Kyushu, will it do both?

"He must hold regiments in position to react to each possibility, and will hardly dare bring up those reserves to fight us."

Smiling grimly, he looked his people over. "Meanwhile there is another army involved that most of you do not know of. By now, Lord Miyagi's fleet should have landed a regiment at Mito, preparing to march against Miyako from the north. And Lord Ibaraki and his allies, who might otherwise contest the way with Miyagi, are in the upper Naka Valley, fighting *daimyo* from northern Tochigi. It is probable that word of Miyagi's landing will reach the Emperor before tomorrow's battle, which should seriously damage the morale of imperial forces."

He grinned at his commanders. "And more! Miyagi will also land two battalions at Hasenhama, on the Kujukuri Shore, if they haven't already done so. Even his commanders at Mito were not to know of this. These battalions will then make a short march by the ancient road over the hills, and appear on the plain just north of the city, probably without having to fight until they reach it. It is even possible that they will find only a garrison left at the palace, and be able to capture it themselves. At least they will sow confusion and dismay."

His expression hardened. "Do not be deceived. The Imperial Army will fight bravely and doggedly, but they lack the spirit of winning. If we attack with that spirit, and with determination, and do not allow ourselves to be disheartened by casualties, we will surely win. Make certain that your men know this, that they feel it in their hearts.

"Brief your commanders before supper. They, in turn, are to brief their officers in the morning. They should already know their positions. Questions . . . ? You are dismissed."

Arakawa and his aide watched them leave. "One thing troubles me," Arakawa said thoughtfully. "Prince Terasu insists on being in the front rank tomorrow. 'To let the men know what kind of samurai I am,' he says. It is dangerous."

The aide nodded. He'd heard the prince.

"I believe in bravery," Arakawa went on, "but we need him

alive. You will assign a squad of my best guardsmen to stay near him, to protect him in case they are needed."

"I will see to it, Arakawa-sama."

"Go then. I will rest—lie down and perhaps close my eyes."

Arakawa went to his room. Even with the sides rolled up, it was hotter than he liked. As he lay down, he thought, *I need you alive, my dear son-in-law, alive until the war is over. Then, when the fighting is done, you must die, because you are less responsible, less fit to rule, than even your brother. And I will rule as regent and* kubo-sama, *until your sons, my grandsons, are old enough to sit on the throne.*

Dusk had interfered with her embroidery, and Mariko had set it aside for her servant to put away. The tent darkened as Prince Terasu blocked the door. He'd removed his armor, and despite being in a war camp had donned a *kami-shimo*. He looked at the maid servant and scowled blackly at her. "Leave!" he ordered pointing, and stepped inside.

The girl looked desperately at her mistress, then bowed deeply, and without speaking, hurried past him and out. The prince examined Mariko without saying anything, as if to heighten her concern. "I am tired of your refusals," he said at last. "I have sent a man back to the battlefield at Momiji, with orders to find your husband's body and bring his head here. Surely that will satisfy your disbelief!"

"I am sorry, but I do not believe he is dead. I believe that the men who told you that were mistaken."

He spoke more quietly now. "Am I not more handsome than your foreign husband was, before a *katana* took his life? Am I not of royal blood, rich and powerful?"

He stepped toward her then, reached out and captured her wrist, his voice taking on a note of honest entreaty. "You are the most lovely and desirable woman I have ever seen. Ever imagined! When I look at you, I feel heat throughout my body! I want to take you in my arms and cover you with kisses! If you will have me, I will make you my empress, and you will want for nothing."

"I am not worthy of the love of a man who will be Emperor. My husband is more than I deserve. I—"

Terasu grabbed her roughly and pulled her to him, pressing against her, and kissed her long and hard. She struggled to push free, exciting him, then turned her head and cried out for help.

He stepped back and slapped her, not very hard, then gripped her shoulders painfully. "You were not born samurai," he hissed, and shook her once, sharply. "I can take you by force if I wish."

"My husband is samurai," she answered defiantly, "and my father-in-law is samurai. And Lord Matsumura, *his* father, is a *tehon daimyo*. I am legally samurai! Lord Tsuyama has told me so!"

Terasu gripped her by the chin with a strong thumb and forefinger, forcing her to look up at him. "Lord Tsuyama will be carrion within the week, and so will that degenerate Hikari. Then *I* will be emperor. I will return to your tent tomorrow after the battle, and make my offer one more time. If you refuse me, I will tear your clothes off and take you by force. Then I will take down your hair and turn you out as a commoner wench. No doubt some of my victorious soldiers will carry you to their tents and require your help in celebrating."

He let her go then, and left.

She did not weep; she'd finished with that. *Tomorrow*, she told herself, *I will not refuse you. I will have* kogo *with you until you cannot do it anymore, and fall asleep. And when you have fallen asleep, then you will pay.*

FIFTY-ONE

The day dawned clear and warm. By midday a fair breeze had risen, discouraging the mosquitoes. Biting flies were active however, drawn by the thousands of horses and sweating men.

There was no eminence from which the commanders could view the battlefield to be, pleasant farmland trampled now by war horses, and soon to be fertilized with blood. His Majesty, the Emperor Hikari, was in the first rank of cavalry, near its center, standing in his stirrups to see what he could. He rode a splendid red gelding that shone from good grain and thorough grooming. Beside Hikari sat Okaya Yari, on a gelding hardly distinguishable from the Emperor's. The two men did not speak.

Neither carried a bow. Hikari had bowmen galore; for his own part, his swords would do. His battle general was Lord Ueda, who was in full charge of the imperial forces; the Emperor himself had only to fight or not, as he saw fit. Almost every cavalryman wore his family's flag in miniature, or his own, fitted into a bracket on the back of his cuirass, to flutter bravely above his helmet as he rode. The Emperor, however, was also accompanied by a standard bearer, carrying the imperial standard on a three-meter staff. Across the field, Hikari saw his brother's upraised standard also being carried into the line— the imperial standard but with a broad golden border. Unfortunately, it was somewhat to the south; they would not meet on the opening charge. Later perhaps, Hikari thought.

Nearby, Lord Ueda barked an order; he would not grant the initiative to the pack of rebel dogs. His trumpeter raised his silver instrument and blew, the sound echoed by others in both directions along the line—be ready! Voices ceased abruptly, replaced by the rattle and squeak of equipment, the stamp of nervous hooves. Then another series of notes sounded clear and sharp, and the imperial cavalry burst forward. Opposite them, other trumpets sounded, but the Emperor, sword enfisted as he surged forward, did not hear them over the thunder of hooves, the roar of battle cries. The rebel line charged to meet them.

Lord Sugimori was on his flagship, riding the gentle swells well off shore. His fleet remained at anchor near the beach. He'd decided to wait till the last minute, in hope that Kyushu would arrive.

And the old warrior had! The appearance of Kyushu's fleet had startled Sugimori, showing him how weak his faith in the *takai daimyo* had become. Now their two flagships met side by side, and grappled together so that Sugimori could cross over and discuss the details of landing.

He knew quite well that Kyushu hadn't liked the plan to land on Sagami Bay. His preference had been to force the Omori Narrows and assault Miyako itself. Arakawa, with Terasu backing him, had applied considerable pressure, more or less forcing Kyushu's agreement. Their argument had been that the Omori Narrows was too dangerous. The imperial fleet could meet them there, loaded with marines, and force a fight far short of Miyako, in circumstances favorable to the imperial defense.

Now Sugimori described briefly and simply his plan for landing. "We must be quick," he finished. "The battle will begin at any time now, if it hasn't already."

Kyushu grunted, staring at him coldly. He'd been alone with his thoughts since leaving Uita, and those thoughts had become increasingly unfriendly to Arakawa. "I am not landing on the Sagami shore," he said. "I have decided to force the narrows by myself, if you are not willing."

Sugimori stood shocked. "But the agreement . . ."

Abruptly the old man's eyes blazed. "The agreement is shit! I reject it! The Emperor knows you are here, and now you say Arakawa's army has already attacked him. Hikari will not expect me to force the narrows. Probably he has drawn a large part of his marines to meet you here."

"But— Arakawa-sama expects us both to land. It was part of the—"

"*Then land!*" Kyushu roared, spittle spraying. "*March north!* I did not come here to argue with some underling!" For a moment he stood glaring, breathing hard. "Now leave this ship, unless you want to come with me." He looked at his captain. "Prepare to let go the . . ."

He stopped, for they'd felt a shock through the hull, followed by shuddering, as if the world were suffering a seizure. A shout came down from the lookout, and all eyes turned westward toward Hakone-san, the volcano above the west shore. Her steam plume had blossomed, was growing into a tall white column. On the bay, the swells jittered at the trembling of the shelf beneath, as if the sea itself was frightened.

Suddenly there was a great jar as the mountain exploded, blowing out the side toward Sagami Bay, and a great cloud of pulverized rock surged upward. Half a minute later, the two flagships jumped forward in the water as the shock wave struck them. Then the men aboard saw a pyroclastic flow, a terrible avalanche of glowing hot dust and ashes rushing down the mountainside toward the bay, the forest on both sides bursting into flame from its heat. At the same time, the lookouts called down that many of Sugimori's ships, those that had been broadside to the blast, had overturned.

The pyroclastic flow had lost considerable of its force and coherence before it reached the fleet, but even so, some of the upright ships burst into flame. Minutes later, even those on the flagships felt the wave of heat, and smelled the stinking gases.

Kyushu pulled his gaze away from the ash cloud that continued to climb, and looked at Sugimori. "There!" he shouted, almost exulting. "Osoroshii-yama has spoken! We were not supposed to land on Sagami Bay! Now, go to your fleet and land where you like!"

With an effort, Sugimori restrained himself from drawing his sword and cutting the old man down. Instead he crossed over to his flagship, separated it from Kyushu's, and began to tack back to his fleet, what was left of it. More ships had been overturned or set afire than were operable. Most of the men

had been lost—drowned or burned to death, or killed by
breathing superheated fumes; almost none above deck had
survived. Sugimori no longer had either fleet or army.

The two ranks of cavalry had clashed, but the infantry hadn't
reached each other yet, when they felt the first quake. For just
a moment it distracted the horsemen, then they fought on, for
quakes were not unfamiliar in Yamato, and this had not been
a severe one. Then the second and greater quake shook the
ground. By that time the infantry had met, with a great crash,
and a roar from many throats, and engagement disallowed
stopping, for those who stopped fighting were cut down. A
minute and a half later they heard the distant boom of Hakone-
san's eruption, and fought through that too, killing and dying.

In the melee, ranks came apart, and groups fought through.
The rebels, though outnumbered, fought hot-bloodedly instead
of grimly, and forced their way forward. The imperial lines
began to give way, but stubbornly, not breaking. Ueda threw
in reserves of cavalry then, like javelins, not to bolster weak
points, but into segments of the rebel line that had not gained.
Two of these thrusts drove through, confusing and distracting
the rebels, until rebel reserves rode into the breaches, striking
with confidence and unrelenting force, snuffing out the imperial
breakthroughs.

For a time, the lines more or less stabilized, until the men
were almost too weary to stand. It was the imperial infantry
who gave way then, but the rebels could only plod forward,
lacking the energy to overwhelm them. The cavalry had been
segmented, and the segments scattered. Then both Ueda and
Arakawa signalled their men to disengage and reform. Men
backed away, arms leaden at their sides, swords seemingly too
heavy to raise again.

It was the imperial troops who continued backing away
though, protected by their still-active cavalry. When the ranks
had reformed, the field was almost carpeted with bodies, and
the imperial ranks were somewhat farther back than they'd
been to start with.

Terasu sat his horse exultantly, spine straight, shoulders back, breathing deeply, and watched the imperial forces withdraw. He had killed men that day. "The first cloth, Yukio!" he said, and without looking, reached out a hand to his aide. The man pulled a cotton cloth from a saddlebag and handed it to the prince, who wiped the blood from his sword, being careful to clean around the small handguard before discarding the rag. "The second, Yukio!" The man drew out a silk cloth then, and Terasu lovingly polished the blade.

He felt god-like, scanning the field, the bodies. Hundreds of bodies, no doubt thousands. Many undoubtedly were not dead; some would no doubt live till night, then try to crawl away. He felt no fatigue, and wondered at the living samurai who, when the fighting had stopped, had thrown themselves on the ground to rest. *They are not of imperial blood*, he reminded himself. *One must make allowance for that.* Overlooking that the infantry had *run* into battle, and that of necessity, their fighting had been much more incessant, more unrelenting than his own.

He discovered, in fact, that instead of tiring him, the battle and blood-letting had stimulated his sexuality again. Turning his horse, he said, "Yukio, tell Koto to stay here and keep the others with him. Then hurry to camp, to the tent of the woman I brought with me. There is business I've left unfinished there, and I may wish your help. This"—he gestured at the battlefield—"this will wait."

Then he kicked his heels against his gelding's ribs, and trotted off briskly toward the encampment less than three kilometers to the rear. *I am a descendant of the sun goddess*, he told himself, *and have blooded my sword repeatedly today, showing myself a hero. It is intolerable that I wait further because of the unwillingness of some girl.*

On both sides, the troops ate and drank in a macabre sort of picnic, then flopped on the ground amidst young barley, or potato hills, or hay stubble greened over with second growth. Many napped, faces turned away from the sun, while to the south, the towering ash plume spread eastward, resembling the anvil top of some large thunderhead. Few paid it any heed, noticing little except their exhaustion and what wounds they had. On the imperial side, the Emperor rode among his guard. His small personal flag showed little life now, for the breeze had largely died. He rode at an easy walk, speaking confidently, assuringly to the men he passed. His armor was blood-splattered, and his helmet had lost most of one simulated water buffalo horn to a sword stroke.

On the rebel side, unit commanders received reports, and passed them on to the high command. They were in no hurry to renew the battle; let the men rest. And, Arakawa thought, let the Emperor's men get word of regiments moving on them from the south and the north. He had no notion of the disaster on Sagami Bay.

Imperial morale must already be stricken, it seemed to him. They would fight, no doubt of it, but only as duty. It seemed to him he could smell their sense of defeat, smell it clear across the field.

At length he'd been brought all the information it seemed to him he needed, and looked around. His eyes settled on Terasu's standard bearer. "Where is the prince?" Arakawa asked.

"Excuse me, your lordship, but Prince Terasu has returned to camp."

The commander looked stunned. "Is he wounded?"

"No your lordship. Captain Masurao told me the prince had something urgent to attend to that would not take long."

Arakawa pressed his lips together and looked toward the bivouac, wondering what could possibly be urgent enough to hold up the battle. Any thought he might ever have had of allowing Terasu to rule had long since died. This simply ratified his decision. Meanwhile he'd wait till the irresponsible fool came back before renewing the attack. Best that Terasu be visible to both sides; it was he who gave the rebellion legitimacy, and his army its sense of mission.

Not long afterward, Terasu rode briskly up, his smirk an irritation. "Have I made you wait, father-in-law?" he asked. "My business in camp has been accomplished, and we have hours of daylight yet." He gestured across the field. "More than time enough for me to kill my vile brother and disperse those vermin before supper."

Arakawa swallowed his anger. He would make sure, he told himself, that this pompous buffoon's sons did not develop their father's insufferable conceit. "Indeed, Your Majesty," was all he said.

"Now," said Terasu, "where is my brother's standard? It is time for me to meet him, and show the armies which brother is the chosen of the gods."

Silently Arakawa reminded himself that the men assigned to ride with Terasu were among the best he had. As the prince rode off with them, the *takai daimyo* turned to his trumpeter. "Call the army to readiness," he snapped.

On the other side of the field, the imperial army heard the rebel trumpets, and were already on their feet when their own trumpets answered. Again it was theirs that first called the charge, and again the imperial cavalry surged forward, the infantry following, their line as long as before, but with fewer ranks.

The Emperor's cavalry moved with as much grim energy as before, but the infantry started sluggishly, and when the trumpets signaled double-time, they ran with less speed. Ahead of them, the mounted forces clashed with an impact seemingly transmitted through the ground. But as before, the battle wasn't really joined until the infantry met, throats roaring, swords and *naginata* clashing.

It was the imperial infantry that began to give way, almost at once. Give way without breaking yet awhile, for to break was to be surrounded, and surely die. Meanwhile, around and amongst them the cavalry fought, their attention on the mounted samurai they clashed with, seeming almost oblivious of the infantry, whose attention in turn was fixed on the foot troops they fought. This was not to say that no mounted samurai struck a man on foot in passing, or that no horse was gutted by some *naginata*, nor hamstrung by some infantryman's sword. But these were mostly incidental.

The front ranks of foot troops melted away, hewed down by the men in front of them, but the casualties were heaviest on the imperial side. Here and there they broke and were overrun, and more and more their line gave back. In the melee, many of the horsemen became more or less separated. Thus the Emperor and some guardsmen found themselves isolated a little from the main body of imperial cavalry. Terasu saw this, and waving, screaming orders through the din, he led an attack on the Emperor's group. Each royal brother was surrounded by guardsmen committed to their safety, but by the time the brothers met, their guardsmen had mostly been cut down, or unhorsed and trampled.

Then Terasu and three of his elite reached Hikari and Okaya Yari, and while the Emperor cut down one of them, his own horse was killed. Somehow he found himself on his feet, surrounded by milling horses and hewing riders. Okaya was already heavily engaged. Terasu shouted that his brother was his, but whether this registered on any of the others is uncertain. He could easily have ridden the Emperor down, trampled him, but instead turned his mount aside, raising his sword, wanting to strike his brother dead by his own hand. Meanwhile, seeing the Emperor unhorsed, Okaya had wheeled and was driving at Terasu, even as Okaya's own adversary struck him from behind with his sword, a thrust that penetrated deeply between the plates of his articulated cuirass. Even as Okaya fell from the saddle, his horse struck Terasu's from behind. The impact nearly unseated the prince, and for just an instant, he struggled to regain his balance.

In that instant, Hikari struck his brother's thigh, cutting it half through despite the chaps-like leg armor, so that the prince fell with a scream. Then supporters arrived, less interested in fighting than in rescuing their royal charges. Sergeant Koto let Terasu's standard fall, and dismounting, lifted the prince. With help he got the seemingly boneless figure across his saddle before being knocked down himself by another horse, and trampled.

Then the brothers were swept away toward the rear, Hikari raging that Okaya had been left behind. Actually he hadn't. Like Terasu, Okaya had been hoisted across a horse, by a samurai with more dedication than good sense. But Okaya had had a lung pierced and his aorta nicked, and been trampled by a horse. Within moments he was dead.

Meanwhile, though the imperial lines had been overrun here and there, the men who overran them were too tired to capitalize on the advantage, while the high commands had lost track and control of their units. The battlefield had become a vast and noisy confusion of men hewing in a cloud of dust. Thus, while the imperial retreat continued, it did not become a rout. Arms and lungs had tired again, severely, and the intensity of fighting slackened. Chests heaving, soldiers often stared unfocused at each other within sword's reach, seemingly unable to strike. Officers shouted, backing their men away, undertaking to reform their units and lines.

It was then that word began to spread through both armies, first that Prince Terasu's banner was down, no doubt trampled on the field, and then that the prince was dead. Hikari, on the other hand, was quick to make himself seen, his color bearer holding his standard high beside him.

Lord Matsumura had ridden into this second fight personally, with his own household troops, including Akira and Hans. He'd fought mightily, for he was a powerful old man, and one of Junichi's heroes at Gifu. After a time, though, things went badly, and Matsumura tired dangerously. Then Hans had been a tower of strength. The enemy wasn't used to a man with a shield, and Hans was young, and superbly conditioned. He believed that Nils had been killed in the Battle of Momiji, and fought in a cold rage, protecting his adoptive grandfather.

Then the two sides had separated. Matsumura's household troops were fewer now, and tired, and many had wounds, but the report of Terasu's death had fired them. Indeed it fired the entire imperial army, whose officers harangued them. Their Emperor had personally killed the traitorous prince, they said. Now it was time to destroy the prince's army.

The report of Terasu's death had fired Ueda, too, or at least inspired decision. He gave his men only a few minutes' rest, then called for another attack. There was no groaning at the order. Once more the cavalry surged across the field while the infantry strode forward. And bit by bit, Arakawa's troops, uncertain now, and lacking focus, gave way.

Despite his fatigue, Matsumura himself led his samurai in this new attack. With the battle tide changing, his grandson fought like a berserker, reaping rebels as he might have sugar cane. At one point, seeing Matsumura outmatched, he surged to him, hewing the old *daimyo*'s opponent from the saddle. Then a sword stroke cut through Hans's hauberk at the shoulder, and his sword flew from his hand. Another struck his helmet, cutting it open, and he fell from his horse like a sack of stones.

Close at hand, Akira dismounted, and hoisted the youth onto his own mount, then swung up behind him and rode back to a place of relative safety, not knowing if Hans was alive or dead.

The rebels began to break and flee, singly and in clusters at first, but soon en masse, with imperial troops in pursuit, their cavalry avid for vengeance, harassing the rebel flight and killing stragglers.

Kyushu's fleet continued sailing eastward across the forty-kilometer-wide mouth of Sagami Bay. An hour after leaving Sugimori behind, Kyushu felt an aftershock. A still later shock, perhaps unrelated, was far enough southward that he never felt it. It sent a great submarine mudslide, an avalanche-like turbulence flow, surging down the long steep slope of the South Honshu Marine Ridge into the Bonin Trench.

The air was thick and gritty with ash sifting down from strong upper tropospheric winds. The spreading ash cloud had turned the afternoon to dusk, and the old *takai daimyo* peered impatiently eastward, watching for Miura Point.

The young eyes of a lookout, elevated some meters above the deck, spotted the point before Kyushu did. Or rather, spotted the peninsula; Kyushu's admiral veered them south a bit then, to round the point. Now would come the moment of truth: was an imperial fleet waiting in the narrows? They tacked northward, Kyushu standing at the very prow, his brows beetled in concentration as his fleet followed. Ahead of them—nothing except water, water and the narrowing entry to Omori Bay. No fleet, beyond a few picket ships.

It was then the lookout shouted: "*Astern! Astern! Tsunami!*"

It took a moment for the words to register on Lord Kyushu Tadaki. Then he turned, clambered down from the elevated forecastle deck, and pushing through the gaping soldiers, hurried to the poop, where he stared in disbelieving shock. The bottom had shelved, and the giant wave behind them had become a steep, froth-rimmed, comber eating his ships. As the old samurai stared, bulge-eyed, horrified, it rushed upon his flagship, looming till he was staring less back at it than up.

Then it broke, crashing down, crushing down, smashing the flagship to matchwood and overriding it, to rush foaming through the narrows and into the bay. There, its size and force reduced, it nonetheless destroyed the imperial fleet at its anchorage and docks, and swept to the head of the bay, carrying with it the debris of ships and dockside buildings. Then came the backsurge, which destroyed nothing, because nothing undestroyed was left within its reach.

A pyre had been lit on Miura Point, to signal the imperial marines to load—that an enemy fleet was approaching. But the ashfall had caused the signal to go unseen. Thus the marines at the naval base in Omori Bay had not loaded, and only the men on dock watch had been caught and killed.

Those of Kyushu's ships which hadn't rounded the point, fared no better. The great breaker smashed them against the rocks of the peninsula.

On the east side of the Boso Peninsula, the tsunami swept north along the Kujukuri Shore. At low tide, Lord Miyagi's second fleet had grounded on the beach called Hasenhama, appropriately enough,[33] and was unloading its two battalions when the monster wave struck. The fleet was destroyed utterly. Some two hundred infantry escaped.

Miyagi's larger fleet, at Mito, was somewhat sheltered, and the destruction was not complete. Also, its troops were already inland, fighting, and the loss of men was mainly of ships' crews.

---

[33] Hasenhama means "shipwreck beach" in Yamatoan.

FIFTY-TWO

Mariko and her maidservant heard hooves, and peering out, saw mounted men gallop up to the prince's nearby tent. The girl Kiku was only fourteen, and began to cry. She'd been raped earlier, though not violently, by the prince's aide, while the prince, in his own tent, had *kogo* with a seemingly willing Mariko. Now they stood, Mariko holding the girl to comfort her. They weren't sure what was happening.

No one seemed interested in them now, and after a few minutes, Mariko crossed the intervening ground to see. A samurai, posted by the entrance of the prince's tent, scowled as she approached.

"What is the matter?" she asked. "Is my lord wounded? I am his concubine, Matsumura Mariko."

The man grunted; this was no woman to stare insolently at. "He has been badly cut," the guard said, "and has lost much blood, but he is a strong man, and it is said he will live. Captain Masurao is having his wound properly dressed before we take him to Momiji Castle to recover."

With a cry she pushed past the guard and threw herself on Terasu, sobbing, kissing him. "Oh!" she cried, "please do not die, Your Majesty! It would be more than I could stand!"

He opened his eyes and smiled vaguely, faintly, the shock of his wound and blood loss too deep yet for pain. She knelt beside his pallet then, holding his hand and kissing it.

They prepared a litter for him, with three sets of carriers to take turns. To take him to Momiji Castle by horse seemed impractical. He needed to lie down with his leg raised; nor could he hold himself upright in the saddle. A properly-built litter, properly carried, would be much more suitable, and Mariko and Kiku could walk beside and attend him.

That plan lasted only a dozen kilometers. Then a group of cavalry came riding down the road from the east, the remains of a platoon. Captain Masurao stood in the middle of the road, waving wildly to halt them, and unwilling, they almost ran him down before they stopped, more to curse and threaten than comply. Masurao cursed them back, and told them who lay on the litter.

The cavalry lieutenant in charge blanched, and slid off his horse to kneel, his troopers quickly following his example.

"Please excuse me," the lieutenant said. "My behavior was beyond pardon. It is intolerable that I should have spoken as I did. I can only say that we did not know it was His Majesty you carry."

He waved toward the east. "In the battle, he was said to be slain. The Emperor's army has broken our own, and everyone is fleeing for their lives. You cannot possibly move fast enough on foot like that. Either His Majesty must be taken on horseback, or you must conceal him somewhere."

As the lieutenant spoke, he seemed extremely ill at ease. His men kept looking back eastward, as if expecting pursuers.

Masurao conferred briefly with two of his own men, then looked back at the lieutenant. "Woods grow along the river there," he said pointing. "Stay here as if resting, while we take him there and hide. If someone comes—the enemy or our own people—you must distract them. Lead them away if they are hostile. And tell no one—no one!—that the prince lives. Let the enemy think he lies on the battlefield, among the heaps of dead. Then they will not search for him here."

The lieutenant bowed. "Of course, Captain. We are deeply honored to be of assistance."

Masurao exchanged the prince's large and gaudy silk tent for one of cotton, small and plain. Then the royal party turned south across fields toward the strip of woodland little more than a kilometer away, the litter-bearers jogging with their burden as smoothly as they could. When they reached the woods, Masurao had the guardsmen set up the drab, newly acquired tent, and conceal it with saplings. When they were done, he ordered them to hide in the brush. Mariko and Kiku he allowed to stay by the prince.

Dusk had begun to settle prematurely, for the ash cloud had spread far enough to cut off the late sun. Potatoes baked the evening before were taken from saddlebags, to be eaten cold with barley cakes. When Terasu wakened a little, Mariko tried to feed him a bit of potato, but he pushed it away weakly.

"Let it be," said Masurao. "Weak as he is, it would not do for him to vomit.

"We will stay here no longer than need be. We must get him away to a place where he can be properly cared for until he is strong enough to ride. Then get him to Osaka. As long as he lives, it will be possible to rise again and depose the degenerate who sits on the throne. And when Prince Terasu is Emperor, he will remember those of us who stood by him in this time of great danger."

It grew darker, and Masurao knelt behind Kiku, putting his hands inside her kimono and fondling the girl, then took her to his own tent, leaving Mariko alone with the prince. When he was gone, she continued to sit quietly.

After a while, visibility inside the tent was nearly zero. Mariko didn't know whether the guard outside was awake or sleeping, or whether Masurao would be back. A quilt had been spread over the prince. Now she folded it, laid it over Terasu's face, and held it down hard with both hands. The spring-blade knife Chiyoko had given her, she had inside her kimono, beneath the sash, ready to use if Terasu was strong enough to struggle.

He wasn't. She held the folded quilt in place for fifteen minutes or more, to be entirely sure, then spread it over him again and tried to sleep. They would think the prince had died of his wound, died of blood loss, she told herself. She would wait where she was till daylight. Masurao would discover the prince's death then, and she could wail, pretending grief.

But as minutes passed, she began to worry. What if Terasu's eyes had bulged out during his suffocation? Or his face had turned blue? Masurao would suspect, and she'd be killed, perhaps tortured by the soldiers.

Almost holding her breath, she crept to the door, listening.

She was nearly certain the guard there was asleep. She could see him, a vague dark form. But was an arm or leg sticking out where she'd bump it? Perhaps step on it? Or might she step on a dry stick in the blackness?

She chanced it, and a few minutes later was in the field again, stumbling in the dark. The air felt strange, smelled and *tasted* strange. She paused, wiped at a mosquito on her face, and found fine dust. After a bit she reached the imperial road and began to hike eastward in the night, hoping to reach imperial soldiers.

She hadn't gone far when she heard hoofbeats ahead.

FIFTY-THREE

Nils had walked and occasionally jogged, sleeping more by day than night. For the ash cloud had been blown eastward out to sea, and napping in the sun was warmer and more pleasant. Nor had the air been dusty, this far west.

He was wakened by the sound of hooves, a number of them, and rolling to his feet, moved crouching to a thicket of young pine from which he could see the road. Clouds had moved in, the sun had newly set, and dusk was beginning to settle. Shortly, horses and riders trotted by, and he read an officer's mind as they passed. They were rebels. Rebels in defeat.

When they were past, Nils trotted to the road, then eastward again toward Momiji Castle. Almost at once, however, he heard more riders coming, and took cover. These too were fleeing westward toward Osaka. They belonged to one of Arakawa's own regiments, and had confidence in their master. From the protection of his Black Castle, he would reorganize and recoup, they had no doubt. He'd establish security and autonomy there, and raise Terasu's sons with their dead father's ambition.

Then they were past, but still another group approached. In less than half an hour, four groups had ridden by, all rebels, all fleeing.

Shortly afterward came a fifth group, a somewhat larger group, also rebels, one of particular interest. After they'd passed, Nils followed them at a trot.

Even on campaign, Lord Arakawa Hideo was used to much more comfort than this hasty camp afforded, hidden a hundred meters back from the imperial highway. His was one of the few tents—actually some junior officer's tent, by no means a pavilion. At least it had mosquito netting. He grunted inwardly;

331

the questions and second guesses cycling through his mind promised to do what the mosquitoes couldn't, threatening to fend off sleep till morning, tired though he was.

Amida alone knew what the casualties had been at Nabemura. The infantry must have been nearly wiped out. Butchering them would account for the lack of sustained pursuit—that and defeating Sugimori's and Miyagi's forces. (Arakawa still knew nothing of the fleets' destruction by the mountain and the tsunami; he visualized hard fighting, and Hikari's victorious forces far weaker than they actually were.)

The foremost question dogging him was actually more a recrimination, for he had no answer to it: *Why, having foreseen the danger, had he allowed that irresponsible fool Terasu to enter the battle?* He'd already seen abundant evidence for the man's self-centered lack of reality. And conceit! He'd demonstrated his swordsmanship more than once, and while it was very good, it was no better than you might expect, considering the quality of instruction he'd had as child and youth. And anyone with any sense knew that a battle was far different than fencing in the *dojo*. Yet the arrogant fool had shown no appreciation at all that he could be killed or maimed: No one but his father had dared hurt him as a child; no one at all would dare hurt him as a man.

And if the report could be believed, Hikari himself had killed him! Hikari *unhorsed* had killed him! Somehow, Arakawa found in that a certain perverse satisfaction. If it hadn't been for that accursed Okaya Yari . . . Hikari had his good points as emperor, but his relationship with Okaya Yari could not be forgiven! Even his misguided tolerance and patience could be forgiven, but not his degenerate behavior with the sodomist! And even if he, Arakawa Hideo, should forgive him, few others would. That by itself disqualified him for the throne.

No, Arakawa told himself, Hikari would be brought down sooner or later, by some alliance of *daimyo*, under some *takai daimyo* like himself. But if it was to be soon, he himself would have to lead it; no other existing *takai daimyo* had the necessary combination of skills in diplomacy, organization, and leadership. Somehow he needed to survive this; survive and bring up Terasu's twin sons. And perhaps the infant in Setsuko's belly would prove to be another boy. An insurance boy; there'd be no further.

But the difficulties! Hikari would never again be reluctant to act. Not that reluctant. And secrecy would be almost impossible now. Also, the other *daimyo* would not soon trust his judgement again in such a matter. They'd relied on him once, and it had all gone to ruin.

If only he hadn't trusted Terasu as he had! How could the cretin have risked himself so recklessly? All he'd needed to do was display himself. Do some token fighting at most. The man had been a fool, lacking any sense of responsibility! He'd destroyed the whole thing. If . . .

A sudden snore interrupted Arakawa's mulling, and he glared toward the bodyguard he shared his tent with, a man invisible in the darkness. Perhaps he should make him move out; he couldn't put up with such noise, and in a place like this, on so dark a night, he didn't need his protection. The first loud snore had settled into a coarse but even sound, less startling, but it seemed to Arakawa just as impossible to sleep with. He raised up on an elbow, moving a hand as if to dislodge his mosquito bar, to get off his pallet and waken the man. But no doubt that would let mosquitoes in, to be dealt with one by aggravating one after he'd crawled under the netting again. So instead he spoke sharply in a sort of articulated hiss.

"Hey! You! Kirisaki!"

He sensed, rather than saw the sergeant jerk upright, no doubt fumbling for his sheathed sword.

"You were snoring! How am I to sleep, with such a racket? Stay awake now, until you hear me sleep!"

"Excuse me, Arakawa-sama. To disturb you is the last thing this unworthy servant wishes to do."

"Do not lie back down until I am asleep! Otherwise you will only fall asleep again and continue that horrible noise!"

"Of course, Arakawa-sama. I will sit upright and remain alert."

"Good." Arakawa lay back down, not actually feeling "good" about anything, especially not the snoring. But it was as if the interruption had freed him from the cycle of errors, blame, and worry. Somehow, he told himself, he would come through this. He'd rebuild his forces before Hikari could recover his own strength sufficiently to come to Osaka and punish him. Meanwhile he would also send messages of regret and self-abasement to the Emperor, promising loyalty, and obedience in all things. Claim that Terasu had told him stories which had made his brother seem utterly unfit, a disgrace to the imperial family. At first, of course, he hadn't believed, but bit by bit, hearing them over and over ... Arakawa looked at the argument critically. It wouldn't be very convincing, but to someone like Hikari, who would rather believe than take forceful and unpleasant action ...

He began to construct a scenario, which drifted into semi-dreaming and then into sleep. His last coherent thought was that he could do whatever was necessary. He'd awake in the morning with a plan; it would all turn out as he wanted.

Two meters away, Sergeant Kirisaki Hoshin heard the changed sound of his master's breathing. Still he remained upright awhile, just in case. Then he found his head dropping to his chest, and muttering, lay back down. The land here was not wet, and the river was swift. Such mosquitoes as there were were no great problem to him, and the sergeant was soon asleep.

Twenty meters away, hidden by the darkness of a cloudy, moonless night, Nils Järnhann lay on pine needles. When Kirisaki had fallen asleep, he slipped unerringly and silently to Arakawa's tent. Its sides had been left rolled up for whatever breeze and light might penetrate the trees, and to Nils's vision, darkness was no barrier. He left the sergeant unmolested—there seemed no need to kill him—and moved directly to the sleeping Arakawa.

Carefully he used his knife to slit the netting, then poised its tip above Arakawa's right eye. This would have to be done skillfully, or some noise might waken the sergeant, and cause an uproar. Waiting till the instant that an exhalation had been completed, he thrust deeply into the brain, while a hand pressed down hard over Arakawa's mouth. The body shuddered and went slack.

Now, with the heart stilled, the head could be cut off without creating a fountain of sticky blood. Briefly he watched Kirisaki's mind. For a long moment it shimmered like a disturbed water surface, then the psychic agitation stilled, settling again into normal patterns.

There was no room in the tent to wield a sword without disturbance, so Nils began to cut Arakawa's head off with his heavy belt knife.

FIFTY-FOUR

Nils put more than twenty kilometers between himself and Arakawa's camp. Then early dawn dissolved the grip of night, and he left the road, hiking up a brook and into a ravine. There he hung his trophy from the branch of a tree to keep it from small animals, and took a silk bag of barley cakes from inside his shirt; he'd left Arakawa's tent with more than a trophy. After eating four of them, he lay down to sleep, as little discomforted by the hard cold ground as a wild animal would have been.

Five hours later he awoke, stretched enormously, relieved himself and began to hike, carrying his trophy wrapped in a blood-crusted sleeping kimono.

Actually, if circumstances had been different, he could have hiked and trotted the remaining distance in six or seven hours. But one group after another of riders came west. In every case, he left the road to avoid being seen, though the last group was a troop of imperial cavalry, out to harry and kill. Thus it was late evening again when he arrived at Momiji Castle. Those rebels well enough to march or ride had left, though the badly wounded still were there.

Matsumura's surviving troops had newly returned from the front. The gate guards recognized Nils at once, of course, and let him in. He got from them a brief summary of what had gone on, then bloody and filthy, went to the guard room instead of to Chiyoko. It was nearly full of tired and sleeping samurai, for most of the returnees were lodged at the castle until the situation settled out. He washed his hands and face at a basin, then went to the kitchen and wakened the kitchen boy, who gave him cold beef and barley, and a bowl of hot *sake*. With his hunger dulled, he returned to the guard room and bedded down on a futon, to sleep till after daylight.

When he awoke, he went to a storage room and stashed his now smelly trophy. Then, returning to the guard room, he stripped to the waist and bathed more thoroughly. That done, he went to the room he shared with Chiyoko, and knocked on the door.

"Who is there?"

"Your husband."

In hardly a second, the door slid open, and a wide-eyed Chiyoko stared at him as if she hadn't believed her ears. She made a small cry and fell into his arms, where she began to weep.

He laughed quietly. "I'm glad you're so happy to see me. You're soaking my shirt with tears."

She looked up at him, for the moment both laughing and crying, and buffeted his thick arm. "I didn't know whether . . ." Her fragile smile dissolved into weeping again, and he held her close, but gently, given that she was nearly eight months pregnant. After another minute more she stepped back from him, gripping his sleeve, and pulled him into the room, sliding the door shut behind him. Her gaze found the blood on his sleeves.

"You are hurt!"

"No." He shook his head. "Someone else was hurt. Not hurt, exactly. Dead."

She nodded soberly. "Where have you been? Your father thought you'd been killed in the first battle."

"I've been—to the mountain. To see the man who . . . It is difficult to explain. Perhaps, after you have borne our child, we can visit Juji Shiro. Perhaps he can help me talk about it to you."

She looked at him earnestly, then nodded again. "Have you spoken with your father? He returned yesterday before dark. He told me that Hansu was wounded. Badly but not dangerously."

Nils shook his head. "You are the first person I've talked to except guards and the kitchen boy." He spread his arms as if for inspection. "I arrived much dirtier even than you see me.

And hungrier. And it was late at night; I thought it best to sleep in the guard room, and come to you today."

She looked critically at him. "You need to be scrubbed, then soak in a hot bath," she said, and calling a serving girl, ordered hot water prepared for the tub, and some in a basin. While they waited, she unbraided her husband's hair. Then the basin arrived for the preliminary scrub. Nils stripped, and she scrubbed him with soap and a cloth, then rinsed him. "You are aroused," she observed.

"So it seems. But it would not do to have *kogo*. It might injure our child."

She kissed him. "There is another way," she murmured, and kissed him some more.

Afterward he soaked in the tub, and while he dried, someone rapped. "Chiyoko! Chiyoko! I've come home, and my husband has come home with me!"

Chiyoko opened the door, and Mariko came in, hands fluttering with excitement. "He is wounded but not mutilated. And Matsumura-sama embraced him! He said—"

She stopped in mid-sentence, for there stood Nils, a clean kimono draped around him. "Nissa-san!" she said. "Where have you been?"

"It's a long story, and difficult to tell."

Someone else looked in through the door then. "Nissa!" It was Matsumura. "Where have you been?"

"That's a question everyone asks. I have been to the mountain."

For just a moment, Matsumura-sama looked puzzled. Then he frowned. "We had thought you dead; it seemed impossible that you could have escaped. I'd planned to send out men today to find your body and bring it home." He frowned again. "Are you wounded?"

Nils knew the old *daimyo's* thoughts and feelings, and didn't grin as he might have. "Not a scratch," he answered.

"Then why were you not at the Battle of Nabemura? Where the enemy was broken! Your son was there, and made a name for himself. And Mariko! She killed Terasu! Men found him just where she told them. If she were a man, I would present her with the two swords and a *kami-shimo*."

Now Nils did grin. "I've been hunting," he said, "and brought you something. A present. Come!"

Gently but firmly, he took Matsumura's arm in one huge hand and led him down the hallway to the storage room. The two women peered into the hall after them, and heard Matsumura cry out in surprise, then listened to an indistinct exchange of words. A minute later the two men emerged, Matsumura talking excitedly. "The Emperor must be informed. In his camp by the road, you say! Incredible! I'll have the brains removed, then soak it in brine and dried, to keep it recognizable. What were you doing there?"

"I went to the mountain. It's a long story, and hard to tell; what happened after that is too strange. Perhaps Juji Shiro can be prevailed upon to visit us. He can help me tell it."

He changed the subject then. "Perhaps you will allow me to take Arakawa's head to the Emperor myself, when it has properly dried."

They agreed that Nils and Akira would deliver the head to Miyako. An escort would go with them, though armed escorts were harder to provide just now, with most of Matsumura's battalion dead. But meanwhile, with the war over and won, Nils had another trip to make while Arakawa's head went through its preservation treatment.

FIFTY-FIVE

This time, though he traveled alone again, Nils went with five spare horses and well-supplied saddlebags. He expected to return with two companions. He found the hut still there; it was safely northwest of Hakone-san.

He dismounted when he saw it, and led the horses. Achikh squatted before the door, watching him with mild curiosity.

"Where is your master?" Nils asked.

Achikh gestured toward a mound of stones a little distance from the hut.

Nils squatted beside him. "What did he die of?" This time he spoke in Achikh's native Buriat dialect.

Achikh blinked, then shrugged, answering in the same tongue. "I do not know. First the ground shook, then it jumped very hard, and my master gave a great cry and pitched forward, dead. Moments later there was a monstrous thunderclap, the loudest I've ever heard, the great god lamenting my master's death."

Nils nodded sympathetically. "Come with me," he said. "We will leave your master with the mountain, which he greatly loved."

Achikh shook his head. "My master told me I must never leave him."

"Ah."

Nils said nothing for awhile, simply squatting, staring at the mound as Achikh was. When he spoke again, it was in Yamatoan. "What did your master say to you that made you his servant?"

Achikh replied in the same language. "I do not remember."

The question brought the hypnotic commands into Nils's view, though of course not into Achikh's. Nils pulled them like a thread, scanning them: not only the first hypnosis of

340

Achikh, but the rat's nest of commands given him later, after he'd been preconditioned.

Finally he whispered into Achikh's mind, using the command Satoru had used, once he'd conditioned him. <<Achikh, you are sleepy . . . Sleeepy . . . Sleeeepy . . . You are asleep, deeply asleep.>> The Buriat's head had slumped, his chin resting now on his chest. <<On the count of five, you will wake up. When you've awakened, you will be able to remember all the commands your master gave you while you slept, all of them, and none of them will have power over you. You will also remember the commands I've given you here. I will count now. One. You are starting to wake up. Two. You are becoming aware of the world around you. Three. You are wakening. Four. Your eyes are open. Five.>>

The Buriat looked around, his gaze stopping on Nils. For a long moment he stared, eyes widening in remembrance. Many remembrances, old and recent, were stirring. He began to shudder, shook like an aspen leaf for a long minute, then rose to his knees. Nils stood, and Achikh got up the rest of the way, stiffly, as if his knees hurt. Then, throwing his strong arms around the Northman, he wept loudly for two or three minutes, the first time he'd cried since he was three years old.

When he'd finished, Nils spoke again. "When did you eat last?"

Achikh gestured at the mound. "Before—he died."

"I have food with me." Together they went to the horses, and Nils took one of the ubiquitous barley cakes from a saddle bag, giving it to Achikh. One wasn't much, but it seemed best to start by eating lightly.

"I'm married," Nils commented.

"You told me. Long ago. Or it seems long ago, so much has happened. Her name is Ilse."

"I've married again, this time a Yamatoan named Chiyoko. I also have a Yamatoan father now." Achikh looked a question at him. "He adopted me. Come. We'll go to his home and I'll introduce you to both of them."

They got on horses then, and started for Momiji Castle.

FIFTY-SIX

The monsoon arrived on the same day that Nils and Achikh did, and they entered the castle soaking wet. To Matsumura-sama, Nils explained Achikh only as someone who'd arrived on the sky boat and been lost—the friend Hans had told about. Hans was walking around by then, with his right arm immobilized and his head bandaged, but his reunion with Achikh was warmer than any of their previous times together.

"Nils tells me you're a dangerous fighter now," Achikh said. "It looks as if you've learned one of the lessons of war: he who strikes is apt to be struck."

Hans smiled lopsidedly. "I was struck often enough in training, but that was different. The swords were wooden, and I got only lumps and bruises." He looked curiously at the Buriat then. "Where did they take you, after you were captured in the village?"

Nils interrupted. "That's a long story. Can you wait to hear it until after supper? Matsumura-sama will want to hear it too, and our wives."

Then the two travelers bathed. Achikh had been brought up bathless, and the hot tub, after the first scalding moment, seemed to him an experience well beyond the shower in the pinnace's sanny.

After supper, the exchange of stories went on till Matsumura-sama's head and eyelids drooped hopelessly. Nils still hadn't explained Satoru, and Achikh himself knew nothing of what the Hokkaidoan had been doing during his trances.

The Buriat was perhaps most impressed by Mariko's killing of Prince Terasu. Mongol women could be fierce, and such ferocity was admired, but this small and seemingly delicate woman ... From the way Matsumura-sama acted toward her, he never suspected the old lord had once despised the girl.

Nils was at home for two days. Then, with Achikh, and Akira, and the salted and dried head of Arakawa Hideo, he started for the capital, with a squad of Matsumura Shinji's samurai as official escorts.

On the road, both days brought rain, but Arakawa's head traveled in state, inside a cedar chest to keep it dry. The fields were vivid green, and mosquitoes flourished. In Miyako, the canals were fuller of water than Nils had seen them before. The Emperor had known that Nils would bring Arakawa's head—Matsumura-sama had sent advance word of it—yet the Northman was met only by a servant. The room assigned to them, though, was relatively large and airy, and Sugitani Katsumi came to see them as they changed into dry clothing.

Katsumi exchanged bows with Nils and Akira. "Nissa-san!" he said. "Your sister-in-law's husband, Lord Ibaraki Katana, is here! With friends of yours! And something more."

Nils grinned at Katsumi. The manner of their reception— as if other matters totally preoccupied the court—had caused him to read the people around him, and he already knew what Katsumi referred to. Nonetheless he asked, "What more?"

"More foreigners! They came in a Heaven Boat, coming to ground on the drill field! They are excited that you are here, and wish to see you at once."

Nils laughed, clapping the young noble on the shoulder. "Thank you for bringing such wonderful news! Stay a minute until we've finished dressing. Then we'll all go."

Matt and Nikko would know only Achikh, and Alex Malaluan would know neither of them, but Northman courtesy dictated that he include Akira as well. When they were dressed, they followed Katsumi through corridors and up stairs, to a luxurious suite normally reserved for visiting *takai daimyo*. That the visitors were lodged there told something of their welcome.

A guard announced them, and a serving man bowed them in. A grinning Matthew greeted them, and Nikko gave Nils a hug. Alex Malaluan shook his hand. The Earth historian was a wiry, fortyish man with old-style glasses perched on the bridge of his nose.

"The *Phaeacia* is back," said Malaluan, spreading his arms a bit, displaying himself as evidence.

"But Ilse is not," Nils said.

"Right. She stayed on New Home. She's teaching there; her lectures are very popular, and she has several personal students she's training in psionic skills. They depend on her. She's had more impact than any of the expedition members— almost as much as the information we took back with us." Malaluan shrugged. "I tried to think of a good way to tell you, but there didn't seem to be any. And knowing you . . . She said you'd understand."

"She and I are much alike," Nils said, "but also much different in some ways. By nature she is an observer, with a hunger for knowledge, while I am a warrior, with a hunger for experience. It's not surprising that our paths have parted."

Malaluan nodded.

Nikko and Matt had looked a bit uncomfortable at the exchange. Now Nikko turned to Achikh, perhaps partly to shift attention from Ilse's absence.

"I suppose you went back to where we let you out, and found us gone," she said.

"Not for weeks," Achikh answered. "It is better you weren't there." He didn't elaborate; Matt made a mental note to ask him about it sometime soon.

"And what of Ted?" Nils asked.

It was Matt who answered. "He went up to the ship with the *Beta*, after it let Alex off here. He needed some teeth repaired. Badly. Matt and I have been here for—this is the third day. We came with Lord Ibaraki, who we understand is your brother-in-law."

Alex's head snapped around. "Brother-in-law?"

"Have you forgotten?" Matt said. "Northman marriage customs are different than ours. A warrior can have three wives."

Nikko continued, bypassing the diversion. "The *Beta* showed up yesterday. The *Phaeacia* had arrived off Earth the day before, and picked up our finder beam. They sent Alex down this morning. You only missed Ted by a few hours."

"We've had some hard months since we saw you," Matt
said. "But ours were a vacation, compared to Ted's."

They sat down then to continue their conversation.
the time they'd been sent for to dine with the Emper.
they'd pretty much filled each other in on what had happened
with them since the previous September. Nils, however,
said nothing about Osoroshii-kami. It would have been a
bit much for Matt and Nikko to handle, and entirely beyond
Alex Malaluan.

Alex was shocked enough when, after supper, Nils presented
the Emperor with Arakawa's head.

Two days later, the *Beta* returned. The *Alpha* had been
repaired on the mountain by a work boat, and was back aboard
the *Phaeacia* again, being reconditioned and upgraded. The
Beta then shuttled Nils, Achikh, and Akira to Momiji Castle,
landing on the mustering ground inside the wall. Matsumura-
sama was deeply impressed. He didn't say so, but it seemed to
him that the coming of the Star People would impact the empire
in ways no one could foresee.

Hans had already decided he had things he needed to say to
Nils. Basically, he wanted to stay in Yamato with Mariko. "Not
forever," he told Nils when they sat down alone together. "I mean,
I want to stay with Mariko forever, but someday I'll want to go
home, too." His expression was troubled as he said it.

Nils grinned, and reaching, tousled his hair. "And I," he
said. "I will stay here with Chiyoko. To see our children born;
she carries twins, a boy and girl. And then to stay longer; to
see what more I may learn through Ojiisan. The time will
come, though, when I will leave here, perhaps not so long
from now."

Then, knowing that Hans would repeat all this to Mariko,
and Mariko would tell Chiyoko, he added: "And when I leave,
I will want to take Chiyoko. If she cares to go. Perhaps it will
not be necessary to live in a log cabin, butchering, dressing
hides, making soap and carrying water."

Achikh too decided to stay, "At least long enough to find
out if I like it." Matsumura-sama had made a samurai of him—

ualties in the brief war had left abundant room for new recruits—and assigned him to serve as bodyguard to Nils.

Ted too would stay, despite his bad experiences. He wanted to compile an ethnology of Yamato. He had a new commset, and so did Nils, allowing them to keep in touch with the expedition and each other, if one went somewhere. A new ship was being built on New Home, somewhat larger than the *Phaeacia*. The intention was to keep one of the two parked off Earth at all times, to maintain permanent research programs on the planet. Shuttle services would be available to Ted pretty much as needed. And an interstellar courier-shuttle would be ready within two years, to carry messages and personnel as necessary, between the Earth-side projects and New Home.

Chiyoko gave birth in July, to Matsumura Axel and Matsumura Fujiko. Also, Juji Shiro came to Momiji Castle to see Ojiisan and Nils, and helped explain to Matsumura Shinji why Nils had gone to the mountain instead of to the battlefield.

THE END